Sarah Duncan trained as an actress and has worked in repertory and West End theatre as well as television. She is best known for playing the part of Rodney's girlfriend (the one before the one he married) in the BBC's only *Only Fools and Horses*.

When she gave up acting and moved to the country from London she wrote and published six books on careers in theatre, film and television before writing her acclaimed first novel, *Adultery for Beginners*. She now lives in Bath.

Also by Sarah Duncan

Adultery for Beginners

Nice Girls Do

Sarah Duncan

headline
review

First published in 2006
by HEADLINE REVIEW
An imprint of HEADLINE BOOK PUBLISHING

First published in paperback in 2006
by HEADLINE REVIEW

3

0 7553 3096 X (ISBN-10)
978 0 7553 3096 6 (ISBN-13)

Typeset in Garamond by Avon DataSet Ltd,
Bidford on Avon, Warwickshire

Printed and bound in Great Britain by
Mackays of Chatham plc, Chatham, Kent

Headline's policy is to use papers that are natural, renewable and
recyclable products and made from wood grown in sustainable
forests. The logging and manufacturing processes are expected to conform
to the environmental regulations of the country of origin.

HEADLINE BOOK PUBLISHING
A division of Hodder Headline
338 Euston Road
London NW1 3BH

www.reviewbooks.co.uk
www.hodderheadline.com

For Nicholas, who lights up my life
even if he won't read my writing

Acknowledgements

I am indebted to Dr Timothy Mowl of the MA in Garden History at Bristol University for sparing me the time to discuss landscape gardens and garden historians, and for helping me create an imaginary garden. Dr Rowena Fowler and landscape architect Andrew Grant generously answered many niggling questions, and an Arts Council grant helped with research costs. My agent, Lavinia Trevor, has been brilliant at coaxing the manuscript out of me and my editor at Headline, Marion Donaldson, has been wonderful at sorting it out. Some writers work on their own; others need the support of friends. I'm lucky that Rachel Bentham, Sue Swingler, Linnet van Tinteren, Nancy Kinnison and Sarah Stone continue to put up with me. Finally, I'd like to thank Menna and Eric for being the best parents in the world and Nicholas and Isabel for being the best children.

Chapter 1

S ex.
 Anna felt a moment of panic. What if she'd already had the last time ever, and couldn't remember it? It wasn't like smoking, where you ceremonially flushed the rest of the packet down the loo at ten past midnight on New Year's Eve. You wouldn't know that it had been the last time. Had it been any good? Probably not. If it had been good, Richard wouldn't have left. She could feel the skin contract across her cheekbones, tight with remembered pain.

She stared out of the sitting room window at the rain-blurred garden, then turned back to flicking through the Sunday supplement, where everything was about sex. Dossiers were sexed up, buildings were orgasmic, even dishwashers, which had once been plain old white goods, were now transformed into sexy desirables in gorgeous finger-lickin' hues. Then there were all the things that were better than sex. Chocolate. Yoga. Football. Gardening was the new sex, and history was the new sex, even newer than gardening. Anna sighed. If that was true, as a garden historian she ought to be awash with sex, whereas here she was, sitting in her parents' house watching the rain dribble down the window, not even able to remember the last time she'd done it.

'Can you see them?' Anna's mother Valerie bustled into the sitting room, wiping her hands on her apron, the flowery, frilly retro sort that were popular at the moment with young women playing housewife. Anna knew it was original fifties and worn without irony. 'We'll eat as soon as they arrive. I do hope they come soon, or the roast potatoes will be like mash.'

'Clare's always late for everything, you ought to know that by now,' Anna said, as Valerie crossed the room and peered out of the window into a rainy Sunday. Valerie's hair, neatly set at the hairdresser's, had escaped in the warmth of the kitchen, giving her the look of a startled cockatoo. 'It used to drive me mad at school, having to hang around at the end of the day for her. We were always missing the bus.'

'You were the eldest, it was up to you to help her.' Valerie's tone was as sharp as lemon.

Anna clasped her hands together, knuckles whitening. You're twenty-nine, not fifteen any more. There's no point. But still her teenage self howled in her head: why do I have to help Clare organise her homework, why do I have to wait when she's got detention, why why why? Just because I'm two years older than her. Adult Anna reasserted herself. 'The thing is, Mum—'

Valerie's face lit up. 'Is that Steve's new car? It's very smart.'

Anna looked out as a sleek silver-grey saloon drew up next to her own insignificant hatchback. 'Yes, that's them.'

Valerie rushed out of the sitting room but Anna stayed behind, counting raindrops, letting her mother enjoy greeting her sister and boyfriend on her own. As Clare shared Anna's house in Bath, seeing one another was not a novelty. She heard Clare bounce through the front door. 'We're not late, are we?'

'Darling, not at all.' A pause for kisses all round, Anna guessed. 'It's so good to see you, you're looking so well. And Steve too! Come on in out of the wet.' Valerie bustled into the sitting room, beaming in a way that Anna couldn't remember from her own arrival. 'I expect you're starving.'

'We've got something to tell you,' Clare said, dragging Steve into the room. The freckles scattered across the bridge of her nose added a deeper toffee shade to her tanned face, and her curly hair was streaked gold. She lifted up her left hand and waggled it so the ring on her finger caught the light. 'We're getting married!'

'Darling!' Valerie's voice shot up the scale. 'I'm so thrilled for you.' She rushed to embrace Clare, then Steve. 'Gordon, Gordon,' she called up the stairs. 'Oh my goodness, I can hardly speak. Clare darling, you must tell me all about it. When did you decide? Gordon, do come down, Clare and Steve are here. Drinks! Oh darling, you should have told me before, I'd have got some champagne in. I'm not sure we have any.'

'I'll go to the shop and get some,' Anna said, getting up. 'Congratulations, both of you.' She kissed Steve, then her sister, feeling the soft warmth of Clare's ribbon-trimmed cardigan against her hands, smelling her familiar flowery scent. Of course Valerie and Gordon would be pleased, this was what girls were supposed to do: get married and have children, not become academics with letters after their names.

Anna slipped through the front door, escaping from the ecstatic scenes in the sitting room redolent of the Second Coming, and walked up the muddy lane that led to the village, rain trickling down her neck. She was pleased for Clare, of course she was. And Steve. They were a great couple. Nine out of ten people would say they were made for each other. They were young, good-looking, fresh, dynamic. She was thrilled for them. The rain trickled down the back of her coat, leaving soggy patches on her thighs. It was just that it was hard to be thrilled when only ten days ago her divorce had come through. Such an ordinary piece of paper to sum up the failure of one's life.

Anna bought the best – the only – bottle of champagne the local shop had to offer and returned to her parents' house. 'Sundowners' was the sort of pebbledashed, half-timbered house you could find in any town or village anywhere in the UK, perhaps with cherry trees lining the street and privet hedges around the neat front gardens. Comfortable, not too large, not too small, and utterly conventional. It didn't feel like home.

Her father was having a man-to-man chat with Steve, the pair of them leaning against the mantelpiece as if propping up the golf club bar, while Valerie and Clare were busy discussing the wedding plans – dresses, bridesmaids, flowers, cake, cars, dates, churches, venues – skipping from one subject to another like a swirl of confetti in a whirlwind. Steve, a stocky young man who played rugby for the Old Boys and would have been excessively butch if it weren't for a preposterously small button nose that Anna was secretly amazed he could breathe through, was nodding at everything Gordon was saying. He fitted right in. Anna caught sight of herself in the mirror above the fireplace, dark wet hair straggling around a thin white face, unlike any of them. She started opening the champagne bottle, carefully twisting the cork and easing it up with her thumbs.

'Get Steve to do that for you,' her father said, frowning, born into a world where women didn't open bottles and squeaked girlishly when the cork exploded with a pop.

'I can manage,' Anna said, just as the cork came out with a suppressed sigh that couldn't have been bettered by the sommelier at the Ritz. She poured, then distributed the glasses among them.

'To Steve and Clare,' her father said, raising his glass. Anna and Valerie echoed his words and gesture. Steve was pink with embarrassment, and Clare could hardly stand with excitement.

'My turn,' she squealed. 'To my family, and to Steve, who puts up with me.' She took a swig. 'Aw, Mum, don't say you're going to cry!' Clare said, sounding hugely pleased at the thought.

'I'm sorry, darling, it's just, it's just . . . my little girl's leaving home.' Valerie blinked furiously. 'Oh dear, the apple crumble's going to be ruined.'

But the crumble survived, and Clare's wedding was the only topic discussed throughout the meal. She was intent on a summer wedding, ultra traditional. At this point she looked sideways at her father, who was obviously going to be expected to pick up the bill, but he was too busy concentrating on his lamb to notice.

Valerie did notice, because she said, in a slightly higher-pitched voice than usual, 'You must have whatever you want, darling.'

Anna looked across at Valerie and Clare, sitting next to each other, their postures and expressions identical. The same way of sitting, one small foot curled round a neat ankle. The same plump hands, both glittering with rings, and the same nails under the layers of varnish. The same tilt of the head, the same retroussé nose, the same slightly protruding lower lip. Soft, plump, girlish women, stamped from the same mould. Anna realised that whatever she did, she would never be part of their inner circle. Perhaps she would feel differently if it was her own wedding they were discussing, but she doubted it. She and Richard had been so wrapped up in each other, they hadn't felt the need for ceremony. Instead they'd slipped away on their own, with their respective best friends from university as witnesses, and not for the first time, Anna had disappointed her mother.

But it didn't look as if Clare was going to disappoint. No, Clare was going the full meringue, by the sound of it. Steve looked mildly surprised at the elaborate wedding plans, not dissimilar in expression to a Hereford bull suppressing hiccups.

Anna leaned across to him. 'Have you decided yet if you and your best man are going to have matching or toning cravats?'

He grinned at her. 'Jury's still out on that one.'

She'd spoken quietly, not intending her voice to travel, but Valerie's radar ears picked it up. 'There's no need to poke fun,' she said sharply. 'Just because you didn't want a lovely wedding—'

'I had the wedding I wanted,' Anna said, keeping her voice level.

'And look where it got you!'

Under the table Anna squeezed her hands into fists so her fingernails dug into the soft flesh. Don't cry. It's only because she's upset about the divorce. She managed a smile. 'I don't think a big wedding would have made any difference,' she said quietly, although her mind boiled with all the things she wanted to say.

'Not that you gave it a chance,' Valerie said. 'Poor Richard. Having to go abroad, and you too busy rushing about with your career to go with him. A man needs looking after, he needs support from his wife. Hardly surprising he—'

'Now, Valerie,' Gordon said, glancing at Anna, reprising his role as ineffectual peacemaker. 'We've talked this all through many times before, and now isn't the time to start again.'

Valerie's mouth was set in deep lines of disappointment, as if the muscles involved with smiling had atrophied. 'It's her own fault. She had a perfectly good husband and she threw it all away for the sake of her career. Career! In my day . . .'

'So I walked out,' Anna said to Bronwen at the bar the next evening, tucked away at the back at their usual table. 'Childish, I know, but . . .' She hugged herself tightly, as if she was a badly wrapped parcel that might disintegrate if she let go her grip.

Bronwen patted Anna's hand, the bar spotlights catching on the big resin rings in the vibrant rainbow shades she liked to wear. 'She does know what happened, doesn't she?'

'That Richard left me for someone else? Oh, sure. But she's always seen my career as a criticism of her life, and now she's been vindicated. She's convinced that if only I had been a better wife he wouldn't have gone off, and she wouldn't have had a divorce in the family,' Anna said, swirling a cocktail stick round in her glass to create a vortex of orange juice and ice. 'According to her, if only I'd had babies it would all have been okay.' Perhaps her mother had been right. Perhaps she should have given everything up and followed Richard. Perhaps she should have been more like Valerie.

'Babies aren't the answer to everything,' Bronwen said, smoothing the red velvet dress that stretched over her bump. No discreet pussy-cat bows and floral prints for Bronwen. Instead she had pink streaks in her hennaed hair, and a cleavage like the Great Rift Valley. She might have been an unlikely candidate for Earth Mother when Anna had met her as a paint-splattered student ten years before, but now she looked like the Fertility Goddess personified. Her bump was enormous, large enough to house a small cetacean rather than a baby.

'How many weeks have you got to go?' Anna asked. It looked as if it might pop out at any minute. That'd give the jostling throng at the bar something to talk about, although judging from the noise bouncing off the steel surfaces, they weren't short of things to say. I ought to find somewhere quieter to hang out, she thought.

'It's supposed to be pitching up in six weeks,' Bronwen said. 'Though as Toby was late, I'm expecting to be pregnant for ever this time round.'

'Perhaps this one'll be early – do you know what it is yet?'

Bronwen shook her multicoloured head. 'No, we decided we'd rather have a surprise. You mustn't let your mum upset you,' she added. 'At least you got married. My mum's still dropping hints about Nick making me an honest woman.'

'No wonder we've always got on – you're living in sin, and I'm damaged goods,' Anna tried to joke. She sent the vortex in the other direction.

Bronwen squeezed her hand. 'You're still the same lovely person I met on my first day at uni.'

Anna leaned back against the wall, determined not to cry. Why was it so much harder when people were nice? 'I was terrified of you,' she said, smiling at Bronwen. 'You seemed to know everything and everyone. I was sure you were a third year.'

'All a front. I was scared of you too, you were so cool and calm. And it was obvious from the first tutorial that you were going to get a first. I don't know why the rest of us bothered.'

'Much good it's done me.' Anna stretched out her hands and

looked at her fingers. Long and thin, bare of any rings or adorn-
ment, nails short. Clare's ring had been a traditional solitaire, the
diamond huge. Anna rubbed her left hand, feeling the waisting on
her fourth finger that still remained from where her wedding ring
had embedded itself into her flesh, a permanent reminder of her
marriage. She turned her hands over, the creases red on her pale
palms.

Bronwen took her hand. 'I foresee a shining future,' she said in a
singsong voice. 'With fourteen children.'

'No thanks.' Anna took her hand back. 'I'll leave that to you.'

Bronwen gave her famous laugh, dirty enough to plough. 'I'm
never having sex again after this one.'

'Join the club,' Anna said.

'Oh Anna, sex is something you give up when you're married, not
when you're single.'

'Yes, I remember that. Trouble is, I seem to have got stuck in
married mode.' It was hard not to think of herself as Richard's
partner. He'd been so much part of the person she'd become, even if
the feeling wasn't reciprocal.

'Well, find someone else.'

'Jeez, Bron, I've only just got divorced. It's been two weeks.'

'You've been separated for ever. The divorce was just the
paperwork.' Bronwen dismissed two grand of legal bills with an airy
wave, then stabbed at the dish of stuffed green olives, managing to
get two on her cocktail stick. 'I love being pregnant, you can eat like
a pig and no one raises an eyebrow.' She popped the olives in her
mouth. 'Let's face it, you separated years ago. Getting divorced
wasn't exactly unexpected, was it?'

'I suppose not.' She and Richard had pulled away from each
other slowly, like Velcro coming apart. Richard had decided to
chuck in his Ph.D. after two years and go into business management, of all the unexpected things, but they'd carried on as usual.
Or rather, she'd thought they were carrying on as usual, but the

cracks were forming, tiny, divisive, inevitable. She went freelance, setting up work, writing her thesis. Then he was transferred to the Zurich office. Richard not being around had seemed a blessing, to be honest. She'd been away a lot that summer, garden tours and lectures, willing to travel anywhere just to get established, and every spare moment she was frantically finishing her Ph.D. The phone calls got fewer, his weekends were spent skiing – well, you had to take advantage of the opportunities when you were out there. And how. Opportunities in the shape of one of his co-VPs or whatever they were called. Anna massaged the back of her neck. No, she had to be fair. Richard's affair was a symptom, not a cause.

'You ought to be going out more. Get back in the swing of things,' Bronwen said with the confidence of someone who had never been out of the swing of things. 'I mean, you haven't been out with anyone since Richard.'

'I don't meet people. Men.'

'You don't meet men hiding away with your books. Look, let's go and talk to those guys at the bar.' Bronwen started to slide out from behind their table, no easy matter.

Anna panicked, knowing that her friend was more than capable of accosting any number of strange men on her behalf. 'Don't you dare.' She tugged Bronwen's sleeve. 'Sit down. Please.'

To Anna's relief Bronwen settled back down. 'You're pathetic,' she said, shaking her head.

'Yes, one hundred per cent pathetic. It's stamped through me like a stick of rock.'

'What about the internet? Or speed-dating?' Anna looked at her; Bronwen obviously read her mind. 'Well, what about someone at work – how about a nice gardener?'

'I don't want to go out with anyone involved in gardens. Or an academic. But that's all I meet. I want . . . I want someone who'll whisk me off in his helicopter for a weekend in the Bahamas.' Anna gave a snort. She might as well say she'd like to go out with a

Martian. Still, it'd stop Bron from threatening to drag her to meet someone at the bar.

'I don't know why you want to go to the Bahamas when you never sunbathe,' Bronwen said, frowning at her.

'There you are,' Anna said cheerfully. 'I told you I was hopeless.'

'Who said you were hopeless?' Gwyn, Bronwen's older brother, plonked himself down in the seat opposite Anna and distributed a round of drinks.

'My mother.' Anna smiled. 'Thanks for the drink – it's needed.'

'Sorry it took so long,' Gwyn said, indicating the bar. 'It's busy for a Monday.'

'See? All that talent going to waste . . .' Bronwen raised her eyebrows at Anna and looked meaningful. Anna shook her head at her.

'Your mum's still upset?' Gwyn asked, raising bushy eyebrows.

'Dreadfully.' Anna sipped her drink, feeling the ice slivers catch at her throat, numbing her tongue with cold. 'You'd think she'd be happy, considering that she didn't want me to marry Richard in the first place. And hey, now I'm not. There's hope for me yet to grab a nice accountant or doctor.'

'Give her time, let her get used to it. How's your dad taking it?' Gwyn examined one of the olives, his fingers surprisingly elegant for such a bear of a man.

'Disappointment all round, I think.' Anna shrugged, feeling that above her lurked a little cartoon cloud with 'Gloom' written across it in shaky grey lettering. 'Let's change the subject. I don't want to bore you both.'

'Don't be silly, love.' Bronwen patted her knee.

'Perhaps you ought to go away for a bit, take a holiday,' Gwyn said, his face concerned.

'Can't. Freelance life – it's either too much work or not enough money, blah blah blah.'

Gwyn nodded. 'So what else have you got on?'

'There's some guy who wants me to prove he doesn't have a historic landscape.'

'Developer, is he?'

'Got it in one. And tomorrow I'm going round a garden – Templecombe Manor, have you heard of it?' Gwyn shook his head. 'Me neither, but the owner says it's an eighteenth-century landscape garden. Hopefully she'll want the works on that, which will see me through until June, when I'm doing the usual study tours and garden visits, then nothing. Destitution looms.' Clare would be moving out of the house after the wedding in July, so she'd have to find another lodger or she'd have difficulties paying the mortgage. Oh God, destitution did loom.

'I heard there may be some work for a garden historian on a television project. Bit of a last-minute job, I gather,' Gwyn said. 'I could put you in touch if you like. You might become a celebrity.'

Anna shifted in her seat. 'Oh yes, and that's likely.'

Gwyn looked serious. 'It wouldn't hurt, you know. Recognition is half the battle in this business. Make a name for yourself in ten years through writing carefully researched articles for the Garden History Society, or in ten minutes through an appearance on *Gardeners' World*.'

'Hmm. I don't want to be famous, but I could do with the money.' And how.

'I'll pass your details on then.'

Gwyn and Bronwen started to talk about summer holidays past and future, while Anna watched them fondly, the family resemblance as strong as when Anna and Bronwen had shared a higgledy-piggledy house as students and Gwyn had come round to visit. The Edwards siblings swaggered through life radiating vitality and confidence.

She'd met Gwyn soon after getting to know Bronwen. He'd originally trained as a surveyor, then moved into landscape design working for one of the big London companies. Anna's history of art degree had covered garden history, and when she graduated, there he'd been, perfectly placed to offer her a job while she studied for a Ph.D. part time. Richard had had a grant for his Ph.D. – 'Crabbe's silences: Muted Voices in the Agrarian Text' – and worked at the university. Some time in the future she'd imagined them, Dr and Dr Fielden, working side by side, experts in their respective fields. She sighed. Not to be. Richard had given up on Silence and had joined what he called the real world of commerce, flipflopping from academia to worldliness with surprising relish. She'd worked elsewhere, for various heritage organisations, but always in the background was Gwyn. Her mentor, she supposed. Without his help, his innumerable contacts, she might not have managed the transition into freelancing. Thinking of which . . . Anna slid off her chair.

'I ought to prepare for tomorrow.' She kissed Bronwen goodbye.

'Now don't forget, you've got to get laid!' Bronwen said in a loud voice that made heads turn and Anna want to curl up and die.

'I'll walk you to your car,' Gwyn said, getting up.

'It's just outside.' Anna rolled her eyes. 'I'm not going to get mugged, you know.'

'Yeah, yeah.' He squeezed Bronwen's shoulder. 'Back in a tick.'

The night air was sharp, not yet warm with summer. The new leaves hardly showed on the trees, spiked silhouettes waving menacingly, dark against the starless sky like a study in shades of black. Deep, deeper, deepest. Anna shivered and wished she'd worn her winter coat. She tucked her hand into Gwyn's arm, grateful for his reassuring presence as they crossed the nearly deserted car park.

'This is me.' Anna stopped by her car.

Gwyn sighed. 'It looks like something you'd get for forty-five quid from a car auction.'

'It's a means of getting from A to B, not a projection of my inner self,' Anna said, conscious of the rust patches around the wheel arches.

'You can always come back and work for us, any time,' Gwyn said, thumping the bonnet. 'Get yourself a decent car.'

Regular income, no more worries about paying bills. It was tempting. Then she remembered the office politics, the repetitive work, the pressure to give the 'right' answers. 'Thanks, but I'll be my own boss for just a little longer. And don't thump it, it might fall to pieces,' Anna said, unlocking and opening the door.

'It's a death trap, you know.' Anna faked a yawn and Gwyn laughed. 'Drive carefully.'

Irritatingly, it took two goes for the ignition to spark, the engine coughing and spluttering like a walrus with bronchitis. But at last the car rattled into life and she drove off with a quick wave at Gwyn.

The next day Anna's car rattled over a cattle grid as she swung between two pillars topped with stone pineapples. Symbols of friendship, she thought, hoping she was in the right place, hoping the owner, Mrs Davenport, would be friendly. It would be hard going if she wasn't. Perhaps I should have taken up Gwyn's offer, she thought. Gone for security. She winced as she bounced out of a particularly large pothole that defeated her car's springs. Please don't break down. With a regular job she could afford a new car, one that didn't threaten to give up at the smallest challenge to its suspension. She dropped her speed to a crawl.

Oh but it was hard being on your own. When she'd gone freelance Richard had been there, his regular salary a stopgap. She hadn't realised how much that knowledge had played a part in her decision. And now that stopgap had gone, along with all the emotional security she'd felt being with him.

Beech trees lined the drive, fresh green leaves mingling overhead to make a tunnel with patches of sunlight filtering through, and sheep grazed the fields on either side. Anna gripped the steering wheel as she bumped and jolted down the potholed drive, eager for her first glimpse of Templecombe Manor and the garden. With luck she'd get the job and that would keep her going for a few months. She bit her lip. She shouldn't need luck. Her CV should speak for itself. But when Richard had packed his bags, her confidence seemed to have slipped in with his luggage and jetted off to the land of cuckoo clocks, where it had undoubtedly put on a dirndl and tied plaits around its head.

She'd expected the house to be at the end of the drive, but it was hidden behind a large beech hedge. The drive turned sharp right and Anna gasped. Ahead was nothing but vast sky, and a dilapidated balustrade was all that prevented her from driving straight over the edge.

She had come to the end of the world.

Chapter 2

Anna got out of the car, tucking her briefcase under her arm to prevent the broken clasp from opening and papers cascading out, then walked to the balustrade, feet scrunching on gravel, and peered over, seeing the sweep of the valley smothered by trees and vegetation. The sky was a clear blue with little wisps of cloud high, high up. The air seemed silent, but as the voice in her head subsided and the swirl of anxieties about Richard and money and work diminished she began to hear small noises: birds stirring in the hedge, the wind rustling the leaves, making abstract ripples across the wooded valley.

A feeling of calmness descended on her, a sense that in this moment she held the future in her hands, that it stretched out in front of her like the sweeping landscape. I will make a success of my life, she thought. I will. It's bad right now, but I can do it. This time next year I will have forgotten about Richard, I will have more freelance work than I know what to do with, I will have my life in order. She closed her eyes and gripped the briefcase tightly. I can do it. I will do it.

A bird whirled past, wings disturbing the stillness, breaking the moment, bringing her back into the present. Anna leant forward over the balustrade, trying to discern features amongst the dense tree cover, but there was no sign of anything resembling a landscape garden.

'Don't jump.'

Anna stood up sharply, hand on heart.

A man was standing watching her, his back to the sun so she had to scrunch up her eyes to see him. He'd obviously been working in the garden; his clothes were liberally sprinkled with bits of shredded leaf and his tanned arms and face glowed. His hair was dark blond with sun-bleached highlights that would have cost a fortune in a hairdresser's salon, although the cut looked as if he'd hacked it himself with the chainsaw that dangled from one hand. He wiped the other on his shorts, then held it out. 'Dr Carmichael, I presume.'

Anna nodded and shook his hand, feeling absurdly formal. 'Anna.'

'Will Sutton.' He checked his watch. 'I was hoping you were going to be late, give me a bit more time. Never mind. I'll take you up to the house.'

Anna turned and looked across the drive to the house, a classic two-storey limestone affair with recessed wings to either side, topped by a slate roof. An arch in a high wall to the left suggested a stable block and possibly a walled garden. Much of the central part of the house was covered with the heavy foliage of a magnolia grandiflora that twisted itself up to the eaves. Buttery flowers the size of gigantic teacups gave off a heady scent. Where the magnolia hadn't spread, soft gold-grey stone glowed in the sunlight. Above the entrance porch, supported by a pair of columns, stood a crest, weathered now, but a prancing animal was still distinguishable. Because of her job Anna saw many desirable houses, but she'd never seen one so immediately appealing.

'It's lovely,' she said.

'It's falling down,' Will replied, swinging the chainsaw up on to his shoulder.

As they walked towards the front door, Anna's enchantment with the house faded. Ivy had smothered one of the wings and was creeping over to the central part of the house, lifting the slate tiles on the roof. Ragged black plastic flapped at a window, a forlorn attempt to block three broken panes. Weeds grew through the gravel. If Will Sutton was the gardener, she didn't think much of his work. All around were signs of decay and neglect. Despite the sunshine she shivered.

Will pushed the front door open and called, 'Peggy? Dr Carmichael's here.' He turned to Anna. 'Peggy's the one in charge here, as you'll find out.'

A woman in her sixties, Anna guessed, came to the door. She wore an old-fashioned apron that defined her waist in the same way the equator defines the globe.

'What do you mean, Will, leaving Dr Carmichael on the doorstep? Do come in, Mrs Davenport's expecting you.' She ushered Anna into the house, talking all the while in a soft West Country burr. 'I'm Mrs Hughes, the housekeeper here, but everyone calls me Peggy. We're all looking forward to your visit. Now, Will, don't you run away, madam wanted you to wait.'

He tugged at his dirty T-shirt, his expression worried. 'But I was going to—'

'You're going nowhere, you just stay here.' Peggy turned to Anna. 'If you'd just wait here a moment.'

She tapped at a door, then opened it and went in. Anna waited, not sure if she should start a conversation with Will. He'd propped his chainsaw in the porch, and was now rubbing his hands together and looking decidedly nervous. Anna felt sorry for him: he'd obviously been working hard in the garden, judging by the patches of sweat on his clothes. And there was something about his downcast eyes, an air of sadness, of vulnerability. I must look like that sometimes, she thought, before stopping herself. Nonsense. The man's just longing for a cold drink and a shower. She looked around her.

Grey stone flags anchored a double-height hall. A honey stone staircase curved up to a gallery, the sweeping line emphasised by the mahogany banister rail. The walls were hung with oil paintings, portraits mostly but one particularly striking Dutch still life of a vase of flowers, complete with butterflies and caterpillars. A mahogany grandfather clock ticked the hours away, and on a side table a real vase of flowers scented the air.

The housekeeper emerged and smiled at Anna. 'If you'd like to go in . . .'

Anna stepped into a room with faded blue walls, more oil paintings and patched velvet curtains. The floor was of wide dark oak boards partially hidden by an Aubusson carpet, fraying round the edges. Gleaming furniture lined the walls. Mrs Davenport was sitting regally in a high-backed chair.

'Forgive me for not getting up. Arthritis, damn it,' she said, leaning forward and offering her hand, her face creased with age into a million lines like a Welsh quilt. 'I have been looking forward to your visit.'

'I hope it won't disappoint you,' Anna said, taking her hand. It was wrinkled and gnarled, the skin caught in whorls on the knuckles and folded on the back of the hand, but her grip was firm.

'I'm sure it won't.' Mrs Davenport smiled, her face serenely confident, and let go of Anna's hand. 'Would you like tea?' She reached for a small silver bell.

Anna shook her head. 'If you don't mind, I'd prefer to walk the garden first. Then we can discuss my preliminary findings, and you can decide if you wish to go ahead with the full report.'

'Which I will do.' Mrs Davenport rang the bell.

Anna felt a glimmer of unease. 'It's best not to make too many initial assumptions . . .' she was starting to say when the door opened and Will Sutton came in, hugely out of place in his scruffy clothes and boots. He hovered on the edge of the delicately patterned carpet, as if he should have been standing on a folded newspaper.

Mrs Davenport's lips twitched, and she glanced up at Anna with a mischievous expression. For a second Anna saw the attractive young woman she must once have been. 'Of course, it's years since

I went into the garden. My hips, you know. I'm afraid it's very over-grown – before the First World War my grandfather had eighteen gardeners working here, and even my father had a garden staff of six. Now there's only William. But he's been clearing it, ready to show you round. William, you could have taken the trouble to change.'

Anna felt for the man, caught in his working clothes. He gave a sheepish smile. 'I was going to, but . . .'

'There's no need to change on my account,' Anna said quickly. 'I'd rather walk round on my own.'

Mrs Davenport raised her eyebrows. 'But how will you know where to go?'

'I have a copy of the 1900 Ordnance Survey map,' Anna said. 'I should be able to work my way round from that. Unless it's drastic-ally changed,' she added.

'May I see?'

Anna pulled the map from her briefcase and spread it across Mrs Davenport's lap. The plan of the garden was simple. Templecombe Manor sat at the head of a steep-sided valley. A meandering path led down the valley to first a small round lake, then a much larger oval one. Only three buildings were shown on the map. The first was between the two lakes, an irregularly shaped building which she'd thought might indicate a waterfall, imagining a rustic arcade with water tumbling over it. Now, looking at it again, she realised it could equally be a field shelter for animals, or a farm labourer's hut. The other two buildings were on opposite sides of the large oval lake: a small square on the east side and a large rectangle opposite it. Neither building was named.

Mrs Davenport peered intently at the map through a magnifying glass suspended from a gilt chain round her neck. 'Yes,' she said slowly. 'That's right. It's all here.'

'The buildings?'

'Yes, although only that one' – she pointed to the large rectangle – 'could really be called a building. We call it the pavilion.'

'And the other two?'

'The square building opposite the pavilion is a funny little thing. This is my family home, not my late husband's, so I was brought up late here. When I was a child I used to pretend it was a castle keep, because it doesn't have a roof, but I'm not sure what it's supposed to be. And the bit in the middle between the lakes isn't a building at all.'

'A waterfall?' Anna said hopefully.

Mrs Davenport shook her head. 'No, not a waterfall. I don't really know what to call it. But you'll see when William takes you there.'

'I'm sure I can find my own way round.' Anna said, folding the map. She hated having her first visit supervised by the client, their speculations interfering with her own impressions. Gardeners could be just as bad. Even if their ideas were good, she worried they could influence her own opinion. 'And I expect he's very busy – the walk could take two hours. Even more.' She glanced up at Will's face, which gave no sign of minding either way.

'No, William will show you, and then you will come back and tell me what you have found.' Mrs Davenport relaxed back into her chair and closed her eyes, dismissing Anna. Will held the door open; Anna hesitated, then went out.

Once in the hall with the drawing room door safely closed behind her, she turned to Will. 'You really don't need to bother,' she said. 'I'm sure you've got other things you'd rather be doing.'

'On the contrary, I'm at your disposal.' He smiled gently, but Anna wished he would dispose himself elsewhere. 'Mrs Davenport has asked me to show you round the garden, and that's what I'm going to do.'

'Do you always do as she says?'

'Invariably. Here, let me take that for you.' Will held out his hand for her briefcase.

'Thanks, but I'm okay.' She didn't want to risk it spilling its guts out in the hall. 'Look, I don't want to sound rude, but can you not tell me things about the garden. Old stories, legends, myths, things like that. If Mrs Davenport decides to proceed after the initial survey, I'll want to know all that sort of information, but right now I'd like to come to it fresh.'

'Fair enough. Follow me.' Will walked on, holding the front door open for her.

Anna followed, slightly surprised that he had accepted what she said. In her experience clients were usually bursting with information about their gardens, whether in the family for centuries or newly acquired. And there was nearly always some particular story that had caught their fancy which they would hang on to, even if she proved conclusively that it was false.

They stopped at the car for Anna to change into walking boots and swap her briefcase for a rucksack, then crossed the circular gravel area in front of the house and started to walk down a path littered with clippings from an overgrown box hedge on one side of the path. Presumably this was where Will had been working, a hot, thirsty job. She glanced up at him, thinking he could have modelled for the Jolly Green Giant or one of those westerns where steers get roped and women wear gingham, and a man's gotta do what a man's gotta do and has a secret past.

The path sloped gently down, and the land on either side became rougher, trees reaching up and arching overhead to make a roof as elaborate as any Gothic cathedral. Anna could glimpse chinks of sky through the leaves. A tree had fallen across the path, the bark gnarled and deeply scored, mossed over in places. The root bole twisted skywards, straggling roots grasping the air like desperate hands. It seemed almost indecent to see the roots exposed. Anna placed her hands on the trunk, letting her fingers settle into the deep green moss.

'I would have had a go at this with the chainsaw, but I thought there were other priorities,' Will said, slapping the trunk. His voice was loud, his cheerfulness piercing the wood's melancholy stillness.

She could just imagine him saying, 'Ho, Ho, Ho,' so it was almost a surprise when instead he said, 'Shall I give you a leg up?'

'No thanks, I can manage.' She gripped the mossy trunk, finding a foothold in the roots shooting out from the base of the tree, and then she was over. Will landed heavily beside her, rubbing his hands to get the green moss stains off.

Beyond the fallen tree the path narrowed and veered to the left, dropping down the valley. Brambles fit for Sleeping Beauty's castle arched among the trees, all leaning at precarious angles like drunks at a party.

Further on the path became a broad walk with the remnants of a beaten gravel surface visible under a thick layer of moss and decomposing leaves, punctuated by the occasional ash sapling. On either side the brambles had nearly taken over, thorny stems as thick as thumbs stretching into the trees and smothering any undergrowth. She scuffed the path with the toe of her boot to see if she could find the surface under the layers of leaf mould and moss. It was more like a woodland walk than the entrance to a landscape garden, but if it was a woodland walk, there should be some specimen trees. Anna looked around, recognising ash and sycamore, the usual suspects, though there was no sign of laurel or rhododendrons beneath the green gloom of the tree canopy, and nothing older than fifty years max.

They walked on to a point where the path divided into two, one fork going straight ahead, the other branching left. Amid the noise of wind in the leaves and the rustling of birds was another sound, a low chuckle. 'I can hear water,' Anna said.

Straight ahead was what had to be the first lake shown on the map, although it was anything but lake-like now, more like an elephant wallow, about thirty feet of stagnant water overhung by bushes. The edge of the pond was covered in layers of green algae, indicating that once the water level had been higher. A high bank had been built around it like encircling arms, with an opening marked by two large rocks directly opposite where they were standing. Immediately she wanted to get across to explore the opening, but how? There were no signs of a bridge or stepping stones. And where was the sound of water coming from? Something to explore later, if Mrs Davenport decided to continue with the research beyond this initial stage.

Anna and Will retraced their way back to the point where the path had split. The other fork led to steep steps up the bank, then further up the valley side until the path levelled out. They were still in woodland, but now Anna could catch glimpses of something shining through the trees: the second lake. She checked the map. The small square building should be near here. She looked ahead, and there it was, smothered in ivy. A castle keep, Mrs Davenport had called it. Anna approached and reached up, trying to feel the stone under the ivy. Her fingers caught what felt like ridges carved into the stone. It could be natural weathering, she thought, before ducking under the ivy and going in.

Light filtered down from the sky on to a square chamber about ten feet across. The back wall was solid, but the other walls had openings formed by two pillars with a large lintel on top. She peeped through the one opposite, and saw the path continue ahead round the edge of the lake. Then she tried the opening to her right. This led to a flat area covered with a mat of fallen leaves and branches, surrounded by brambles. She knelt and tried to clear away some of the debris with her hands and found flagstones. Through the trees and across the lake she could see something else. 'Is that the building Mrs Davenport calls the pavilion?'

Will nodded. Anna walked round the edge of the flat space in front of the building, then stopped at the furthest edge. Where the brambles weren't as thick, she could just make out steps going down to the lake. Something else for Will and his chainsaw to clear if – IF – Mrs Davenport decided to proceed.

Back on the path that circled the large oval lake, Anna tried to make sense of what she'd seen, fit it into previous gardens, known patterns. It obviously was a landscape garden, but as to the date, plan or purpose, she couldn't tell. Maybe it was just a couple of buildings placed around a lake. The area by the muddy pond was intriguing, but there didn't seem much evidence beyond that.

They had circled the top of the oval lake and in front of them was the third structure shown on the map, a stone building with a portico and a set of steps descending to the water's edge. It reminded Anna of paintings by Claude Lorrain, of imaginary classical cities, the water lapping at the base of temples and palaces. The portico had four columns supporting a triangular pediment above, a scaled-down version of a classical temple. Will slapped one of the columns. 'This has got to be something special, don't you think?'

'Well . . . to be honest, pavilions like this aren't that unusual.'

His brow creased with anxiety. 'I don't want Mrs D to be disappointed.'

'I'm sorry.' Anna made a gesture of apology with her hands. 'I can only report what I find. I can't make it up.'

'No, I can see that. It's just . . .' Will rubbed the back of his neck. 'She's been good to me.'

'The area round the pond is the most intriguing thing here. I'm sure that's worth investigating further,' Anna said, and was rewarded with a grin from Will. 'Do you know if there's ever been a bridge there, or stepping stones?'

'I thought you didn't want me to comment.'

Will sounded innocent enough, but Anna could detect a twinkle in his eyes. He was quite nice-looking when he wasn't sad. 'Make an exception.'

'Okay.' He looked around. 'I haven't a clue.'

That made her blink. 'I'm sorry?'

He shrugged his shoulders. 'I haven't a clue. No idea. Your guess is as good as mine.'

'But . . .' She stared at him. 'Aren't you the gardener?'

'Sure, but the first time I've been this way was last week, when Mrs D told me to make sure the paths were clear for your visit. I didn't even know there was a garden here, to be honest.'

Anna blinked. 'So you know as little about it as I do.'

'I hope not. You're supposed to be an expert.' Will grinned at her, and she smiled back, thinking how nice it was to be teased again. It had been a long time since anyone had talked to her like that.

There were French doors between the central pillars, and three windows to either side, the paint peeling off the frames exposing rotting wood. Anna rubbed at the glass with her sleeve to clear the grime, feeling a little like Howard Carter peering in at the tomb of Tutankhamun. 'What can you see?' they had asked him, and he'd replied, 'Wonderful things.' Anna peered and saw a jumble of odd bits of furniture, tennis racquets, old lamps, croquet mallets, even a boat, all shrouded by cobwebs. Not wonderful, but they conjured up images of carefree sunny days, pre-war perhaps, of tennis parties and croquet on the lawn, cucumber sandwiches and Earl Grey tea poured from a silver teapot into china cups.

She had pushed all thoughts of Richard out of her mind during the walk through the garden, losing herself in work, but now they flooded back, intense and insistent. A wave of sadness came over her, sadness for what had been and what might have been. She steadied herself, one hand on a column, and looked out across the lake. Her spirits lifted. Here was a landscape garden, waiting for her. The surface of the lake shimmered and sparkled in the summer sunshine and the air was fresh and new. I am so lucky, she thought. I'm here, in this beautiful place, and it's work. It's time for me to let Richard go. I have to move on and leave the past behind me. Start something new.

Chapter 3

Anna smoothed the 1900 Ordnance Survey map across her desk. Now . . . The day before she'd been to the county records office and the local museum looking for information about Templecombe, but had drawn a blank. The National Records Office in Swindon was next, but she had a nagging instinct that there was going to be nothing there. Still, at least Mrs Davenport had said there were boxes of estate papers relating to the house and garden up in the attics. Perhaps she'd find some information there.

The crash of the front door announced her sister's return. When Clare goes, Anna thought, looking up from the map, I shall have to get a lodger who appreciates words like fragile and subtlety. Thump, thump. Clare was apparently dragging a corpse up the stone stairs.

The study door burst open. 'I'm back,' Clare said.

'So I heard,' Anna replied, knowing that irony was another word Clare didn't have much time for. She stretched, easing her neck and shoulder muscles. Perhaps she should take up yoga.

Clare slumped on a chair. 'God, I'm exhausted, you've no idea what it's like. Non-stop emails, the phones ringing all the time, we're in a complete state of panic, what with that new restaurant opening – I'm sure I told you – and the photographer didn't turn up so the boss was not a happy bunny, but hey, at least the press was there, so the client can't complain too much. Not that that's going to stop him. I've never seen such a hissy fit. God, my feet hurt.' She slipped one foot out of its kitten heel and rubbed it. 'Mmm, speaking of which, I must get my wedding shoes sorted out. You could come and help me choose, if you like.'

'Okay,' Anna said absent-mindedly, thinking that tomorrow she'd go to Templecombe and search the attics for documents.

Clare looked over her shoulder at the map and giggled. 'It looks like a sperm,' she said, pointing to the curving path winding to the oval lake. Anna had to admit she was right. 'Any news about Bron?' Clare added.

Anna stopped rotating her right shoulder. 'What do you mean?'

'Nick called me at work – didn't he ring you?'

Anna shook her head. 'I turned the phone off so I could concentrate. What is it?'

'He rang ages ago – Bron's gone into labour.'

Anna grabbed the phone and turned it on. 'Are you sure? The baby's not due for six weeks.'

Clare shrugged. 'He probably left a message on your answer machine.'

Anna listened. Two messages. First Nick's voice telling her that Bronwen had been taken into hospital, and he'd call when there was any news. The second message was from a breathless girl saying she'd call her back soon. Anna checked her watch. Five hours since Nick had called. 'Aren't second babies supposed to be quicker?'

Clare shrugged. 'Search me. Look, there was something I wanted to ask you . . .'

'Sure,' Anna said, her mind on Bronwen. What was she doing now? Puffing and panting, or writhing in agony? Or sitting up and having a cup of tea, a neat little bundle wrapped up and tucked into the crook of one arm. She could call Nick's mobile – no, didn't you have to turn them off in hospital? She drummed her fingers on the table. She'd phone Gwyn. He'd know how Bron was.

She was about to dial Gwyn's number when the phone rang. She clutched the receiver, her hands shaking. Please let Bron be okay.

'Is that Dr Anna Carmichael? I'm calling from Balfour Productions.'

'Sorry?' Anna tried to concentrate.

The girl at the other end repeated herself. 'We're planning a series on historic gardens. Your name was given to us as someone who might be able to help.'

'Yes . . .' Anna struggled to pull herself together. 'I'm sorry, who did you say you were?' The girl repeated herself a third time, and this time the penny dropped. They must be the television company Gwyn had mentioned. She turned her back on Clare and tried to sound businesslike. 'What exactly are you looking for?'

The girl outlined their series, and then added, 'The thing is, we thought the presenter would be able to act as the consultant for the series, but it's, um, well . . .'

'Who is the presenter?'

'Hamish McCarthy.' She paused as if Anna should be impressed, but got no response so carried on. 'We've got a bit of a tight schedule. Would it be possible for you to come to London to discuss it further – we'd pay your expenses.'

'I don't see why not.' Anna picked up her diary and arranged a date for the following week.

When she put the phone down she turned to Clare. 'Have you ever heard of someone called Hamish McCarthy?'

'The TV gardener?' Clare said, her eyes lighting up. 'Oh, he's gorgeous, fab eyes and a great bum. A bit like Diarmuid Gavin, but wild and hairy.'

'What about the gardening?'

'He does that programme *Fantasy Gardens*, you know, they transform someone's suburban semi into an oasis in the Sahara complete with stuffed camels. And disco lights. I think he's got a bit of a thing about disco lights.'

'He doesn't sound like someone who'd present a historical garden programme,' Anna said.

'Is that what the call was about? He'd be fabularoony. You'd get people my age watching instead of all the old codgers.'

'Perhaps that's what they're thinking.' Gwyn had said ten minutes on television was worth ten years of careful research.

'Are you going to be on the box?' Clare asked.

Anna shook her head. 'Just being the consultant, helping to write the script, that sort of thing.'

'God, wouldn't it be brilliant if you got on the telly, even if it was a gardening programme. Hey, I'll come and do your clothes and make-up if you like – I know, you could leave your bra off like—'

The phone rang again, cutting Clare off. Anna grabbed it. 'Hello?'

Nick's voice came down the line. 'Just letting you know Bronwen's had the baby and everything's fine.'

'Thank God.' Anna gave a thumbs-up sign to Clare. 'How are they?'

'The baby's tiny compared to Toby, so tiny she almost fits into my hands. It was really different this time, much quicker – it's funny, you'd have thought second time around wouldn't be as exciting, but – of course, it was different, what with being an emergency . . .' He talked for a little while, his excitement bubbling, and Anna listened with relief. Extraordinary to think of Bron going through all that while she'd been sitting quietly working in her study. Nick added that the hospital wanted Bron and the baby to stay in for a few days, and suggested that Anna might visit the day after tomorrow.

'I'll do that. Ah, Nick, I'm so pleased for you both.'

'Gotta go, Anna. I just rang to let you know.'

'Send them my love.'

She put down the receiver and turned to Clare. 'It's a little girl, just under six pounds, and they're both fine.'

'Brilliant.' Clare stretched, and headed for the door. 'After all this excitement I'm going to collapse into a Malibu and Coke. Want one?'

The attics at Templecombe turned out to be extensive and crammed with boxes and wardrobes and enough trunks to sink the *Titanic* even if the iceberg hadn't been around. But that was the nature of these old houses, Anna thought, although her heart sank at the sight. Generations of wealthy families, each discarding items no longer in fashion, the cast-offs accumulating in layers in spacious attics and cavernous cellars. She looked around her. Where to start?

She decided on a large steamer trunk with initials picked out in round-headed nails. As she lifted the lid, a familiar thrill ran though her. What would be there? She plunged her hands into the trunk, like a glorified lucky dip, and sneezed as clouds of dust rose up. Inside was a dinner service interleaved with layers of *The Times* for protection. She checked the masthead: 4 April 1947. She sneezed again, eyes watering from the dust, and stood up, needing to open a window.

The attics followed the square design of the house, with dormer windows facing outwards to the garden. There were also two glazed doors for access to the central flat roof. Anna tried the handle of the nearest. Locked. She could imagine the servants meeting out on the leaded roof, perhaps sharing a furtive cigarette. If she'd been born two hundred, even a hundred years ago her world might have been contained within walls like these, freezing in winter and boiling in summer. It was certainly stifling now.

She crossed the attic and tried one of the windows. She didn't think it was locked, but layers of paint had jammed it into place. From up here she could see along the valley towards the landscape garden. She peered out, trying to see more, and caught a glimpse of light reflected off the lake, but the garden was virtually hidden, even from this high vantage point. Strange to make a garden on such a scale but keep it so private. But rich people were able to indulge their whims. The Duke of Portland – she couldn't remember if he'd been the fifth or sixth – had been so obsessed by privacy that he'd virtually rebuilt his house underground, complete with ballroom and billiard room. Not that she'd ever managed to see it: the house and estate were now a training centre for the MOD, who were as keen on Keep Out notices as any eighteenth-century duke.

Her eyes narrowed. A man – no, two men were coming out of the trees along the path. Was it Will the gardener? She rubbed the glass with her sleeve but only succeeded in making it smeary as well as grubby. They'd stopped to talk and were looking up towards the house. She stood on tiptoe, craning her neck. They were below the ha-ha, and almost out of sight under the overhang. One of the men was bald, she thought, and the taller one seemed too dark for Will. And they were wearing suits . . .

She jumped as she heard a noise behind her. 'D'you make a habit of sneaking up on people?' she said, cross at being caught snooping.

Will grinned at her. 'Nope, just with you.'

'Well, stop it.' So it wasn't Will in the garden. But who then? 'Will, come here a sec and tell me—' She looked back out of the window, but the men had disappeared from sight.

'What?' Will stood next to her and peered out.

'Nothing.' She felt strangely disappointed, although it was none of her business who was walking around in the garden. Will, next to her, was still looking out. He seemed cleaner and tidier than on her previous visit, less scruffy and sweaty. Perhaps he'd tidied himself up for her, she thought with a spike of interest. No, he was probably married. She checked his hands, strong and capable. No wedding ring. Not that that meant anything. Richard hadn't worn one either. She brushed her hand over her eyes. The attics were stifling.

'Do you think you could get this window open?' she asked Will. 'I tried, but it's jammed.'

Will tugged at the sash, then leant into the window like a rugby player joining the scrum, and gave a mighty heave. The window flew up and fresh air rushed in. 'There,' he said, rubbing his hands together. 'Mrs D. sent me up to help.'

'I thought you were the gardener.' Anna leaned out, but the men had gone from view.

'Gardener, chauffeur, odd-job man. Attic sorter. Whatever she wants me to be.'

Anna nodded. So not a professional gardener.

'Where shall I start?'

She ran quickly over the sort of things they were looking for: estate papers, maps, inventories of what was in the grounds, purchase ledgers showing how much the labourers were paid or the cost of damming the lake, old photographs that might show the garden as it had been, diaries, letters describing the place. 'Oh, and don't forget there might be something in the packing, so you need to check that too.'

They worked solidly for the next two hours, pulling open drawers, checking wardrobes, opening boxes. Anna yearned to explore further: a trunk full of tureens wrapped in hand-stitched quilts; a box of Victorian prints which she'd got excited about until she realised that they weren't of gardens but of Scottish attractions such as Arthur's Seat and Fingal's Cave; the contents of a doll's house; old tennis rackets and a croquet set, a collection of lead crystal mille fiori paperweights. If you had the space, you could save everything, she thought, the heavy weight smooth and firm in her palm.

The morning light streamed through the windows, casting squares of light on the dusty floors that moved round the attic as they worked. Will showed Anna anything he thought might be of interest. He seemed less sad today, and although they didn't talk much, Anna felt comfortable and pleased to have his company. She accumulated a large pile: a stack of old ledgers to check through, several sheaves of letters bound with faded ribbon, papers tied with battered string. And other treasures: a baby's satin shoe, tied with finely knitted thread that was like a whisper, a tortoiseshell comb with silver inlay, a linen handkerchief with a hand-stitched monogram. She traced her fingers over the letters. JF.

'What about these?' Will held up a small suitcase stuffed with a tumble of black-and-white photographs.

'You've found photographs! Brilliant!' She was across to his side of the attic in seconds. The first photographs appeared to show a house party of some sort. The men were in high-waisted, pleated white trousers with tennis rackets slung over their shoulders, the girls in drop-waisted dresses and white stockings. Lives caught and frozen in time. Anna studied the background. In one, a group of young men and women were lounging on what had to be the pavilion steps, but the photographer had cut off the pavilion itself. In another, a couple dressed in sheets posed as if statues, wreaths around their hair, but Anna couldn't make out anything in the background beyond generic hedge.

'Any good?'

She put the photographs back in the suitcase. 'Not enough of the garden. And they're nineteen-twenties or -thirties, judging by the clothes. I'd really like to find something earlier, anything that would give an indication of when the garden was built.'

'Aren't there records?'

'Not a sausage so far.' She picked up a box of papers and began to look through them. 'We only know the things people have written about. If no one's kept a diary, or letters, then how can you tell? And we may be looking in the wrong place. A hundred years ago, one of the children may have got married and gone to live in Norfolk, or Cumbria, taking their granny's diary with them.' Her heart leapt as she spotted a bound book in the pile of papers, but it was too modern, 1950s she guessed, flicking through. 'So perhaps in some attic in Norwich or Carlisle there's a load of estate documents about this house. Or they might have ended up the local county record office. Either way, we won't know.'

'Aren't all the records on line?'

Anna laughed. 'That would be way too easy. It's a question of money. As ever.' She glanced up to catch Will looking at her. 'There's nothing here,' she said, putting the book down and feeling suddenly shy. He was attractive, she supposed, if you liked the outdoors type. Go on, have a bit of rough, she could imagine Bronwen saying. Anna inwardly shook her head. No, no gardeners for me. But then Will said he wasn't a gardener. She glanced at him, and wondered what he was if not a gardener. Mrs Davenport spoke to him as if he were her social equal, which was strange. Yet he described himself as the odd-job man. He didn't seem like an odd-job man, she thought. He seemed too, well, educated to be that. Perhaps he's done something terrible in the past and is on the run, she thought, then smiled to herself at the fantasy. Whatever, it's none of my business.

There was a noise behind her, and she turned to see the housekeeper, Peggy, at the attic door.

'Goodness, but it's a long way up here,' Peggy said, out of breath. 'How are you doing?'

Anna glanced at Will. 'Not too bad.'

'Mrs Davenport says to tell you that lunch will be ready in twenty minutes.'

'Lunch? I hadn't realised it was so late.' Anna's stomach gave a rumble. 'But I wasn't expecting to be given lunch. I've brought sandwiches.'

'Mrs Davenport has told me to prepare lunch for you.' Peggy spoke firmly.

Anna gave in gracefully. After all, with Will's help she had got further than she had expected. 'That sounds lovely, Peggy,' she said, conscious of her dusty hair and dirty hands. 'I'd better wash.'

After a session in a bathroom that could have doubled as an ice house despite the summer sun, Anna felt she looked almost presentable. As she came downstairs she saw the top of Will's blond head disappearing through a door under the stairs that she assumed led to the kitchen area of the house, but when she followed him Peggy shooed her away, directing her to the dining room. Obviously the spirit of *Upstairs, Downstairs* reigned at Templecombe. Anna crossed the hall, not sure that she wanted to be classed as Upstairs, and pushed open the door Peggy had indicated.

The dining room had a look of having been furnished in 1890 and not changed since, just polished and buffed to keep up appearances. The mahogany table was laid with three places, complete with silver cutlery and linen table napkins. Anna's heart sank. Please don't let this go on for ever, she thought. I want to finish in the attic and go home, preferably with a good-sized box of inventories or diaries. She looked around the room at the portraits lining the walls, leaders and commanders all, judging by the number of medals festooning the scarlet coats.

She went to the end of the room to the long windows looking out on to the garden at the back of the house, a lawn enclosed by a high wall with a gate set in it. Beyond she could make out a church spire. Clare was planning a church wedding, possibly the biggest, most traditional wedding in the country. She picked at a bit of flaking paint on the window frame. Perhaps Richard and she would have stayed married if they'd had a big church wedding rather than a few minutes in a registry office, both of them delirious with the secrecy, the lack of ceremony. She rested her forehead against the cool glass of the window and stared unseeingly into the garden. They'd been so happy that day, or so she'd thought, whatever Richard said later.

No, this had to stop. I must stop thinking about him. I must move on. She smiled, thinking of Bronwen urging her to play the field, have a good time, go mad for a change. I'd love to see her face if I did go mad, if I turned up with a Hell's Angel, say, riding pillion on his chopper with a skull and crossbones on my crash helmet.

Hey, why not go really wild, ditch the helmet and ride with the wind in my hair?

Hmm. She ran her finger over the flaked patch, feeling the roughness of the bare wood underneath. Perhaps not. But someone different from her. Perhaps she ought to consider Will the gardener. He was attractive, seemed a nice guy, so why not? She tried to imagine what going out with him would involve. Trips to the local agricultural show, evenings out with the Young Farmers, pints of scrumpy, raw and fresh enough to take a layer of skin off the top of your mouth, then bumping home in a beat-up Land Rover with no suspension to speak of. Ah, that was unfair. She'd only just met the guy. He was probably married already and lived in a cottage with pink rambler roses round the door, lots of tousle-haired toddlers and a pretty blonde wife called Rosie. All the best men were taken. Besides, she wanted to move outside her own little world, someone not involved with gardening or heritage. I wish, I wish, I wish.

The door creaked behind her and she turned, expecting to see Mrs Davenport. Instead a man entered the room as if he owned it. He was dark-haired, like one of the portraits come to life, but instead of a soldier's jacket and a row of medals, he wore a striped shirt open at the neck and a charming smile.

'Hello,' he said, strolling towards her. 'I didn't know we had company.'

Chapter 4

A nna stared at him, her mind in overdrive. The appearance in the dining room of a good-looking man when she'd been expecting an elderly lady had completely thrown her. Who was he?

'I'm Anna,' she said. 'Anna Carmichael. The garden historian.' Damn. Her voice had gone up at the end as if she wasn't sure.

'Ah, the expert,' he said, holding out his hand. 'Oliver Davenport. Not an expert at anything.' He smiled as he shook her hand, grey-blue eyes looking directly into hers, and Anna was furious to realise she felt pink all over. 'My grandmother told me she'd asked someone to look at the garden. I imagined a tweedy lady in half-moon glasses with strong views on compost and pillar-of-the-community stamped across her forehead.'

So he was Mrs Davenport's grandson. Things were looking up. It must have been him she'd seen from the window, she thought, though he'd ditched the suit jacket. She realised she was still holding his hand and snatched it away, then tucked her hair behind her ears as if that was what she'd meant to do all along. Then untucked it.

'And have you yet found anything worth researching?'

'It's early days,' she said, wishing fervently she could think of something witty and interesting to say to get a conversation going, but her brain seemed to have seized up. Thankfully the door opened and Mrs Davenport entered, saving her from the immediate need to contribute anything.

Oliver immediately went and helped his grandmother into the chair at the head of the table, tucking a shawl around her shoulders and making sure her stick and handbag were within reach. Then he pulled out the chair to Mrs Davenport's left for Anna.

'Thanks,' she mumbled, feeling self-consciousness settle on her like an iron overcoat. Oh to be the sort of person who knew what to say, who could talk to anyone, who didn't feel their brain shrivelling up to the size of a walnut while their tongue and hands grew to gargantuan proportions. Oliver settled himself opposite her.

'I'm so pleased you are able to join us, Dr Carmichael,' Mrs Davenport said, pressing what looked like a doorbell on the table. A faint buzz sounded in the hall. 'Tell me, have you discovered anything up in the attics?'

Peggy entered and distributed plates of sliced melon while Anna gave a brief report on the morning's activities. 'But there's still this afternoon to go. There are some interesting things up there,' she added.

'Such as?'

'I saw a box filled with paperweights, for instance. I'm not an expert, but some looked like Baccarat.'

'Ah, yes.' Mrs Davenport leaned back, a distant look in her eyes. 'A great-aunt of mine collected them – my mother's side of the family, Oliver, the Leicestershire Naughtons of course, not the Norfolk Naughtons.' She talked about family relationships for a little while. Oliver, eating melon, nodded politely but appeared uninterested in the difference between the Leicestershire and Norfolk Naughtons.

'My mother kept a few out on display.' Mrs Davenport's face lit up. 'I think they're in the vitrine. Oliver, be a darling and look for me.' She pointed to a small glass-topped table and Oliver obediently went to it. Mrs Davenport leant towards Anna. 'Typical man,' she said in what she obviously thought was a quiet whisper. 'Not interested in his heritage. It's always the women who keep these things together.'

Anna glanced at Oliver, who had lifted up the top of the vitrine and was taking out some small objects. He looked amused, obviously unfussed by his grandmother's assessment. 'There. Enough trinkets to sink a small ship.'

He had brought over a collection of small pillboxes, a couple of paperweights, and some pieces of silver including a miniature chest of drawers and chairs scaled to suit Thumbelina. Anna picked up one of the paperweights. 'Lead crystal millefiori work,' she said. 'Lovely.'

'What's that?' Oliver said.

'Millefiori. Look.' She held out the paperweight and he took it. 'The glass rods are rolled and twisted together, then cut so it looks like millions of tiny flowers.'

Oliver cupped the paperweight in his hands. 'I suppose it's one up on a Santa in a snowstorm.'

'Bad boy,' Mrs Davenport said, her voice dripping with indulgence. 'I know you're only doing it to tease.'

Anna picked up the box nearest to her and examined it. The oval lid was made of ivory painted with glowing washes of delicate colour and depicted dancers dressed in togas, hands joined to form a circle: a Dance to the Music of Time, a favourite theme in the eighteenth century. Each figure represented a season, Spring young and fresh-faced, Winter old and white-haired, and in the background the dark figure of Death lurked among the trees. She felt a brief pang of envy that if she'd been looking at her mother's trinkets there'd be nothing as delicate as this, more china Siamese cats with glinting glass eyes. She picked up another box; this time the pattern on the lid was formed from various shades of gold. Technically clever, but not to her taste. The third box looked of a later date, with a geometric pattern set with glittering stones. She squinted at the underneath. 'I think that's the Fabergé mark.'

Oliver stopped munching. 'Fabergé?' he repeated.

'I think so,' Anna said. 'But it looks quite late, more deco.'

'It must be worth a fortune,' Oliver said taking the box from her. 'Are the stones real?'

'Probably.'

Oliver examined the box more closely, his demeanour reverential. Anna watched, amused at his intent expression. Brand names bestowed glamour, regardles of artistic worth. Clare worshipped at the altar of Prada and Dolce and Gabbana. It was the same with antiques: Chippendale, Sheraton, Hepplewhite. 'If you had to pick one, which would you choose?'

'This one, of course.' He looked surprised that she should ask. 'The Fabergé.'

'And if I say that I think the oval box is worth more?' Anna looked across at him.

'You're too clever for me,' Oliver said, laughing and putting the box down. 'You're quite right, I was assuming that something by Fabergé would be worth a bomb. You've exposed my shallow superficiality.' He shook his head as if in sorrow, although the expression of mischief in his eyes gave no indication of repentance.

Peggy brought in the main course, roast beef, and laid dishes of roast potatoes, cabbage and peas on the table. It was just like Easter Sunday at Anna's home, except they'd had lamb. The fatted calf might have been more appropriate, given her mother's delight in Clare's engagement. She wondered if Mrs Davenport ate like this every day, or if it was for her benefit, or Oliver's. He was making sure his grandmother had everything she wanted: gravy, mustard, salt. She liked him for it, and the way he'd laughed at himself.

Mrs Davenport started on a long tale about the village, something to do with avocados and the WI, and Anna and Oliver both listened, Oliver apparently engrossed by the saga, asking questions every now and then about the characters, his tone one of affection. Mrs Davenport was flushed with his attention, and Anna wondered if she was lonely. That might explain why she was so friendly with Will. But there was no doubt she was enjoying Oliver's company now. It was good the way he was concentrating on his grandmother, drawing her out rather than rushing in with his own stories. Physically he reminded Anna a little of Richard, both of them being tall and dark-haired, but if Richard was a watercolour, Oliver was a confident oil. She could imagine him being painted by John Bratby, bold sweeps of colour applied thickly with a palette knife.

She stabbed a bit of cabbage with her fork. It didn't matter if she liked him; there was no way someone like that would be interested in her. He probably had a girlfriend already, with long brown legs and sunglasses holding streaked blonde hair off her face, and a dinky little handbag that couldn't take anything more than a credit card, lipstick, and the smallest of mobile phones.

He suddenly glanced across at her and she immediately looked down at her plate, wishing she could think of something to say, anything other than sitting mute like a dummy. But now the conversation was coming round to things she knew about, houses and gardens, the past rather than the present, and she felt able to join in, gradually gaining confidence. By the time Peggy cleared their plates away, she felt more at ease.

'Did your friend like the garden?' she said.

Oliver looked startled. 'What?'

'Your friend. It was you in the garden earlier this morning, wasn't it?' She had a picture in her mind of the tall man in the suit standing with the bald man. 'This morning, when I was in the attics, I looked out and saw—'

'Not me, I arrived just before lunch,' Oliver cut in, shaking his head. 'Maybe it was that layabout Grandma wastes her money on.'

'Oliver.' Mrs Davenport's voice was sharp.

'Come on, Gran. The place is falling apart.'

'And would be worse without William's help.' Mrs Davenport's face was stern.

Oliver looked as if he was going to say something, then checked himself. He took his grandmother's hand in both of his.

'I worry about you,' he said gently. 'The house, the garden. It's too much with just Peggy to look after you – and she's getting on. What if you fell, or had some sort of accident?'

'William would be here.'

Anna looked from one to the other, Mrs Davenport's expression stubborn, Oliver's charming. She could feel the currents between them, but had no idea what they might mean.

'We don't know that. He turned up out of nowhere, he could go tomorrow. You've no idea what he's doing; he could be inviting anyone on to the estate.' He swept his hand through his hair. 'Next thing we know, we'll have a travellers' camp here.'

'It couldn't have been Will I saw this morning,' Anna said. 'He was helping me in the attics. I thought it was you . . .'

'Maybe you were mistaken,' Oliver said, with an easy smile.

Anna frowned. She could see the men in her mind's eye, but she could have been wrong – the glass had been dirty, the men a long way away. 'I must have been,' she said, puzzled.

Peggy brought in a silver bowl of sugared almonds and a pot of coffee, which Oliver served. 'Was the man you saw bald?' he said suddenly. Anna nodded. 'Mystery solved. It must have been Bob Henderson, collecting for Christian Aid. I bumped into him as he was walking through the garden back to the village.'

'You should have asked him in,' Mrs Davenport said. 'I haven't seen Bob for weeks.'

'I did, but he wanted to get on. He said he'd got the rest of the village to do.'

Anna thought of pointing out that she'd seen the men much earlier on. If Oliver had only just arrived, the timing was wrong. But

Mrs Davenport was looking drawn, so she decided to say nothing.

'If you'll excuse me, I'm going to have a little lie-down,' Mrs Davenport said, getting to her feet. 'Oliver darling, I want you to help Dr Carmichael up in the attics.'

Oliver looked across at Anna. 'I'd love to,' he said.

Oliver stood in the dusty attic, incongruously clean and elegant amid the higgledy-piggledy boxes and suitcases.

'You don't have to help,' Anna said, amused by his horror.

'I can't leave you to do all this on your own,' he said. 'You might never emerge again, swamped by all this junk.' Anna raised an eyebrow. 'Come on, it *is* junk. My inheritance, what's more.'

'Is it?' Anna said, curious to know more.

'It's either me or the cats' home. There's no one else,' Oliver said. He leaned over a box and with one finger cautiously raised the lid. 'We're not prolific breeders in my family,' he said, peering in. 'If anything, the opposite. And we're rather prone to dying young. But don't worry, I don't propose to die just yet.' Oliver sneezed, and let the lid flop down. 'Although I might suffocate. Surely you're not going to waste time going through all this rubbish.'

'It's my job.'

'Hmm. And are you happy in your work?'

'Very,' Anna said with emphasis.

'God, I wish I was,' he said as he moved across to the window and peered out. There was an elegance about him that wasn't just down to the expensive clothes he wore so casually. There was an economy of effort, the sense that he was gliding through life. Anna sat back on her haunches. Easy enough to glide if you were rich.

'What do you do?' she asked.

'Insurance.' He leant languidly against the window frame, reminiscent of the Hilliard miniature of a young aristocrat at the court of Elizabeth I – good-looking, confident, although minus the dangling pearl earring. 'It's very boring.'

'Why don't you leave?' Anna said, surprised that he should continue with a job he didn't enjoy. Fair enough, some people didn't get the choice, but surely with his background he could do what he pleased.

'It's the family firm, and anyway, insurance is very lucrative.' Anna could see that it was; a sleek veneer of wealth covered him. 'Is garden history lucrative?'

'Not at all,' Anna said, thinking of the sorry state of her bank account. 'But it's never boring either.'

'But dusty.' He glanced around at the boxes and trunks.

'Sometimes,' Anna conceded. 'And muddy and wet and cold at others.'

He smiled at that but said nothing as he left the window and strolled the length of the attic, looking into opened boxes, flipping the lids of suitcases. Anna thought he was like a cat in new surroundings, sniffing, staking out territory. At the corner he paused, before turning round and marching back to where Anna knelt on the floor. 'Right. I'm at your command. What do you want me to do?'

'I'm looking for any papers and documents relating to the garden. Your grandmother says she can remember a box filled with them, but can't help me any further. There might be paintings or photographs or maps – anything that might help with how the garden looked before it became overgrown.'

'Can't you work it out from what's left?'

Anna shrugged, a large platter in her hands. 'Buildings may have vanished, statues may have been moved, coppiced trees become overgrown.'

'So if you don't find anything up here, you're scuppered.'

'Oh no, there are other avenues to explore. But it would help a great deal. If you could do those . . .' She pointed.

Oliver tugged an imaginary forelock. 'Yes, m'lady.'

Anna watched him cautiously open a suitcase and rummage gingerly through the contents. Strange to think that a hundred years ago if she'd been a servant she'd have kept her eyes lowered as he passed, yet here she was telling him what to do. The servants then would have slipped warming pans between the starched linen sheets of his bed, heaved copper buckets up to his room for his bath and never mind the splashes of boiling water on hard-working hands. They would have known everything about him, and yet he would have known little about them. He'd never have come up to these attics, unless it was to seduce one of the maids, creeping up the narrow stairs after a good evening at the brandy. Poor girls; there were so many stories about young maids being led astray by a gentleman then abandoned with a baby on the way.

'That was a big sigh.'

Anna sat up, practically dropping the platter. 'I was thinking . . .'

'About what?' His eyes held hers.

She began wrapping the platter up in newspaper again, hands working fast, keeping her head down so he wouldn't see her blush. 'Nothing. Nonsense.'

The attic door opened. 'Will!' Anna exclaimed with relief at a diversion from the confusion of Oliver's presence.

Will's broad smile faded as he clocked Oliver. 'I came to see if you needed help.'

'That'd be great. You know what to do,' Anna said, waving her hand at the boxes, trying to make him feel welcome.

Will hesitated. 'It's probably a bit crowded with three. I've got other stuff to be doing.'

Oliver straightened up. 'A priority would be to clear the ivy from the front of the house. It's going to have the roof down soon.' He spoke pleasantly, but Will's face stiffened.

'I can't do everything,' he said.

Both men appeared relaxed, but Anna sensed a charged atmosphere between them, like two dogs circling each other deciding whether to fight. Perhaps Will resented Oliver for being the owner's grandson, for belonging despite rarely being here. She'd worked in other great houses and knew that not everyone was as loyal as their employer might have wished. Underneath the deference corrosive envy sometimes lurked. Not that she'd thought Will was the sort to be bitter, but then she hardly knew him.

'No one's expecting you to,' Oliver replied, smooth as cream on apple pie. 'If you think your time's best used up here, then be my guest. Alternatively, I'm sure there are things Dr Carmichael would like done in the garden.'

'Well . . .' Anna looked from one man to the other, Oliver silkily in control, Will wrong-footed and out of place. 'If you were going to clear ivy, I think there are some carvings on that sentry box thing opposite the pavilion—'

'The gateway,' Oliver interjected.

'Of course,' Anna said. How stupid of her. Oliver probably knew the garden as well as anyone. 'Is that what it's called?'

He smiled back. 'I don't think that's its official name, just what I called it as a kid.'

Anna realised she was staring at Oliver as if he'd just made the most profound comment in the history of the universe. With a conscious effort she shook her attention away from him and back to Will. 'It would be brilliant to see what's underneath.'

Will shrugged. 'That's what I'll do then.' He paused, as if waiting for someone to say something. Anna had that feeling she could remember from school, of someone wanting to come and join in a game, but hovering on the edges, not invited in.

'Only if you want to,' she added quickly.

'It sounds like a job that needs to be done for you to continue your research,' Oliver said.

'Yes, but I'm sure Will has other things to be doing, more important things . . .' She didn't want to sound as if she was ordering Will about, but Oliver had no such qualms.

'Then it might as well be done now.' His tone was pleasant, but final.

Will looked at Anna, who looked at the floorboards. She didn't want to hurt his feelings, but it would have to be done at some stage and it was logical for him to do it now rather than look through the attics for papers, especially as Oliver was helping her. And it was Oliver's family history, not Will's. But she felt guilty about turning down his offer; if Oliver hadn't been helping her, she'd have been glad of Will's company. She said nothing.

Oliver waited until Will had gone and they could hear his boots clattering down the stairs. 'I don't know how my grandmother puts up with him. Or why.' Anna made a little gesture with her hands, reluctant to talk about Will behind his back. 'He pitched up here four months ago, no experience, no background, no references, and she took him on. He's got some sort of hold on her.'

'Surely not,' Anna said, startled. But then, only earlier that day she'd been wondering about Will, about who he was and the relationship between him and Mrs Davenport. Perhaps Oliver was right.

'Since he's been here things have changed,' Oliver said.

'Like what?'

'Lots of things. This research, for example. Getting her all excited for no purpose.' He pushed his hair off his forehead. 'Look, I don't mean to knock what you're doing, but I'm not convinced it's worth-while.'

Anna gasped. 'Don't you – don't you want to know about the garden?'

'Up to a point, yes, but there's nothing left, is there? You've seen how rundown the place is. Nothing personal, but I can't help but think the money she's spending on your research would be better spent on fixing the roof. And even if you do discover there was something here two hundred years ago, it doesn't change anything. Anyone can see it would cost hundreds of thousands of pounds – probably millions – to restore, let alone the maintenance.'

Anna knew what he said was true. 'But that's nothing to do with Will.'

He sighed. 'Since this man's been here, a lot more money's been going out of my grandmother's account and I'm worried. I hope it's going on the maintenance of the house and garden, but who knows? I can't be down here all the time.' He looked up as if struck by a thought. 'Look, I don't want to put you in an awkward position, but would you – well, if you saw anything untoward, would you let me know?'

'You mean spy on Will?'

'Of course not. Just . . . if you saw anything, or heard anything.'

Anna hesitated. Will struck her as being a good person, gentle and considerate. On the other hand, there was a haunting air of sadness about him hinting at something more complicated than what was on the surface.

'I'm really worried about my grandmother,' Oliver said softly. 'I wouldn't ask otherwise.'

Anna nodded slowly. 'I'll let you know if I think there's anything going on.'

'Thank you,' he said, and despite her misgivings, Anna's heart gave a leap of excitement.

Chapter 5

'Whatever you do, don't make me laugh,' Bronwen said. 'Or I'll burst my stitches.'

Anna didn't like to think about which bits might have needed stitching. 'Can we pretend I'm a man,' she said. 'A gay man.'

'Squeamish?' Bronwen asked.

Anna nodded, feeling enclosed by the curtains that had been pulled round the bed, shutting out the bustle of the hospital ward. She concentrated on Bronwen. Despite her defiant dyed-plum hair and her electric-blue nightdress Bron looked tired, less than her usual vibrant self, Anna thought with concern, noticing the dark shadows.

'When you've had all those doctors lining up to pull the baby out of you like the story of the giant turnip, you become the woman that shame forgot.' Bronwen looked down at the baby tucked into her arm. 'Do you want to hold her?'

The baby seemed very small, wrapped tight in a bright flannelette blanket like a startling pink enchilada. 'Didn't swaddling go out in the Middle Ages?' Anna asked.

'Babies like being wrapped up, it makes them feel secure. If you don't, they wave their little arms and legs about like upturned beetles and wail. Here . . .' Bronwen held the bundle out to Anna. 'Don't drop her.'

Anna held the baby, worried she might do something wrong. One tiny fist clutched the edge of the blanket, the size of a fifty-pence piece. With a hesitant finger Anna stroked the baby's hair. Her skin was a delicate pink and her hair golden wisps finer than thistledown. A small mouth opened into a gaping yawn then relaxed into little sucking movements. 'She's lovely,' Anna said, enchanted. The baby had an expression of great determination as she began to wave her hands beyond the top of the blanket, fingers poking through the filigree pattern of her woolly jumper, which Anna gently disentangled. 'She looks like you,' she added, glancing at Bronwen.

Bronwen beamed. 'All newborns look like wizened shrimps, and she's no exception,' she said, the pride in her voice giving the lie to her words. 'Worse, because she was so early.' She lay back against the pillows with an air of great satisfaction. 'We'll probably have to stick around here for a bit, which is a bore, just to check she's feeding and doing all that baby stuff.'

'Poor you.' The baby stirred, made pouting motions. 'I think she's waking up.'

'Quick, pop her down in the crib, and perhaps she'll sleep for a bit longer,' Bronwen said, showing she was a fully paid-up member of the good-enough-mother club.

Anna carefully put the baby into the crib at the foot of the bed, relieved not to be holding her in case she did something wrong, but also missing the warmth of the tiny body against hers.

'I got you these,' she said, draping a bunch of grapes over Bronwen's bedside locker next to the present she'd brought for the baby. She'd hardly settled on the sole chair before the curtains round the bed were swept back with a flourish.

'So how's the new mother?' Gwyn swooped in, kissed Bronwen, then Anna, nicked a handful of grapes and leaned over the crib. 'Hello, sweetheart, it's your wicked uncle here,' he said, making a clucking noise to the sleeping baby. 'She's just like you, she doesn't listen to a word I say,' he pronounced, plonking himself down on the end of the bed. 'But with Nick's nose.'

'She hasn't, she's got a darling little nose,' Bronwen said, sitting up.

'Nah, she's definitely Nick's daughter.' He fed the grapes into his mouth, rat-a-tat, then reached across for some more.

'Don't jog around so,' Bronwen said, clutching her tummy. 'Respect my stitches.'

'I've got to eat the grapes,' Gwyn said, in mock horror. 'It's compulsory for visitors to eat all the patient's grapes.'

'Sit here, Gwyn,' Anna said, getting up from the chair, worried about Bronwen's stitches.

'You can sit on my lap,' Gwyn said, patting his knees. Anna gave him a look, and perched on one of the chair arms while Bronwen filled him in on what had happened. Anna noticed she gave him the U-certificate version. She wondered if when men got together they discussed their prostates and hernias in glorious Technicolor. The only thing she knew about prostates was they could become enlarged, which as she didn't know what size they were to start off with didn't help much. An enlarged one could be the size of a walnut or a football and she would be none the wiser. She smiled. Funny how discussions of men's bits ended up in a discussion of size. In fact, everything desirable for men seemed related to size. Bigger car engine, bigger skyscraper, bigger boobs. She looked down at her own. Perhaps I should get a Wonderbra.

'How are things?' Gwyn said, jerking her away from the possibilities of making mountains out of molehills.

'Fine. I've started researching a new garden. Very overgrown, but I think mainly eighteenth-century. There's an odd area that I think might lead to a tunnel or a grotto.' Gwyn sucked in his breath and opened his mouth but Anna beat him to it. 'And no, I won't go exploring any tunnels unless I know it's quite safe.'

'Much documentary evidence?'

Anna shook her head. 'I spent all of yesterday going through the attics in search of some papers that were supposed to be up there, but I couldn't find anything.'

'A whole day wasted,' Bronwen said sympathetically.

'I didn't mind,' Anna said, thinking of Oliver. He'd been useless at searching, but good at making her laugh. 'Anyway, the owner's commissioned a full report with a view to restoring the garden to its former glory.'

'What are the people like?' Bronwen said.

'Nice, but a bit *Upstairs, Downstairs.* The owner is very old – I think she might be in her eighties or even nineties – and the place is falling to pieces, everything is patched and mended.' Anna remembered Oliver talking about how he was worried about his grandmother's money, how it was disappearing from her account.

'Is it just the old lady? No dishy sons for you to fall in love with?'

'No sons, but there's a grandson, and a gardener.' She casually ate one of Bronwen's grapes, feeling her cheeks flush.

'Aha!' Bronwen said, sharp as ever. 'Is he nice?'

'Who?'

'Either!'

'They're both nice,' Anna said primly, thinking that Oliver Davenport was definitely more than nice, but way out of her league. She wondered if he would be staying at Templecombe for the weekend.

'But which one are you going to fall for?' Bronwen's face was alert.

'Neither.' Anna shook her head. 'Have you decided on a name for the baby?'

Bronwen gave her a look that said, I know you're distracting me but I'll let you. 'Not yet. Nick wants to call her Imogen, I want to call her Angharad and Toby wants to call her Parsley after the cat.'

'Good thing the cat's not called Tiddles,' Anna said. 'Tiddles Thompson.'

'I was at school with someone called Courtney Fish,' Bronwen said. 'I think that's mean, I really do.'

Anna suddenly remembered. 'I forgot to tell you – I've got some news.'

'What?'

'Guess.' She couldn't keep the grin off her face.

'Some mug's offered to buy your car?' Gwyn's suggestion.

'Ha ha, very funny.' She was bursting for them to guess.

'Give us a clue. You're all lit up like a Christmas tree.'

'Well, it's something to do with . . . appearances.' She looked at Bronwen, willing her to guess right.

Bronwen frowned. 'I can't think. Pregnancy's turned my brain to mush. Umm – you're getting your hair cut.' Anna pulled a face, tossing her long straight hair back over her shoulder. 'You ought to, you know. All that hair hanging down makes you look mousy.'

'It's not my hair. Something serious.'

'Something to do with television?' Gwyn said, his tone arch.

'You knew.' Anna stared at him. 'That was quick. I only heard myself the day before yesterday.'

'A little bird told me.' He looked smug. Gwyn was famous for his little birds; he could have stocked an aviary.

'What's this about television?' Bronwen said, eating a grape.

'They want me to help write the script for a television series on historic gardens.' Anna laughed. 'I think they were a bit desperate.'

'But that's brilliant. Will you still know us when you're famous?'

Anna snorted. 'Don't be daft, I'm not presenting it. They've got some guy called Hamish McCarthy for that.'

'Oh, I love him! He's gorgeous,' Bronwen said. 'There you are, your big chance to have his babies.'

'He's not my type,' Anna said, thinking of Oliver. She'd do the garden survey on Monday. Maybe he'd still be there.

*

To Anna's disappointment, Oliver wasn't at Templecombe on her next visit. Still, she couldn't imagine him helping her the way Will was doing, standing patiently holding the sighting target steady with one hand and the measuring tape with the other, while Anna squinted through her inclinometer to measure the fall in gradient. She wrote down the measurement, then checked the direction with her compass.

'Have you come to any conclusions yet?' Will asked. 'About the garden.'

'Not yet,' Anna mumbled, holding her pencil between her teeth as she flipped to the next page of her notebook. 'The only thing is that I think this was designed as a private rather than a public space. Is the tape taut?'

Will nodded. 'Surely all gardens are private.'

'Not necessarily. In fact the tourism industry started in the eighteenth century with gardens. Garden owners wrote guidebooks, sold tickets, set up tea rooms, just like today.' She jotted down the distance. 'Mind you, some were private. There's a garden that's rumoured to have been built deliberately so the gentleman of the house could visit his mistress, a beautiful gypsy girl. The access to it is steep and extremely narrow.'

'So?'

'His wife was supposed to have been a rather large lady, too large to get down the path.' Anna folded up the tripod stand and slung the inclinometer back into her rucksack.

'I don't know if I'd go to such lengths to keep the wife away,' Will said. 'What about you?'

'Divorce wasn't an option in those days,' Anna said. 'But it does seem extreme.' She tried to keep her voice light, but Will must have picked up something, because he turned to look at her, a questioning expression in his eyes.

'Sorry,' she said. 'My husband – my ex-husband – went off to another country to get away from me. My sister says it's, like, sooo fashionable to have a starter marriage.' She imitated Clare's voice. 'Ah well, that's life. Gotta take the rough with the smooth.' She tried to think of other clichés to make a joke of it, so Will would know it didn't matter.

'I'm sorry,' Will said simply.

'Yeah, well, there it is . . .' Sometimes it was easier to talk in clichés; you didn't have to say anything that might hurt. Anna stared at the compass as if it would give her the right direction. North south east west. The compass point wavered. No she'd decided to move on, not think any more about Richard. 'Let's get going,' she said, shaking her head. 'I've finished here.'

She headed down the path towards the first lake, the boggy pond, Will silent beside her. His presence was comforting and she instinctively knew he'd be sympathetic and kind, the perfect shoulder to cry on. But she knew nothing about him. Nor did anyone. Oliver had said he'd turned up from nowhere, no history, no past. She decided to try a little detective work.

'Have you been a gardener for long?'

'It's my first gardening job. I'm having a mid-life crisis, ten years early.' Will spoke lightly, but she felt deflected. Still, not much of a detective if she gave up at the first attempt.

'So how come you're here?'

'I saw Mrs Davenport's ad in a shop window in Milbridge.' He spoke gently, as ever, but in a way that made it clear he didn't want to talk further.

All right, don't tell me anything, she thought as she strode towards the pond. Perhaps Oliver was right to be suspicious. Will was being distinctly cagey. Maybe he really had done something dreadful and was on the run. She glanced at him, wondering how she'd know. It wasn't as if he'd be wearing pyjamas with arrows all over them, or had a mask and a sack marked 'swag'. Will looked eminently trustworthy as he walked beside her.

'An international man of mystery,' she said, trying to appear casual.

'To be honest, there's not much mystery and none of the international bit,' Will said with a sigh. 'I was taking time out, seeing a bit of the country. That was fine for a few months, but then it was November and freezing. The ad said accommodation was provided so I got in touch. And here I am.'

But that hadn't really answered her question. Taking time out could mean anything. She wanted to trust him, but surely he'd be open about what he'd been doing before he came to Templecombe, unless it was something disreputable. After all, 'What do you do?' was the most obvious question of all time. Oliver was right. Will did appear suspicious. They had reached the boggy lake and she felt a frisson of fear. What if he was a rapist? They were a long way from the house. She mentally shook herself. No. He couldn't be. Rapists were . . . well, she didn't know what they were, but she was sure Will wasn't one. But there was definitely something about his past he wanted to hide.

She took out a folding knife from her knapsack, flicked the blade into place to lock it and started to cut away at the overgrown vegetation round the lake, revealing a series of stones making a definite edge. She inched her way around, hanging on to branches with her left hand while she slashed at the overgrown vegetation, until she reached the far side, where there was enough room for her to set up her equipment. 'Stay right there,' she called. Will obediently stood with the pole while she measured the distance across the pond.

Now to investigate the tunnel. She turned to go between the rocks.

'Hang on . . .' Will was edging round after her, balancing precariously on the stones.

'Careful you don't fall in,' Anna called out, laughing as his feet slipped perilously close to the muddy black water.

'I can swim,' he said as he joined her.

Anna turned and edged through the opening. The ground sloped down, curving to the right, and at the bottom there was a brick archway set into the bank, large enough for a man to walk through. She peered inside but could see nothing but darkness, and she shivered despite the sunshine on her back. She longed to go in and explore, but the sensible bit of her knew the tunnel was likely to be unsafe. Water trickled somewhere in the distance. She raised her head and listened, trying to work out where the noise was coming from. The large oval lake was on the other side of the bank, but that sounded more like a spring.

She took out her notebook and started to write.

Pool – bridge over? Or stepping stones? Rocks – check cleft. Pilgrim's Progress? Date? Reference? Seven steps down. Significant?

She sucked on her pen, trying to think what it reminded her of. Not quite like this, but there were echoes. She could feel her mind reaching for the name, then added:

Hawkridge Caves, Shropshire? Connections with family? Tunnel – poor condition, probably unsafe. Leads to? Lake? Spring? Nymphaeum? Possible.

'What's a nymphaeum?' Will was looking over her shoulder.

'It's where nymphs hang out.' Anna snapped her notebook shut. If Will wouldn't answer her questions properly, there was no reason why she should answer his. She sniffed, scenting the air. There was no earthy smell that would indicate a roof fall. She rummaged in her rucksack to find her torch and turned it on. 'If this collapses on me, tell them I died happy,' she said, glancing back to Will. 'Don't follow me in.'

It was wet and cold and dark, but she was able to straighten up. She swung the torch upwards and saw an arching vault, brick walls either side and ahead a curving tunnel.

'It's bigger than I thought,' Will said behind her, his voice low.

She jumped, surprised into fearfulness. Her breathing seemed suddenly loud in the blackness of the tunnel and her heart was thumping. She flashed the torch at his face, and thought how honest and dependable he looked. 'I said not to follow,' she hissed, angry with herself for imagining that Will had evil intentions. 'I was relying on you to get me out if the roof collapsed.'

'It hasn't collapsed yet. Tell you what, after I finish work I usually go down the pub. If we get out alive, do you want to come too?'

It was completely unexpected. 'What, after we've done the survey?' She stared at him in the darkness. She hadn't gone out for a drink with anyone for ages. Her mind tumbled with possibilities, which she quickly squashed. It was just a drink after work, no big deal. Perhaps he'd tell her more about himself over a drink. 'Sure, why not.'

'Good.' He exhaled as if in relief, and Anna let the torch drop away, confused by the connection she felt between them. She swung the beam of light up at the roof of the tunnel as she tried to recover her professional self.

'I wonder if this is an ice house.' It would fit, being close to the coolness of the lake, but it was quite a long way from the house. She walked forward, her senses alert for any signs of danger, eyes straining for any clues to the building's function, forgetting about Will as her torch beam swung from side to side. Her heart beat faster as she came to the corner, thinking about what might be there . . . a grotto perhaps. Round the corner and—

'It's a dead end.'

She moved the torch over the wall in front of her, hoping to see modern bricks, anything to indicate that there was something behind. But no, the bricks were exactly the same as those forming the rest of the tunnel. 'Damn.' She could have wept.

They retraced their steps. As they left the tunnel, Anna wiped her hands on her trousers, oblivious to the slimy green muck she was depositing on them, then consulted her map. 'I don't understand what's going on,' she said. 'Why would anyone build such an elaborate tunnel and then just end it?'

'Perhaps they ran out of time, or money.' In the short time they had been in the tunnel, moisture had settled on Will's hair, a fine mist of sparkling drops. Anna shook her own head to scatter any drops that might have settled.

'I want to take some readings from here.'

Will edged back round the pond and took up sighting target and tape again. Anna measured various levels and distances, noting particularly how the tunnel opening related to the surrounding landscape. It was strange the way the bank had been built . . .

'Hang on a sec.' She edged a little to her left, then scrambled up the bank, slipping and sliding on the vegetation until she reached the top. From here she could see the lake on the far side. No sign of any opening from the bank into the lake, though. Perhaps the tunnel was simply a dead end. 'Can you go a bit further back along the path, to where it joins the other one?'

Will did as she asked, and Anna took more readings, then she looked along the bank, tracing the curve around the edge of the lake with her eyes. Maybe the tunnel did continue round. She was about to walk along the bank to see if she could see any signs of it when she heard the muffled noise of her mobile. She dug it out of her pocket. 'Hello?'

'Oliver Davenport here. My grandmother gave me your number.' She turned back towards the lake, instinctively moving away from Will as Oliver continued. 'Listen, I was thinking . . . I was very dismissive about your garden research the other day. I wondered if you'd like to have dinner with me and tell me about it.'

She pressed her ear to the phone. Stay cool, stay cool. 'When were you thinking of?'

'Would tonight be any good? I'm staying overnight in Bristol for a meeting early tomorrow morning, so I thought I could go there via Bath. I could pick you up at, say, seven thirty?

Her mind began to calculate. Finish the survey, get back, wash hair – yes, she could do it if she hurried. 'Can we make it eight?'

'I'll pick you up from your place then.'

Anna gave him directions, then said goodbye and slipped the phone back into her pocket. Well. That was a surprise. Oliver Davenport. She looked out across the lake, the ripples sparkling like candlelight on crystal. Silly to be so pleased, but she couldn't help smiling. She half scrambled, half slid back down the bank, and then round the pond edge to where Will was waiting patiently. 'Sorry to keep you.'

Anna finished the rest of the survey as fast as she could, knowing she was usually more thorough, taking more readings and double-checking all the results, but she hadn't got the time, not if she was to get back. Ivy still covered the gateway building.

'I would like to see what's underneath,' she said, patting the stone walls. 'If it were possible.'

Will smiled. 'You're the boss.'

'Give me a ring when you've done it and I'll come down again.'

She hummed tunelessly on the walk back to the house, Will helping to carry the kit. What should she wear? Smart? Casual? There was that designer hand-knit cardigan she'd got in the sales half-price. Sort of 'smart but I haven't made any effort'. And her newest black jeans. Jeans . . . too casual? Perhaps. But she could wear them with those jewelled sandal things Clare had passed on to her; they were quite dressy. But plain earrings, so it wouldn't look as if she was trying.

Anna loaded the equipment into her car and slung her rucksack in. 'Thanks for helping,' she said to Will. 'I can do it on my own, but it's much easier if there are two.'

'No problem.' Will checked his watch. 'It's quite early, but I expect the pub'll be open.'

Drat, she'd completely forgotten about the drink. She couldn't be late for Oliver. 'I'm sorry, I can't, Will. Not this evening. That call . . .' She brushed her hair back off her face, frantically thinking of an excuse – she couldn't say it was Oliver. 'It was my sister, she needs me to come back to, um, help sort out her bridesmaids' dresses.'

'What, tonight?' Will looked disbelieving, as well he might.

'Yes, um, something about the fabric having to be ordered tomorrow.' She couldn't meet his eyes. 'Look, I'd love to come for a drink, but another time. What about when you've cleared the ivy – okay?'

He shrugged. 'Sure.'

'I'm really sorry, but . . .' She bit her lip, not wanting to hurt Will's feelings, but also starting to worry about the traffic and whether there'd be any hot water in the house for washing her hair.

'Hey, it was just an idea.' Will stepped away from the car.

'Another time,' she said, getting in and starting the ignition. She didn't look back as she drove away.

Chapter 6

Anna hadn't known quite what to expect when Oliver said he'd pick her up at eight. What she hadn't imagined was a drive in his sleek black car, whizzing down country lanes while she clutched the soft leather edge of her seat and prayed he had good brakes. He slowed to take a left turn and she saw an illuminated sign for a hotel and restaurant.

'But this is really smart,' she said, recognising the name.

'Is it?' Oliver said, negotiating a cattle grid. 'God, I hope it's not too pompous. I just looked it up in a guidebook.'

Anna smoothed her palms over her legs. This was a little-black-dress sort of place, perhaps accessorised with an elegant but discreet string of pearls. Hair up, even. A place for anniversaries and special birthdays, for proposals and congratulations and extraordinary announcements – Darling, I've got something special to tell you. What, darling? Well, darling, it's . . . it's . . . (shy smile, demurely downcast eyelids) I'm going to have a baby! Not a place for black jeans, however new, and a cardi in shades of bubblegum, no matter how hand-knitted. She went cold. Perhaps jeans were banned. You couldn't just borrow a skirt in the way a man could borrow a tie. Worse, in the hurry to wash her hair, she'd forgotten to shave her legs. No, surely they couldn't, wouldn't make a fuss? Oliver wasn't wearing a tie, but he looked smart; they wouldn't turn him away.

They drew up outside the hotel, gravel scrunching with an expensive sound. Anna slunk out of the car and trailed behind Oliver, hoping to be invisible next to his aura of confidence as he confirmed the reservation. It appeared to have worked, as no one looked at her. Ouch – a sharp bit of gravel had lodged under the ball of her foot. She wriggled her toes in her sandals, trying to dislodge it. No, she'd have to pick it out. Trying to be discreet, she balanced on her good foot and slid her hand down her leg to try and flick the stone out with her fingers, all the while staring ahead with what she hoped was a nonchalant expression on her face.

'Are you all right?' Oliver was frowning at her.

Anna stood up straight, suppressing a yelp as her weight landed squarely on the bit of gravel. 'Of course.'

A waiter led them to their table at the far end of a large dining room heavy enough on the soft furnishings to absorb the noise of a posse of thundering cowboys, complete with horses and steers. Not that such a thing would ever exist here, as the room consisted mainly of couples talking in hushed voices, the life drained out of them by the oppressive haberdashery. No wonder interior designers called gold fringing bullion, it was draped around chairs, cushions and curtains like chains of wealth. Anna, hobbling behind, couldn't help noticing the other diners clock Oliver as they passed, and felt a frisson of pride. As they sat, Anna surreptitiously flicked the gravel from her sandal. Bliss. Then she looked at the menu, blinked, and looked again. The prices! Each main course was what she'd expect to pay for an entire meal. She looked at Oliver, who gave every appearance of unconcern.

'I really wasn't expecting – all this,' she said, looking around the room and shifting uncomfortably in her chair as if the seat was stuffed with gravel.

'I know – eighties time warp. I thought about Babington House, but it's that much further from Bath,' he said, leaning forward. 'Anyway, I expect you go there all the time.'

Babington House. Clare had been a few times and had come back with stories of who she'd seen, rock stars and TV presenters and celebrities Anna had never heard of. She didn't want to appear completely the unworldly academic, living like a dormouse in some dusty turret, so instead of being truthful, and saying she'd never been, she said, 'Not often.'

The waiter came over to take their order. Anna quickly looked at the menu. 'I can't decide. It all looks wonderful.'

'Red okay for you? Do you like champagne?'

Anna nodded, bemused. Champagne, posh restaurant – it wasn't what she'd been expecting at all. It felt like years since she'd been out with a man to a place like this. Hang on, it *was* years. She and Richard had always been too broke at the beginning, and then when Richard had started to make money, it'd been too late.

Oliver ordered the wine and asked the waiter to come back in a few minutes for the food, then leant forward. 'So tell me about garden history and being a garden historian.' The pupils of his eyes were velvety black, and the blue shaded into a smoky grey line.

'Goodness, I don't know where to start,' Anna said, trying to rearrange her thoughts into more professional patterns. 'Do you want a potted lecture on the basic history, or . . . ?'

'Start with you,' he said as the waiter returned and poured champagne the colour of palest straw into tall flutes. 'Have you always wanted to be a gardener?'

Anna shook her head. 'I'm not a gardener at all, I'm a historian. I read history of art at university and ended up specialising in garden history.'

'So you don't get your hands dirty?' He rested his chin on one of his own hands, the nails perfectly shaped, not too long, not too short, a healthy pink against the tan. Anna put her hands beneath the table, conscious of her bitten nails. From tomorrow she'd follow Clare's advice and start having weekly manicures.

'Apart from in your grandmother's attics, no.' She sipped her champagne, feeling the cool liquid seep through her body. 'And I'm not a designer either. I know nothing about plants. Well, that's not entirely true. I know about the history of plants, what species were introduced when, but I couldn't tell you what to put in your borders.'

Oliver shook his head in mock dismay. 'And there I was hoping to get some free advice.'

'Unless you have a Jekyll garden. I'd be able to tell you then.'

'A Jekyll garden?'

'Gertrude Jekyll – she was a hugely influential garden designer working in the Edwardian period with the architect Edwin Lutyens.'

'I think I've read something . . . Is that how you pronounce the name, not like Dr Jekyll and Mr Hyde?'

'Mmm, rhymes with treacle.'

'You learn something new every day.' He sipped his champagne, looking as if he was interested. She wished she knew if he really was. She didn't want to be blathering on about gardens if inwardly he was dying of boredom. Not that he gave any sign of it, she had to admit. He'd said he was bored with his work, she remembered. Perhaps he was thinking of getting involved in the garden restoration at Templecombe.

The waiter came back and hovered. Anna frantically read the menu.

'I can always ask him to come back later,' Oliver said.

'No, no, I'm ready. I'd like crab cakes to start, but I can't decide between the duck and the lamb,' Anna said, flustered at having to make an instant decision.

'Why not have both?'

'Both?'

Anna watched in amazement as Oliver ordered a starter each and three main courses. 'You can choose which you prefer when they come.'

'But that's . . .' Extravagant? Wasteful? She'd never heard of someone ordering two courses before, just because they couldn't choose. And at these prices. 'I'll have the lamb,' she said quickly to the waiter, who bowed and left.

'You didn't have to do that,' Oliver said.

Anna drew in a breath and let it out. 'Oh, I did. I couldn't . . .'

'Hey, it's only money.'

'I suppose.' It was difficult to put a finger on what it was that disturbed her about the extra order. Yes, it was only money, and not hers at that, but it seemed so needlessly wasteful – of food, of money, even of respect for the chef, for his or her time and skill.

'You're upset because I've broken the rules,' Oliver said, a teasing note in his voice. Anna protested, not liking the idea it might be true.

'It's only convention that decides how we eat: first course, second course, pudding to follow,' he continued. 'I've seen menus for dinners at Templecombe that mix up all sorts of different dishes, all coming together with no distinction between them. Bit like a buffet, I suppose.'

'Certainly that was true in the eighteenth and nineteenth centuries . . .'

Oliver stretched. 'Why should you have to make a decision about what you want to eat based on simple description? How many times have you ordered something and been surprised at what you've received?'

Anna shrugged. 'Lots of times, but—'

'Or those ghastly Christmas office parties where you have to decide what you're going to want to eat two months before the event. I mean, how the hell should I know? I might have become a vegetarian by then.' He grinned, showing strong white teeth. 'Although I will concede it's unlikely, I'm very much a carnivore.'

Anna had a mental image of him tearing off hunks of flesh from a haunch of venison with his teeth, then tossing the bone over his shoulder to a wolfhound. She dragged her mind back to the present and Christmas parties. 'You have to sympathise with the restaurant staff, it must be difficult . . .'

'You're obviously a kinder person than I am. They're offering a service, simple as that.'

Anna rubbed the back of her neck with her hand. She could see his point, and she supposed in a way he was right. But the world would be a very harsh place if everything was reduced to financial transactions and there wasn't room for consideration for others, service or not.

Oliver spoke again. 'In my business I see a lot of people covering up for shoddy work or saying it can't be done, simply because it's inconvenient for them.'

'I don't know much about insurance,' Anna said with an apologetic shrug. Judging from appearances, she didn't think Oliver was at the call-centre end of the business; more like something in the City. Through work she came across plenty of people working in finance with newly purchased estates and gardens to research, but she'd never been particularly interested in exactly how they'd acquired the wherewithal.

Oliver twisted the signet ring on his little finger, the gold catching the light. 'Insurance is a kind of legalised gambling. You make a bet, give a quote, get the stake; if they claim, you lose, if they don't, you win.'

'That doesn't sound boring.'

Oliver shrugged. 'I've being doing it for too many years. My father started the company, but now he's gone . . . I'm thinking about maybe selling up, moving on, doing something else – but what? Any ideas gratefully received.'

The waiter arrived with crab cakes for Anna, foie gras for Oliver, then left.

Anna leant forward. 'Why don't you restore your grandmother's garden?'

'I suppose I could . . .' Oliver spread foie gras liberally on a piece of toast. 'Go on, tell me why I should.'

'Well . . .' Anna dunked some crab cake in the sauce. 'I think Templecombe might be very special.'

'But there's hardly anything there, just the pavilion.'

'It's the positioning of the structures, that tunnel area. I think . . .' She paused. 'Well, I'm not sure if I'm right or if it's just wishful thinking, but I think it may be symbolic.'

'Symbolic? You mean like trains rushing into tunnels in old films?'

Anna practically choked on her crab cake with a spurt of laughter. 'No. Well, yes, that is symbolic, but I didn't mean – not that sort of thing.' She took a deep breath, and tried to recover her composure. 'Symbolism isn't always about sex,' she said. 'Gardens could be about all sorts of things: retelling classical stories like Aeneas and the flight from Troy, for example, and some were political—'

'Political?' Oliver's expression was one of amused disbelief. 'Now you're pulling my leg.'

'Not at all. Stowe and Chiswick House were both built by republican Whigs and they put up statues of classical republicans like Plato and Seneca alongside other statues – at Stowe there's a Temple of Classical Virtue next to one of British Worthies who all represented Whig supporters. People at the time would walk round and get the references as they were brought up on Latin and Greek stories. We're ignorant peasants in comparison.'

'I certainly am,' Oliver said cheerfully. 'I find it hard to believe Templecombe has some sort of political message.'

Anna tucked her hair behind her ears. 'The themes aren't always political; they could be religion, or love, or anything really.'

'Including sex?' He looked at her sideways, eyes devilish.

Anna laughed, and gave in. 'Yes, including sex.'

'So the next time I walk through a tunnel in a garden I'm having sex with it. Entering Mother Earth, I expect.'

'That could be a valid interpretation,' Anna said, as straight-faced as she could manage and wondering how to steer the conversation on to safer ground. It was dangerous talking about sex with a man like Oliver. But fun, and she hadn't had fun for such a long time.

Oliver laughed. 'Come on, this is like looking at a pile of bricks and seeing a sweeping condemnation of capitalism.'

Anna felt compelled to try and explain why these gardens were so special. 'I could take you to a symbolic garden, in the same condition as it was originally made, and show you.'

'You're very passionate about this, aren't you?' His eyes searched hers. 'Okay, I accept your challenge. You're going to show me round a garden and try and convince me that it means something.'

The waiter brought their main courses and broke the conversation. Anna felt elated. She would show him round a garden and convert him. She was sure all it needed was for him to get involved, understand a little. Where would be best? A political garden like Stowe or a thematic garden like Rousham? Rousham was most like Templecombe. She'd take him to Rousham and then . . . her mind conjured up a picture of them walking through Arcadian glades, the sun shining, Oliver listening attentively while she explained why the garden was so important. Her imagination fast-forwarded and they were at Templecombe, supervising the restoration together, standing close as they examined a survey plan, his shirtsleeves rolled up. She looked across the table and the vision popped. He didn't look like the Oliver in her imagination, too good-looking, too smooth. Her sense of excitement faltered. He wasn't interested in gardens. He was just being polite. Well-mannered. He would forget about it. She picked up her knife and fork and started to eat. Enjoy the food, because this is as far as it goes, she told herself.

'You don't regret not having the duck?' Oliver said.

She shook her head. 'This is delicious.'

SARAH DUNCAN

'I eat out so much on business, I sometimes long for something simple,' Oliver said.

'Like what?'

'Beans on toast,' he said, a faraway look in his eyes. 'Beans on toast with a dash of Worcester sauce and some grated cheddar on top. Or scrambled eggs made with lots of butter and a stack of toast. Or cheese pie.'

Anna laughed, the contrast between his list of wish food and what they were eating was so great. 'What's cheese pie?'

'Something disgusting we used to make when we were students. Mashed potato, grated cheese, onion and ketchup all mixed together. He laughed. It looks disgusting, but take my word for it, it's delicious.'

'When did you last have it?'

'Years ago. Longer than I want to remember.'

'What were you studying?' Finance, she thought, or maybe something esoteric like Russian history.

'Law. It's what my parents wanted, and I didn't particularly want to do anything else, so . . .' He took a mouthful of venison. 'What about you? Were your parents academics?'

Anna smiled. 'No, not at all. No, I think they found my going to university as bizarre as if I'd announced I was going to be an astronaut. They live in a neat little house, and have neat little lives and neat little minds.' She drank, spilling a little. 'When I got my Ph.D. I thought they'd be really proud, and they were, but I overheard my mother on the phone to one of her friends. "Of course she's not a real doctor," she kept saying. "Not a proper one."' She tried to smile at Oliver, to show it didn't matter.

'That must have hurt,' Oliver said gently, his eyes dark.

'I shouldn't take things so seriously.' She gave a brief laugh. 'Story of my life so far. Don't be so serious, Anna, don't take everything so seriously.'

'Don't change,' Oliver said suddenly. 'There are enough frivolous and shallow people in the world.'

••• 70 •••

'It's boring being serious,' Anna said, smoothing her napkin over her knee in little jerky movements and wishing she could make bright, witty small talk.

'It's charming.' Oliver's eyes held hers.

Anna picked up her glass, to hide her awareness of that sudden change when the air has become charged with meaning. But it was empty.

'Here, have some more.' He reached for the bottle.

'No, I've had enough.' More than enough, she thought.

'There's only a little left and I'm driving, so . . .'

'Okay,' she said. She watched him pouring the rest of the bottle into her glass. What was she thinking of, telling him about her parents? She didn't know what to do with her hands, which seemed to have grown to vast proportions. She clasped them in front of her, then thought it might look as if she was praying and put them in her lap. Like a good girl. But then she'd always been a good girl, obeying the rules. She looked across the table to Oliver, who had obviously never obeyed a single rule in his life, and suddenly she longed, yearned to be bad, to be the sort of person who did what they pleased, when they pleased. Not to ride roughshod over others, but to decide for oneself what to do, and do it, regardless of whether it made you stand out from the crowd. Since Richard had left she'd felt stuck behind a glass wall, able to see, unable to connect. Oliver looked as if he shattered glass walls every day, simply by the force of his self-assurance.

'Do you have brothers or sisters?' he asked.

'One sister.'

'Is she an academic too?'

Anna shook her head, amused at the thought. 'Not at all.'

'You get on with each other?'

'Most of the time.' She fingered the stem of her wine glass, not wanting to talk about Clare. 'What about you? Do you have brothers and sisters?'

'Nope.' He shook his head. 'No family left, apart from my grandmother. My father died last year.'

'I'm sorry.' God, she sounded pathetic, so banal.

'Yeah, well. I wouldn't say we were close, but, you know, he was my father. He was young too, only in his sixties. We die young in my family. Except for my grandmother, of course. I expect she's going to last for ever.' He shrugged, as if to show it didn't matter, but it made Anna want to reach out and touch his hand in sympathy. Instead she clasped her hands tighter in her lap.

'Did . . . did he love Templecombe?'

'It was part of him. It's part of me.' Oliver started to talk about growing up in London but spending holidays at Templecombe, and of what it had been like then, a child's-eye view of the beautiful, dilapidated house. Anna registered that he didn't mention his father: obviously it was too painful a subject to talk about with a stranger. She watched him as he talked, fascinated by what he was saying. But he could have been reciting football fixtures and she'd still have been fascinated. She rested her head on one hand, elbow on the table, and watched him as he talked, the way the light fell on his high cheek-bones, the line of his jaw, and his eyes, the pupils large and almost covering the blue with velvet darkness, as secret and mysterious as the garden he was describing.

'I always felt that the garden was my magic kingdom. I used to pretend it was an undiscovered country and claim it for myself. My new-found land.'

He spoke softly and their eyes met. My new-found land. Anna felt he was an explorer searching for something, someone, some virgin territory waiting for him to plant his flag and claim it for his own. She mentally shook herself. Get real, Anna. It's not going to happen.

'Is that why . . .' She blinked, brain struggling to get back on the professional track. 'I'm sorry, I may have got this wrong, but I got the impression you're not keen on the idea of restoring the garden. Do you think that might be why?'

'Spoiling my private kingdom?' He shrugged. 'Maybe. I must admit, I don't like the idea of it being manicured. I like the wildness. Do you want anything else? Pudding? Coffee?'

She shook her head. 'Everything's been perfect.'

Oliver turned, and at his gesture the waiter came. Anna was struck by how easy he appeared, how everything he did was effortless. He turned; the waiter came. Richard had never managed that trick. But then everything about Oliver was unlike Richard. Richard was at heart a rule-obeyer, a follower. She supposed she was too; conventional and obedient. She watched Oliver, the way his mouth curved as he signed the flimsy strip of paper to pay the bill, the way his hair flopped forward over his forehead. He caught her eyes and smiled, his face lifting.

Anna dropped her gaze, unable to meet his, heart beating faster. *If he tries to kiss me on the way back, I'll let him. It's unprofessional, and I shouldn't. But I will.*

On the way back to Anna's house they talked about Bath, and how Anna liked living there. 'I went to uni in Bristol, but I prefer Bath. It's smaller, but if you ever want something edgier or more urban, you can always go to Bristol.'

'Which is where I'm staying tonight.'

'Do you go away much on business?'

'The odd night here and there. I've got a trip to Prague coming up at the end of May. It's the bank holiday so I might stay a few extra nights.' He shrugged, as if deciding to stay extra nights meant nothing.

Anna felt a pang of envy. Not that she'd have swapped her Ph.D. for any amount of travelling, but studying had meant she'd missed out on that aspect of student life. 'I'd love to go to Prague, everyone says it's beautiful.'

'Isn't Bath considered one of the most beautiful cities in the world? I'm ashamed to say this is the first time I've been here.'

'Really? You ought to visit it properly. Now's quite a good time of year – not too many tourists.' She inwardly winced. It sounded like she was fishing to show him round. Hell, she *was* fishing.

'You'll have to tell me what I should see,' Oliver said, concentrating on the road ahead.

'There's the usual things like the Royal Crescent and the Circus, and . . .' Go on, suggest you show him round, you've got this far, just do it. 'And you should see the Abbey and, and, um, there are loads of things,' she finished lamely, mentally kicking herself for not offering her services as tour guide.

'Why don't you show me now?'

He'd caught her off guard. 'Now? It's the middle of the night.'

'Even fewer tourists.' He glanced across at her, and she would have happily given him a guided tour of a coal cellar.

Oliver parked opposite Anna's house, and they walked up through Royal Victoria Park to the Avenue. Although it was dark, the majestic sweep of the Royal Crescent above could be clearly seen. They reached the top of the park and stood on the broad flagstone pavement at the entrance to the Crescent.

'I had no idea,' Oliver said, sounding impressed. 'What does one of these go for?'

'They're mostly divided into flats, but a whole house is, I don't know . . . three, four, five million? Out of my league, anyway.'

They walked along Brock Street towards the Circus, moths fluttering in the warm orange glow of the street lamps. Anna felt she was a moth drawn to Oliver, but he appeared oblivious to her, just listened politely as she told him a little about the history of Bath. She kept glancing up at his face, trying to work out if he was bored. It was hard to tell. He nodded, and asked polite questions, but that could mean anything. And she longed for it to mean something more. Anna Carmichael plays the starring role of herself in the major motion picture Desperately Fancying Oliver.

'And here's the Circus.' The tall terraced houses formed a

complete circle, pierced at three points by roads, with a central round patch of green where five plane trees swayed in the breeze. So much for deciding she'd let him kiss her; he showed no sign of interest in her as they walked round. Perhaps it was for the best. She was supposed to be there in a professional capacity, trying to make Oliver understand why the garden at Templecombe mattered, especially if it was a symbolic garden.

'Do you see the frieze that runs round the top of the ground floors?' She pointed to the carved symbols that circled the buildings like a belt. 'Each section is different.'

Oliver lounged against the iron railings. 'Do they mean anything?'

'There isn't a secret message, if that's what you mean.' He looked disappointed. Anna wanted him to appreciate it, not be disappointed. She continued hurriedly. 'At the time people were really interested in things like alchemy and hermeticism, and published books of symbols, which is where most of these come from. So there's a Masonic symbol, the triangle and all-seeing eye. That one with the snake eating its tail, that's ourobouros, meaning eternity—'

'Hang on a sec.' He touched her arm and it stopped her dead. 'Alchemy I've heard of, but hermitism?'

'Hermeticism.' He wouldn't ask if he wasn't interested. Would he? She took a deep breath of the cool night air. 'It's a development from alchemy. They loved all that stuff in the eighteenth century. John Wood, who was the architect of all this' – she waved her hand to indicate the Circus and the sweep of the Crescent – 'was obsessed with King Bladud, who was the legendary founder of Bath, and with druids. The Circus is the same diameter as the outer ring at Stonehenge, and if you look up . . .' Anna said, pointing, 'I don't know if you can see, the light's not very good, but look at those things on the top of the houses.'

'What are they?' Oliver said, squinting up into the night sky. 'Urns?'

'That's what they traditionally would be, but here they're acorns. The oak is the sacred tree of the druids.' She rubbed her arms where they were goose-pimpled.

'So more symbolism, like the gardens.'

'Not all eighteenth-century gardens are symbolic, but some are, yes.'

'And Templecombe might be one.' In one fluid movement he slipped his jacket off and draped it over her shoulders.

'No, I'm fine,' Anna said, feeling she had to protest, feeling overwhelmed, feeling – oh, excited and hopeful and worried that she was reading too much into a kind gesture. She could feel his warmth from the silken lining.

'You're shivering,' he said. 'Go on, I haven't got fleas. I hope.'

They started to walk down Gay Street to Queen Square. A couple were kissing passionately in a doorway, their bodies pressed together. As they walked past, the couple separated, and the girl laughed then said something in a foreign language. Tourists, Anna thought. In love. She glanced at Oliver, but he appeared not to have noticed.

'This is Queen Square. The north side was the first of the new buildings to be built.' They turned right along the north façade. Anna thought of the tourist couple, the girl's beaming smile, the gurgle of laughter. It was a long time since she'd felt like that about anyone, that feeling of sheer delight at being with someone else.

'If Templecombe turned out to be a symbolic garden, it'd be quite a discovery for you,' Oliver said suddenly.

Anna looked up at him, his jacket wrapped around her like an embrace. 'It's the sort of thing you dream of.' She paused, gathered her thoughts. 'That's why I have to be so careful with the research. It's very easy to believe something is there just because you want it to be.'

'Like life,' Oliver said.

'That sounds profound.'

'Profound? Not me.' He shook his head.

They went the long way back through the park rather than the direct route along the main road, their steps slow as if matching the stillness of the night.

Oliver looked back up at the Royal Crescent. 'My mother would have loved this . . . this order. Everything in its place, all planned and designed. When she died I always thought what she really minded was that the cancer and being ill was so bloody untidy.'

Anna floundered, trying to think of something that was sincere but not trite. To lose both your father and your mother seemed desperately sad. Poor, poor Oliver. 'I'm sorry.'

'No, my fault. I shouldn't have said anything. Sorry. I'm boring you.'

'Oh no, you couldn't,' Anna said spontaneously, then cringed at how naïve she sounded.

He paused. 'You're very sweet.'

Sweet. Anna didn't want to be sweet. They had reached his car. 'Would you . . .' She caught her breath. Go on, say it. 'Would you like to come in? For coffee?'

'Thank you, but no.'

Her ego crashed to the pavement. The moment had gone, and Oliver was going. She was sweet and he wasn't interested. She slipped the jacket off and handed it back, formally polite to hide her disappointment. 'Thanks for the loan. And for dinner.'

'My pleasure. Thank you for the guided tour.' He put the jacket back on, and she wondered if he noticed that now it carried her warmth.

'Drive safely.' She thought about kissing him on the cheek, but he was too tall for her to reach without grabbing his lapels and hauling herself up. Not a good idea. None of it was a good idea.

Oliver fiddled with his car keys. 'I'll wait until you're inside.'

'You don't need to, it's quite safe.' She crossed the road, unlocked the front door and stepped in, then turned and gave a little wave. 'Goodnight.'

'Anna . . .' She waited as he crossed the street and came to the door. 'I've got to be up early. Otherwise I would have liked to come in.'

'Oh.' She felt about sixteen, hovering on the doorstep at home. 'Well. I've got to be up early too – I've got to go to London to see some people about a television job.'

'Good luck.' He touched her cheek with his finger. 'Goodnight.'

He got into his car and zoomed off, the engine noise disturbing the night-time quiet. Anna shut the front door behind her and leant back against it, confused and restless. She closed her eyes, feeling again his finger on her cheek. Did that mean he was interested? Or not?

Chapter 7

Anna tried to be interested, but there was a limit to how much shoe talk she could take. She sat in the bridal shop wondering how on earth she'd managed to let Clare persuade her to come with her and why on earth Clare had wanted her in the first place. It couldn't be for advice. She must have decided it was a sisterly thing to do together, without thinking it through. It probably suggested bonding over kitten heels in the latest edition of *Celebrity Brides Illustrated,* a fun thing for sisters to do.

There was another couple in the shop. The young woman was trying on a pair of sequinned flip-flops – at least that was what they looked like to Anna. She met the young man's eye and realised that he was thinking flip-flops too. 'They look great,' he said whenever his opinion was asked for. 'The thing is, it'll be hot, really hot, even at the castello,' the woman said, which made Clare's lips twitch. Anna knew she was toying with the idea of giving up her traditional English wedding for a castello.

I shouldn't be here, Anna thought. I should be working. But it was Clare's big day. Anna tried to look interested in a ribbon-tied sandal with preposterously high heels, nodding as Clare ran through the pros and cons of wearing high heels. None of this seemed important when Richard and I got married, she thought. We were in love, and that was all that mattered.

Clare started a discussion with the shop assistant about the possibilities of dyeing shoes to match her dress, and Anna sank back on her chair. Thoughts of Oliver seeped into her brain. Perhaps he was still in Bristol. She stroked the plush velvet with a finger, smoothing the pile. He might call in on the way back. She sighed. He didn't even attempt to kiss you, she told herself firmly. He's obviously not interested. Not even a peck on the cheek. Perhaps I should have . . . No, too much like throwing yourself at the man.

Clare flopped down in the chair next to her. 'Chosen?' Anna said brightly.

'Heavens, no. She's gone to get me some things to try on.' Clare pulled out a pink binder and consulted a long list. 'Oh, I know what I wanted to ask you. Would you please please please, lovely big sister, please organise my hen party?'

Anna blinked. She didn't know anything about hen parties, let alone the sort of thing that Clare might want to have. 'Why on earth do you want me to organise your hen party? I must be the worst person in the world for that. What about getting Jackie or Helen to do it?'

'But you're my sister,' Clare said, pouting. 'It's better if you do it, it'll mean more. Besides,' she added, suddenly more businesslike, 'if I get Jackie or Helen to do it, I'll end up getting what they want. If you do it, I'll get what *I* want.'

'I suppose I could do it,' Anna said, frowning with anxiety. 'But I really wouldn't know where to start.'

'Don't worry about that,' Clare said, clicking open the file and handing Anna four sheets of paper before slipping on a satiny shoe. 'It's all there.'

Anna scanned the pages. Day at a spa, dinner, club. It was all written out in Clare's big round writing with little Os dotting the Is, where she wanted to go, who she wanted invited, what she wanted – Anna was to make a spontaneous speech about how wonderful it was having Clare as a sister. She could see why Clare hadn't wanted her friends to organise it; all too tempting to sabotage her ambitions.

'You want Bron to come; that's nice.'

'I thought you'd want someone to be grown up with,' Clare said over her shoulder, hopping around with one foot four inches higher than the other. 'Anyway, Bron's fun.'

Anna looked at the list again, wondering if all little sisters thought their older sisters were grown up and boring. Probably. 'I'll have a go.'

'Brilliant,' Clare said, giving Anna an exuberant hug. 'Do you think I ought to go for a bigger size? My feet might swell on the day.'

'I don't know. Try the other one on.' Anna's phone started ringing and she scrabbled in her bag to find it, relieved of the interruption.

'Hi. It's Oliver.'

Her heartbeat went from nought to sixty. 'Hi. Thanks for dinner.'

'How did it go with the television company?'

He'd remembered. And he was calling. Anna thought she might have heart failure. 'They offered me the job: six programmes on great garden designers.'

'Including Jekyll?' He pronounced the name correctly.

'Including Jekyll.' Anna pressed her ear to the phone, feeling she might melt down it. 'And your meeting?'

'Yeah, it went well, just doing the paperwork now I'm back in the office.'

Quick quick, think of something to say. Her brain felt scrambled with the pressure to come up with something. Clare was looking at her now, which made her feel doubly self-conscious.

Oliver broke the pause. 'At dinner you were talking about a similar garden to Templecombe, and I was wondering . . . well, I expect you're very busy . . .'

She could hear the I'm-about-to-ring-off note in his voice. The words gushed out. 'No, no, I'm not, I'd love to show you round.'

'Great. I was wondering if you wanted to make a date for that.'

A date? A DATE. No, no, calm down, he doesn't mean that sort of date. She cranked her brain back to something approaching normal speed. 'There are a couple of gardens I could show you. There's Rousham, which is outside Oxford, but Chiswick House in London might be easier for you. Or Stowe? That's in Buckinghamshire.'

'Which is best?'

'Rousham probably, in terms of comparing with Templecombe.'

'Okay. What about this Friday?'

Friday. She'd intended to go to Templecombe to check out the tunnel area, but . . . 'That would be fine,' she said. They arranged to meet there, and he rang off. Evening sunshine flooded the shop, the last rays of a glorious, fabulous day.

'You look pleased with yourself,' Clare said. 'So who was that?'

'No one.' Anna knew she was grinning like a sick cat.

'What's he called?' Clare's face was brimful of questions.

'Oliver Davenport.' Anna immediately regretted saying his name. 'But it's business, I'm showing him a garden, you know, professionally.'

'Anna Davenport – sounds great,' Clare said. 'Oh, is he the gardener at that place you're researching?'

'No, that's Will. Oliver's someone else, but really, Clare, it's business.'

'Is he the guy you went out to dinner with?' Clare's eyes narrowed.

'Yes, but . . .' Don't tempt fate, she thought. 'I don't think he's interested.'

'But you are – oh, you've gone the same colour as those shoes.' Clare giggled. 'Tell you what, why don't you ask him to the wedding? He's bound to make a pass then – weddings do that to people.'

'That's two months away. I'm hoping . . .' She stopped and fiddled with a strap.

'Hoping for action before then?' Clare said.

Anna laughed. 'I'm not saying.'

Oliver swung his car into the stable block and parked next to Anna's. 'Not many people here today.' he said, getting out.

'No, there never are,' Anna said, suddenly conscious of her car's rust patches and mismatched front panel next to his gleaming bodywork. 'They don't let children in, so it's really just garden enthusiasts and artists who come.'

He kissed her cheek in greeting. 'It's good of you to show me round.'

'Not at all,' Anna said calmly, as if he hadn't brushed his cheek with hers. All week she'd been playing this moment over in her mind, what to say, what to do. Now it had come, she felt self-conscious, as if Oliver could sense her foolish daydreams. You're on a mission, she told herself, a mission to convince Oliver that gardens are worth restoring.

They walked back through the stable entrance and bought tickets from a machine that looked more like a parking meter, then crossed in front of the house, scattering brightly coloured bantams with fluffy pantaloons for legs, who had been pecking at the gravel. They turned right and walked down the side of the house, stopping briefly to admire a paved courtyard crammed with pots of geraniums basking in the sun. At the back of the house, a formal lawn led to a central statue of a lion attacking a horse. Beyond, the ground dropped away and the valley spread out before them.

'That's a bit like Templecombe, the bit in front of the house,' Oliver murmured. 'When I came on visits with my parents I thought it was the end of the world.'

Anna nodded, recognising her first impression. 'There are similarities. It would be interesting to know if whoever designed your garden had ever visited here,'

'My grandmother's garden. Not mine.'

Anna sighed. Fair enough, it was technically his grandmother's, but his family had made it.

Oliver moved towards the statue of the lion and horse. 'Not sure they've got the scale right.'

'I've never thought of it like that,' Anna said, surprised. 'I suppose it would have to be a very large lion.'

'Or a very small horse. More of a Shetland pony, in fact.'

Anna wasn't sure Oliver was treating the statue one hundred per cent seriously. 'It signifies the domination of Rome – that's the lion – over Tivoli – that's the horse, so it's not surprising the lion is scaled up.'

'Go on,' Oliver said, looking at Anna sideways. 'Tell me who it's by.'

'Scheemaker,' Anna said, not without a hint of smugness. 'It's a copy of the original Roman statue at Tivoli.'

'Very good,' he said, giving her a little clap. 'Of course, you could be making it all up.'

'How dare you?' she said in mock horror. 'I'm a known expert. People pay lots of money to be shown round a garden by me.'

'Yeah, but I bet you make it up sometimes.'

'Never,' Anna said, frowning at the suggestion. How could she make it up?

Oliver laughed. 'Don't worry, I won't tell anyone.'

'No, really . . .' Anna started to protest, but Oliver touched her arm.

'Come on, show me the rest.'

Anna shook her head. 'You've got to look at the eye-catcher first.'

'The what?'

'The eye-catcher. Look, there on the horizon.' She pointed to the other side of the valley. 'Do you see that thing that looks like a castle? It's a fake, like a stage set. It's designed so that when you stand here you have something interesting to look at. Also it gives the impression that the garden stretches as far as the other side of the

valley, whereas in fact it stops this side of the Cherwell.' She was
aware of Oliver standing close to her, his proximity emphasised by
the expanse of terrace stretching either side of the statue and the
sweeping view below. He was squinting at the eye-catcher, hand
over his eyes like a ship's captain on the bridge, or a pirate. He must
have hundreds of women chasing after him, Anna thought, and felt
a guilty thrill that he was here with her.

'What's it supposed to be?' Oliver said, oblivious to her thoughts.

'A Gothic triumphal arch. And if you look below, you can see
Cuttle Mill. Kent – that's the man who designed the garden – added
gothic details to that too.' She looked sideways at him.

'Clever,' Oliver said.

'Mmm, the whole garden's clever. It's actually quite small, but
because you keep on doubling back on yourself and getting different
views, you feel it's much bigger. Let's go on.'

They walked across the lawn to a gravel path that led through
dark evergreens. At the end of the woodland they could see the
silhouette of an urn on a pedestal, caught in darkness against the
sunlit glade beyond. Since Oliver's phone call she'd been thinking
about this visit. Usually when she went round it was as the guide to
a tour, normally a group of interested ladies well informed about
gardens and eager for more information. She could quote from the
relevant texts, give dates and figures, cite references. But was that
what Oliver wanted? What *did* he want? They rounded the corner
to an arcade tucked into the slope of the hill.

'This is called the Praeneste, after the temple at Praeneste,' Anna
said. Oliver made no comment as he walked into the shade of the
arcades. Anna followed him, uncertain if he wanted more
information. What was he thinking? He walked along the stone
pavement under the arcade, looking through each arch at the view
down to the Cherwell. She hoped he was thinking of Templecombe
and how wonderful it would look if restored. But he said nothing.
They reached the last of the six arches and walked through to the

next patch of woodland, the dappled light shining on Oliver's dark hair.

'Which way?' Oliver was standing with his back against the light, outlined like the urn. Not quite as tall perhaps as Richard, but more substantial. Sexier. Anna was thankful for the shade of the trees, which hid her expression.

'Oh, to the right. The lower path,' she said, thoughts racing as they walked into another glade. I mustn't think about him like that; he's my employer's grandson and I'm trying to convince him that landscape gardens are interesting. The fact that he's sexy and attractive is neither here nor there. This is a professional visit. Think about Kent. William Kent. Dates 1684 to . . . to . . .

Oliver had stopped in front of a large circular pond where golden orfe floated mysteriously under the lily pads. Further up was a small rustic temple with a statue on the apex of the roof. He was smiling at her. He'd got a fantastic smile, warm and friendly and . . . 1684 to . . . to . . . 1748. Architect and garden designer. Did furniture too. Come on, Anna, sort yourself out. She looked up at the temple.

'This is called the Vale of Venus,' she said, and immediately regretted it. Venus, the goddess of love. Why hadn't she said another goddess: he wouldn't have known the difference. She should have said it was someone intellectual like Athena, she could have made something up about wisdom. 'The garden symbolises different types of love,' she went on, thinking that she should have taken him to see Stowe. Talking about politics would have been easier than love and romance.

At the far end of the pond there was a small waterfall, the culmination of a stream flowing along a small channel about six inches wide cut into the centre of the gravel path. They followed the path into a dense area of evergreen woodland, one on either side of the channel as it curved round the contours of the land. It was cooler in the shade, and Anna realised she had forgotten how the trees dipped down, enclosing visitors in their own world. Oliver was walking further away from her now, on the other side of the channel, but she felt as conscious of his presence as if they were holding hands. That's what they ought to be doing, swinging their hands together, keeping the physical connection although they were separated by the stream. Holding hands. Anna shoved hers deep into her jeans pockets.

'This stream is called a rill,' she said.

'I always wanted to know what a rill was,' Oliver said to her surprise. 'There was a bit about one in some poem I had to learn at school.'

'Coleridge. "Kubla Khan",' Anna said, her memory locking in. 'I had to learn it too.'

'I liked it because it stops so suddenly, when he was interrupted.'

'The person from Porlock.'

The path widened round an octagonal pool and they came to a halt beside its cool green depths. 'I can remember thinking it was great he got away with such a pathetic excuse,' Oliver said. 'You know, the dog ate my homework.'

Anna laughed. 'I thought you said you didn't have a dog, just a cat.' The trees surrounded them. They could have been the only people on the planet. Anna's heart beat faster.

'You've got a good memory,' he said, looking at her. Their gazes held, for way longer than they should. Then as if by mutual agreement they started walking again, more slowly than before, the rill still trickling between them.

'Isn't it ridiculous, getting children to memorise poetry when they don't know what the words mean?' Her voice sounded high-pitched.

'But it sounded good. Look at us, we can both remember it. Or most of it. Perhaps it doesn't matter not knowing.'

'Is that what you'd say about this garden? That you get as much pleasure from just looking, rather than knowing all the names and the symbolism.'

'If you know something about it, or you're with someone who

does,' and he flashed a glance across to her, 'you can appreciate the garden in different ways, but that doesn't mean necessarily you get more pleasure than from just looking at it.'

Anna felt her heart flicker with nerves. 'Are you enjoying it?'

Oliver smiled at her. 'Oh yes,' he said softly.

Surely he was interested. But what did she know? Before Richard her dates had been along the lines of trips to the cinema, where a casually placed arm across the back of the seat had been enough to indicate interest.

They had come out of the dense woodland now and stood in the final glade, headed by a small classical temple. Anna led Oliver a little way down the path to where a classical statue stood on a plinth. Behind it, the woodland had been cut back to create a view right up to the Praeneste, lit by the sun beyond the dark trees.

'Look.'

Oliver was standing right beside her. She could feel the heat of his body. 'I didn't think we'd walked that far.'

She put her fingers on the edge of the statue's plinth, squeezing the cold stone tight to bring her away from her awareness of Oliver. 'It's an optical illusion. The path narrows at the end, so it looks as if it's further away from where we're standing. Kent used to be a theatre designer, so he's good with sight lines. And this statue is of Apollo, the sun god, and he's looking across the Vale of Venus, who's associated with the moon, up to the Temple of Good Fortune.' As a chat-up line she knew it was sadly lacking. Perhaps I should simply have said, come up and see my temple, she thought as they walked across the grass towards it.

They entered the temple through a portico supported by two columns. A bench ran round the back which Oliver sat on. Anna sat beside him.

'What do you think?'

Oliver leant back against the temple wall. 'It's very beautiful.'

Beautiful. Of course the gardens were beautiful, but there was so much more to them. Anna felt disappointed, as if he'd missed the point. 'These gardens are meant to be a physical expression of the idealised landscape that continental painters such as Lorrain and Poussin were painting in the early eighteenth century.'

'Anna?'

'Yes?'

'Shut up.'

'Oh.' Oh God, Anna thought, I've been boring on like an idiot.

Oliver stood up. He held out his hand, and as if it was the most natural thing in the world, Anna took it. He led her to the front of the temple, between the two columns, and stood behind her.

'What do you see?'

Anna was puzzled. 'The garden,' she said, uncertain as to what he wanted her to say, and superconscious of him standing behind her.

'Go on.'

'Well. There's the lawn going down to the river, past the statue of Apollo, across the Cherwell, and then the countryside beyond the river.' She sighed. 'Look how clever Kent's been, he's got a whole series of contrasts in this view: formal and informal, arcadian and rural, the dark evergreens and the light glades.'

'You're talking like a guidebook,' Oliver said, his voice a warm and amused buzz against her ear.

'It's my job,' she said crossly. 'What do you want me to say?'

'It's a garden. It's trees and grass, nothing more.'

'But that's like saying a painting is just pigments ground into oil smeared on to canvas.'

'You said it . . .'

Anna twisted round to face him, then relaxed. 'You're teasing me.'

'A little.' He frowned. 'But I'm not sure you've convinced me. Oh, it's clever, I'll give you that, but it's also fake. Manufactured.'

She was conscious they were standing only inches apart. Practically touching. She didn't step back. Nor did he. All she had to do was lean forward just a little . . . 'But you said it was beautiful,' she said, feeling breathless.

'Mmm, but I prefer my beauty to be a little more natural.' Oliver touched Anna's hair, a loose strand that had escaped being swept back. 'A little ruffled, a little disordered, a little less controlled.'

'Shall we look at the rest of the garden now?' Anna walked down the temple steps, not looking to see if Oliver was following her. She felt shaky and confused. I'm behaving like an idiot over someone I hardly know. This isn't real; this is fantasy, this is the garden working its magic. It's what it's supposed to do, lure you into believing in romance and true love and that life can be perfect. It's meant to be walked through hand in hand, and I'm reacting to it. She ignored the fact that she'd been to the garden many times before and had never had the urge to kiss one of her companions before.

At the river she stopped and waited for Oliver to join her. He strolled down the lawn to where she stood, relaxed and amused, as if he knew exactly what he was doing. And he did, she realised, feeling uncertain and out of her depth yet excited at the same time. He was the hunter, she was the prey, and she didn't care.

At the water's edge he paused. I should be telling him about the bridge over the Cherwell, she thought, as the world held still. Then he leant forward and gently kissed her lips.

Anna closed her eyes and kissed him back. Gently at first, lightly, softly, feeling Oliver's hands cupping her face, his mouth on hers; then harder, as if she would die unless she could become part of him, her hands clutching at his arms, all thoughts of Kent and perfection and gardens driven out of her head, just the absolute necessity of being with Oliver. And then, pulling away, becoming gentle again, kissing his chin, his cheek, his neck with tiny nuzzling kisses, inhaling Oliver with every breath until she felt she would never forget him.

Chapter 8

They didn't talk much after that first, delicious kiss. Or rather, they talked of nothing, of dragonflies skimming the surface of the river, the way the reeds shimmered in the current, the clouds suspended in the sky. The old Anna reasserted herself and started to tell Oliver about the Bridgeman Theatre, but Oliver kissed her and she was lost in the new Anna, who didn't need to disgorge information. They strolled hand in hand, Anna swinging her hand like a child, caught up in the novelty of it all.

Then through an elaborate wrought-iron gate set within a curved stone surround, to the herbaceous borders, with clouds of pink, mauve, white and blue flowers, some spilling over the path and some standing six feet high and getting tangled with clematis and climbing roses that rambled over the supporting pergola. Bees buzzed industriously, butterflies collected nectar and a peacock called in the distance. Anna's hand rested around Oliver's waist. She could feel his body under his shirt and felt weak with wanting him. Too fast. It was all happening too fast. She didn't care.

A plainer gate led to a small church yard, sprinkled with grey stones mottled with yellow lichen. Two larger granite gravestones intruded, too glassy for the muted soft tones of the other stones, but Anna forgave them. A husband and wife, married for so many years they didn't want to be parted in death. She felt solemn as she read the inscription, and excited because Oliver had just kissed the top of her head and she knew he wanted to kiss her just as much as she wanted to kiss him.

They drove in tandem to a nearby pub and ate, Anna teasing Oliver about his dreams of beans on toast as he tucked into home-made Lancashire hotpot.

'Nearly as good,' he said, with every sign of enjoyment.

Anna could have been eating spinach for all she cared. Everything tasted delicious, wrapped in the haze that was Rousham and Oliver.

In the car park afterwards they stood by their respective cars and Anna said, casually, 'Do you want to come back to my place for coffee?' as if Bath was just round the corner instead of sixty miles away.

'I'd like that,' he said, and they drove back, Anna torn between pushing her car to keep pace with his and worrying about the engine seizing up. If her car went, it would be difficult to do her job, let alone the expense of repairing it, which she couldn't afford. Oliver's black BMW accelerated. Anna metaphorically crossed her fingers, offered up a prayer, and put her foot down.

The engine survived the journey, to Anna's relief. The lights were on in the house, which meant Clare was in, although Anna prayed she'd gone up to her room to watch television leaving the lights on downstairs. Clare was casual about electricity. Anna was conscious of the electricity between her and Oliver as she rummaged in her bag to find her house keys.

Suddenly the door opened and Clare stood in the light. 'There you are. I've been waiting for ever. You've got my – oh.' She stopped, her eyes wide.

'This is Oliver,' Anna said. 'My sister, Clare.'

'Hello,' Oliver said, shaking Clare's hand. Anna felt a glow of pride as she saw Clare give him the once-over and her eyes widen.

'The kitchen's just through here,' Anna said.

'Where did you find him?' Clare mouthed to Anna as Oliver

went past. 'Mind your own business,' she mouthed back before following Oliver into the kitchen. She didn't want Clare muscling in on him.

'And this is Steve.'

Steve had obviously just emerged from under the sink and was wiping his hands on a tea towel. 'I'd shake hands but . . .' he said with a smile. 'Clare managed to drop her ring down the sink.' He held it out on the palm of his dirty hand, a shining band of gold complete with solitaire diamond.

'My hero,' Clare said, giving him a kiss. She slipped the ring back on her finger and waggled it. 'We're engaged,' she said to Oliver, coquettish as a TV gameshow assistant. Anna scowled at her. You'd have thought it was enough that she'd got Steve on toast; she didn't need to flirt with Oliver.

'Congratulations,' he said, so charmingly that Anna burned. She'd forgotten how it was. She'd bring someone home, all excited by the possibilities, but then they saw Clare and forgot Anna. 'When's the wedding?'

'Not for ages,' Clare said, leaning against the sink and twiddling one of her curls around her finger. 'Ages and ages.'

'Three months,' Anna said, shoving the kettle under the tap. Water splashed everywhere. 'Drat.' Why did Clare have to be there? Anna knew she was being unreasonable, but right now she wished that she had chosen the castello option and was somewhere in Spain or Italy.

'You'll have to come,' Clare said, big-eyed. 'Anna's going to be a bridesmaid.'

Anna glared at her. It had all been going so well, and now Clare was shoving herself into Anna's magical day. I am not a teenager, Anna told herself. If Oliver is more interested in Clare than me, that's how it is and he's not worth my interest. Rise above it. She took a deep breath and turned to Oliver.

'Do you want decaff or the real thing?'

'The real thing,' Oliver replied, looking at Anna in a way that made her want to burst out singing.

'Oh, are you making coffee?' Clare said cheerfully. 'I'd love some.'

'I thought you'd given it up as part of this diet,' Steve said.

'Not all the time,' Clare said with a sweet smile. 'Just not late at night.'

Steve checked his watch and raised his eyebrows. 'It's gone ten.'

Clare pouted. 'I hope you're not going to be this bossy when we're married.'

Steve laughed. 'Let's go and leave these two in peace,' he said, practically pushing Clare out of the room.

'Byee,' Clare called to Oliver as she disappeared through the door. 'See you around.'

'That's my sister,' Anna said to Oliver. 'Sometimes I wish she was a million miles away.'

'You're very different.' He raised an eyebrow at her.

'I know.' Say it before he can. 'I'm the clever one, Clare's the pretty one.'

'I didn't mean that, I meant how you behave. And anyway,' Oliver touched her cheek, 'you're much better-looking than she is.'

'Really?'

'Really.' He ran his hands over her shoulders, his expression concentrated. Anna was at the top of a rollercoaster, those moments before it topples over the edge. He touched her face, her neck, her hair as if he was a blind man, the tips of his fingers light, delighting every nerve ending more than a rougher caress. Anna closed her eyes, giving herself up to the feel of another person's skin against hers.

'I read once that if babies are deprived of physical contact they die,' she murmured.

Oliver ran his index finger over the outline of her upper lip then gently pressed the centre. 'Sshhh,' he whispered, sounding like the murmur of waves lapping the shore. 'You think too much.'

'I'll try not to.'

He bent and ran the tip of his tongue from the base of her throat round to her ear, and Anna unconsciously flexed all her fingers in sympathy with the sensations he was producing at the back of her neck. God, but he was good at this. She felt like a marionette on strings, her nerves being played by an expert. Any minute and she'd dissolve in a little puddle on the floor.

She pulled away. 'Coffee,' she said brightly, trying to hide the fact that she was breathing heavily.

Oliver looked around the kitchen, taking in the mishmash of cupboards, the old range she'd reclaimed from a skip. 'Clare says it's like living in a museum.' Anna said, taking cups and saucers down from the china cupboard and getting the milk from the fridge, all the time achingly conscious of his presence. 'I don't like fitted kitchens.'

'So I see.' He lounged against the small table.

Anna's hands trembled as she shook coffee into the cafetiere and the grains scattered across the scrubbed beech worktop. Drat.

'I'm making a mess of this,' she said, smiling in his general direction but unable to meet his eyes. The kitchen was a small room and Oliver made it seem smaller. She picked up the tray.

'Allow me.' He took it from her, his hands touching hers. 'Lead on.'

Like most Georgian houses, the sitting room was on the first floor. Anna quickly cleared the magazines off the table to make space for the tray, then closed the shutters on the tall windows facing the road.

'Original?' Oliver said.

'Of course. When I came here they were hidden under hardboard panels and buckets of purple gloss paint.' She swung down the bar that kept the shutters in place. 'They're not as cosy as curtains, but I prefer them.'

She didn't want to be as pushy as to sit next to Oliver on the chaise longue, so she perched on the edge of the armchair. It was amazingly comfortable if you wanted to snuggle up with a book, but required serious consideration getting in and out of as the springs dipped down under your weight.

'Did you enjoy Rousham?'

'Very much so,' Oliver said. He looked amused, and Anna felt herself blush.

'I meant . . .'

'The gardens are spectacular, and I enjoyed being shown round them,' Oliver said, before suddenly grinning mischievously. 'Though I'm not convinced that Templecombe ever looked like them, or ever could. I also expect it has a team of gardeners, and Templecombe only has one, and a pretty dodgy one at that.' He raised his eyebrows at the thought of Will.

'But didn't you see . . .' She was stunned. How could he not be convinced?

'I can see that there are a few similarities, the positioning and so on. But Anna, you've no evidence there's ever been anything beyond that.'

'The buildings . . .'

'What, the pavilion?'

'Yes – and the gateway thing, and the area by the first lake . . .'

'All there is is a rather grotty damp hole.'

'What you call grotty, I might call a grotto.' She sat as straight as she could in the collapsing armchair.

Oliver laughed. 'Very good,' he said. 'Let's not talk about it now, there are far more interesting things to discuss.'

'Such as?'

'Like why you are sitting over there when you should be sitting here.' He patted the chaise longue next to him. Anna hesitated, then went over to him. 'That's better.' He stroked her hair. 'Who was it who said something about a chaise longue? The something of the chaise longue after . . . ?'

'Mrs Patrick Campbell. "The deep calm of the marriage bed after the hurly burly of the chaise longue." '

'It's like having my own personal encyclopedia,' he said, drawing her to him. 'My very own, very pretty . . .' His voice trailed away and he began to kiss her with a proficiency that made Anna quiver from her toes up. She kissed him back, small kisses on his mouth, his chin, his cheeks, butterfly kisses that nibbled the skin, each one teasing the softness inside her lips, making her wait for his mouth, greedy to have him, wanting him. She slipped her hands inside his jacket, skimming them over his shirt, coming to rest in the small of his back, pulling him to her, as if without being anchored by her hands he might sail off over the horizon and out of her world.

'They must have had comfier chaises longues in those days,' he said. 'I'm going to be on a permanent contract at the chiropractor at this rate.' He eased his neck as if he'd got a crick in it.

Anna thought of where else they could go. The kitchen – nowhere to sit; the dining room – too formal, like an interview. The only place was her bedroom, and that was an invitation. After Richard had left, she'd read all the books about Life after Divorce. All had the same two messages: Don't Rush and Never on the First Date. And then there was her mother: Nice Girls Don't. She looked at him. 'If we go up to my bedroom . . .' He stood up and took her hand. 'It's not an invitation to . . .'

Or was it? On the stairs up they stopped to kiss three times, so the climb to her bedroom took a delicious five minutes. The bedside lamps washed soft arcs of light against the walls as she closed the shutters. There was a loud creak from the bed. She turned to see Oliver stretched out, hands above his head.

'That's better,' he said, snuggling down with his shoulders. 'You've got to get some comfier furniture.'

'What, just for you?' She perched on edge of the bed.

'No, for you. I'm sure it's not good for your character to have nothing but uptight furniture. Take this bed, for instance,' he said, bouncing on it so the slats creaked.

'What's wrong with it?' It was late Georgian; she'd bought the frame at auction.

'Too short,' he said, paddling his feet against the bars at the end. 'And creaky.'

'We can always go downstairs again.' Anna made to get up, but he lunged and caught her.

'Not downstairs, please, not downstairs. Not the chaise longue, don't be so cruel.' His arms were round her waist, like a supplicant.

'Shut up,' Anna said, laughing despite herself.

'Please, Anna, please.'

'Don't be so silly.' She pushed him away from her, and somehow found herself lying across the foot of the bed with Oliver's face hovering above hers.

'So who are you calling silly?' he said.

'You.'

'Me?'

'You.'

And as she looked up at him smiling above her, their eyes meeting, the atmosphere went from hysterical laughter to something more serious. Oliver wasn't smiling any more; his eyes were searching hers, and she put her arms up round his neck and drew him down to her.

'I really shouldn't be doing this,' she whispered to him after they'd kissed.

'Why not? Nice girls do, you know.'

'You're sort of a client.'

'Not really.' He stroked her face, inches from his.

His eyes were the most fabulous smoky blue, she thought.

'I expect I'll be drummed out of the garden history society.' She raised his hand and kissed his palm, keeping her eyes locked to his.

'Only if I tell.' His fingers were stroking the back of her neck.

'Do you think you will?' She ran the edge of her teeth down his thumb.

'I might,' he murmured. 'And then again, I might not.'

Their mouths were so close, Anna felt they were sharing the same breath. 'What do I have to do to buy your silence?' she said, feeling the blood whoosh around her system. She lifted her mouth to his, and they touched. Softly. Exploring. His arms around her, hers around him.

Her shirt had come loose when he'd tickled her and now she could feel his hand warm against the skin of her waist. She arched her back with pleasure as his thumb massaged just the right vertebra at the base of her spine, and then realised her bra was undone and his hand was on her breast.

She paused. 'You did that very neatly.'

'Years of practice,' he said, before lowering his head to her breast, the buttons on her shirt having magically come undone. She pressed her fingers into his thick hair and involuntarily raised her hips against him, feeling desire flood her arteries, spreading to every fibre. Strange to be with someone other than Richard, unfamiliar and different. For a second she felt as if she was somehow being unfaithful although Richard had gone long ago. But no, she was free to please herself. And what pleased her was Oliver.

Never on the First Date. Nice Girls Don't.

She hesitated. Did she want to? Oh, yes.

She pulled his head up and kissed him deeply. She felt as if a different Anna had taken over, an Anna who was daring, who took risks. She undid his top shirt button, then the next one, their eyes locked together. She slipped the shirt off and ran her hands over his shoulders, her fingers down his spine, then shrugged off her own shirt and bra.

'Dr Carmichael,' Oliver said, caressing her back as she started to undo his belt. 'Are you seducing me?'

Anna felt her heart beat faster. 'I hope so,' she murmured.

'Isn't it very unprofessional to seduce clients?'

She paused. 'Very. Do you want me to stop?'

Oliver ran his fingers down her spine. 'Oh no. I have no, um, ethical or moral objections to being seduced. Please. Carry on.'

She unbuttoned her jeans, slipped them off together with her pants, feeling dizzy, light-headed. Driven. She pushed at his trousers as he kissed her neck; she kissed him and the kiss became harder, more passionate, his hands on her waist, her back, her body pressed to his, now his mouth on her breast so she arched her back to him, then reached out to him, feeling how much he wanted her. His tongue ran a trail to her navel while his hand traced circles on the inside of her thigh. Then up. Her fingers tightened in his hair as his reached inside her, tight, yielding. His tongue moved further down. She pushed against him, his mouth and fingers hot, tantalising, teasing, soft, hard, unutterably, exquisitely, painfully pleasurable.

'Too fast,' he murmured.

'Not fast enough,' she replied, pressing her hips to his, rubbing herself shamelessly against him, not caring for the consequences. Consequences. Her brain stirred its from its woozy deliciousness. 'Hang on.'

She slithered across so she could reach the bedside table and scrabbled in the drawer. With any luck . . . but her fingers found nothing, not even at the very back. 'Damn.'

Oliver stroked her back. 'Luckily I was in the boy scouts.'

She watched him in the soft light as he reached over the bed to his trousers in a heap on the floor. She should have guessed he'd be prepared. A flicker of anxiety ran over her. Was it good he had been certain enough to be prepared? She lay back on the bed. I don't care. If I am foolish, at least I am being consciously foolish. I know I am rushing in, breaking the rules. This is my choice, to sleep with a man who may well leave after this evening. This is what I want.

He came back to her side, and stroked her, his fingernails tracing patterns on her skin that made her quiver, then stretched his hand across her breasts, as if measuring her proportions, and smiled as if they were just right. She let him study her, raising her arms above her head, leaving herself defenceless and open, and the stroking grew faster, closer, further, and she arched to meet his hand, feeling she was falling, falling. His tongue rasped against silken, sensitised skin, his weight shifted on top of her, her fingers on the curve of his shoulder blades, the muscles taut. Opening like a sea anemone, mouth and fingers, his skin salt on her tongue, lips tender, her hands guiding, showing, him sliding inside, a sharp intake of breath, then plunging, touching deep, touching her heart, and ebbing like the tide, and she on the crest of discovery, as if this was the first time, and it was the first time, and, and she was losing control, losing herself, and inside her a chrysanthemum flowered, bursting into colour and light, shooting stars, then subsiding into glowing warmth and Oliver's arms around her.

She opened her eyes and he was watching her.

'Good?'

'Mmm.' She felt stroked inside and out, skin sheened with sweat, her very soul undone. Very good indeed.

Chapter 9

Anna opened her wardrobe doors in search of something smart. Really smart. She ran her hand over the clothes. Her suit and a couple of shift dresses she wore for presentations and job interviews. No good. Her hands paused on a cotton summer dress printed all over with tiny bunches of lily of the valley. She'd married Richard in that dress. Nothing special, just a pretty dress. Next to it hung a dress splashed with poppies. She'd bought that on their honeymoon in Paris. She hadn't worn either in years. Carefully she slipped them off their hangers and folded them on the bed. Time to put them away.

That done, she went back to the wardrobe. A little black dress was the obvious solution, but she didn't have one. She didn't lead a little-black-dress life, that was the problem. She led a jeans-and-jumper life, in country shades of mud, sludge and khaki. If Oliver had said she should wear something suitable for a weekend on a pig farm, she could have filled several suitcases. As it was . . . She shut the wardrobe door and went upstairs to Clare's room.

'Clare?' She knocked on the door loudly to be heard above the music. 'Clare?'

Clare emerged wearing what appeared to be a plastic shopping bag on her head, under a woolly hat. 'Hi there,' she said.

'What are you wearing?' Anna said, eyes riveted to her sister's head.

'It's a deep-conditioning hair mask. I'm keeping it warm.'

Logical, if bizarre. Anna dragged her eyes away from the woolly hat. 'Oliver's asked me to a black-tie thing in London on Saturday.'

'Wow, that's great. I thought you were having a good time – we didn't see you all weekend. Did you ever get out of bed?'

'Clare!' Anna was embarrassed and pleased at the same time, jumbled up with swirls of how wonderful the weekend with Oliver had been. Her body was inwardly singing the Hallelujah Chorus. And he wanted her to spend the next weekend with him in London. 'This thing is really smart, and I've nothing to wear. I couldn't borrow something, could I?'

Clare took her arm and drew her into the room. 'Of course, help yourself. What are you looking for?'

'I don't know. Glamorous. Sexy, if possible. But definitely smart.'

'You don't want much.'

'Smart then. I don't want to look like a hick from the sticks.'

'I know, let's go shopping!'

Anna shook her head. 'I don't want to spend money on something I'll only wear once – there's not much call for posh frocks in garden history.' She had a brief image of herself dressed in tiara and taffeta surveying the garden at Templecombe with Will. 'Hiring's expensive too.'

'I thought you were rolling in it, what with this TV job.'

The incongruous image vanished. 'It's not that well paid, and if I spend money on anything, it ought to be on my car, which is about to die on me. Oliver said black tie. D'you think that means long?'

Clare, fashion arbiter, personal dresser and woman with a supermarket plastic carrier bag on her head considered. 'Not necessarily, but definitely dressy. Now. What about . . .'

Clare had strewn what looked like her entire personal possessions over the floor – magazines, books, CDs in a bright jumble, with as many clothes outside the wardrobe as in it. Anna stood in what felt like the only available floor space while Clare rummaged in the wardrobe.

'What about this, and this, and this?' She seemed to have an endless supply of smart clothes. Anna stripped down to her underwear and put on an emerald silk dress, ignoring Clare's comments about the state of her bra and the fact that it was a miracle she'd ever pulled wearing knickers the colour of dishcloths.

The sisters stared at Anna's reflection in the mirror. Anna could see why the dress suited Clare, with her roses-and-cream colouring and her compact body, but she thought she looked washed out and grey.

'There, that'll do,' Clare said with triumph.

'I'm not sure about the colour . . .'

'Oh, you just need the right make-up.' Clare peered at Anna's face. 'I'll give you a makeover if you like.'

'Thanks . . .' Anna studied herself in the dress. She could see that it was smart enough, but she was a different shape from Clare, which no amount of making over would deal with. She tugged at the skirt. 'It's a bit short.'

'You've got great legs! God, I've always wished I had your legs. Try on something else, be my guest, but please, please, please . . .' Clare cocked her head to one side, the carrier bag tilted fetchingly over one ear. 'Get some new underwear.'

Anna dropped off Clare's dress at the dry cleaner's, then walked up Milsom Street to the department store. She wasn't sure about the dress – it was such a vivid shade of green, one of Anna's least favourite colours, although it was smart. It would do if she couldn't find something else, that was the main thing. Perhaps if I went to smart places I'd be more interested in smart clothes, she thought, trailing listlessly through racks of dresses, mostly variations on a gypsy theme in honey browns or turquoise and hot pink. She sighed. Men were lucky, all they had to do was put on a suit and a tie.

She crossed the road and went into a shop that had a likely-looking dress in the window. The assistant gave her a supercilious look as if she could tell at a glance that Anna was not their usual sort of customer.

'Can I help?'

'The dress in the window,' Anna mumbled, suddenly conscious of the hole in the toe of her left plimsoll. The assistant directed her to the right clothes rail and hovered as Anna looked at the dress. Would it make Oliver proud of her, pleased that he'd asked her along? She let the silky fabric run through her fingers, imagining Oliver taking it off her. The weekend had been . . . She looked at the price tag and crashed back to reality. Surely not! That was two months' mortgage. For just one dress? She turned the tag over in case she'd got it wrong and was reading the bar code or something. No, that was the price. And the dress wasn't that wonderful either. She dropped the tag and left, trying to look as if she'd just remembered an urgent appointment elsewhere.

She traipsed round a few more shops, getting increasingly depressed. The expensive dress became more attractive. Oh, but it would be nice not to have to worry about the cost, just for once. To say, sod it, this is what I chose when I went freelance, feast or famine, and as it's feast time, I'll treat myself to a dress. But she couldn't justify spending that sort of money for the sake of something she'd wear once, especially when there was a perfectly good dress at the dry cleaner's. No, she'd just have to hope Oliver was a not-noticing sort of man.

When she got home she phoned Bronwen and told her about the dress, or lack of one.

'Cariad, you're welcome to something of mine, but you'd look like a pin in a tent. And I doubt I have anything grand enough. The last black-tie thing I went to was the All Saints Parents' Association Dance. I don't think it sounds quite in the same league, somehow. Who are you going with?'

Anna was torn between discussing him and keeping him secret, just to herself. 'He's called Oliver Davenport.'

'And is he gorgeous?'

Anna curled up on the chair. 'Utterly,' she said.

Bronwen whooped, then shushed herself. 'I mustn't wake the baby.'

'How is she?'

'Fast asleep, that's why I can talk. Now, tell me about this gorgeous man.'

'There's not much to tell, really,' Anna said, knowing that if she started talking about Oliver she might not be able to stop. She refused to give in to Bronwen's pleas for more information. 'I don't want to tempt fate, it may all go wrong. Tell me about the baby instead.'

Bronwen sighed. 'It's funny, having already had a baby doesn't make you ready for the second one. They come with their own little quirks and personality. Toby, now, he was never still, wriggled like a sand eel, but this one, she just tucks into your arm as quiet as can be.'

Anna smiled at the image of Bronwen grappling with a sand eel. 'I haven't seen Toby for ages. Why don't you all come round for lunch one Sunday? What about the sixteenth?'

'Make it the twenty-third. It'll be Betty's first outing.'

'You decided against Parsley then?'

'It was a close-run thing, but yes. And speak of the devil . . .' Anna could hear some squeaks over the phone. 'Must dash, motherhood calls,' Bronwen said. 'I'll see you then – enjoy your weekend.'

'Wow.'

Anna gazed at Oliver's flat, the expensive limestone floors stretching throughout the open-plan space, the leather of the low-rise sofas gleaming under carefully placed lighting, the wraparound windows giving the most spectacular view over London, the gleaming steel kitchen – at least she thought it must be the kitchen, although there were no visible appliances, just a single arched tap over a circular sink.

She turned to Oliver, who was looking distinctly smug. 'It looks like something in a magazine.'

'Actually, it has been in several magazines.'

She walked out across the expanse of floor. 'Where do you store stuff? Don't you have any clutter?'

Oliver touched what she'd thought was a wall. A floor-to-ceiling section swung out as easily as if it had been made of paper, revealing shelves neatly stacked with boxes.

'Television?'

He picked up a remote control. The section of wall above the fireplace slid up soundlessly, revealing a flat screen flush with the wall.

'That's about the size of the screen at the local cinema,' Anna said, giggling. She looked round the room. 'What else does it do?'

Oliver spent the next ten minutes showing her the flat's tricks – remote-controlled shutters for the windows, retractable glass ceiling complete with rain sensors, concealed this, automatic that.

'It's like the baddie's lair in a James Bond film,' she said, laughing. 'Come on, it's such a cliché, the bachelor penthouse with all the gizmos.'

'Maybe,' he said, looking a little sheepish.

'Ah, it's fabulous,' she said, kissing him. 'Just – unbelievable.'

'Come and see the bedroom.' He picked up her weekend bag.

She followed him along a hall lit with uplighters set in the floor, washing the walls with colour. 'I hope you haven't got a circular bed with black satin sheets.'

He turned round, his expression one of horror. 'Oh no, you've caught me out.'

'Twit.' She hit him playfully on the arm.

His bed wasn't circular but was extremely large, with white bed-linen. He patted it. 'Care to try?'

Anna was too busy touching the walls to pay him attention. 'I bet you've got cupboards somewhere.'

He shook his head. 'Wrong.' He pushed open a concealed door flush to the wall. 'Walk-in wardrobe.'

Anna peeped inside. Tiers of shelves, drawers, a rail of jackets, racks of shoes, each with a wooden shoe tree, all the accoutrements fitted in burr walnut. 'It's like something in a film.' She touched the nearest garment, almost expecting it to be fake; it was all too perfect. But no, she could feel the soft texture of cashmere between her fingers. Did real people live like this?

'And if madam would care to see the bathroom . . .'

She stared speechless at a bath the size and shape of a small galleon, the glass basins apparently floating in space, the shower head the size of a flying saucer. All immaculate, the surfaces un-smeared, untouched.

'Do you actually use this?' she said, trailing her fingers over the marble walls.

He shrugged. 'Course. Do you want to use it now? You've had a long journey.'

'Bath to London's not that far, and the train wasn't bad . . .' Her voice was muffled as he lifted her shirt over her head.

'Don't be dense.'

Thoroughly soaped, cleansed and moisturised in places she didn't usually moisturise, Anna lay on the big bed wrapped in Oliver's dressing gown, staring at the ceiling. She was glad to see there wasn't a mirror set into it. Instead, tiny spotlights twinkled like stars. She felt like Marlene Dietrich, Jean Harlow and Marilyn Monroe all wrapped up into one. No wonder Oliver found her house shabby and uncomfortable. Not that he'd said that, of course, but he'd been distinctly grumpy last Saturday morning when the shower had been more of a trickle and the hot water had run out. Here the hot water gushed out at a rate that made the Angel Falls in Venezuela look pathetic.

Oliver came in with a glass of champagne. 'You look edible.'

Anna rolled over on to her front and took the glass from him. 'You've already tried that.'

He tapped her bottom. 'Naughty. Have you unpacked yet?'

'Give me a chance, I've only just come.'

'In more ways than one, I hope.' He kissed the top of her head. 'I was wondering what you were planning to wear tomorrow.'

She scrambled up, unzipped her bag and held up the dress. Even through the dry cleaner's bag it looked horribly vivid, like an Amazonian tree frog.

'What's it like on?'

She showed him. 'It's not mine, actually. It's Clare's.'

'Mmm.' He circled her, assessing with his eyes. Anna felt like a pony gone to market. She almost expected him to feel her fetlocks. 'Tomorrow we're going shopping.'

Anna was baffled when Oliver pulled up on double yellow lines outside an apparently empty shop.

'Is this it?' she said, peering out at a window swathed in oyster satin held back by black velvet ribbons to reveal – nothing. There wasn't even a name written on the shop front, just a small brass plaque by the door.

They got out and Oliver pressed a bell. After a few moments the door buzzed and they went inside, Anna wiping her feet several times on the doormat although it wasn't raining. She felt she should be standing on newspaper, the carpet was so thick and creamy. They went through into what had perhaps once been someone's front parlour, knocked through to the back room. Everything was in shades of cream. The area at the back was sectioned off as a changing room, fabric doors looped back with more black velvet ribbon. Anna was relieved that the place at least resembled an ordinary shop in that it had some clothes hanging from rails along the sides. Not many, though.

An assistant came through looking smarter than Anna had ever looked in her life. Make-up, hair, clothes, shoes – everything was immaculate. Oliver explained what they were looking for and the assistant listened carefully before turning to Anna and looking her up and down. Anna felt she could see right through her clothes. At least she'd got new underwear.

'Please, take a seat,' the assistant said, indicating a cream chenille sofa, before turning on her perfect legs and gliding through a door into the back.

Anna perched on the edge of the sofa. 'This is a black-and-cream version of what I imagine brothels look like,' she whispered to Oliver.

'Relax and enjoy it,' Oliver said. 'I thought all women enjoyed shopping.'

'Women vary, and besides, I'm not convinced this *is* shopping. Not as I know it, anyway.' It made the posh dress shop in Bath look like Woolworth's. 'God, I hope you're not a secret white slaver.'

'I intend to sell you off to the highest bidder,' he said, giving her an amused look.

The session did have some resemblance to a slave auction, Anna thought. The assistant brought several dresses which Anna put on, then paraded in front of Oliver. She was disconcerted to find it wasn't an entirely unpleasant feeling, sashaying up and down, swirling round at his bidding, like a doll. It helped that the dresses looked and felt fabulous, red-carpet dresses for the glitterati, not garden historians. Anna was amazed to discover they all had built-in underwear, although it was invisible from outside.

'That's the secret of these dresses,' the assistant said. 'It's not so much what you can see as what you can't.'

'What's this fabric called?' Anna asked, running it through her fingers. It looked a bit like satin, but was soft and floaty.

'Silk charmeuse. Gorgeous, isn't it?'

She hadn't thought she could look like this, like an illustration in an Aubrey Beardsley drawing, all froth and femininity. Last week she'd been a humble garden historian; this week she'd become more glamorous than Clare. She did a twirl in front of the mirror and the dress swirled out around her in waves and folds. Good thing she hadn't gone for that drink with Will. Half a pint of scrumpy and a roll in the hay. She turned to Oliver, who was relaxing in the sofa like the master of all he surveyed. 'What do you think?' she said.

Oliver put his head on one side. 'It's good, but I prefer the blue one. Put that one on again.'

Anna obediently tried on the blue dress. Gorgeous, but not as fabulous as the Beardsley one, she thought. 'Don't you think it's a bit, well, low-cut?' she said, tugging at the empire-line front where she felt overexposed. Not that she was in danger of flopping out; she was held firmly in place by invisible boning. Too firmly, almost. She felt her breasts were being thrust on display as part of an anti-gravity demonstration. All very well if you were Nell Gwyn, but it wasn't a look she was used to.

'No, it looks great.'

'What about the other one?' she said, looking wistfully at the gentle folds of silk charmeuse over the assistant's arm.

'No, this is the one.' He kissed her neck, his hand tracing the sweep of her breast.

'Oliver!' Anna hissed, pushing him away, pink with embarrassment that the assistant might see. But she had turned discreetly away, which made Anna feel even more embarrassed.

'Eminently fuckable,' Oliver murmured in her ear, his hand continuing its journey. 'Just as it should be.'

'Stop groping me,' she whispered, torn between outrage and excitement.

'I bet they've seen worse,' he said.

'You don't know that,' Anna shot back, pushing his hand away.

She wasn't going to be groped in a clothes shop, no matter how posh. 'Not now,' she said firmly.

'You're such fun to tease,' Oliver said as he sat back on the sofa and crossed his legs. The assistant came back into the room. 'I'll take that one,' he said, pointing to the blue dress.

Anna hesitated. 'I like the other one.'

'I don't remember the Fairy Godmother getting this hassle from Cinders,' Oliver said.

'If you're my Fairy Godmother, then where's your wand?'

His lips twitched. 'Come and find out . . .' Anna rolled her eyes in mock despair as he handed his credit card to the assistant. 'Comes in plastic nowadays.'

She looked at herself in the mirror, glowing as if sprinkled with fairy dust. None of this is real, she thought. This place, this dress, it's like a fantasy world. She looked again, and a new, different, eminently fuckable Anna looked back.

Anna felt like a princess as she swanned into the ballroom of the Dorchester, her fabulous dress on and her hand tucked into Oliver's arm. She thought Oliver looked utterly gorgeous in black tie and she was inwardly bursting with pride that she was with him. She could tell by the way heads turned that they were the most glamorous couple there, and that was a new feeling.

Oliver scanned the room. 'Let's mingle,' he said, taking two glasses of champagne and handing her one.

Anna soon realised Oliver was on a mission to speak to everyone in the room, shaking hands with some, clapping others on the back, handing out cards. Some of the glamour began to seep away. She'd never been very good at drinks party chit-chat, even when she knew people, but here most of the talk was 'shop' and very soon she gave up trying to follow what they were talking about. It wasn't that anyone was unfriendly, in fact they were unfailingly polite, but they all seemed to know each other. And as the noise levels rose, she often couldn't quite catch what people were saying. After a while she got bored with saying 'What? Sorry? Can you say that again?' so she just stuck close to Oliver, nodding away like a dog in the back seat of a car when anyone addressed her, an inane grin on her face.

She'd not worn anything so low-cut before. When Oliver introduced her to a man, she could see his gaze flicker over her chest. Most of the men would then resolutely raise their eyes and stare fixedly at her face, but one or two never got further than her chest, sticking there as if glued. She had swept her hair back from her face with combs, but after one man had all but drooled down her cleavage, she surreptitiously removed the combs and shook her hair out so she felt a little less naked. It was a relief when they sat down at a table, not least because her new high heels were hurting.

Oliver introduced her to the others as Dr Anna Carmichael, which made her feel less like a sex object, but most of the guests didn't or couldn't grasp that she wasn't a medical doctor. She had to be quite firm with one man, who started to tell her far too many details about his hernia. Over the course of dinner she had the same conversation four times – no, not a medical doctor, a doctor of philosophy. No, not garden design, garden history. Yes, it is very interesting. And what do you do? Oh, insurance. How interesting.

One of them commented: 'Oliver's going up in the world, I thought models were more his type. His last girl – now she was a stunner. Legs up to here . . .' and he indicated a level that would imply Oliver's previous girlfriend had been a spider. He must have registered Anna's expression, adding in a kind voice, 'Of course, looks aren't everything,' which deflated Anna even further. She'd assumed Oliver's previous girlfriends would be stunning, but it wasn't great to be reminded that she was playing way out of her league.

Later on there were interminable awards to be handed out. Anna listened, feeling she was losing the will to live, clapping when everybody else clapped. Oliver was shortlisted for something, she didn't catch what, but he didn't get it. She could tell by a tightening of his jaw that he'd wanted to win, but he was laughing and clapping with everyone else. She murmured an excuse, not that anyone was listening, and left the room, then traipsed down what seemed to be endless corridors to find the Ladies, her new shoes slipping on the carpet.

She was about to wash her hands when another woman touched her arm.

'You've come with Oliver Davenport, haven't you?' She was blonde, with eyes bright as stars and lips so big they could suck the chrome off a Cadillac. 'Lucky you, he's gorgeous.'

Anna nodded, turning the taps on, trying not to look smug.

'Who's gorgeous?' Another blonde had come out of the loo, smoothing her dress down. Anna felt uneasy. Perhaps these were the model-types Oliver usually went out with. Neither of them resembled spiders; they were more like flamingos, with teeny brittle legs supporting generous curves that promised a lifetime of backache.

'Olly Davenport,' the first blonde said, applying another layer of glossy lipstick.

'Oh yeah, gorgeous.' They both studied Anna with measuring looks, as if they could tell she was an impostor despite her gorgeous boyfriend and gorgeous dress. She squirted soap on to her hands, recognising the brand as something smart Clare used. Odd to have strangers tell you how gorgeous your boyfriend was.

The second blonde was adjusting her cleavage, which stuck out at an improbable angle from a chest so bony Anna could count her ribs. 'Are you 'n' Olly going to the hospital after?'

'I wouldn't have thought so,' Anna said, surprised at the question.

'Everyone's going.'

'Oh.' Anna dried her hands very carefully. Mass food poisoning? She couldn't think of another reason why everyone would need to go to hospital. Was it some weird insurance thing?

'I hope you feel better soon,' she said before escaping into the corridor.

Oliver was lounging against the wall. He straightened up when he saw her, and gave her a hug.

'Everything okay?'

'Mmm,' she said, not wanting to admit how bored she was.

'I'm sorry, it must be very dull for you,' he said. 'But you're doing brilliantly. Franklin can't stop talking about you.'

'Is that good?' Anna wasn't sure which one Franklin was. The hernia man? Or the one with the beard that fringed his chin in a neat reversal of the absence of hair above his domed forehead?

'Of course,' he said. 'He's one of my biggest clients.'

Anna leant against the wall, calf muscles aching in her new high heels. 'Are we going to go soon?'

'Everyone's going on to a club . . .'

'Oh please, Oliver, let's go home.'

He kissed the top of her head. 'I know they're not in your league brains-wise, but I work with these people.'

The two blondes came out of the Ladies and stopped when they saw Oliver. Double air kisses all round.

'You going on to the Hospital, Olly?'

Oliver glanced at Anna. 'Not sure.'

'You must. Everyone's going.' The one with the lips pouted, giving her a distinct resemblance to a carp. 'Don't be a bore, Olly.'

'Of course you're going,' the other one chimed in. They tottered off down the corridor in their absurdly high heels, calling, 'See you later.'

Oliver shook his head, his expression amused. 'They're not as dumb as they look,' he said to Anna.

They couldn't be. She had a sudden thought. 'Is the Hospital a club?' He nodded. 'Oh shit. I didn't realise. No wonder they looked puzzled.'

'What did you say?'

'I said I hoped they'd get better soon. I didn't know . . .'

Oliver gave her a hug. 'That's so sweet. You are funny.' Anna wasn't sure she liked being funny in the circumstances, let alone sweet. 'You'll have to come now, got to see what it's like. Have you been to a club before?' he added kindly.

'Yes, of course,' Anna said crossly. 'I'm not something you discovered under a stone, you know.'

'Of course not, I'm sorry.' He looked contrite. 'Come on, it'll be fun.'

'I'm really tired,' Anna said, knowing that the last thing she wanted to do was go to a club with the blondes – who were probably at this moment telling everyone what she'd said. The last bit of her veneer of sophistication evaporated and suddenly she wanted to go home, away from this alien environment.

Oliver glanced quickly up and down the corridor, then grabbed her arm and pushed her back into the Ladies and into one of the cubicles.

'Oliver,' Anna said, half laughing, half shocked. She turned her face up to be kissed, not at all averse to being ravished.

Instead he took out of his inside pocket a small flat silver box like a cigarette case and flipped it open on top of the cistern. The inside was mirrored and there was a packet of white powder which he shook on to the mirror surface. He chopped at it with a razor blade several times, making four thin white lines, then rolled up a new twenty-pound note and held it out to her.

'But . . .' She stared at him. 'I've not . . .'

'You'll love it, you'll see. Look . . .' He pressed a finger over one nostril, put the rolled note to the other, and sniffed up one line, then repeated the procedure on the other side. 'Mmm.' He gave himself a little shake. 'It's easy. Just don't blow out.'

She looked at the rolled note in his hand, then at the white lines. She'd never been part of the druggy set at school or university, never dropped acid, never smoked dope, certainly never taken coke.

'Isn't it addictive?' she whispered.

He shook his head. 'Not if you're careful and just keep it to the weekends. Bit like alcohol. Go on.' He pushed the note into her hand and she took it, feeling she was teetering on the edge. This is illegal. This is forbidden. Aren't I supposed to just say no? Her heart was racing with the mere thought, it might explode if it went any faster. But she didn't want to appear provincial, a hick from the sticks, so she quickly bent her head, put the note to her nose and sniffed, first one side, then the other, just like in the movies. She straightened up, feeling as if her nose was going to explode.

'Good?'

She didn't know about good. She felt most peculiar.

'You're not going to be sick?'

Was she going to be sick? She thought hard, then shook her head, speech having deserted her.

Oliver led her out of the Ladies and back to their table. She'd found them boring before, but obviously she hadn't got to know them properly. They were actually fascinating people, and she could talk to them, really talk to them, like they were her best friends. She was the Anna she was supposed to be, not shy and inhibited, but outgoing and confident.

They didn't go to the Hospital in the end, as another one of Oliver's friends was opening a club. Becky, one of the blondes, pointed people out to Anna. A list, B list, Z list. Anna nodded happily, not having a clue what Becky was talking about.

'Ooh, look. She's always in *Heat*, you must have heard of her,' Becky said.

'I don't watch much television,' Anna replied, which had Becky shrieking with laughter. Anna joined in. She realised that Becky and Della, the other blonde, actually *were* her best friends, her bestest ever friends. They had so much in common, they worked in insurance, and she was seeing Oliver who worked in insurance, which was an amazing coincidence. And it was extraordinary, she'd not met them before and yet they were the best friends a girl could have – they'd gone to the loo together, and afterwards Della had told her to check her nose, which was just so funny. At one point someone – Johnnie, Harry? – asked Oliver where he'd found her.

'In my grandmother's attic, covered in dust,' he said. 'Scrubs up well, doesn't she?' and everybody had laughed, Anna most of all. God, he was great, she hadn't felt like this about anyone before, not Richard, not anyone.

'Let's go home,' she whispered in his ear, pressing herself against him.

They took a taxi back to the flat.

'It's light,' she said, peering out of the cab window.

'It's four thirty,' Oliver mumbled, his head down over her breasts, hand up her dress.

'It's amazing, it must be dawn,' she said, smiling at the cab driver, who was checking his rearview mirror with astonishing frequency. 'I haven't seen the dawn for years and years. I ought to see it more often, it's amazing. Olly, Olly, look at the dawn, it's amazing, you've got to see it.' Oliver grunted. 'Really, Olly, you ought to look, the colours, there's pink and green and blue and a sort of silvery silver, it's amazing.'

Back at the flat the sex was amazing too, on and on, this way, that way, they kept changing positions as if Oliver had a Kama Sutra diary and had decided to tick off a whole year's worth in one night. On and on, but strangely unsatisfying. And when they stopped, almost arbitrarily, neither of them having come, Anna found her eyelids were unable to close, so she stared at Oliver's ceiling, physically exhausted, mentally zooming, holding on to the side of the bed in case she might fall off.

Chapter 10

Anna woke up feeling as if someone had taken her eyeballs out, rolled them in pepper and popped them back in their sockets. She stared at the lights set in the ceiling, not sure that she would ever be able to move again. Everything ached: her throat, her cheek muscles, everything. I am never, ever doing that again, she told herself.

Oliver came out of the bathroom, a towel wrapped round his middle, and sat on the edge of the bed. 'How do you feel?'

'Odd.' Strange how even the balls of her feet were sore.

He stroked her forehead. 'Did you get any sleep?'

'Not much.' Too busy dancing – that was it! Dancing to the rhythm of the music (although perhaps not entirely with it), spiralling away like a drunken daddy-longlegs wearing high heels on a hard tiled floor. So not a bizarre side effect after all.

'Best thing is to get up now, and have some lunch.'

Anna dragged her body to the bathroom and showered, cowering under the weight of water that fell on her head. They walked to a nearby brasserie. Oliver knew a couple who were already there, and they joined their table. Anna hid behind a pair of Oliver's sunglasses, which were too big for her and kept slipping down her nose. Other people joined them, moving tables together, until there were eleven of them there, laughing, talking, drinking. The men were all tall and good-looking, the women blonde and slim. Piers, Amanda, Rupert. Charm bracelets dangled from tanned wrists, designer stubble was well groomed. It was like being in an animated Boden catalogue, Anna thought. Caro, Charles, Venetia. They exuded success, good health and glamour. They weren't the only people eating lunch in the garden, but they dominated it, other couples looking enviously across at them, the charmed inner circle. And Anna, the silent outsider, pale as a lamprey.

She pushed her food around her plate, feeling as lumpen as the mashed potato she'd thought would be the least inflammatory item on the menu. Bangers and mash with onion sauce. The sauce looked like tapeworms.

Oliver stroked her hair. 'Okay?' he whispered. She shook her head.

He passed her, quite openly, the flat silver case and she shoved it in her bag, terrified that the drugs squad might suddenly leap out from behind the plumbago tubs. Oliver looked in his wallet for a new note from the cashpoint, handed it to her. 'Go on. You'll feel better.'

Anna looked around, but none of the others seemed to have noticed, they were all chatting and laughing. She edged off her seat and went to the loo, all the while expecting a large hand to descend upon her shoulder and a voice to declare: 'You're nicked.'

Her face in the mirror matched the dishcloth knickers. Perhaps just a little would help. It had been wonderful the night before; she'd felt a whole new Anna had emerged from a chrysalis. Just a little. She entered a cubicle.

Back round the table, she sat next to Oliver, his hand casually on her shoulder, and it was easier. She didn't feel intimidated by his friends' glossy surfaces and was able to talk a little. Piers was a television producer and interested in her programme. Madeleine edited a magazine, and suggested she might like to write an article about historic gardens, nothing too academic, of course. Anna nodded, as if article commissions were run-of-the-mill, and suggested sexual imagery in gardens without a flicker of embarrassment. Madeleine seemed to think that was a good idea. Anna relaxed. This was how life was supposed to be: a leisurely Sunday lunch in the sunshine, surrounded by friends. She stroked Oliver's thigh. And a lover.

When the coffee arrived, Rupert brought out a box of Trivial Pursuit, to groans from Clemmie. 'Not this again . . .'

Rupert ignored her. 'The usual?' he said, looking round at the group.

'Make it five,' Oliver said.

'You're too competitive,' Clemmie complained, tapping her manicured nails on the table. 'Count me out.'

'I'm in,' Piers said

Amanda, Clemmie and Madeleine took their coffees to the far end of the table, but the rest made two teams of three, with Anna and Oliver a pair.

'But I don't know how to play,' she whispered in Oliver's ear.

'You're lovely,' he said, pulling her on to his knee. 'It's very easy. Just answer every question you get asked.'

And it was easy. She didn't know anything about sport or television or pop, but Oliver answered those. Anna thought the questions pretty basic, although the others struggled. At first she thought they were putting it on, but then she realised they genuinely didn't know the difference between Dali and Magritte, or that Charles II was nicknamed Old Rowley after a stallion in the royal stables. She started to add little qualifying statements – well, I'm not sure, but I think it might be – even when she knew the answers. They won easily.

Rupert shook his head. 'How come you know so much useless information?'

'I don't know,' Anna said, blinking at his opinion of her knowledge. 'I just remember things.'

'She's got a Ph.D.,' Oliver said casually.

This led to a chorus of exclamations. 'You bastard,' Piers said. 'You brought a ringer.'

'Davenport, you're a toad.'

'No wonder he wanted to play for five,' Marcus said.

Oliver grinned. 'Pay up.'

To Anna's surprise, they started to get out wallets and chequebooks.

'So what's a clever girl like you doing with a dimwit like Oliver?' Rupert said, passing Oliver a cheque. Anna gasped when she saw that it was for £500. 'D'you ever manage to get a degree, Ol?'

'Very funny,' Oliver said, folding up the cheque and slipping it into his wallet. 'You know I got the same as you.'

'Pass degree, wasn't it? Didn't even scrape a third,' Marcus said.

Oliver smiled, unruffled. 'I earn more than you,' he said lightly.

Marcus flushed, and handed Oliver a cheque, which Oliver took with a bow.

The afternoon was obviously over; everyone started to get up, collect bags, make arrangements to meet up, ask if there was a lift going to the Henbury party.

'I'll pick up the tab,' Oliver said. 'In the circs.'

'Someone throw something at him,' Madeleine said.

Anna stood too, uncertain of what she should be doing. Several of the men kissed her goodbye and told her she was wasting herself on Oliver. Madeleine handed her her card. 'Don't forget that article.' And then they were all gone and she and Oliver were walking back to his flat.

'Did you gamble on me knowing everything?' He nodded, and put his arm around her shoulder. 'But I might have been useless.'

Oliver kissed her. 'That's why it's called gambling. I made a guess, raised the stakes, and you were brilliant.'

'You didn't tell me. I couldn't have afforded to lose.' She felt sick at the thought that she could have lost £500.

'We won, so there's no problem.'

'I wouldn't have played if I'd known.'

'Which is why I didn't tell you. Thought it might put you off.' He stopped. 'Look, we normally play for money. It's usually a hundred, and I hardly ever win. So yes, I gambled that you'd be good, and raised the stakes. Those guys have been quite happy to take money off me before, so this is payback. They got screwed.' He laughed. 'Did you see Marcus's face? He hated giving me that cheque. Supercilious sod.'

'Isn't he a friend?'

'Sure. I was at school with him.'

She thought about this conversation several times in the coming weeks as she got to know Oliver's friends. There were enough of them: the skiing crowd, the university crowd, the school crowd, the City crowd, the clubbers, the insurance lot. He had many different circles of friends, all overlapping, acquiring names in his BlackBerry like other people acquired CD collections. Some he didn't seem to like much, like Marcus, but that didn't make any difference; they were part of the crowd and that was enough. Anna wondered whether if she hung around long enough she'd become part of the crowd too.

The following two weekends she spent in London, with Oliver and his friends, going clubbing, going shopping, things she never usually did but which acquired a charm because she was doing them with Oliver. Swinging shopping bags over one shoulder, hands entwined as they strolled around The Cross, looking in shops of the kind she'd always avoided before, she thought she'd never been happier.

Oliver was as acquisitive for shiny new gadgets as a magpie, but he liked buying generally. He enjoyed an audience for trying on clothes, and Anna was keen to oblige, stroking fabric to gauge the quality – she quickly learnt the difference between two-, three- and four-ply cashmere – picking off imaginary loose threads, anything to touch him. She felt drunk with his presence, and with the whole feeling of being her when she was with Oliver. She imagined other people envying them, this glamorous, exciting couple, hopping into taxis, not being able to decide between colours so having both, carrying armfuls of fresh flowers for the flat.

She decided to spend her share of the Trivial Pursuit winnings on clothes, stifling any qualms about wasting money that should have been spent on keeping her car on the road. She tried on things she'd never have dreamt of before, tight, short and fitted, parading in front of Oliver in her turn, like a game. If she decided against something he liked, he'd often buy it for her. She tried to explain that she hadn't decided against it in the hope that he'd buy it for her, but he laughed and said not to worry. He looked at labels, Anna checked out prices. She protested at spending £98 on the tiny wisps of lace and gauze and satin that made up a minuscule bra, but he bought it for her anyway. Her underwear drawer staged its own version of the Velvet Revolution.

The weekends fell into a pattern. Anna went up to London on Friday afternoon and Oliver met her at the station. They went out to a drinks party or a private view, or met his friends for a drink, then dinner as part of a big group, ending up in a club. Saturday was spent shopping, Saturday night was a repeat of Friday, and then it was Sunday lunch at the brasserie before catching the train back to Bath on Sunday evening. The first time, she'd slept so deeply on the train home, she'd woken up in Cardiff.

Sleep. Anna had never had problems with sleep before. They slept Saturday and Sunday mornings away, or rather Oliver did, no matter how many lines he'd taken. But Anna couldn't get to sleep, or when she did she kept waking up, only dozing off when the light filtering through the blinds showed that dawn had arrived. She wanted to say no, but the evening she did, she ended up slumped on a banquette, yawning, before they'd even gone on to a club. Bored, and boring. She found it hard to keep up with Oliver's friends' conversations, almost as if the were talking in a strange language. Celebrity gossip, designers, gadgets, cars, films, television, money – she didn't know the vernacular, and by the time she'd caught up, they were on to something else, talking in loud, confident voices that made her want to shrink. Coke fixed that. Oh, she still didn't know the difference between a Beemer and a BlackBerry, but somehow it didn't matter; she could join in as loudly and as confidently as anyone else. Work hard, play hard, she said to herself as she accepted a line, echoing Oliver.

Work was demanding. Back home, she dragged herself into her study every day, rubbing her eyes and wondering if she was going down with a cold. Her nose was running, she had the beginnings of a sore throat and she didn't feel quite like her usual self. But the cold never seemed to develop beyond those symptoms, so she vaguely thought she was getting off lightly. She yawned as she flicked through her in-tray. There seemed to be so much to get done, and she felt so tired. Prioritise, she thought. The television script had to be written. And the article for Madeleine – it seemed too good an opportunity to miss. Perhaps it would open up a new area for her. Then there were the notes for her garden visits in June and the preparation of handouts. People liked handouts. Further down the list came a speech at a conference Gwyn had roped her into – more than a month away, but she needed to prepare and organise the slides – and then there was Templecombe.

Oliver said to write up the report based on the material she'd already got; she could hardly be expected to invent what was missing. Anna knew he was right. She also knew she should investigate the gateway building more, and the tunnel area. But that would take a whole day, which she felt she couldn't afford. I'll do it later, she told herself, feeling a little guilty that she was taking advantage of Mrs Davenport's kindness. But Oliver said not to worry, so she wouldn't.

Three weeks passed. The television script went through several

SARAH DUNCAN

drafts, as did the article for Madeleine – 'Too academic. Sex it up a little, mmm?' Anna wrote up her lectures and prepared the handouts and slides; she drew out the Templecombe survey, wincing inwardly when she realised that she'd hadn't taken as many target points as she usually worked with, concentrating furiously to get as much done as possible. Work hard, play hard, she kept saying. And at the weekends she became a different Anna: sexy, confident, urban. An Anna transformed by her glamorous, gorgeous boyfriend into someone who was at home in a magical world. Richard had never made her feel like this. Richard was provincial, unsophisticated, quiet, ordinary and everyday. Being with Oliver was like moving from black and white into glorious Technicolor.

Back home, torn between tiredness and lack of time, the repeated redrafting of the television script, the conundrum of how to sex up an article on garden history, it was easier to forget about Templecombe.

The Friday before the television programme filming was due to start, Anna was heading downstairs, case thumping on the stairs behind her, about to walk to the station to catch the train to London, when the phone rang. She paused. I'll miss the train, she thought. But it might be Oliver. She ran upstairs to her study to answer it.

'It's Will.'

'Who?' She frowned, not able to place the voice or the name.

'From Templecombe.'

'Oh, that Will,' she said, as if she knew hundreds of Wills.

'Yeah, that Will.' He sounded pissed off, and she felt a wave of guilt about Mrs Davenport. 'You wanted to know when the ivy was cleared from that gatehouse. I've done it, and I think you ought to come and see.'

'That sounds brilliant, but I'm about to catch a train,' she said. I can't come next week, I'm filming' – God, how glam did that sound?

– 'so it'll have to be the week after. I'll let Mrs Davenport know. I must go.' It would be dreadful if she missed the train; Oliver would be waiting for her. He made a special effort to get back from work early on Fridays. Just thinking about him made her stomach contract. She dragged her mind back to what Will was saying.

'She was hoping you'd have finished your report by now.'

'I'm working on it,' she lied. 'Look, I must go or I'll miss my train.'

She put the phone down and ran out of the house and all the way to the station, case clattering behind her like an outsize toddler toy. Safely on the train, rushing towards London and Oliver, it was only once past Chippenham that she realised she'd forgotten to say goodbye.

Chapter 11

Anna stood on the terrace at Keyningsham and stamped her feet, chilled from hanging about in the early-morning sunshine for over two hours. In front of her the landscape swept in a series of gentle curves down to a serpentine lake, and silhouetted against the landscape was Hamish McCarthy.

He spread his arms out, his eyes twinkling in that lovable way that had made him the housewives' favourite TV gardening presenter. 'This is the story of an incredible journey, a journey that would start in a simple cottage in 1816 and would end here—

Anna nudged the director. 'Sorry, but it should be 1716.'

'Cut,' he yelled.

Hamish pulled a face. 'What's wrong?'

'It's 1716, not 1816.'

'I said that. I did, I said it.'

The director sighed. 'From the top, if you will . . .'

Hamish stomped off and kicked at a stray tuft of grass. Anna could hear him muttering, '1716, 1716.'

'Places.'

'Ready, Hamish?'

'I'm ready, I'm ready. 1716, 1716.' He went back to his mark.

'Okay . . . and action.'

Hamish spread his arms out, his eyes twinkling again in that lovable way that had made him the housewives' favourite garden presenter. 'This is the story of an incredible journey, a journey that would start in a simple cottage in 1716 and would end here . . .' He paused. 'What the fuck's this place called anyway?'

'Cut.'

'Keyningsham Park,' Anna called out.

'Keyningsham Park, Keyningsham Park, 1716,' he muttered.

'From the top . . . and action.'

Once again Harnish spread his arms out, his eyes twinkling in that lovable way that had made him the housewives' favourite. Incredible how he could do it every time, just the same. Like magic. 'This is the – ah, fuck, could I not just ask her questions?'

Everyone looked at Anna.

'Me?' She clutched her chest, thinking her heart might stop right now. 'I couldn't. I'll write something else, something easier.'

'We don't have time,' the director said. 'Look, jot down some questions for Hamish to ask you, and we'll take it from there.'

'But I can't go on television.'

'Don't worry, we'll cut away from you most of the time, just have your voice.' He took her arm as if to lead her across the terrace.

'No,' Anna said, shaking him off. 'Really. I don't want to do this.'

Everyone looked at her again. The cameraman rolled his eyes at the sound man. The director rearranged his features into something approaching charm. He put his arm around Anna's shoulders and led her away from the rest of the group. 'Dr Carmichael. We've got time pressures. The gates are going to open to the public in exactly' – he checked his watch – 'twenty-three minutes. It would be very helpful if you would do this little thing.'

'It might be little to you, but I'm not, um, comfortable with the idea.'

He patted her shoulder. 'Everyone wants to be on television.'

'I don't even have a television, let alone any desire to be on it.'

'I admire you for that, I really do.' He didn't look as if he meant it. 'But we've already wasted a morning and I haven't got anything to show for it. You'd be helping me out of a big hole.'

'Sorry.' Anna shrugged apologetically. 'But I'd really rather not.'

He puffed his cheeks out. 'Double your fee?'

'Sorry?'

'We can't go higher, we spent most of the budget on getting that pillock.' He gestured to Hamish McCarthy, who was sitting on the balustrade, a light breeze ruffling his hair, a faraway look in his eyes. All he needed was a Border collie at his feet and he could have been presenting *One Man and His Dog*.

The word no was on the tip of her tongue, but she stopped herself. It couldn't be that bad, could it? She'd know what the questions were going to be, and what her answers were. And she'd written an awful lot of cheques recently.

She exhaled to keep the nerves at bay. 'Okay, I'll do it.'

Anna got back on Friday evening, exhilarated. The filming hadn't been as bad as she'd expected; she'd just talked directly to Hamish and pretended the camera wasn't there. She chucked her bag over the newel post, then made herself a cup of tea, thinking about the weekend. She'd got it all planned – Oliver was coming to Bath in the morning, they were going to Templecombe in the afternoon, then home for dinner, and then on Sunday she was going to show him off to Bronwen and Nick. Oliver would be charm itself, and she would be the perfect hostess. The whole weekend was going to be perfect. She hugged the idea to herself, anticipating the expression on Bronwen's face, then rang Oliver's mobile.

'Great to hear you.' There was lots of background noise and she had to press the phone to her ear to hear his voice. 'How was the filming?'

'I ended up doing some stuff in front of the camera.' She wished she could see his face as she told him.

'Hey, you're going to be famous.'

'I doubt it.' The kitchen seemed empty and prosaic compared to the buzzing energy that fizzed down the phone. 'Where are you?'

'At the brasserie, with the usual crowd. Say hello to Anna, guys.' He had obviously held the phone up, because she could hear various voices chorus 'Hi Anna'. Oliver came back on the line. 'I've missed you. Why don't you come up tonight?'

'You're coming down here, remember?' Anna said, laughing.

'Shit. Is it that weekend already?'

Anna stopped laughing. 'We're going to Templecombe tomorrow, and then I've got friends coming for lunch on Sunday. You can't have forgotten.' She cradled the phone into her neck.

'Shit. I've got the dates mixed up. I said ages ago I'd go to this party on Saturday. Never mind, we can both go and then get to Bath in time for your friends.'

'But I've got to get lunch ready. And what about Templecombe?' She felt cold with disappointment. 'We agreed . . .'

'All work and no play makes Anna a dull girl.'

Anna hesitated, playing with the idea of going to London on Saturday. It'd mean dropping Templecombe, but she didn't want to be a dull girl. Clare clattered on the stairs, and Anna reached over to push shut the kitchen door. 'You said you were coming down. Don't you want to see me?'

'Of course I want to see you, that's why I want you to come up. Come on, it'll be fun.' He sighed as if she was being tiresome and difficult, and guilt stabbed her.

'I'd love to come, but I can't get up to London for Saturday night and be back in time to get lunch ready here on Sunday.'

'Never mind. It's just bad timing, I guess.' There was a brief pause. 'Look – you know I'm going to Prague next week. I thought you could come too.'

Anna bit her thumbnail. 'I'd love to, but I can't afford it right now,' she said. She *was* being dull, no to this, no to that.

'My treat.'

She wanted to go, but she had so much work to do. She hesitated. 'Do I have to decide now? I just thought, if I work flat out tomorrow, then I might be able to spare the time . . .' She'd have to pay, of course, she couldn't let Oliver pick up the tab for everything, but maybe she could manage.

'Tell me on Sunday. What time?'

'Twelve.' She deliberately told him half an hour before she'd asked Bronwen. She wanted him to be there when Bron and Nick arrived, there and helping, handing round drinks so Bronwen could see that they were a couple.

'I'll be there. And Anna . . .' His voice dropped. 'Love you.'

He'd never said it before. She curled the phone wire round and round her fingers. 'Love you too.'

Right. Plan of action. Get the house ready, get the shopping done, prepare the food, get a week's worth of work done in a day. Love you. She hugged herself. Love you love you love you. She decided to wash her hair. Head upside down over the bath, she sang, 'I'm gonna wash that man right out of my hair'. She didn't know all the words, so happily jumbled half-remembered snatches of lyrics with la-la-la-ing.

'You sound cheerful,' Clare said, coming into the bathroom with what appeared to be a disc of white polystyrene in her hand.

Anna stopped, head upside down and conditioner dripping into her ears. 'I might be going to Prague next week.'

'With the gorgeous lover?'

Yes, he was gorgeous, and he was hers. Love you. 'The very same.'

'Lucky you.'

Yes, she was lucky. She couldn't believe how lucky. Of course she'd go to Prague with him, she'd just have to work harder now. She began to plan her schedule – she'd have to postpone the Templecombe visit until the following week. 'You look as if you're enjoying that,' she said as Clare munched.

'It's like eating solidified insulating foam, but I've decided to lose a stone before the wedding.' Clare licked her fingers, perched on the edge of the bath and opened her pink wedding file. 'Now, I wanted to sort out some stuff with you. Have you booked the minibus? And the spa? Vicki says she can't come after all, but she will come to dinner and the club.'

'Yes, yes,' Anna said, running the water again and drenching herself in the process. She felt like one of the little pigs being besieged by the big bad wolf. Thinking about the rows they'd had as teenagers. Clare was more than capable of huffing and puffing and blowing her house to pieces, if not actually down. Easier to fall in with her plans. 'Yes, yes, yes.'

'Oh, and I saw this shop in Bristol that'll print up T-shirts. Can you do some for me – I want something like "I survived Clare's hen night" – and then there's the dress, d'you think you could come to a fitting with me next week?'

'Expect so. Clare . . .' Anna wrapped her head in a towel and stood up, tucking the towel ends into a turban shape. 'If I gave you a list, could you please please go to the supermarket and get my shopping. I've got to work all day tomorrow otherwise I can't go to Prague.'

Clare looked surprised. 'I thought Oliver was pitching up tomorrow.'

'Change of plan. He's coming on Sunday.' Anna undid the turban and started to rub her hair dry.

'So how are things going?' Clare said, eyeing Anna's hair. 'You'll get split ends if you carry on like that.'

'Wonderfully.' Anna stopped rubbing her hair and examined it. 'What should I do?'

'Squeeze it,' Clare said, showing her. 'See? That way you don't rub up the follicles.'

'Aren't the follicles where the hair comes out of your head?'

'Whatever. Squeeze the moisture out, don't rub it.'

Anna stared at herself in the mirror. 'Actually . . . I think I love him.' I think I love him, she repeated in her head, feeling surprised at having said it.

'Wow. That's a bit soon.' Clare blinked.

Anna sat on the edge of the bath, glowing inside. 'I know, but everything's different with him, I'm different, I feel like someone else. We're always doing stuff, and going out – I've been to more clubs in the last month than I've been to in my entire life.'

'No wonder you're wrecked when you're here,' Clare said. 'Why don't you try some of this on your hair?' She held up a small plastic bottle.

'I've not been wrecked, just really busy work-wise.' Anna squinted at the bottle. 'What is it?'

'Serum.' Clare squirted a bit on to her palm, rubbed her hands together then stroked them over Anna's hair.

'After Richard, and the divorce, I felt I'd never have fun again. But with Oliver everything's fun,' Anna said, thinking of their weekends together. 'It's so different. I feel I've been living a half-life, and I didn't know it.'

'You've always been very academic,' Clare said, shrugging. 'I thought you didn't like going to parties.'

'I don't really, but with Oliver it's like I'm someone else.'

'Now brush it through.' Clare handed Anna the brush. 'Is being someone else a good thing?'

'Oh, yes. I was so naïve, so stupid – I can't believe how little I knew about everything, and now . . .' Anna could see Clare reflected in the mirror, watching her brushing with an appraising eye. 'Do you know what a Rabbit is?' Clare nodded. 'I didn't. I thought this girl was talking about her pet.'

Clare gave a shriek of laughter. 'You didn't!'

'How was I to know? I'm always getting things wrong like that. Oliver says it's funny, but it's embarrassing.' She gave a sheepish grin as her eyes met Clare's, but Clare had stopped laughing and her face was serious.

'You will be careful, won't you?'

'What do you mean?'

'It all seems to be happening so fast.' Clare pressed her lips together. 'You've only just got divorced.'

'I love him,' Anna said, smiling at her reflection in the mirror, and her reflection smiled back. 'I love him.'

On Sunday Clare was sprawled over the kitchen table, picking at the bunch of grapes in the fruit bowl. Anna watched the plucked stems emerge like a handful of spindly jacks.

'If you want some, why don't you take a bunch?' Anna asked, glancing at the clock. Twelve fifteen, and no Oliver.

'I don't really want any,' Clare said, pushing them away. 'You're not supposed to eat fruit on this diet.'

'It doesn't sound a very healthy sort of diet if you're not allowed fruit.'

'You sound just like Steve.' Clare began peeling her nail varnish off, Day-Glo shreds falling on to the table.

'D'you mind not doing that?' Anna could hear the tension in her voice.

'I don't know why you're so uptight, you've been ready for ages. I mean, look at it, it's like a cookery show.' Clare gestured at the plates and dishes covered with newly laundered tea towels. 'You're as bad as Mum, cooking the veg hours before.'

'I'm not,' Anna said. 'I'm not like Mum at all.'

'Whatever.' Clare yawned extravagantly so Anna could see all her fillings. 'When's he coming?'

'They,' Anna looked at the clock, 'they are coming in about fifteen minutes.' That meant Oliver was late. But only a little bit. She couldn't expect him to be exactly on time. Traffic could be tricky on the M4, she thought, suppressing the thought that it was Sunday morning, hardly a prime time for traffic jams.

Clare bounced out of her chair. 'Great. I've got time to wash my hair.' She scuttled off, her two-at-a-time progress up the stairs reverberating through the house.

Oliver would be here soon. The sun was shining, the sky was blue and Oliver was coming. She could imagine him in his car, roof down, turning heads along London Road as he came in. Yes, that was it, the traffic was always dreadful there as it funnelled into Bath. She tidied up the bunch of grapes, but no amount of artful draping could make them look anything other than lopsided, so instead she divided them into little bunches to scatter around the cheeseboard, then checked the clock again. Twelve twenty-two. She should have given him directions to come via the back road. He'll be here any minute, she thought, smoothing her hair and thinking about what to do next. Upstairs she put out bowls of olives, crisps and some Bombay mix, thinking how the colour of the Bombay mix set off the green olives, and the crinkly texture of the crisps was a pleasing contrast to their glossy roundness.

The doorbell rang. At last. She ran downstairs to answer it, but it wasn't Oliver.

'Bronwen, hi,' she said, kissing her friend's cheek and trying to ignore the internal thud of disappointment. 'Where's Nick?'

'Cleaning the car. Toby was sick on the way,' Bronwen said, coming into the hall with Toby tucked under one arm and heading for the stairs. 'I'll have to mop him up.'

'Um, I think Clare's in the bathroom,' Anna said, standing well back to let them pass. Toby seemed a lot bigger than she remembered. The smell made her feel queasy too.

'I'll use the kitchen then.' Bronwen wheeled off to the right-hand door. 'Lucky we brought a change of clothes!'

'Oh dear,' Anna said, trailing after her. Oliver was due any minute. 'I'm sure Clare'll be finished soon.'

Bronwen was briskly stripping Toby off. 'Don't worry about us, we're fine, though a bin bag would be good.' Anna got one out and handed it to Bronwen, who was feeding Toby's arms into a clean T-shirt. 'Oh, pop his stuff in, would you, that'd be brilliant.'

Anna looked at the pile on the floor. So many clothes for such a small person, and all of them damp. Holding them by the tips of her fingers and at arm's length, she dropped the clothes into the bin bag, then tied the top and held it out to Bronwen, who took it. 'Great,' she said, stuffing it into a bulging candy-striped bag. With one easy motion she swung Toby up and settled him on her hip. 'Now, say hello to Auntie Anna.'

'Hello, Toby,' Auntie Anna said, taking a step back despite the fact that Toby now looked reasonably cherubic and clean. Toby was obviously blessed with ESP because he clutched his mother's hair with fat fists and screamed. Bronwen's hearing must have been set to a different decibel threshold from Anna's, because she appeared oblivious to the noise.

'He's got a bit of a bug, poor poppet,' she said, a broad smile on her face. 'I did think of ringing and cancelling, but hey! I didn't.'

Anna took a deep breath and squared her shoulders. 'You're here, and it's lovely to see you. Both,' she added after what she hoped was an infinitesimal pause. 'Let me get you a drink.'

'An enormous glass of whatever's going, please.'

'Champagne?'

'What's the celebration?'

'Nothing.' Anna shrugged, feeling a pleasant frisson of superiority. Oliver and his friends drank champagne all the time and never needed a reason. The frisson turned into a glow. They were in love. 'What about Nick?'

'What about Nick?' said a man's voice behind her. Anna turned and did a double-take, for at first it looked as if Nick was taking part in a sci-fi movie. A baby dangled face forward from his chest, head lolling and limbs protruding in a starfish shape, limp as sausages. It looked bizarre and extremely uncomfortable for the baby. Anna was uncertain if she should kiss him in greeting, worried about squashing the baby, but Nick had no such qualms.

'Good to see you,' he said, giving her a hug and a whiff of sour baby sick together. 'I was just saying the other day how I hadn't seen you for ages.'

'Too long,' Anna said. 'Champagne?'

'Great – what's the celebration?'

'Nothing,' she said. Dear Bron and Nick, just a little provincial.

'And the real thing too,' Nick said as she filled the glasses. 'Garden history's obviously doing well.'

'And Toby?' He had quietened down and was now staring at her with big eyes, one finger in his mouth. He did look quite angelic, Anna thought, but Rubens not Raphael, with scarlet cheeks. 'Apple juice?'

'I've brought some cartons,' Bronwen said, waving the bag. 'They're easier.'

'You're looking smart,' Nick said, appraising Anna. 'Think it's the first time I've seen you in high heels.'

Bronwen peered at her. 'That colour really suits you,' she said, almost surprised.

'Oliver chose it,' Anna said, wishing he was there. 'Shall we go up?'

They trooped upstairs carrying enough baby paraphernalia to stock an expedition to Everest, and Bronwen let Toby down to the floor.

'So where's Mr Wonderful?'

'He'll be here any minute,' Anna said, hoping it was true. 'How are things with you?'

Nick started to talk about work while he unstrapped the baby from his chest and settled her in a Moses basket. Anna listened with a very small part of her attention. Perhaps there had been an accident. A motorway pile-up. Oliver always drove too fast. She watched Toby stagger to the coffee table and examine an olive. He picked one up with a delicate pincer grip and bit into it with two small white teeth. Then he screwed his face up and dropped the olive, which rolled under the chaise longue, bite marks clearly visible. Anna picked it up absent-mindedly, ears on the alert for the sound of a car pulling up. Toby took another olive and repeated the procedure. Anna waited for Bronwen to restrain him, but Bronwen seemed to be thinking of things far away.

On the fourth olive Anna picked up the bowl. 'Perhaps Daddy would like some,' she said in what she hoped was a kindly voice, prising Toby's surprisingly strong fingers from the edge of the bowl and passing it to Nick.

'You ready for Steve and Clare's wedding? I hear you're running the hen party,' Nick said, helping himself to a couple of olives. 'What've you got? Stripping Tarzans?'

'No, I—' Toby had grabbed a fistful of crisps and was trying to shove them in his mouth all at once. Visions of greasy crisp particles lingering for ever in the carpet stung Anna into action. She grabbed at Toby's hands, which made his face turn lobster and his mouth an ominous square shape as he took a mammoth and apparently everlasting intake of breath.

'Oh God, I'm sorry,' she cried, looking at Bronwen and Nick, knowing she had just committed the most heinous of crimes, that of laying her hands on another's child.

Toby's lungs expelled air and crisps at full throttle. Bronwen clasped him to her chest, Avenging Madonna con Ferocious Bambino.

'Thank heavens you stopped him,' Nick said, to Anna's surprise. 'Really?'

He clicked his tongue and shook his head. 'All that salt.'

All eyes turned to Anna's bowl of hand-cut crisps made from organic Charlotte potatoes sprinkled with natural sea salt and cracked peppercorns as if it was one of Satan's offerings.

'And fat,' Bronwen added, pressing Toby's tear-soaked face to her chest, where the vibrations must have been worth several doses of ultra-high-frequency massage. 'And E numbers. Poor baby doesn't want all those nasty chemicals in him, does he?'

'They are organic,' Anna ventured, but Bronwen and Nick looked at her with expressions that convinced her this wasn't an argument to even try winning. 'I'll take them away,' she said humbly. 'And everything else.' She picked up the untouched Bombay mix – think of how many additives that must contain – and stacked the offensive crisps on top, sandwiched by the olive bowl. 'Back in a sec.'

She ran downstairs and dumped the bowls on the side in the kitchen. Better check on lunch. The duck was crisping up nicely on its wire rack, the skin dark and caramelised, fat draining into the roasting dish below. Where was Oliver? He should have been here by now. She put the dish on the side to let the duck settle before carving, then went back upstairs.

Clare had come down from the bathroom, hair fluffed up by vigorous use of the hairdryer, and was telling Bronwen and Nick about her wedding plans.

'I've always liked a wedding,' Nick said. 'Everybody in their best kit, getting drunk.'

Clare checked her watch. 'I hope he pitches up soon, I'm going to have to go.'

'He'll be here shortly,' Anna said, standing by the window, praying Oliver would miraculously appear on the pavement. 'Anyway, Clare, I thought you were going over to Steve's.'

'I am, I am. Just wanted to see the fabulous Oliver again.' Clare laughed. 'Hey, it was a good thing you didn't go to that party, wasn't it, or we'd have been here waiting for you.'

'Yes, wasn't it,' Anna said. Her hands trembled on her glass. 'Shall we go downstairs and start?'

It doesn't matter, she told herself, as she hacked the duck into pieces in the kitchen. It doesn't matter that he hasn't come, it's lovely to see Bronwen and Nick. Stupid of me to want to show him off in the first place. She bit her lip. He promised he'd be here. Noises on the stairs warned her Toby and entourage were approaching.

'Go straight in,' she called out from the kitchen. She took three deep breaths to steady herself, then carried the plate of duck into the dining room. Unable to afford a Georgian table, she'd bought a rectangular piece of thick MDF, then balanced it on top of an ugly but sturdy table she'd found in a junk shop. It was impossible to tell it wasn't the real thing under her starched white linen tablecloth. She plonked the duck down in the centre.

Nick had fixed some sort of chair on to the side of the table and was lowering Toby into it. Toby was sticking his legs out and kicking when his father tried to bend them in the middle.

'I don't think that's a good idea,' Anna said. Nick looked up. 'Really, I don't think it's strong enough to take his weight. It's only a bit of MDF underneath. I think it'd tip the whole thing over.'

They looked at the table laden with glasses, cutlery and side plates plus two small vases of flowers.

'We didn't bring his high chair,' Bronwen said, rather sharply Anna thought. It wasn't her fault she couldn't afford a proper table.

'Can't he sit on a normal chair? I brought down some cushions,' she said.

Bronwen sighed. 'I suppose we can try,' she said, settling the Moses basket down. Anna peeped in for a second. The baby was still sleeping, which was extraordinary given the volume emitting from Toby's lungs.

'Come on, Toby, you come and sit here,' Anna said, piling cushions onto the only armed dining-room chair she had.

Nick lifted him up and plonked him down on top of the pile. Toby looked like an infant pasha surveying his court. He picked up a spoon and rapped it on the table, the noise somehow amplifying to that of a jackhammer.

'I'll get the pancakes,' Anna said.

Bronwen had told her they were trying to introduce Toby to as many different flavours as possible so he wouldn't be a faddy eater. Anna had decided, rather cunningly she thought, on Peking duck, as there wouldn't be any gravy to slop around and everything could be prepared beforehand. No bones to choke on, no need for cutting up. Toby could fill up on the little pancakes or eat the cucumber strips, and it didn't matter if he used his hands.

'Everybody help themselves,' she said.

Clare plonked herself into the place laid for Oliver and was starting to roll a pancake when her mobile went. 'Steve,' she said, checking the display and getting up from the table.

Toby seemed to like the pancakes and the cucumber, but baulked at trying any of the duck. Nick tried to tempt him, pretending to be an aeroplane zooming a morsel of meat to Toby's lips. It looked as though it was going to work, but at the last moment Toby flung his head back and Nick narrowly missed feeding his ear.

'Have you decided yet if you're going back to work?' Anna asked Bronwen, trying to appear nonchalant.

'And here comes the plane again – chugga chugga chugga zoom – and there it goes, open wide, neow, and here we go . . .'

'I don't know. I told Nick I was going to, but now . . .'

'Never mind, old boy, let's have another try. Chugga chugga chugga . . .'

' . . . it hardly seems worth the hassle. Practically all my salary would go on childcare, so you think, what's the point when you could be at home with the babies?'

'Next time round, okay? And here comes the plane . . .'

'But don't you miss work?'

'Sure, but – oh, give me the spoon, Nick, anyone can see you're not going to get anywhere like that. Now come on Toby, come on, sweetheart. One for Mummy!'

Anna watched as Bronwen and Nick cajoled, tempted and pleaded with their son to eat just a teeny weeny bit for Mummy, please, while their own food lay untouched on their plates. For a horrible moment she wondered if Bronwen and Nick now called each other Mummy and Daddy.

'Perhaps I could get him something else?' she suggested.

'Anna, you'd be an angel. Do you have anything like,' Bronwen shrugged, obviously casting her mind about, 'spaghetti in tomato sauce?'

Anna blinked. 'You mean tinned?'

Bronwen picked up on the surprise in her voice. 'I was forgetting this was a child-free zone. Some cheese, perhaps?'

'Cheese, yes, I've got lots of cheese.' She went to the kitchen and brought out the cheeseboard, sweeping off the damp tea towel that had covered it. 'Da-da! Cheese.'

'Oh.' Bronwen's eyes swept across the board. 'Haven't you got any ordinary cheese, Cheddar perhaps?'

Anna surveyed the selection, all Oliver's favourites. 'The vacherin's very mild,' she tried.

'Perhaps a tiny sliver.'

Anna cut a piece and put it on a plate. 'Some grapes?'

'I don't want to upset his tum. But a banana, perhaps?'

'I think so,' Anna said, mentally checking the fruit bowl before trotting off to the kitchen again.

Clare was sitting on the stairs curled round her mobile. 'It's dreadful,' she was saying with obvious glee. 'He hasn't turned up.' She caught Anna's eye and went scarlet

Anna bolted into the kitchen, blinking rapidly to keep back the tears. There must be some completely logical reason for Oliver being late: his car had broken down or something. She tried not to think of him out partying into the dawn light. He'd promised to be here. Bron and Nick were pretending everything was okay, but Clare was right. It was dreadful. It was a disaster.

The doorbell rang.

She rushed to the front door. 'You're late,' she said, and immediately regretted it as Oliver's expression behind his sunglasses became sulky.

'I'm here, aren't I?'

She kissed him. 'I thought you weren't going to come.'

'Wish I hadn't after that welcome.'

'Don't be grotty, it's lovely to see you.' She looked at him more closely. He looked less than his usual immaculate self. 'Were you late last night?'

'I drove straight down,' he said, yawning.

'You mean you haven't been to bed yet?'

He shook his head. 'You wanted me here.'

Anna wanted to ask him more – what had he been doing all night for a start? – but she was so relieved to see him, she would have forgiven him anything. And in a way it was rather romantic, staying up all night and then driving down to visit her rather than going to bed. She suppressed the thought that he shouldn't have gone to the party in the first place. 'Come on in and meet my friends.'

She took his hand and led him into the dining room. 'This is Oliver,' she said, beaming. 'Nick, and Bron. And that's Toby. And Clare's around somewhere . . .'

'Hi, everyone,' Oliver said, waving a hand vaguely. 'Have you got a drink, hon?'

She scuttled into the kitchen and found the champagne bottle was empty. Perhaps she should open another. But what if he didn't want it? It'd be a waste of a whole bottle – the booze side of the shopping list had made up more than half of the cost of lunch as it was.

When she got back, Oliver had sat down as far away from Toby as possible. Someone – she guessed Bronwen – had pushed the serving dishes containing the duck and pancakes up his end, but his plate remained empty. He'd still got his dark glasses on.

'We've moved on to red, but I can open another bottle of champagne if you want.'

'No, red'll do.' She poured out a glass for him. 'Thanks.'

'And something to eat?' Anna said, determined to maintain the perfect hostess role in the face of a distinct lack of encouragement. 'There's duck, and pancakes . . .'

Oliver surveyed the table. It did look rather a mess, post-Toby. 'Some cheese, please.'

Anna passed him the cheese and the bread, which he took. 'Thanks.' Monosyllable man. He prodded the cheese with his knife. He looked, if not actually mad, certainly bad and dangerous to know.

'So how did you meet Anna?' Nick asked, after a short pause, with the air of someone filling a social breach.

Oliver put his knife down with a sigh. 'She's researching my grandmother's garden,'

'Great.' Nick pulled his earlobe. 'So . . . what sort of garden is it?'

'Overgrown.' He hunched in his chair like a bad-tempered hawk.

There was a silence. Anna caught Bronwen and Nick exchanging glances.

Toby squished his cheese down on his plate with both hands, rather as if playing mud pies, then licked them. Anna thought of the cost of artisanal vacherin from the specialist cheese shop and sighed. At least he was enjoying himself, which was more than she was.

'Did you ever find that banana?' Bronwen said brightly.

'I'll get it now.' Anna nipped into the kitchen and returned to more silence. Oliver had acted like a fire blanket on Nick and Bronwen. She handed over the banana. What was the matter with him? He was Mr Sociable usually; she was the one who found meeting new people difficult. And he was never hungover like this. It was she who felt washed out by Sunday lunchtime.

A crash made them all look up. 'Clare's gone out,' Anna said.

Nick resumed rolling a pancake around some congealed duck. 'What about you, Anna? What are you working on?' He'd obviously decided to ignore Oliver.

Anna picked up his lead. 'Various bits and pieces. Hey, I'm going to be on TV.'

Bronwen peeled the banana. 'I thought Hamish McCarthy was presenting.'

'He was, but it was a bit of a disaster. In the end they ditched the script and he just asked me questions.' She smiled, grateful that normal service had been resumed.

Bronwen handed the banana to Toby, who grabbed it with both fat fists. 'That sounds good. Must pay well.'

'Not really . . .' Anna said, watching as Toby stubbed the banana out on the tablecloth.

Bronwen smiled encouragingly at Oliver. 'Has Anna discovered lots of interesting stuff about your grandmother's garden?' she said.

'No.' Obviously Oliver didn't want to be encouraged.

Bronwen looked as if she was about to say something sharp.

'It's early days,' Anna chipped in. 'The gardener rang me the other day saying he'd uncovered something, so that's quite exciting. I'm hoping it's going to be a symbolic garden—'

'Let's not get carried away here,' Oliver drawled, putting his hand firmly on Anna's. 'Whatever may have been there two hundred years ago isn't there now.'

'Will said—'

'Whatever.' His hand was hot and heavy on hers. 'We don't want to bore everyone with the garden.'

'I think it's fascinating,' Bronwen said, sitting up, alert as a Jack Russell that's just seen a rat. 'I'd love to hear more.'

'It's only me speculating,' Anna said, loving Bronwen for being about to launch in on her behalf, terrified she'd carry on. 'Oliver's right, Bron. There isn't any evidence.'

'You just haven't found it yet.'

'I'm going back next week, so maybe . . .' Her voice trailed away as Oliver didn't succeed in hiding a stupendous yawn behind his hand.

Nick put his hand on Bronwen's arm. Bronwen pursed her lips and glared at Oliver. Another silence, which Nick again attempted to fill. 'What do you do, Oliver?'

'God, that's got to be the world's most boring question,' Oliver said. He sounded amiable, but Bronwen spluttered like a Catherine wheel starting up.

'He's in insurance,' Anna said. She cut herself a thin slice of dolcelatte, hoping that if she appeared unconcerned, Bron and Nick would magically not notice Oliver's rudeness. 'But not cars and houses,' she added. 'More planes and ships. It's really interesting.'

'Insurance.' Nick paused, as if turning over cutting remarks in his head. Anna pleaded with her eyes. Don't, please don't. Nick swallowed. 'I suppose someone's got to do it.'

'Too right.' Oliver swigged his red wine.

'Tell me how it's going at the gallery. What's the next exhibition going to be?' Anna said in her brightest hostess-with-the-mostest voice. Mostest to cover for rudest boyfriend.

Nick look relieved. 'Really exciting, got this great group of artists coming in, working in various different media.' He started to talk about the artists, his thin hands waving as he got enthusiastic and Bron prompting him when she thought he'd missed out an important bit – which was frequently. Anna smiled and relaxed; she really was desperately fond of them both, even if they were shifting from bohemia to suburbia. It struck her that she was making the reverse journey, from the cosy, settled world of academia and Richard to something edgy, vibrant, exciting and—

A noise made her turn. Oliver was snoring.

Chapter 12

The house seemed empty once Bron and Nick had gone. Anna cleared the dining room, trying to keep the clatter of plates to a minimum so as not to disturb the sleeping Oliver. His dark glasses had slipped and were skew-whiff on his face. He looked both comical and rather sweet. On her last trip she gently eased the glasses off his head and folded them on the table. He looked peaceful, his face relaxed into vulnerability. Endearing. Love means never having to say you're sorry, she thought, scrubbing at a plate over the kitchen sink. Which means I shouldn't expect an apology from Oliver, I should just love him as he is. He bloody well should apologise, squeaked the childish bit of her brain, to be squashed by the adult side. No, it was my fault, I shouldn't have insisted. And he did drive all the way down from London. But . . . but . . . but.

She put the plate on the draining board and picked up another. But he ought to apologise. He was unbelievably late, and then rude to Bron and Nick. Unforgivable. She swooshed the plate in clear running water to get rid of the soap bubbles. Stand by your man. She had an image of herself giving cups of tea to waiting journalists, being charming, smiling bravely, while Oliver lurked in the background. But he hadn't been unfaithful, had he? Her heart contracted. Or had he?

She shook her head and tipped the water out of the washing-up bowl. No, she was imagining things, putting the worst possible interpretation on his absence. He'd wanted her to go to the party. She should have gone. Then she would have made sure they'd left early enough to make it to Bath on Sunday morning. It was her own fault, in a way. Poor Oliver. He'd probably wake up feeling dreadfully guilty. She laid a tray with paracetamol, a glass of water and a cup of tea, perfect hostess and perfect girlfriend, and took it into the dining room.

'Oliver?' She stroked his hair gently. 'Darling? I think you ought to wake up now.'

He screwed his face up, much as Toby had done before yelling. But instead he shook her hand off and dropped back to sleep.

'Oliver.' She gave his shoulder a shake, and he started, putting his hands up to his face. He looked around the room, puzzled, then blinked, registering where he was, who she was.

'I must have dropped off . . .' he said, rubbing his eyes like a small boy.

Anna felt indulgent. 'You've been asleep for hours. Look, I've got some paracetamol.

He shook two tablets from the container and gulped them down. 'Jeez, those people were boring,' he said, scowling. 'No wonder I went to sleep.'

Anna stood, indulgent feelings evaporating. 'They're my closest friends.'

'I can't help that. God, they were provincial. All that Mummy and Daddy stuff.' He yawned. 'D'you think they call each other that in bed?'

Anna felt a surge of guilt that he'd mirrored her own thoughts. 'You were bloody rude,' she said, anger at herself mixing with anger at Oliver. 'So what if they're a bit—'

'Dull?' Oliver rolled his eyes.

'I make an effort for your friends; you could at least make an effort for mine. You come down unforgivably late—'

'I'm here, aren't I? I've driven all the way, given up my Sunday – I'm not like you, I can't choose the hours I work and take days off; my weekends are precious.'

'So are mine. I work too, you know. I ask you to spend one weekend here, and you go to some party instead of coming down, then you turn up late, way after lunch has finished, humiliate me in front of my friends, are rude to them, and then you pass out. I don't know why you bothered coming at all.' She stared at him, breathless, as an anger she hadn't known she'd possessed bubbled up.

'I'll go then, as I'm obviously not welcome.' He got up, knocking the chair back so it crashed on the floor. His face was set, the muscles in his jaw taut, his eyes hard and fixed on hers. Anna knew she was supposed to beg him to stay. She looked away.

'Right.' He swept out of the dining room and she heard the front door slam with a crash.

She dropped her head into her hands. What a disaster.

Oliver rang on Monday, full of apologies, although Anna wasn't sure he sounded especially repentant. She listened with an aching heart, wanting to forgive him, wanting also to stay cool. He'd behaved badly so he ought to be apologising. 'I was so knackered,' he said. 'I need you to keep me on the straight and narrow.' He promised they'd do whatever she wanted the next weekend.

'I thought you were going to be in Prague,' she said, waiting for him to ask if she was coming, no, beg her to come too.

'I'll change the flight and make sure I'm back by the weekend.' Had he forgotten he'd asked her? 'Look, I'm sorry about your lunch. Say you'll forgive me. I love you.'

She forgave him. She loved him.

Bronwen was less amenable when Anna phoned to apologise on Oliver's behalf. 'He's said sorry, and I've forgiven him,' Anna said sharply.

'If you think that's good enough . . .' Bronwen said, in a tone that implied she certainly didn't.

'I do. I've got to go now,' Anna said, and hung up, her hands shaking.

She felt scratchy and irritable for the rest of the day. She made strong coffee to try and perk herself up, but the restless feeling wouldn't leave her, not letting her settle to work. She went for a long walk in the pouring rain, then spent the afternoon shivering over her desk.

On Tuesday, a bouquet of flowers arrived, what seemed like at least a hundred exotic or scented blooms, spiky plants with heads like vicious beaked birds, white lilies with the pollen stamens snipped away like floral vasectomies, dyed green amaranthus drooping like gangrenous turkey wattles. *Sorry sorry sorry love Oliver*, the accompanying card read, with the 'love' underlined three times.

'The common name for this is love-lies-bleeding,' Anna said, as the amaranthus quivered fatly under her fingers. He loved her.

'More like snot-lies-dripping,' Clare said.

'He's gone to Prague today,' Anna said dreamily.

'You're mad.' Clare snorted and stomped upstairs.

The next day the rain stopped and Anna decided to go to Templecombe. She rang the doorbell several times, but no one responded, not even Peggy. Perhaps it was her day off. Drat, I should have rung beforehand, she thought. She ripped a page from her notebook and scribbled, *Will, if you see this in time, I'm checking the location of the tunnel. An extra pair of hands would be a help, Anna.* She folded it, wrote his name on the front and tucked it under the front door, then walked into the garden.

The heavy rain the night before had made the path slippery and her wellies had hardly any grip. But the air felt fresh and the sun was trying to come out from behind the clouds. Here and there thin shafts of light penetrated the green roof overhead, dappling the brambles and nettles into an impressionistic glow of golden green. Will had chopped up the tree that had once blocked the path. She felt a pang. If Mrs Davenport went ahead with the garden restoration, this area, however romantic, would have to be cleared.

She strode down the path to the point where it separated and took the route to the left going down to the pool rather than the right turn going up towards the gateway. Someone – Will presumably – had been at work down here. She could see the fallen vegetation slashed back away from the edge of the pool. The rain had filled the pond, making it more lake-like than bog-like, and a dragonfly darted across the surface, blue-green wings shining in the sunlight.

She tested the depth with her pole. Down in the sludge there appeared to be a ledge about eight inches below the surface. She tried various areas of the pool, and yes, there was definitely a ledge lurking under the black surface. She stepped on to it, first one foot, then the other, carefully transferring her weight, always alert in case it started to give way. But it held firm.

The watery mud was about two inches below the top of her boots, but whatever she was standing on was solid. She felt around with the pole. About two feet from the side of the pool the solidity ceased, became nothing. She tapped the edge with her pole, rolled her sleeves up as high as they would go, then plunged her hands into the pool. Slime slipped through her fingers as she felt her way round the ledge, probing, stretching forwards and sideways. Her heart started to race. It was man-made; she could feel the grooves where brick abutted brick. There was the corner, a distinct right angle. Her fingers reversed the journey until they found the other corner, six brick-lengths away. It had to be the foundation for a bridge stretching over the pool.

She stood up, black mud dripping off her hands, stepped back to dry land and picked up her notebook.

Brick pier. Too narrow for stone bridge. Wood? Explains why no trace. 19th century – Monet's garden at Giverny. Japanese bridges.

She bit the top of her pen, trying to think of wooden bridges.

Mathematical Bridge – at Cambridge? Something to do with Isaac Newton? Newton = late 17th century.

Now to work out the line of the tunnel. She started to climb up the slope of the bank, scrabbling through the tangle of jasmine interwoven with brambles, occasionally pausing to check the relative location of the arch. Her hands were scratched by the time she reached the top. It wasn't very high, perhaps ten feet or so above the level of the pond, but from here she could see how the overall design worked. The lake was in front of her, with the pavilion to the left. To her right, the steps wound up towards the gateway.

She could hear water trickling. That had to be the outflow of the spring into the lake somewhere near where she was standing. She'd written *nymphaeum* in her notebook when she'd first seen the area, more in hope than anything else, because she couldn't believe anyone would build such an elaborate entrance only for it to lead to a dead end. It would be an ideal place for a nymphaeum, what with the flowing water and the dark tunnel. She looked at the encircling bank. Surely the tunnel continued, following the line of the bank around the edge of the lake.

She pushed down her measuring pole and heard a satisfying clunk as it hit the brickwork of the tunnel. She took two paces and pushed down again. Clunk. She carried on round the bank, guessing that she'd hit the dead end soon. She paused, breathing heavily. It was hard work, but at least the heavy rain of the past couple of days meant the earth was soft. It would have been impossible if the soil had been baked hard. Push. Clunk. It must be the dead end by now. She took two paces forward, said a short prayer and pushed.

Clunk.

Her heart rate rose. The tunnel continued round. Push. Clunk. Her boots squelched on the sludge of fallen leaves as she took more readings. Thin branches whipped back and forth as she passed, arcs of sound slicing the summer stillness, scattering raindrops. Push. Clunk.

She was about halfway round the bank when suddenly the ground under her boots was not there, disappearing from under her, and she was falling. She grabbed at what she could, but the branches whipped through her hands, shedding leaves, while rock and earth slithered down into darkness and brought her with them, down into a crash of sudden sharp pain like a fireball shooting up her leg. And then nothing.

Chapter 13

Anna opened her eyes. Then closed them. It made no difference to the darkness. She kept them closed and tried to sleep. But she wasn't supposed to be sleeping, she was supposed to be getting up, she could hear her alarm ringing. She reached out for her alarm clock, but everything she touched was cold and clammy, and crumbled under her fingers like earth. She tried to struggle out of bed, pushing the sheets off her, but it wasn't sheets and blankets weighing down on her, but bricks and earth. She was lying on the floor, and when she began to pull herself up, her ankle exploded and she screamed with the shock of the pain. She collapsed back against the floor, trying to suck air into her lungs, but the air had thinned as if the oxygen had leached out, and she had to take ragged gasps to draw in enough to breathe. Gradually the pain from her leg subsided, became a throb to match the one that bounced on the back of her skull.

This time when she opened her eyes she kept them open. I must have been hallucinating, she thought, hallucinating that I was home. She thought back over what she could remember: the scramble to the top of the bank, the ground giving way under her feet. Grey light was filtering through a ragged hole above her head; she could vaguely make out branches and tufts of couch grass silhouetted against the overcast sky.

It took her a moment to realise what was wrong. The sky was the grey of dusk, and what she last remembered had been the warmth of a late spring afternoon. How long had she been in the tunnel? She peered at her wrist, but couldn't make out the hands of her watch. She tried lifting herself up so the maximum light fell on the watch face. Warning pain shot up her leg as she moved.

She put her left toe at the base of her right heel and gave a gentle push to try and ease the boot off. The pain shot in immediately. A wave of nausea surged over her, and she squeezed her eyes tight until it passed. The thumping headache settled into a rhythm: don't be broken don't be broken don't be broken. She tried again. This time she was sick, retching a gobbet of sour mucus on to her chest.

The nausea passed. She took a deep breath and cautiously moved her hands down her right calf, bracing herself against the pain she knew was coming. Whatever she had done to her ankle was serious. Her leg had swollen to fill the boot, but it didn't feel wet inside and her fingers, when she licked them, tasted of earth and mould, not the sharp iron of blood. So whatever damage she'd done was internal. She wouldn't be bleeding to death just yet. She had time. Time to think about rescue.

Will. He'd see the note and come. But then why wasn't he here already? Doubt started to creep in. A scrappy bit of paper, pushed under the door, perhaps slipping beneath the mat. Maybe Will didn't even use the front door. Nor would Peggy, not if she came up from the village. That left Mrs Davenport. Anna couldn't see her registering a grotty message torn from a notebook. My car, she thought, hope rushing in. They'll see my car up at the house and wonder where I am. But hope subsided as quickly as it had come. She'd parked round the back of the disused stable block, where no one would go.

Oliver. Her hopes rose, then sank again as swiftly. In Prague for the rest of the week. Clare would worry, but she might not notice Anna's absence immediately – and what if she decided to stay over at Steve's? She sometimes did midweek. Anna hadn't spoken to Gwyn for ages, and Bronwen wouldn't be expecting a call since their spiky conversation on Monday. Her parents hardly noticed her presence at the moment, let alone her absence. No one would realise she was missing.

Hot tears squeezed out from her eyes, big childish drops rolling down her cheeks, wetting her face. Her mouth puckered and she wailed, a wordless cry that voiced her fear that she would die here in this tunnel, alone and in the dark. The sound echoed round the chamber, rolling off the walls in echoes that pressed against her, then receded like waves. Her sobbing became less intense, became a hiccupping cough, then sniffs.

After the noise of her crying the tunnel seemed very quiet. Anna felt in her pockets and found a used tissue. She blew her nose and felt better, more like herself. Crying won't get you anywhere, she thought. Crying won't help. Think. But it was hard to think when she was so cold.

The tunnel was quiet but not entirely silent. There was a trickle of water somewhere near her left hand, and further on she could hear a heavier gush which must be the spring or stream she'd heard by the entrance. The fading light from the roof showed that the hole she'd fallen down was about seven feet above her. Perhaps if she'd spent all her spare time doing press-ups she could have managed it, but sitting in front of a laptop had done little to improve upper body strength. Seven feet. Not far to fall, but too high to jump and get out, even if her ankle had been sound. No, the logical thing was to sit it out and wait for rescue.

Then, suddenly, there it was again, the noise she'd thought was her alarm clock. No, not an alarm clock, a mobile phone. Of course, why hadn't she remembered it before? It had been in her pocket. Desperately she patted the ground with her hands, chucking broken brick and lumps of mortar to one side, making sweeping arcs in her search of the tunnel floor, praying for the ringing to continue. Her hands touched something smooth. There, there it was.

'Help,' she panted without preamble, not caring who it was. 'Help.'

But there was no one at the other end. She pressed the call button and the screen lit up, revealing that her battery was nearly dead. She punched in 999 but there was silence at the other end. No signal. Nothing.

'You bloody useless thing.' She threw the phone into the darkness, where it hit the wall and dropped with a splash on to the floor. 'You blood stupid, useless . . .' She rubbed her eyes but only succeeded in getting earth into them, which made her cry even harder. She could feel panic bubbling up, hysteria waiting to overtake her. She pressed her hand against her mouth in an effort to control herself. It will be all right. They will come for me. I just have to wait, and they'll come. Forty-eight hours maximum. Probably less. Will. He'd notice her car, he was bound to. And then he'd come looking for her. The panic subsided as she held on to the thought of Will coming to find her, setting up a search party. He was a rescuing sort; if he were a dog he'd have a brandy bottle around his neck and big shaggy paws.

It was now very dark in the tunnel. The temperature seemed to be dropping as night fell, and her bottom, soggy in the puddle, was especially cold. But this was England in the spring, and whatever the vagaries of the weather, it was unlikely she would get frostbite or hypothermia. Having had the thought, she started to doubt it. Frostbite she was pretty certain she was safe from, but hypothermia? She had no idea at what temperature that kicked in. Without thinking, she gave a little whimper, and it bounced back at her along with some other rustling noises. She sat still, completely focused on the sounds. Rats. Rats scrabbling around, rats with long tails and sharp teeth. Something fell on her, and she screamed, swatting at her head in an effort to ward them off. But she felt only earth.

Her shoulders sagged in relief. Stupid, it was only a slight earth fall from the edge of the hole. The pattering noise continued. Another scurry of earth came down. But if it wasn't rats, what could it be? More earth.

At that point she realised the roof was likely to collapse.

*

Anna concentrated on what she knew. The tunnel was blocked off at the pond end, but it had to lead somewhere. Even if there had been a roof collapse, there was a good chance she would be able to crawl through. So. Plan A. Investigate the tunnel exit. Plan B. Mmm. She decided to think about Plan B only if Plan A failed.

She shuffled forwards on her bottom, trying to ignore the jagged surge of pain each time she bumped her leg. It might only be a few inches at a time, but at least she was going somewhere. She ignored the patter of earth falling, the clatter of rocks and brick. There was nothing she could do about that, she thought, strangely cheerful. She realised that since she had devised a plan and was doing something about it, she hadn't felt anxious at all. It didn't matter if no one came to rescue her: she would rescue herself. She pushed on, feeling more optimistic. She'd wanted to know what lay at the other end of the tunnel, which was why she was in this mess. If she was going to die, smothered by earth, she might as well have her curiosity satisfied. Curiosity killed the cat, but maybe satisfaction would bring it back.

Anna laughed aloud, high-pitched, hysteria near the surface. The noise echoed round and she stopped laughing, suddenly sober, her senses alert, then made another noise. Yes, the echoes were different. Her eyes strained in the darkness. She couldn't see anything, but the sound of splashing water was louder. Perhaps she was coming to the end of the tunnel.

She set off again, invigorated by the knowledge that soon she'd know exactly what her situation was, dead end or exit. In her haste she bumped her ankle, but ignored the pain shooting up her leg she was so excited. And then she put her hand out and instead of earth or brick it plunged into cold water.

Using a combination of feeling with her hands and listening to the water and the echoes, Anna worked out that she was in a large chamber with a brick floor laid in a herringbone pattern, extending, judging by the echoes, quite a long way beyond and to the right of the pool of water in front of her. A spring bubbled up somewhere to her left. Dead ahead of her on the far side of the pool she thought she could make out an arch. It was difficult to tell, but it seemed lighter underneath and she could just make out the surface of the pool as it skittered with ripples from the falling spring water. It had to lead to the lake.

Which explained why they hadn't been able to see an exit before. She'd been looking too high up. Someone lower down, perhaps sitting in the pool, could look through. Perhaps this had once been a bathing pool, where people could sit and contemplate the view, then swim out into the lake. She felt a surge of excitement. Academic speculation aside, this was her way out. All she had to do was lower herself into the pool and swim out through the arch into the lake, then to the bank. She touched the cold water, imagining her wellies filling up, dragging her down, down until she drowned. Her bloated body would float out into the lake and people would assume she'd killed herself over love for Oliver Davenport . . . Oh, what nonsense, she snapped at herself, trying to dampen the fear she felt. The pool was unlikely to be more than a few feet deep, and she could take at least one of her wellies off.

It was difficult taking off the wellie on her good leg when she couldn't use the other foot for leverage, but she managed, then shuffled forward and swung her good leg into the water. The cold made her inhale sharply. She kicked out, trying to feel the bottom, but couldn't reach it. A deep plunge pool, obviously, but it might be okay when she stood up. In some ways deep was better; the water would support her bad leg and she could hop along the bottom. She swallowed. What if she had to swim, with one boot dragging her down?

More earth fell, splashing into the water, accompanied by a shifting, moaning sound. Anna looked up into the darkness. If the roof collapses, I'm dead. Using both hands on her thigh, she swung her bad leg into the pool. The cold water was blissful on the burning pain. She shuffled right to the edge, her feet still not touching the bottom. If the pool was deeper than five foot she would sink, the water rushing over her head, and she would be unable to swim up to the air with her wellie filled with water. She teetered on the edge, paralysed by indecision. To have come so far, inch by painful inch, but still to fail was impossible. And yet she hesitated, afraid of the black water, afraid that when she pushed off the edge she would plummet down and drown.

As Anna dithered she caught a wisp of sound above the bubble of the spring and the patter of earth. Something different, something with purpose. It couldn't be . . . She strained her ears. A thread of sound, moving up and down a scale. It was getting louder, more distinct, moving from being a snatch of melody to a man's voice singing. And singing the blues, what was more.

'Will!' she screamed. 'Help!'

The sound paused. She called his name again, her lungs bursting with the effort of making herself heard above the water.

'Hello?' His voice sounded hesitant, as if he thought he was being addressed by the spirit of the lake.

'Will, it's me, Anna. I'm down here.'

A long pause. 'What are you doing?'

Why were men so stupid? 'I'm stuck. The tunnel's fallen in, and I can't get out.'

'Oh. Okay. Do you need help?'

'Yes,' she yelled. 'Get me out!'

'Hang on.'

Silence. Then a slithering sound and a shout, followed by swearing. A few pebbles scattered over the water, but now that Will was here, she didn't mind the idea of the roof collapsing.

'I'm at the edge of the lake, but I can't see you.' His voice sounded nearer.

'There's an arch that leads to the lake. I'm there, inside the bank. You've got to get me out of here,' she babbled, words tumbling over each other like stones in an avalanche.

'How d'you get there?'

'I fell. I think I've broken my ankle. Can you see the arch?'

'It's pitch black out here, I can't see a thing. Hang on, I'll go back to the house for a torch.'

The thought of him leaving made her desperate. 'No, don't go.' She knew she wasn't thinking straight but she was sure that if he left her he'd never come back, never find her again. 'Don't leave me here.'

'I'll be back soon.' His voice was faint.

More pebbles pattered on to the surface. 'The roof's going to cave in,' she screamed, beyond caring what he thought of her, just needing him to stay. 'Please, Will, don't go, don't leave me.'

Silence. Then, 'Okay. Tell me where you are.'

'There's an arch that leads out to the lake. It's about two feet above the surface. Can you see it?'

'Nope. I'll have to swim round,' A splash, and then: 'Shit, that's cold.'

She couldn't hear the sound of him swimming above the sound of the spring water splashing softly, so it came as a surprise when suddenly his voice was in the chamber with her.

'Anna?' She could just make out his shape against the arch.

'I'm here, I'm here!'

Then he was with her, and she could feel his shoulders bobbing against her legs. She reached out for him, relief and joy mixed equally. But her outstretched arms tipped her weight over the edge, and she lost her balance and slithered down into the water, black water filling her eyes and ears and mouth, dragging her down. And then up to the surface, gasping for air, Will's arms around her. She clung to him, coughing, trying to get her breath back.

'So tell me, Dr Carmichael, do you always work this late?'

She shook her head, laughing, crying, shivering, she didn't know what.

'I think I've broken my ankle.'

Will paused, as if he was assessing the situation. 'I could carry you, but there's a lot of weed and muck at the bottom. It'll be easier if I swim, and you hang on.'

She nodded, then realised he couldn't see her. 'Okay.'

'You'll have to let go for a sec.'

Let go of him? She couldn't, she wouldn't. With a conscious effort she released her grip so he could turn.

'Arms round my neck then.'

She clasped him again, her chest against his back, determined never to let go.

'Relax.' Will gently loosened her grip a little, and they were off. Her legs trailed out behind. It hurt when his legs kicked hers, but the pain seemed distant, almost as if it was happening to someone else. She let her head flop on his shoulders, feeling the movement of his arms. Four strokes and they were through the arch and out into the lake. There was fresh air in her lungs, like being reborn after the depths of despair.

The cold night air had never felt so good. She half slipped off Will's back, going into the cold water, panicking as she realised the weight in her boot was dragging her down. Reeds and water weed thickened the water, twisting round her feet. He moved away and she grabbed at him, flailing in the murky water.

'Hey, don't strangle me.' He gripped her wrists, breathing hard. 'I've got you.'

The panic subsided.

'Okay?'

'Okay,' she said, her teeth chattering, aware of how cold she was. Will was no longer swimming and was standing, or rather crouching, in the water.

'Can you stand?'

She tried, but her good leg was numb with cold and collapsed when she tried to put her weight on it. 'Sorry,' she half whispered, half whimpered.

Somehow Will got them both out, pulling her through the reedy sludge at the side, then dragging her up the bank, where she sprawled as flaccid as a flounder on the fishmonger's counter. It was good to feel the tangle of grass under her face, feel the lightest of winds on her cheek, to sense that above her was nothing but the arching darkness of the night sky, sprinkled with stars and a sliver of crescent moon.

'Thanks,' she gasped.

'Think nothing of it,' Will said. 'A moonlit swim was just what I needed to clear my head after the pub. Not that there's much moonlight,' he added. 'Still, enough to see you should be in A and E having your leg seen to. Right, let's get you up.'

After much grunting and manoeuvring and yelping from Anna when he bumped her leg, he managed to get her across his shoulder, bottom stuck ungracefully in the air and legs hanging down. Shame she wasn't some elfin princess who could have been whisked up by the handsome hero and carried to safety, rather than lumbered along like a bag of cement. But at least Will could carry her. He'd swum to rescue her too. She pressed her cheek against his back, arms tight around his waist. It didn't matter that she was being carted along; all that mattered was that she was safe. She tried wriggling her toes, but couldn't feel them. Her legs felt like cement too, the waterlogged boot a concrete lump dragging her down.

Will pushed open the door to the pavilion and went through, catching Anna's dangling foot on the side, making her cry out and dig her nails into his back.

'Sorry,' he said. 'Let's get you down.' He settled her on something soft, she couldn't see what in the darkness, gently lifting her legs up. There was the sound of a match being struck and then the soft light from an oil lamp filled the room in a warm haze of gold and red. Anna blinked. I'm hallucinating. It must be the shock. Instead of the jumble of broken furniture, there were chairs and rugs, tapestry cushions and brightly coloured kelims.

'What's happened?' she said.

'I moved some stuff down from the house,' he said, pulling clothes from a chest. 'You need to get out of your wet things as soon as possible.'

'Okay,' she said, but her hands were shaking too much to unbutton her shirt and Will had to finish taking it off. He had an air of brisk professionalism that prevented her from being embarrassed, although he did momentarily react when he saw what she was wearing underneath – an Oliver special – but his expression was bland as he slung her dripping shirt into a corner of the room. He put one of his own shirts on her, gently doing up the buttons, and then pulled a sweater on top.

'It's too big,' she said, light-headed.

'Better than pneumonia,' he said, briskly rubbing her shoulders and arms to warm her up. He picked up a rug and passed it to her. 'Now get your trousers off and put this round you. I won't look.' He turned his back.

Anna eased her jeans down and got her good leg out, leaving the trousers round her bad leg, then wrapped the rug round her. She was still shivering but at least she didn't feel as cold as she had done. 'I can't get them off my bad leg.'

'I'll have to cut them,' Will said, turning back to her. With a penknife he cut the fabric and eased it off her leg, tucking the blanket firmly round her.

'Warmer?'

She nodded, although she thought she'd never be warm again. He slipped a sock on to her good foot. 'What did you think you were doing, exploring the tunnel without telling anyone where you were going?'

'I didn't mean to explore the tunnel,' Anna said, as indignant as she could be with her teeth chattering. 'I fell.'

'Mmm,' he said, considering her, waterweed still dripping off his mud-spattered torso, looking brown and healthy from working outside in the sunshine.

'You look like a classical river god,' Anna said. 'Nausicaa – no, that's a nymph. How odd, I can't remember the name. You often see statues of him draped in nothing but waterweed, with vines around his head.' She waved her hand vaguely.

'I dare say.' Will pulled a sweater on. 'I think you're in shock.'

'No I'm not,' she said, registering that, now he mentioned it, she did feel strange.

He started to unbutton his wet jeans, picked up a fresh pair, then hesitated.

'I won't look,' Anna said, closing her eyes. 'Will, why is all this stuff here?'

'I've been sleeping down here the last week or so. And a good thing too,' he added, 'or I wouldn't have heard you.'

She peeped through her eyelashes and registered that he had a very nice pair of tanned legs. He pulled up his jeans and she quickly shut her eyes tightly again.

'You can look now,' he said as he came back to the bed with one of the oil lamps and knelt beside her, the light giving him a glowing aura against the darkness like a painting by Caravaggio. No, not Caravaggio, Rembrandt; not hard-edged violence but warmth and compassion. If I say he should have been painted by Rembrandt he'll think me completely barmy, she thought. She almost reached out to touch his hair, to find out if it was real, but realised what she was doing just in time. He wasn't looking at her, but at her leg.

'May I? I won't hurt you.'

'Okay,' she said in a tight little voice as she braced herself.

Will's hands were cool, and managed to be both firm and gentle, but she still winced and caught her breath.

'Are you going to cut my boot off?' she managed.

'No, it's holding everything together. I don't think you've broken your leg, but you might have fractured your ankle.' He sat back and rubbed the back of his neck, ruffling the hair she'd wanted to touch.

'Right. I left my phone with my other things at the edge of the lake. I'm going to call an ambulance.'

'Don't leave me.' She struggled to get up, in panic that he was going.

He sat on the edge of the bed. 'I have to get some help, but I'll be back shortly.'

'Promise?'

'Promise.' He stroked her hair, calming her fears. 'Trust me.'

She let out a breath. 'Okay.'

Peggy met them at the door as Anna struggled out of the Land Rover, not having got the hang of using the crutches they'd given her at the hospital.

'Will, I've put Dr Carmichael in the blue bedroom.'

'I'm so sorry I've caused all this trouble,' Anna panted, as one crutch slipped on the threshold.

'We've got to get you up the stairs,' Will said. 'Can you manage?'

'I feel great,' Anna said, blinking in the light of the hall. She did feel great, although slightly woozy.

'That must be the drugs talking. Let's try and get you to bed before the effect wears off. Come on, it'll be easier if you lean on me rather than the crutch.' Will tried to drape Anna's arm over his shoulder, but the height disparity made it tricky. 'Right.' He picked her up and started up the stairs.

Anna put her arms round his neck. 'You keep on rescuing me,' she said, squinting at him. 'Like a St Bernard. But you haven't any brandy.' She shook her head. 'It's a terrible shame.'

'Last thing you need is brandy,' Will said, putting her down on the landing. 'D'you reckon you can hop across? I'm knackered, carting you around all night.'

'Course I can hop. Look!' Anna said, setting off.

Will caught her before she fell and managed to half carry, half stagger her to the bedroom. 'Peggy will sort you out.'

The thought of Will leaving her made Anna grab his hand. 'Don't go.'

He gently disengaged himself. 'You need to rest. It's going to hurt like hell tomorrow.'

'What exactly has she done?' Peggy asked, bustling into the room.

'Concussion and a partial tear of the lateral ligaments.'

'They cut my wellie off,' Anna said to Peggy, as the housekeeper plumped up the pillows. 'It was quite a new one too.'

'Not a break then?'

'No,' Will said. 'Though I expect it hurts as much. A partial tear can be more painful than a complete rupture, as the ligaments are still under tension, but it should heal quickly. Ice packs, bed rest and painkillers are what's needed.' He yawned. 'I think they overdid the painkillers in the hospital.'

'Never mind that,' Peggy said. 'Now, Will, it's gone four in the morning, you should go to bed. Do you want to sleep at the house tonight instead of the pavilion – the room you were in is all made up.'

'Thanks, Peggy, you're a star.' He gave her a kiss. Anna turned her face up too, but Peggy was shooing Will from the room.

'Get on with you. Dr Carmichael needs some sleep.'

Anna lay back against the pillows feeling let down. 'Call me Anna, please do. And I don't feel sleepy at all.' She didn't, but her words were sliding all over the place like greased ball bearings.

'Mmm.' Peggy surveyed her with hands on her hips. 'Let's get you undressed and then we'll see.'

'This is Will's shirt,' Anna said, as Peggy helped her arms out of the sleeves. 'He saved me.'

'So I heard.' Peggy pulled the shirt off and saw what Anna was wearing underneath. 'Goodness, it'll be a miracle if you don't catch your death of cold wearing something like that. Slip it off and I'll give it a wash fresh for tomorrow.'

Peggy's expression showed such surprise at academic Anna's

choice of garment that she giggled as she undid the catch. 'I think Will was surprised too.'

'I dare say he was. There's not enough fabric to cover a pimple.' Peggy popped a nightdress over Anna's head and threaded her arms through. Anna felt as limp as a rag doll. 'You should have known better than to go poking around a tunnel all on your own.'

'I wasn't poking, I was falling. I mean, I fell.' Anna rubbed her head, wincing as she touched the bump at the back. It felt as if the words were coming from deep underwater, as if she'd drowned. 'I thought I was going to die. Will saved me.'

'You should have told us what you were doing, not gone alone. Now, lift your legs up, there's a good girl.'

'You're awfully kind,' Anna said, yawning. 'And Will's kind too. And strong. I would have died without him.'

'Well, you didn't. You need to sleep now. There's a bell on the side table here, so if you want something you just ring that and I'll come. All right? I'll say goodnight then.'

'Goodnight, Peggy,' Anna said on another yawn. 'And thank you.'

Peggy left the room, turning the lights off, leaving Anna woozily contemplating the soft darkness of her new surroundings. Much nicer than a dank tunnel. And then swimming out on Will's back. Swimming out, like being reborn. Being reborn. She struggled against sleep because she sensed the meaning of the garden was just there, within reach; she only had to think a little more, just a little more, and it would become clear. But she was sinking, sinking into unconsciousness. With one last effort of concentration she turned her side light on, and found a pencil and an old postcard in the drawer of the bedside table. The letters swam before her eyes, and she had to work hard to write them, but she managed, before flopping back against the pillow, clutching a postcard of Brighton Pier scrawled with the single word: HELL.

Chapter 14

In the morning the world was not such a cheery place. The pain in her ankle was excruciating and her body ached all over, despite swallowing as many painkillers as Peggy would allow her. Reluctantly Anna agreed to stay at Templecombe, feeling it was imposing on Mrs Davenport. Will pointed out that it would be Peggy who would be doing the work.

'So it's imposing on her too,' Anna said. 'I ought to go home. I can walk, really I can.' She tried putting her foot to the ground, but recoiled, feeling sick and giddy with pain. Impossible.

Peggy tucked her back in bed. 'The doctor said to rest, and rest is what you'll have.'

Anna relaxed on to her pillows, secretly relieved that Peggy and Will wouldn't let her get up. 'I suppose I could work from here for a day or so. Oh!' She sat up in a panic. 'My rucksack – it's got all my stuff in it . . .'

'I'll see if I can retrieve it,' Will said, and she was reassured. Will would get it.

'Certainly not,' Peggy said tartly. 'It's bad enough to have one person fall down a tunnel, let alone two. And we'd need the fire brigade to haul you out, you're at least twice the weight of Dr Carmichael.'

'Call me Anna, please.'

'Anna it is.' Peggy nodded at her.

'It might not have fallen down the tunnel. I can't remember . . .' Anna put her hand to her head. It throbbed so. Tears pricked at her eyes.

Peggy patted her hand. 'Well, Anna, you're to stay in bed for the rest of the day and do nothing except what I tell you to.'

She did what she was told. Peggy gave instructions – eat this, drink this, go to sleep – and Anna followed them. She made a token show of protesting each time, but secretly it was wonderful to hand over responsibility for herself to Peggy. It may have been more oo-ah than *ER* but she was confident in Peggy's care. The day passed in a haze of pain. Vaguely she remembered Mrs Davenport coming in to see her, but she was too woozy from the pain to really understand what she was saying. Her ankle hurt, her back hurt, and her head felt as if someone had sawn it across the top using rusty cheese wire.

In the evening Will came in and set a tray down on the bed. 'Cream of chicken soup, buttered toast, poached eggs, more toast, painkillers if you want them and a glass of milk.'

Anna sat up as far as she could. 'Will, I need to contact my sister, let her know I'm okay, she might be worrying.'

He gently pushed her back down. 'Don't panic. Mrs D. rang and left a message.'

'Thanks.' Anna took his hand, feeling a wave of emotion come over her, her eyes welling up. 'I don't think I said thank you properly this morning. You saved my life.' Her voice trembled as she thought of how close she had come to entombment in the tunnel.

'You save mine, and eat all this up.' Will smiled at her, his hand warm in hers, reassuring. 'You've got to finish it, or else I'm in trouble with Peggy.'

Anna pressed her hand to her eyes. 'I'm sorry, I seem to be crying all the time.'

'You've had a shock,' Will said gently. He passed her the

painkillers and a glass of water. 'Take these and then eat something. You'll feel better.'

Anna swallowed the painkillers. 'You'll have to help me. I'm not very hungry.'

Will took a spoonful of soup. 'Open wide.'

Anna managed a feeble smile. 'I didn't mean that sort of help. I've hurt my ankle, not my hand.'

'Open wide.' Will waved the spoon.

Anna opened, and he fed her. 'Mmm. It's good,' she said.

'And again . . .' He scooped up another spoonful.

She opened her mouth, but added as Will went for another spoonful, 'I can do it myself. Really.' She picked up the spoon. Will watched her, his bee-brown eyes concerned.

'You're very good at looking after people,' she said.

'It's Peggy who's done the looking after,' he said quickly.

'No, down at the pavilion, I meant.' Anna took a spoonful of soup. 'I thought you were staying in the house.'

'Oliver Davenport made a fuss about me being here, so it seemed simplest to move out.'

Anna spluttered her soup. 'Sorry, went down the wrong way.'

Will passed her a napkin. 'He doesn't seem to like me for some reason.'

Anna wanted to say something about her and Oliver but didn't know what. 'I think you should know we are lovers' sounded both prim and conceited. And it was really up to Oliver to tell his family first, not her. She concentrated on her soup. It was none of Will's business anyway, she rationalised, ignoring the fact that she felt uncomfortable with the idea of telling him, given the antagonism between him and Oliver.

'When I first came here the house was in a terrible state,' Will said. 'No one had done anything for years. Peggy was doing her best, but Mrs D. was living in a couple of rooms. But you know, it wasn't difficult to set the basics right – clear the ivy, get the electrician round, mend the hole in the roof, sort out the heating, fix the broken windows, that sort of thing. Sure, it's still falling to pieces, but at least she can carry on living here in comfort.'

'But Oliver doesn't object to that, surely.' Oliver, her Oliver, was always keen on comfort and luxury.

'It seems he does.' Will shrugged. 'Get on with your soup. You've not eaten any toast.'

'I can't manage any more.' She flopped back on the pillow, waiting for the painkillers to kick in, not wanting to talk any more. 'You'll have to eat it.'

Will picked up a bit of buttered toast. 'The thing is, he could have organised all that stuff himself, but he didn't.'

Anna frowned, knowing she ought to stick up for Oliver. 'He's in London most of the time. And I don't think he does DIY.' She'd certainly not seen any signs of Oliver doing anything domestic for himself; he paid other people to do that for him.

'You don't need to be a DIY genius to pick up the phone, and get someone in, do you?'

'I suppose not.' She searched her aching brain for excuses. 'But that sort of thing's hard to organise if you're not around.'

'He comes often enough when it suits him.'

She ran her hand over the coverlet, fingers picking at a carefully darned patch. Oliver hadn't come to Templecombe when she'd wanted him to. In fact, if they'd come when she'd originally planned, she wouldn't have fallen down into the tunnel. But I've forgiven him for that, she thought, like I've forgiven him for his behaviour at lunch. It occurred to her that Oliver was quick to take a dislike to certain people – Bron, Nick, Will. Perhaps he doesn't like sharing people, Anna thought. Me. His grandmother. He is an only child. She looked up at Will. 'Why do you think he objects to you organising it?'

'Seems pretty obvious to me.' He munched a piece of toast. 'I thought you were supposed to be clever.'

Anna shook her head. She couldn't say about Oliver not liking to share people.

'It showed him up for the sort of person he is,' Will said. 'It didn't take much to get this place up and running, and he doesn't seem short of cash.'

No, he wasn't. Anna thought guiltily about all the clothes he'd bought her, the meals they'd eaten, the fabulous dress for the dinner dance. They must have cost thousands. 'Perhaps he didn't realise . . .'

Will snorted. 'He knew. He just didn't want to spend the money.'

Her head ached with the effort of defending Oliver. 'Perhaps Mrs Davenport wouldn't let him – old people can be very proud.'

Will looked at her, as if slightly puzzled. 'Are you playing devil's advocate?'

Anna shook her head. 'There are always two sides – neither of us knows the whole story.' Oliver's not a bad person, she wanted to say, not in the way you're making him out to be. He has lots of good qualities – he's funny and energetic and generous, and I know he loves his grandmother. She's his only family, I'm sure he would have done something if he'd known. 'Perhaps he didn't realise . . .' she said, her voice trailing off.

'Maybe I am being a bit hard on him.' Will shrugged. 'And Mrs D. is as proud as they come. But it's not just about money, it's about having the will.'

'Or a Will?' Anna said, managing a smile although she felt in more pain now despite the painkillers.

He smiled, then became serious again. 'I think it suited him to have her living like that.'

'What do you mean?'

'She couldn't have managed another winter here. As it was, she was struggling.'

Anna stared at him in horror. 'What are you saying?'

'Not my place to say anything.' He munched on the toast. 'But the sooner the old lady goes, the sooner Oliver Davenport gets his hands on her property.'

She slept fitfully that night, tossing and turning in her sleep, and each movement jarred her ankle, a spike of pain that made her cry out. She dreamt she was back in the tunnel, trapped, not able to escape, with no one to hear her cries. The roof was falling on top of her, pressing down, filling her mouth with earth.

'Will, Will,' she screamed. 'Save me!'

And then he was there, his hands on her shoulders. 'It's okay, sshh, it's okay.'

'The roof's coming down!'

'I won't let it,' he said, stroking her hair. 'Go back to sleep.'

'Don't let it fall,' she murmured, snuggling back into the pillow.

'I won't.'

She sighed and closed her eyes. Will was there, Will would save her. 'Stay with me.'

'Of course.'

Anna woke to sunlight streaming through the curtains, looking around for Will, confused that he wasn't there. Perhaps it had been a dream. She rubbed her eyes. Weird dreams about Will kissing the top of her head. Her ankle throbbed, but she knew she couldn't stay in bed for another day. She had to get up. She swung her legs out of bed and tried putting weight on the bad one. Agony. But she had to get up, she'd go mad lying in bed.

Peggy was doubtful. 'The doctor said to rest that leg of yours.'

'But I could rest it downstairs, or outside. Please.' She gave what she hoped was an ingratiating smile.

'I don't know.' Peggy shook her head. 'I'll have to see what Will thinks.'

'Will?' Anna said. 'What's Will got to do with it?'

But Peggy had trotted off, leaving Anna to think. Perhaps Oliver was right. Perhaps Will did exert undue influence on the two women. He had tried to turn her against Oliver the day before. Perhaps he was turning Oliver's grandmother against him too. Anna buried her face in her hands. Her head hurt so much, she couldn't cope with thinking about Will and Oliver.

Will duly came up and Anna reluctantly presented her ankle for him to look at.

'Yes it still hurts, and yes it's still swollen, and yes I'm getting up.'

'Fair enough, but there are still a lot of contusions.' Will examined her leg. 'With these sorts of tears it's up to you what you feel you can bear. Just watch out for overdoing it.'

'Since when were you a doctor?' Anna said, cross because Peggy was nodding at everything Will said.

'Me?' He shrugged gormlessly. 'I'm just repeating what they said in the hospital.'

'Well, don't,' Anna said. She felt scratchy and irritable, and the fact that he was being reasonable just made her even crosser.

'Poor Anna,' Will cooed. 'Are you in a lot of pain?'

'It's none of your business. I will get up,' Anna said recklessly. She stood, and pain shot through her leg so suddenly, so intensely that she cried out. She collapsed back on to the bed, crying and crying, and not really knowing what she was crying about. She knew she was being pathetic even as the hot tears flowed down her cheeks. She brushed them away, but they seemed an inexhaustible flow. Then Peggy was holding her, in a way her own mother never had, and it was comforting to be shushed and patted and generally fussed over.

'I don't know what's wrong with me,' she wailed into Peggy's shoulder.

'There now, it's a bit of reaction, I expect,' Peggy said, her voice as cosy as an armchair in front of a fire.

Anna pulled back and wiped her face with the back of her hand. Will silently passed her a box of tissues. 'Sorry to be so pathetic,' she mumbled.

'Never you mind about that,' Peggy said. 'Now, you lie back down and rest for a while, and meanwhile me and Will will see if we can sort something out so you can get up later.'

Anna sniffed. 'I'm being such a nuisance. I don't mean to be.'

'You settle back down like a good girl, and we'll see what we can do.' Peggy got up, the bedsprings creaking in relief.

'Thank you, Peggy,' Anna said in a small voice.

She watched them leave, thinking that there was no way she was going to be able to sleep. The light came through the drawn curtains, giving the room a blue tint, like being underwater. The curtains moved gently in the breeze from the window, making shafts of sunlight ripple on the walls. Perhaps Oliver stayed in this room when he visited. Perhaps he slept in this very bed. She stroked the mattress, thinking about him. He was still in Prague, having business meetings. It seemed a very long way away, as far as the other world he lived in. Hard to believe this house was his world too. She sighed and closed her eyes.

The door creaked open, and the noise penetrated her sleeping brain. Anna squinted through half-closed eyes to see Will.

'Feeling better?'

'I suppose so . . .' She woke up a bit more, checking her head, her ankle. The dreadful throbbing seemed to have stopped. 'I'm really sorry about this morning.'

'Don't be so hard on yourself.' Will stood at the foot of the bed, his hands on the ironwork rail. 'You had a bad fall, you know. A reaction to the shock was only to be expected.'

'It's only a torn ligament, for heaven's sake. How pathetic is that? I didn't even break anything and I'm a wreck.'

'Think yourself lucky you didn't.' Will's face was serious. 'You know, it was sheer luck I happened to be there and heard you. You could still be stuck in the tunnel.'

'I know,' Anna said, feeling the corners of her mouth turn down and the tears on the brink of coming again.

'I've set up a table and chair for you outside,' Will said hurriedly. 'And I'll help you down when you're ready.'

'Thanks, but I can't go out. You cut my trousers up.' Her voice had gone all squeaky. 'I've nothing to wear.'

'Your sister's going to bring some clothes tomorrow, but until then . . .' Will waved something lurid at her. 'Problem solved.'

It looked like a flag from *Braveheart*. 'What is it?'

'Peggy has supplied some of her own redoubtable garments that she thinks might do the trick.' He stopped waving the flag, and it turned out to be a slightly hairy plaid skirt in vivid colours. 'Not a hundred per cent sure about the sizing . . .' he said, his voice amused, as he laid it on Anna's bed along with a flowery shirt. 'Might be a little on the large side.'

Anna thought the skirt would go round her at least three times, but it was something. 'That's so kind of Peggy,' she said, clutching it to her and feeling all soppy.

'I'll go outside, you change, and then call me and I'll get you downstairs.'

When he'd left, Anna quickly stripped off Peggy's nightdress and put on the clothes, turning the waistband of the hairy blanket skirt down several times to try and make it tighter. She discovered that Peggy had discreetly folded her washed underwear inside the flowery shirt, away from Will's eyes. The contrast in style between the skirt and the underwear was startling. When she was dressed, she called Will in.

'Very fetching,' he said, straight-faced. Anna decided that as she needed his help she would ignore his comment. She hopped along the landing with his support, still unable to put her foot to the ground, having to stop every few seconds and clutch the skirt as it threatened to descend. At the stairs Will stopped.

'You know, this is going to be much easier for both of us if I simply carry you.' He scooped her up. 'The skirt fits okay, I see.'

'Very funny.'

'Covers the hidden treasures at least.' His face was bland as a glass of milk.

'You looked,' Anna said, outraged.

'Careful, I might drop you.' He made a little movement, and Anna clutched at his neck.

'You are not a gentleman,' she said, turning her head away from him and feeling like Scarlett O'Hara.

'No,' Will said, laughing. 'I'm not.'

Will had organised a comfortable spot for her on the back lawn under the shade of the cedar tree, with a table and several chairs and a small stool to rest her ankle on.

'Any chance of something to write with?' she said, settling down.

He frowned. 'Don't you think you ought to just rest?'

Anna shook her head. 'I've wasted too much time already. I need to work.'

'I'll see what I can find,' he said.

'Thanks,' she said, smiling at him. 'And – if you don't mind – there's a postcard by my bed. I made some notes last night. No, the night before,' she added. It was easy to get confused; yesterday had passed in a blur of pain. 'Would you bring it, please?'

Will came back with the postcard, a half-used pad of paper and a handful of leaky biros and blunt pencils. Even better, he'd also found a map of Templecombe, not as good as the plan she'd drawn from her survey, but good enough.

Anna wrote down every detail she could remember or estimate from the accident and the rescue: the width of the tunnel, the height, the degree of curve, the archway under which they'd swum. Bees working the flower borders gave a soft, droning hum. Her eyes started to close, the details of the tunnel became woozy, the sun through her eyelids gave everything a warm glow like the pavilion two nights before, and Will half naked, pulling a sweater over his tousled head. She shook herself awake.

'I hope I didn't disturb you.' Mrs Davenport was standing by her chair. 'Am I intruding?'

'No, heavens, no. It's me who's disturbing you.' She rubbed her eyes. What was she doing, dreaming about Will? 'I must have dozed off.'

'I don't want to disrupt your work,' Mrs Davenport said, settling into a chair opposite Anna.

'I'm so sorry about this,' Anna said, indicating her ankle. 'I've caused you a lot of trouble and inconvenience.'

'It's quite all right.' Mrs Davenport inclined her head graciously, then twinkled at Anna. 'Of course, all the trouble and inconvenience has been Will and Peggy's, but at my age it's wise to accept any gratitude that comes your way.'

'You're not old,' Will said, coming towards them with a tea tray.

'Ah, William, if only that were true. Now, we must make sure no one else can have such a fall.'

Will nodded, setting the tray down. 'I've already seen to it.'

'You're a good boy.' Mrs Davenport patted his hand. 'I understand that you will be with us for a few days, Dr Carmichael.'

'If that would be convenient. I think the doctor said it could be painful for the first couple of days, but would probably have healed by the end of the week, if not before.' She looked up at Will. 'Did he really say that or am I imagining it?'

Will nodded. 'The ligaments are partially torn so it's more painful because every time you make a movement you're pulling at the tear. But because it's only partial it should heal more quickly than if you'd fully torn them. So days rather than weeks. He said he knew a marathon runner with a similar injury who was back training within five days.'

Anna shifted her ankle and winced. 'I'm not a marathon runner, though. Still, I do hope he's right. I hate being immobile.'

'It will be an opportunity for you to complete your research,' Mrs Davenport said, smiling at her.

'Yes, I hope so.' Anna touched the postcard. 'In fact, I think the accident's given me an idea. I'd like to ask you some questions about the garden, particularly what you can remember about the tunnel.'

'I don't think I'm going to be able to help you much. Even when I was a little girl the tunnel was blocked off.' Mrs Davenport leant back in her chair, her face lined in the dappled sunlight. 'Although I do remember there being a bridge over the pond.'

A bridge . . . she was right, there had been a bridge. She could feel the excitement welling up. Keep calm, all this is speculation. 'Look.' She picked up the postcard and showed it to them.

Will leaned forward, a puzzled expression on his face. 'Brighton Pier?'

'No, no, it's nothing to do with Brighton, it was the only paper I could find to write on at the time.' She turned it over, wincing as she moved her foot, and showed them what she'd written.

'Hell?' Mrs Davenport said. 'Aren't gardens more about Paradise?'

'Exactly,' Anna said in triumph, looking at them. She registered their blank faces. 'Heaven and Hell.'

Their faces still looked blank. 'I don't see what that's got to do with the garden,' Will said, glancing at Mrs Davenport, who shook her head.

Anna couldn't believe they couldn't see it, it seemed so obvious to her. 'Think of the route through the garden. You go down the path until it splits and you have a choice.'

'Left or right,' Will said.

'Yes, of course, but what else about the two paths?' She looked at them expectantly. Surely Will would get it.

But he didn't. Mrs Davenport said apologetically, 'It's years since I've been down there, my dear.'

'You've just said it – down. One path goes down, and the other path goes up.'

Will nodded. 'So?'

Anna could feel her cheeks were pink with excitement. 'Let's suppose you choose the easy path. You go downhill . . .'

'Fast, in my case,' Will said.

'. . . because it seems the easier option, but instead of heaven you reach the pond. Now, remember that whoever designed the garden almost certainly had been taught Latin and Greek, and would have known the mythology. So . . .' She took a deep breath. 'I think the first lake symbolises the River Styx, which in Greek mythology was the division between life and death. You cross the Styx, and descend into the Underworld.'

'I don't want to sound rude,' Will said. 'But isn't that a bit far-fetched?'

Anna shook her head. 'No, the same symbolism is found in other gardens.'

'But—'

'Wait a minute,' Mrs Davenport said, putting her hand on Will's arm. 'Wasn't the Underworld protected by a dog? Have I remembered rightly?'

'Cerberus,' Anna said, nodding.

'I'm not sure if this is relevant, but I can remember there being a statue of a dog by the bridge when I was a child.'

Anna stared at Mrs Davenport, almost unable to believe what she'd said. 'Are you sure?'

Mrs Davenport frowned with the effort of remembering. 'I desperately wanted a dog when I was a child – my father had dogs for shooting, but working dogs, not pets – and I can remember this statue quite clearly, because I pretended he was my dog.'

'And he was at the lake by the bridge, guarding the entrance?'

'Absolutely.' Mrs Davenport leaned back on her chair, one hand to her heart. 'Goodness, I'd forgotten all about him until now. He was quite big enough for me to sit on, you know.'

'He's certainly not there now,' Will said.

Anna felt like rushing out into the garden immediately to search for the statue. 'Perhaps he's been moved. He might be hidden in the undergrowth.'

Will put his hand on her arm, as if he could read her thoughts. 'I'll go out later and have a look,' he said. 'If I find anything I'll report straight back. Go on with the garden symbolism.'

Anna sighed. She'd have to wait until her ankle was better before she was able to go searching for missing statues. 'So you've gone to the Underworld, and a horrid place it is too.' She felt a frisson of cold as she remembered how it had nearly been her own Underworld. 'The only way out is to be reborn . . .' She suddenly felt self-conscious as it occurred to her that Will might laugh, so she spoke in a rush. 'I think the big chamber at the end is like a womb and you have to swim out through the birth canal to be reborn into the lake.'

Will raised his eyebrows, but at least he didn't laugh. 'What happens if you take the other path?'

'The upward fork symbolises the path of the righteous. It's a struggle at first but it leads to the gateway. Now in my interpretation, that's a bit like Purgatory. It's somewhere to wait, to meditate, to think about your sins, and all the while, across the lake you can see the pavilion which represents Paradise.'

Mrs Davenport frowned. 'Isn't Purgatory Christian rather than Greek?'

'I'm just calling it Purgatory for now. It's quite feasible that whoever designed the garden could have drawn from different mythologies. Lots of ideas got jumbled up together in the eighteenth century. John Wood of Bath was a Christian, but he also believed in druids and King Bladud and mysticism.' Anna remembered telling Oliver about Wood and King Bladud. She bit her thumbnail. She ought to say something, but she couldn't blurt out that she'd been seeing Oliver, it would sound odd. Yet she couldn't think of a conversational opening that would allow her to just mention it in passing.

'What about the symbols?' Will said.

'What symbols?' Anna said, thinking how really it should be Oliver who told his grandmother.

'On the gateway. I told you I'd cleared the ivy away. There are loads of symbols carved into the stone underneath.'

All thoughts of Oliver whooshed out of her head. Anna pushed herself up out of her chair and gave a yelp as she put weight on her ankle. She fell back, gasping, as the pain shot up her leg.

'They won't run away,' Will said.

She glowered at him. 'Why didn't you tell me before?'

'I did. Should have got your act together earlier,' he said smugly. Anna threw her pencil at him.

'Dr Carmichael!' Mrs Davenport looked quite shocked.

'Sorry.' She knew he was right, she should have made time to come and see the gateway. In fact, she should have made time to finish the entire report. It wasn't good enough. 'I'm sorry,' she said, covering her face with her hands.

Will patted her shoulder. 'We'll go and look tomorrow.'

The afternoon light began to fade, the shadow of the house growing longer and thinner across the daisy-strewn lawn. Will carried Anna to the drawing room and settled her on a sofa, then lit a fire. Mrs Davenport joined them, and they talked about the house. Mrs Davenport told tales of the former glory of the house, the house parties and balls it had seen, the men handsome in black tie and tails, the women in satins and silks, diamonds and feathers in their hair. Anna talked about some of the great houses where she'd worked, the unexpected treasures to be found in dusty muniment rooms and ancient libraries. And then she found herself talking about Richard and the whole sad, drawn-out ending of their marriage. Will's eyes were deep with sympathy and understanding as she stumbled through the sorry litany of disappointment and anguish.

A log settled in the grate with a shiver of sparks and Anna stopped talking, embarrassed at having said so much. Mrs Davenport's eyes were closed, her hands fallen open in her lap. 'I've bored her to sleep,' Anna said to Will, feeling more embarrassed than before. 'It's your turn now.'

'What do you want me to say?' Will asked, getting up and putting another log on the fire.

Anna stretched. 'Tell me about your childhood, your past loves, your life. No, tell me what you were doing before you came here.'

Will fiddled with the poker, pushing the log into position. 'You don't want to hear about that.'

'I do,' Anna said, feeling bold. 'I've told you lots about me, and I know nothing about you. Except that you're very good at saving people's lives if they fall down tunnels,' she added.

Will smiled. 'Isn't that enough?'

'No,' she said, shaking her head, completely serious. 'It's not.'

Will said nothing. He stared into the flames as if he could read the future in them. But it's the past I want to know about, Anna thought. Who are you? Where have you come from? Why won't you tell me?

The poker clattered down on to the hearth with a clang. Mrs Davenport woke with a start, one hand on her heart. 'Oh!' she said. 'I must have dropped off. Where were we?' She looked around with blurry eyes.

'I was just going to carry Anna up to bed,' Will said, tidying the poker away on to its stand.

'I can manage,' Anna said, angry with him. He'd dropped the poker on purpose. She stood and tested her ankle, pressing her lips together with pain as she put weight on it. 'Goodnight,' she said to Mrs Davenport, who nodded graciously.

She hobbled to the door, one hand holding up Peggy's skirt, the other clenched with pain. Will followed her to the hall.

'You'll never make the stairs,' he observed.

'Watch me.' She took a deep breath and gripped the banister rail.

Will scooped her up. 'You'll end up spending more time in bed if you push it too far now.'

She turned her head from him as he carried her up the stairs, feeling small and pathetic, once again on the verge of tears, though why she didn't know. He put her down outside her room.

'Why won't you tell me anything about yourself?' she said, leaning against the door for support. His face was in shadow.

'There are some things it's best not to know.' He gently kissed her cheek. 'Goodnight Anna,' he said softly.

Chapter 15

'Wow,' Clare said, letting Anna's weekend bag drop on to the hall's flagstone floor with a loud bump. 'I'm not surprised you're bonking Oliver if he's going to inherit all this. Jeez, I'd sleep with him too.'

'Don't be silly,' Anna said sharply, hoping no one had heard Clare's comment. 'Did you bring my things?'

'And about time too, by the look of you – what have you got on?' Clare peered at Anna's odd assortment of clothes. 'You could always come back with me.'

'Thanks,' Anna said quickly, 'but my ankle should be better within a day or two, then I can drive back. Saves another trip to pick my car up. Besides, there's more to research here.' Will had promised he'd help her to the gateway in the afternoon if she thought her ankle was up to it. She knew she was going, regardless of how it felt.

'I'll say.' Clare peered at the Dutch flower painting. 'Bet that's worth a fortune.'

'Yes, I think it is.' Clare's presence made Anna feel curiously on edge. 'I expect you want to be getting back.'

'No hurry. Go on, show me round your future domain.'

Anna winced. 'Don't call it that.'

Clare peeped into the top of a large Famille-Rose spice jar. 'And where's Mr Gorgeous himself?'

'Prague. I'm not sure when he's coming back.' She realised she didn't really know what Oliver was doing. Prague, London, Oliver, Sunday lunch, everything seemed a long, long way away.

Clare gave up inspecting the paintings. 'Why don't you show me the garden now I'm here?'

'I would but my ankle's really not up to it.' Anna felt a twinge of anxiety that Clare would hang around for ever, saying whatever came into her head. At that moment Will came through the front door, a pile of logs in his arms.

'Hi,' Clare said brightly. 'I'm Clare, Anna's sister.'

'I'm Will. I'd shake hands, but . . .' He indicated the logs.

'Are you the one who saved her?'

'I suppose so.' Will looked embarrassed. He glanced at Anna, who didn't smile back and stared at the flagstone floor. He'd refused to talk about himself last night, had been positively cryptic in fact, so she didn't see why she should be friendly now. 'Were you saying you wanted to see the garden? Give me a chance to dump these and I'll take you round.'

'That'd be brilliant,' Clare said, as Will went into the drawing room with the logs.

'Look, be discreet,' Anna whispered to Clare, conscious of Will stacking logs next door. 'You know – about . . .'

Clare's eyes widened. 'Don't they know about you and . . .'

'No,' Anna whispered back. 'I don't want them to either.'

'Why on earth not?'

'Because . . . it's awkward, okay?'

'Okay.'

Will and Clare went off, Will promising to bring back Anna's rucksack, leaving Anna to fret about what her sister might say. Having kept quiet about her relationship with Oliver so far, she really didn't want it blurted out now. It would be inappropriate, she told herself, knowing deep down that she didn't want any of them to know, not Mrs Davenport, not Peggy, not Will. It wasn't that she was ashamed of Oliver; heavens, how could she be? Just that she felt in some strange way it was letting them down. It was funny, but although Oliver had more right to be there than any of the others, except his grandmother of course, he somehow fitted in least. He was too modern for the shabby old house. She suspected that where she saw the charming patina of the past, he saw only dust.

Her ankle was hurting, so she sat down on the stairs. She touched the elaborate carving of the banisters, feeling the warmth of the wood curve under her hand. The grandfather clock chimed gently and the sun came out, striking the dust motes in a golden haze. Sitting on the stairs with the hall arching over her, she felt enfolded into the house. She had a curious feeling of welcome, of acceptance, and she turned, half expecting someone else to be sitting on the stairs next to her. But there was no one there. She laid her palm flat on the smooth stair, feeling the slight dip where the wood had been polished by the passing of hundreds of feet. She saw them then, the light slippers of the ladies of the house, the sturdy shoes of the maids; women like Mrs Davenport, gracious in rustling silks and diamonds, or like Peggy in starched caps and pinafores. Women loving, cherishing, caring for the house that was to be Oliver's inheritance.

It was decidedly more comfortable being back in her own clothes, although Anna felt less comfortable when Clare stayed for lunch. There was no knowing what her sister would say or do. Luckily she seemed more interested in Peggy's old-fashioned recipes for beauty products.

'If you're that interested,' Peggy said, 'there are some really old books I've got at home, dating back to heaven knows when. I'll search them out for you. They came from here originally, but madam said I could have them. I know there's one with lots of recipes and potions for brides and wedding days.'

'That'd be wonderful,' Clare said, beaming. 'Perhaps Anna could copy some of them out for me before she goes.'

Anna stopped watching Will slice bread into even slices. 'If you want me to I will, but I ought to be checking out the carvings on the gateway.'

'I'll help you get out this afternoon,' Will said, setting the bread knife down. 'Assuming you think your ankle's up to it.'

'Oh, I do,' Anna said eagerly. Will smiled at her, and she smiled back, then remembered she'd decided to be reserved and became confused. Why wouldn't he talk about his past?

'Tell you what,' Peggy said, taking a slice of bread, 'I'm off home after lunch. I'll dig out those old books for you and bring them up tomorrow morning. How about that for a plan?'

Anna smiled at her. 'You're very good at organising me.'

'I wish you'd come and organise my wedding,' Clare said. 'I'd no idea how many things there were to do.'

'When we were young it was just a small thing with a few friends, and maybe a week away at the seaside for a honeymoon,' Peggy said. 'Nothing compared to now. My granddaughter Ginny got married last summer, and you'd never believe the palaver. Weekend with her friends in Newcastle of all places before the wedding – they flew all the way from Bristol, they did – and her dress ordered a year before, and a carriage to take her to the church.'

'But that's lovely,' Clare said, dolloping Peggy's home-made pickle on to her plate. 'She's had a wonderful day she'll remember for the rest of her life.'

'That's as maybe, but it's a waste of good money if you ask me.' Peggy shook her head. 'And her with two kids to look after and another on the way.'

Clare did a double take, but rallied quickly. 'Well, I'm planning to have the day of my life, exactly as I want it to be.'

Peggy nodded. 'And I expect you're used to getting your own way, Miss Clare.'

Clare blushed, then said in an endearing burst of honesty, 'I do try to,' which made them all laugh.

'So what sort of cake are you having then?' Peggy asked.

Clare needed no further encouragement to discuss cakes at length, then flowers – you don't want lilies in church, that's bad luck that is, Peggy said – then the dress and then . . . Anna stopped listening. She chased a couple of crumbs around her plate with her forefinger. This afternoon she'd go to the gateway with Will.

'Is this the sister who said starter marriages were fashionable?' Will said softly to her, and Anna nodded, touched that he'd remembered but slightly resentful that he expected her to answer his questions when he wouldn't give her the slightest bit of information about himself. 'Not exactly tactful, is she?'

'Not exactly.' She sighed, forgetting her resentment in the warmth of his interest. 'I'm used to it, I suppose. Clare's life has always been shinier and glossier than mine.'

He touched her shoulder, and without thinking she put her hand on his and turned to look at him. 'Thank you,' she said softly. 'Thank you for saving my life.'

Will's eyes were warm and welcoming and the world outside receded, lost in that moment, the feeling of recognition, of coming home. What am I doing? she thought in a panic, and dropped her hand from his. I love Oliver. Will's saved my life and I'm grateful, but I love Oliver. She stared at the plate in front of her, her mind racing. I'm confusing gratitude with – well, she didn't know what. Not love. I love Oliver.

Will stood up, pushing his chair back. 'Shall we go and look at the carvings?'

'No, I mean, yes,' Anna said. 'I'm sure I won't need help, my ankle's nearly better.' She stood up too, testing her ankle.

'You want to be careful,' Peggy said. 'You don't want to be twisting it again going up and down those paths. You make sure she doesn't fall down any more holes, young William.'

Clare thanked Peggy for lunch and they went into the hall. She kissed Anna at the door. 'You've done well,' she whispered. 'Ageing retainers, doting gardeners, whopping great house, garden to play with. Better hang on to Oliver!'

'Clare . . .' Anna protested, feeling panic again at the thought of Will overhearing.

'I know, I know, I'm going. I'll see you in a few days – ring me if you need anything else.' She opened her car door, then paused and turned back. 'By the way, where did you get all those sexy undies from? I was amazed!' she said, not bothering to lower her voice. 'Not like you at all.'

'Go away,' Anna said, making shooing gestures with her hands.

Clare drove off with an unrepentant wave. Anna turned round and saw Will right behind her. From his expression, she knew he'd heard Clare's parting comments.

'Don't say a word,' she said. 'Not one.'

'As if I would.' He grinned, eyes twinkling. 'I've got your things.' He slung her rucksack over his shoulder.

Anna found she needed to lean on Will to get down the garden and then up to the gateway. Even so her ankle was hurting almost as badly as it had done in the tunnel.

'Are you okay? You're very white,' Will said, helping her to sit on the path. 'This was stupid, we should have waited until tomorrow.'

'Give me a few minutes.' Anna felt her leg was on fire. She breathed deeply, and the pain started to subside. When she was ready, she looked up.

Will had done sterling work clearing the ivy. The shape of the gateway was now clearly defined, a square block with a central archway. Semicircular bowls stuck out from the wall at waist height, one on either side of the door. What made her jaw drop, though, were the carvings above the door lintel.

She scrambled to her feet, wincing as she put weight on her ankle. Will helped her to get to the wall. She stretched up and touched the carvings, her fingers making out the shapes. A circle, like a door knocker or a wreath. A triangle with a lozenge in the middle. Another triangle, but this time the base line had been lost. In the centre, above the entrance, another circle, with what seemed like horizontal lines either side of the top half. The symbols continued round the two other sides with doorways.

'They're amazing,' she whispered, feeling the excitement rising in her. 'Absolutely amazing. Thank you, thank you so much for clearing the ivy.' She was so excited she could have hugged him. No, she mustn't hug Will, she had to keep her distance. But it was wonderful, this discovery.

Will shrugged. 'It was nothing,' he said, but she could tell he was as pleased as she was. More than pleased. She patted the carvings, unable to stop grinning.

'Right. First thing is to record what's here.' Anna hesitated, uncertain she'd be able to hold a camera still when she was so unsteady on her ankle. She turned to Will.

'Do you think you could take photographs of them for me?'

'Sure.'

'Great. They need to be as close up as possible and in the same order as they go round the gateway. You never know, there might be some significance in their positioning. There should be a camera in my rucksack.' Will nodded, and bent for the rucksack. 'Oh, and if you could take a couple of the structure as a whole so I can place them later? Thanks.'

She turned her attention to the bowls, stroking the surfaces, the stone cold to her touch. Man-made, smooth not rough-cast. Like a basin. She ran one hand around the edge, probing with her fingers for any anomaly. Although the exterior was smooth, the inside was rough, a million tiny pits. Perhaps they had held water, she thought, but there was no sign of an overflow or any drainage channel.

'What do you think those are for?' Will said, pausing from taking photographs. 'They look like those basins you get in Catholic churches, for holy water.'

'I hadn't thought of that.' He was right, that was exactly what they looked like. She rubbed her fingers together under her nose. They felt rough, and smelled of smoke. Cautiously she licked one, tasting something familiar she couldn't place under the green taste of moss. Something burnt.

'I've cleared that front area as well. You were right, there are steps to the lake.'

Anna hobbled through the gateway and out on to the platform. The flagstones were now clearly visible where the brambles and ivy had been cut back.

'You must have worked so hard,' she called to Will, who was still on the entrance side. 'This is brilliant.'

She made her way across the flagstones and saw a series of stone steps leading down to the lake edge. Perhaps there was a landing stage down there, so you could row boats on the lake. She looked up, one hand on a tree for support, and saw the pavilion on the other side to her left. She looked to her right, trying to work out where the outlet of the tunnel was. Yes, she could just about see where it must be, low down in the water and overhung with vegetation. She turned her head back to the pavilion, trying to work out where they must have clambered out. She stopped. Looked right. Then left.

'Will,' she called. 'Come here.'

He came and stood beside her, and she tucked her arm into his, happy he was with her and able to share the discovery. 'Look at the pavilion, and then look where we swam out. Do you see, it's a triangle: the gateway to the pavilion to the tunnel entrance and back to here. A perfect equilateral triangle.'

'What does that mean?'

'It could be – oh, I don't know, maybe it doesn't mean anything . . .' she said. 'But groups like the Freemasons started worshipping God as the Three-in-One rather than God the Father, the Son and the Holy Ghost. The triangle's a Masonic symbol.' She realised she was still holding Will's arm and he was looking down at her. She let go of him and struggled back to the gateway to look at the carvings. 'Some of these are definitely triangles, aren't they?' She felt breathless with the discovery.

Will nodded. 'So does that make the guy who designed the garden a Freemason?'

'Not necessarily, there were other groups that believed in Unitarianism. I need to examine the carvings more closely . . . Will, would you be able to nip into Milbridge and get that film developed today?'

Will got back in time for supper, having found a one-hour developer in Milbridge. Mrs Davenport insisted they eat first, to let Peggy get home. Anna had discovered that they usually all ate in the kitchen, the dining room being reserved for more formal occasions. She sat impatiently, staring at the packet of photographs as if she might develop X-ray vision with enough concentration, unable to eat or join in with Mrs Davenport's conversation more than half-heartedly.

At the end of what seemed like an interminable meal, Will began to clear the table. Anna couldn't wait a moment longer. She ripped open the packet and spread the photos out on the kitchen table, ignoring Peggy's complaints, and looked at each one in turn.

'They're very eroded,' she said, shaking her head. 'The ivy's done a lot of damage.'

'What do they mean?' Will picked up one of the photographs.

'I don't know. They might not have any meaning, they might just be symbols that have been picked from a book – oh!' When had she said that before? It was quite recently, something about random images and then Stonehenge . . . that was it!

'The Circus. I was in the Circus with . . .' She checked herself.

'With a friend. Anyway, the meotopes there are about the same size as these. I wonder if . . .' She picked up a photograph of the symbol like a door knocker and traced it round with her finger. 'Do you think this could be a snake eating its tail?'

Mrs Davenport shook her head. 'I can't see well enough, my dear.'

Peggy, busy washing up, looked over her shoulder. 'That could be anything.'

'Will?'

He shrugged. 'I couldn't say.'

'What about this one then?' She passed round another photograph, then another, but although they studied them closely, no one could suggest a definite image.

'If they were the same as the symbols in the Circus, what would that mean?' Mrs Davenport said.

'It would imply that whoever designed this garden had access to certain books. Which would suggest a date, which is important. I couldn't assume that they had a further significance. There doesn't appear to be any meaning in the placing at the Circus, and this might be the same. But getting a date would be good.'

'I'll be off now,' Peggy said, collecting her coat from the peg on the back of the kitchen door. 'I'll try not to forget those old recipe books for your sister.'

'Thanks,' Anna said absent-mindedly, going back to the photographs.

In the morning Anna's ankle, despite the strain of the previous day, hardly ached at all. She announced at breakfast that she'd go home tomorrow, if it was okay to stay one more night.

'I hope you'll have time to look at them there books,' Peggy said. 'My Frankie gave me a lift up so I could bring them all. They're in the dining room. I didn't want them messing around on my kitchen table.'

Anna registered the rebuke. 'I'll take a look at them now,' she said, getting up and half walking, half hopping to the dining room.

Five cardboard boxes festooned with cobwebs stood on the table. Anna looked at them with dismay. She'd hoped Peggy was talking about one or two books, not boxes of them. She checked the first box and her heart lifted slightly. A Mrs Beeton, and quite an early edition too, but Clare could easily get a copy for herself if she wanted to. The next book was another guide to household management. That looked early twentieth-century, judging by the typeface. She picked it up to check and a scattering of photographs slid out and cascaded on to the table and the floor. She bent and collected them, then realised they were of the garden. They were not dissimilar to the ones Will had found in the attics, but as she rifled through she saw they were more varied. As well as groups of people posing, there were several pictures taken at twilight, the soft darkness lit by Chinese lanterns and thousands of little candles or night lights. In one, someone was rowing a boat across the lake towards the pavilion. Had they left from the landing stage at the bottom of the gateway? She couldn't tell, but guessed from the camera angle that the photograph must have been taken from the platform at the top. She flicked through the book, hoping for more photographs, but there were none.

She emptied the box, checking each book for more photographs and finding a handful, all of a hunt meet. She recognised the front of Templecombe Manor, although the magnolia grandiflora wasn't there. The maids handing round trays of drinks were in ankle-skimming black dresses, white frilly aprons and caps set low across their brows. Nineteen-twenties, she guessed.

She was halfway down the next box, caught up with reading an extraordinary recipe for making boar's-head jelly (*take your boar's head and bury it in the ground for two days . . .*), when Will came in.

'How are you doing? Found anything for your sister? A recipe for hemlock, perhaps?'

'She's not that bad.' She handed the photographs to him, amused at his assessment of Clare. 'I found these in that box.'

He shuffled through them. 'Didn't you say something about rowing across lakes having significance?'

'Did I? Oh, you mean rowing across the water to get to the afterlife.' Anna lifted her head from the book to glance at the photograph. 'I think he's just doing it for fun. Or he's fishing.' She went back to roasting the boar, then paused. 'Even if you've chosen the right path towards Heaven, you still have to cross the water to get there. And the steps are there leading down to the lake. So it does fit the Heaven and Hell theory.'

Will looked pleased. Anna wondered if he was waiting for her to ask him to help with searching through the books. She felt guilty at not asking when she owed him so much, but she didn't want to get too close to him. She loved Oliver, and he didn't like Will. Besides, the way Will blocked her questions about his past made her wary. She felt a twinge of regret. Will felt like a friend, a close friend, but friends shared, they told each other things. He appeared trustworthy, but she knew nothing about him. He could be anything, even a murderer. She put her head down as if reading again, but was very conscious of Will standing next to her. She heard him pick up a book and the crinkling sound as he turned the pages. She tried to concentrate. *Take the boar firmly* . . .

'Anna . . .'

'Yes?' She was surprised that her heart was pounding.

'As it's your last day, do you want to go out for that drink tonight?'

She was about to say yes, then stopped. No. She shouldn't. Except . . . She was saved from answering by the door creaking open and Mrs Davenport coming in.

Anna stood up briskly, as if she and Will had been caught out doing something they shouldn't. 'Oh, good morning,' she said, feeling absurdly guilty. 'I've found some photographs you might like to see.'

Will pulled out a chair for Mrs Davenport and she settled down in it. Anna handed her the photographs.

Mrs Davenport nodded. 'These take me back. That's my father, on a rather nice bay hunter, and that's my mother. Side-saddle was such an elegant way to ride, don't you think?' She looked at a group photograph, young men and women lounging on the pavilion steps. 'Now, where am I . . . yes, there I am, sitting at the top. I'm the only one left alive now.' She rolled her wedding ring around her finger as she gazed at the photograph, her eyes filled with tears.

'I'm sorry, I didn't mean to distress you.' Anna reached to take the photograph, but Mrs Davenport held it with a firm grip.

'Nothing for you to be sorry about,' she said crisply. She pointed at the photograph again. 'That's Quentin Davenport, standing at the bottom, who I was to marry. Oliver looks like him, don't you think?'

It was hard to tell, Anna thought. Both had dark hair and were tall, but beyond that . . . She stared at the photograph, trying to see Oliver's features in his grandfather's face.

'I think Oliver has a lot of his grandfather in him,' Mrs Davenport said, putting the photograph down and picking up the next one, which showed a view of the lake lit by lanterns. 'Now that's a lovely one. It was my family's tradition. On Midsummer's Eve we used to light up the garden with hundreds of lanterns, as many as we could find, and then row across the lake to the pavilion for a feast. It was magical. I'm afraid like so many things we stopped because of the war, and I never had the heart to start again.' Her voice trailed off, a faraway look in her eyes.

They went through the rest of the photographs, Anna asking questions about the garden and Mrs Davenport telling her what she could remember. She didn't think there were going to be any revelations, but the old lady was obviously enjoying herself, reliving the past, and it was better than looking through dusty books for bridal recipes for Clare. Will slipped out, she noticed, and she wondered why. She'd thought he was interested in the garden, in the research and Mrs Davenport's memories. Obviously not.

At lunch she discovered what Will had been doing. Both she and Mrs Davenport had envelopes on their plates. Mrs Davenport opened hers and looked at the card inside. 'Goodness,' she said, looking surprised.

Anna opened hers and read the handwritten card.

Your presence is required at a Not-Midsummer's Eve Feast to celebrate Anna's last night. Please assemble in the hall at 8.00 p.m.

Chapter 16

The grandfather clock in the hall struck eight at last. Anna could hear the soft chimes through the door of the drawing room, where she and Mrs Davenport had been waiting, banned from venturing out of the house since lunchtime.

Anna stood up. 'That's our cue.' She smiled at Mrs Davenport, ready to help her to her feet if necessary. But to her surprise, Mrs Davenport shook her head.

'I'm not coming.'

'But . . .'

'I find I prefer to remember the garden as it was.'

'Will's worked all afternoon. I'm sure you'd love it.'

Mrs Davenport smiled. 'I expect William has made it beautiful,' she said. 'But it's not for an old woman like me. It's for young people.' She patted Anna's hand. 'You go, my dear. You enjoy it for me.' Anna hesitated. 'Go on. Have a lovely evening. And Anna . . .' Mrs Davenport smiled. 'Make a wish on the evening star.'

'I will.' On impulse Anna bent and kissed her cheek, then went into the hall, closing the door behind her. Peggy was waiting.

'And madam?'

'She decided not to come.'

Peggy nodded, unsurprised. 'I thought she might not, in the end.'

She took Anna's arm and led her to the door. 'You're to go into the garden, and follow what you see.'

The setting sun streaked the grey sky with gold and pink and the front of the house was ablaze with light reflecting off the honey stone, but there was no sign of life. Where was Will? She started towards the balustrade, but something flickered in the corner of her eye at the entrance to the garden, so she walked towards that instead. Follow what you see. She saw a night light, flickering in a jam jar, and made her way down the path, slightly nervous because of her ankle. At least it hadn't rained recently. Shadows gathered softly in the corners of the garden, and honeysuckle and jasmine ran wild, while under the arching trees night lights twinkled all along the path. She needed their soft shimmer to see her way through the shade of the trees. At one point there was a moment of complete darkness when she felt a surge of panic. But there was another flickering light, this time in a pretty golden glass, and so she continued until she reached the division of the paths. Left to the pool and tunnel, or right to the gateway.

I'll choose the harder path, Anna thought, and go to Heaven. She smiled to herself as she climbed the steps up into the darkness. At the top there was a larger candle in a hurricane lamp. The air swirled with the scent of jasmine, which had been cleared away from the path. She looked across the lake towards the pavilion, feeling the closeness of the night, the air heavy. Lights lined the steps up to the doors, and the windows glowed.

Anna carried on up the stairs to the gateway and stopped in amaze-ment. The two basins were flaming, flickering against the stone walls. She peeped in, and saw they were filled with oil of some sort, with a bit of rope as a makeshift wick. Clever Will. She walked out to the platform, and then carefully down the stone steps to the lakeside, the scent of crushed thyme rising from under her feet. Two hurricane lamps blazed at the top of the steps, and a small dinghy was moored at the edge of the lake. She stopped, uncertain of what to do next.

'What do you think?'

Will's voice. Anna turned. She could just make him out in the shadows of a great willow tree arching down to the water, his shirt ghostly white in the half light.

'It's magical,' she said, suddenly shy.

He came forward, and after the slightest hesitation kissed her cheek. 'I'm glad you like it,' he said. 'I had Peggy digging in cupboards all morning to find enough jam jars. We're lucky it's exactly the right season. She's nearly finished all of last year's jam and preserves but hasn't yet started making the next batch.'

Anna laughed, to cover her disconcertion over his kiss. 'We'll have to make sure they all go back to her. I wouldn't want her to miss her preserving.'

'Where's Mrs D.? Isn't she with you?'

'She's not coming. She said it was for the young.'

He looked disappointed. 'I wanted her to see it like this.'

'I think . . .' Anna frowned. 'I think she felt she could see it in her memories, and didn't want to risk spoiling them.'

'Perhaps it's for the best.' He went to the edge of the lake. 'To be honest, I wasn't sure the boat was going to manage the three of us.'

'Mmm, it's not quite so romantic if we sink.' She was glad Will couldn't see the blush that spread across her face at mentioning the R word.

'I checked the boat earlier, and it's watertight at least, despite having been in the pavilion for goodness knows how many years. The question now is, is the water deep enough on this side? If not, you'll have to get out and push,' he added, throwing a wicked look up to Anna which she decided to ignore. He climbed in gingerly, then stood in the middle and rocked from side to side. 'Well, it's not stuck in the mud yet.'

Anna hesitated for a second. How embarrassing if the boat got stuck now. She knew she didn't weigh as much as Will, not by a long way, but she was a grown woman, not a featherlight child. Will held out his hand to her.

'Come on. We won't know if we don't try.'

Anna stepped into the boat, which rocked under her feet. 'I think we're okay,' she said, delighted she hadn't sunk the ship.

Will pushed off with one of the oars and the boat slid ten feet away from the side, then stopped. He dipped the oars, and pulled. Fountains of mud shot up.

'Will!'

'Not as deep as I hoped.' Will leant forward, a big grin on his face. 'We're all alone in the middle of a lake, and one of us is going to have to swim to shore.'

'You're not serious,' Anna said, hoping he was teasing but not a hundred per cent sure. After all, what did she know about him? Nothing.

He raised his eyebrows. 'You're in a dress, you could just take your shoes off and wade to the side, whereas I'd have to strip completely. Besides, I've already swum in this lake and it's bloody freezing.' He prodded her side. 'Time to walk the plank.'

'Certainly not,' Anna said, trying to concentrate on their situation rather than on Will sitting so close beside her. 'It's time for a bit of empirical research. We know the water's deeper further out, so it's just a question of where the deeper water starts and how we can get to it from here.' The boat, having travelled about fifteen feet from the edge, was stationary again. Anna looked at the lake side. Not far, but the water looked horribly sludgy and dark. Incredible that they'd swum in it.

Will turned to her, and the mood made one of those sudden shifts, as if the world had stopped breathing as his gaze caught hers. They were alone on the lake with the night lights flickering on the shore and night falling.

Anna dragged her eyes away from Will's. This wouldn't do at all. She stood, the boat rocking with her sudden movement, and grabbed an oar. 'Look, we can pole it across, like a punt.' She pushed the oar in. It went down quite far into the water and she could feel the resistance of the sludge at the bottom, but the boat moved a few feet. She did it again, then Will took the oar from her.

'You're supposed to be lying back, trailing a hand in the water,' he said. 'Imagine you're in Venice.'

Anna sat in the bow of the boat, her hands clasped around her knees, and watched Will pole the boat across the lake. The water didn't so much softly lap lap as noisily gloop gloop as he drew the oar in and out, but the boat moved forward steadily until they were in deeper water and he could sit and row. In the dusk the last of the swallows were out catching midges in extravagant swoops against the deepening blue-black sky. Lower down, where the sky shaded into the last hints of clear blue, a single star hung, shining bright.

'Star light, star bright, grant me this wish I make tonight,' Anna sang softly. I wish . . . I wish . . .

'What are you wishing for?' Will said, his face blurred in the dusk, but she shook her head and wouldn't answer him, just hugged her knees to her chest. She wasn't sure she knew herself.

As the boat neared the other side, she thought she could hear a faint sound.

'Will? What's that? Is it music?'

Will cleared his throat. 'When I left school, I went out to Kenya with a friend to work on a cattle ranch there. It wasn't the Kenya you imagine from seeing safaris on television; it was hard work in a dry and dusty land. After we'd been there about a month, we were invited to a party by Lake Naivasha. We drove up country through miles of scrub, then turned into a long drive sheltered by eucalyptus trees and with lawns on either side.'

It was the first time Will had said anything about his past, and Anna hugged it to herself. Will continued, sounding more confident. 'Music was floating down the drive, twenties music, like Noël Coward. We turned the corner, and there was this extraordinary art deco house, with men and women in evening dress drinking cocktails on the veranda. I've never forgotten it. The whole thing was so incongruous, like we'd time-warped into a parallel universe.'

Anna could now hear the music, light and precise, a stream of coloured notes skipping out from the pavilion. 'And had you?'

'No, the house had been built by an Italian count in the thirties and the family still lived in it. Labour's so cheap out there they could afford to run it.' He was silent, and Anna wondered if he was thinking about Templecombe, the way it was falling apart, or about his past. But this wasn't the moment to ask.

'It's perfect, Will,' she said, turning round to look at the pavilion as they came closer to the landing area. Candles in storm lanterns flickered on the two stanchions beside the steps. 'Absolutely beautiful.'

Although it was quite dark, Anna could sense him looking at her. Then he broke the spell. 'Can you grab the mooring line?'

She grabbed. Will took the line and got out, then held out his hand to her. Anna took it, feeling his rough skin envelop hers. Strong, warm, competent. He helped her out of the boat and they stood opposite each other in the warm darkness. They were at the foot of the steps up to the entrance, each step with its own pair of lanterns so the whole blazed like a river of fire, while the music softly interwove with the scent of plants and nectar in the air. Anna looked back across the inky lake. She could just make out the shimmer of lights at the landing stage.

Will sighed. 'Let's go in and eat, but first . . .' He went to the lakeside, pulled on a string and up came a mud-smeared bottle. 'Not exactly five-star service, I'm afraid, but I'm sure madam won't mind a little mud on the bottle if there's none in the glass.'

They walked up the steps to the pavilion, paces as perfectly matched as Fred Astaire and Ginger Rogers'. Anna felt she didn't need champagne to feel light-headed.

'Oh.' She stopped at the door, astounded by what she saw.

She'd seen it once before, after the accident, but her memory was hazy. She realised Will had brought down old carpets and rugs to lay on the floor and drape over the bits of broken furniture, giving a souk-like quality to the austere classical building, the reds and russets of the rugs glowing in the soft golden light of oil lamps. In the middle was a low table covered with a cloth, surrounded by cushions. She looked again, and realised the table was one of the trunks from the attic.

Anna stood by the door, looking out, a glass in one hand. From the interior, the lake looked black, lit only by the twinkling night lights, like the reflections of a thousand stars. She thought of the hundreds of men who must have laboured to create the garden, digging out the lake, heaving stone and rock and barrow upon barrow of gravel and sand to lay the paths, building the pavilion. Then tending the garden, training the willows so they hung in graceful arcs over the edge of the lake, planting the jasmine and roses that had gone wild, snaking up into the tallest of the trees.

She wondered what Will was thinking as he stared out at the lake and garden. Did he see it as she did, mysterious, beautiful, infinitely fascinating, or was it no more than somewhere to work, to be cleared and tended in a ceaseless round of maintenance? His face gave no clue beyond a nerve that twitched in his jaw.

'It's beautiful,' she whispered. 'Thank you.'

'Yeah, well. Think nothing of it,' Will said, looking embarrassed and pleased at the same time. 'Peggy did the feast part, of course. She said I'd give you food poisoning. Let's eat.'

He sat down on one of the cushions and checked the table, putting serving spoons in the dishes, making sure Anna had cutlery. His face was serious, intent on getting it right, doing justice to Peggy's feast. What a kind man he is, Anna thought, smiling as he handed her the dishes: chicken in a creamy sauce with almonds sprinkled on top, sliced tomatoes and a green salad. 'Help yourself.

I've forgotten the potatoes.' He went off to the back room. Anna settled herself more comfortably on a cushion and started to spoon chicken on to her plate.

Will returned and they ate, talking about the garden, the photographs, Anna's house in Bath. Anna felt slightly self-conscious, just the two of them, alone in the pavilion. Perhaps it wouldn't have been so bad if they had been sitting at a table, but here they were, lolling on cushions like a pasha and his favourite houri from the harem. What would Oliver think if he knew? She bit her lip, knowing that Oliver would be furious. Still, no need for him ever to find out. And it wasn't as if there was anything going on. As they talked, Will again side-stepped questions about himself, giving no clues to his past before Templecombe. On her second glass of wine Anna felt bolder.

'Will, can I ask you something?'

He looked nervous. 'You can ask, but I might not answer.'

'What did you mean when you said that there are some things it's best not to know?'

Will's face closed. 'Nothing.'

'So why won't you tell me?' He shrugged, and Anna could have hit him with frustration. 'What were you doing before you came here?'

'This and that.'

Anna dropped her head. He obviously wasn't going to tell her. It had to be something dreadful. Unless he was one of those irritating people who like to be mysterious to make themselves more interesting, when in fact there's nothing very mysterious to discover after all. It suddenly occurred to her that he might have been in prison. Yes, that would explain why he was so tight-lipped about his past. She was sure he must have told Peggy and Mrs Davenport, and therefore it couldn't be a dreadful crime like murder, but maybe something like fraud. She wouldn't embarrass him by asking again.

'Can I ask *you* a question?' Will said.

She smiled as she replied, 'You can, but I might not answer.'

'Why historic gardens?'

'I don't know,' she said, leaning back on the cushions. 'I think partly it's the scale, seeing the breadth and ambition of the landscape designer. An artist works with pigments and brushes, but here . . . the designer's working with trees and hills and creating something that, while it's artificial, is also natural. It's always changing, and you can walk through the landscape and get different perspectives, see the same things from different angles, and see them differently as a result. The scale of it is so incredible.' She told Will about the ruthlessness with which designers in the past had swept away villages that were in the 'wrong' place, so their landscape vision could remain pure and unpopulated except by the occasional aristocrat playing nymphs and shepherds.

'Bit tough on the villagers,' Will said.

'Yes, but they created model villages instead,' she said. 'Usually far better than they'd had before.'

Will looked doubtful. He was leaning on one elbow, eating with just a fork balanced casually between his fingers. Fingernails short and practical with clear white half-moons, the skin roughened through work. With her eyes Anna traced a blue vein on the inside of his wrist, running across the tendons. She felt an impulse to lean forward and lick the line of the vein, taste the salt of his skin. What? Where did that come from? She sat up straight. The trouble was, gardens at dusk were too romantic, especially when candlelit.

'D'you know, when they dredged the top pond at Heligan they brought out over three hundred tons of detritus and eels.' Eels! What would she say next?

'Eels are remarkable creatures,' Will said. '*Anguilla anguilla.*'

'Sorry?'

'It's what they're called. *Anguilla anguilla.*' His voice was dreamy. 'The European eel. It mates only in the Sargasso Sea. Then the elvers take three years to swim across the Atlantic. Some people call

SARAH DUNCAN

them glass eels, because they're transparent. Country folk used to believe if you tucked a horsehair under a rock in a stream, the next day it would have become an eel. They're as fine as your hair.' He sat up, and for a second Anna thought he was going to touch her hair, but he didn't, just settled himself more comfortably on the cushions before continuing. 'Then, when they reach maturity – which can be anywhere between twelve and thirty years – in the last week in October they leave, and swim all the way back across the Atlantic, to mate and die under the light of a full moon.'

Anna blinked. 'Is that true?'

'Yup. You're not the only one who knows things.' He looked at her sideways. 'Aristotle believed they spontaneously generated out of mud.'

'About the full moon.'

'Current research says so.' He lay back against the cushions, hands behind his head, legs stretched out. 'It's a beautiful night.'

Anna didn't know what to make of Will's eel talk. Was he sending her up? 'Pity there isn't a full moon tonight,' she said, more to fill the silence.

'All the better for seeing the stars.' Night had fallen, the darkness deepening. The music had finished.

'It's a shame it's not Midsummer's Eve,' she said to fill the silence, and she knew her voice was trembling. 'Otherwise we could stay up and see in the dawn.'

'The sun probably rises over the top of the pavilion.'

Anna could tell from his tone that he was teasing her, but she said seriously, 'It probably does.' She shivered.

'Are you cold? You could borrow a sweater . . .'

'No thanks. I think I ought to go back.'

'Not tempted to stay and see the dawn?'

Their eyes locked. For a mad moment she was tempted. Then reality asserted itself. She stood, breaking the contact, suddenly needing to get back to the house, away from the garden, away from Will. ' Well . . .'

'Well . . .' He stood too.

A pause. She was used to awkward pauses. 'I ought to be going.'

'I'll come with you.'

'I'll be okay.'

'Sure?'

She nodded. 'Sure.'

'You'd better have a torch. I expect most of the lights will have gone out.' She waited while he found one.

'Thank you for a lovely evening.'

They walked outside. Although there was no moon, just a thin crescent of light, the stars sprinkled the night sky, turning the garden into a tapestry of black and silver.

'Starlight to walk home by,' she said, turning to Will. She reached up and . . .

She only meant to kiss him on the cheek. That was all. She turned to him, and put her hand on his shoulder to steady herself as she stretched up to touch his cheek with her lips. That was all she meant to do, a simple kiss, a way of saying thank you, the garden's beautiful. But somehow she turned her head and missed his cheek, caught his mouth and kissed him, and without thinking the hand that was meant to lightly touch his shoulder, just to steady herself, clasped him like it might never let him go. And her mouth, which had only meant to be a whisper against his cheek, became demanding of something, Anna didn't know what, only that it asked.

And he answered.

Anna became lost in their kiss, absorbed utterly in what was happening. The past, Oliver, the garden, none of it existed, nothing mattered except that she was here with Will. She slid her hand around his neck, pulling him to her, feeling his arm go round her back, drawing her to him. Bodies pressed together, wanting, yearning, everything forgotten except the way his hair felt between her fingers, the texture of his skin, his jawbone hard against hers, his scent mingling with the perfumed air outside. Her skin tingled all over and she pressed herself harder against him, wanting to absorb him into her, or be absorbed by him, she didn't know which and it didn't matter, and then—

She broke away from him, her eyes wide. This wasn't what she was supposed to be doing. This was Will. She wasn't supposed to be kissing Will.

'Anna?'

'I'm sorry,' she said, pushing past him and running back towards the house, back towards safety.

Chapter 17

Anna woke feeling suffused with a golden glow, and watched through blurry eyes the light filter through the curtains and dance on the walls. It must be early, she thought hazily, content to lie and watch the dawn. The echo of it made her sit up. Watch the dawn. Oh no. She remembered kissing Will, the mad dash back to the safety of the house. How could she have done something so stupid?

She rolled over on to her front, thinking of Will. He'd saved her life, of course she felt something for him, and he'd been so kind and generous. But she was seeing Oliver, she was in love with Oliver. How stupid could she get? She was tempted to sneak out of the house right now, anything to avoid having to speak to him. He'd still be asleep. Her ankle was healed, although it ached a little. Perhaps the mad dash back up the garden in the darkness had strained it again. She buried her face in the pillow. Stupid, stupid, stupid.

In a few hours' time she was going home, and that would be that. There were no more reasons for visiting, as the tunnel area was too dangerous to explore without the proper gear. Simpler – and cheaper – to simply prevent access and wait until the whole garden was being restored. If it ever did get restored. She sighed. It all came down to money in the end.

She rounded up her things and went to the bathroom. She

stripped and washed, shivering in the cold morning air not yet warmed by the sun. Five days of immobility and Peggy's cooking had plumped her up; her arms and belly had a pleasing roundness. She stretched a hand on her tummy. What if a baby was in there? Would she be pleased? Or frightened? Bit of both? She let her hand drop and carried on washing. It was academic; she knew she wasn't pregnant. But would you like to be? nagged the question inside her head, and her internal reply was not the resounding no it had always been before.

She dressed quickly and slipped down the stairs, her bare feet soft on the ancient wooden boards, and into the garden. Pale sky stretched overhead, blush-rose streaks against silver grey. Birds sang, joyful piping voices and the deep cooing of wood pigeons; honeysuckle scent wove through the air, twined with the heady aroma of roses. Anna's bare feet scrunched on the gravel drive, the sharp points digging into the soles of her feet. There seemed to be an echo of the sound, and she turned round to look behind her. Nothing, except a solitary blackbird perched on the edge of the balustrade. As if affronted by her interest, he flew off across the valley towards the farm buildings down below.

Anna walked down the path, the ground cool and damp under her toes. My last day here, she thought. Halfway down, another noise made her turn, thinking perhaps Will was there but all she saw was cow parsley, sparkling with dew in the morning sunshine that filtered through the ash leaves. The thought of him walked with her as she walked towards the lakes.

She reached the division in the path and chose the way to Hell. In the shelter of the bank the pond was dark, more unforgiving than before. The rank smell of rotting vegetation filled her nostrils, making her feel sick with apprehension. The shrubs lurked like nameless black beasts at the edge of the inky water, monsters coming to feed. Was one of them moving? She fled back up the path and climbed towards the gateway.

Here the air was lighter, the scents less oppressive. The first rays of sunlight teased silvered ripples in the lake's surface, where a moorhen shepherded her brood to the safety of the reeds, more like balls of black thistledown than cheeping hatchlings. Dragonflies darted, catching the midges that rose in soft clouds. The pavilion was mirrored in the water, shimmering, a heathen temple in a perfect land.

In the pavilion Will was sleeping.

Anna stood, watching for signs of life, but there were none. The sun was up, the sky brightening into a clear blue. It was going to be a perfect day. She tensed, alive with the sudden impulse to run down to the pavilion, fling open the doors and greet Will with the morning. She rubbed her eyes, her face. She shouldn't have kissed him. Such a stupid thing to do. At least she'd had the sense to run. It was only a kiss, one starlit kiss. It was embarrassing, but she was leaving today. Her work at Templecombe was done, and she would never see Will again. The garden stirred in the dawn breeze, mist rising off the lake.

She waited, uncertain of what she was waiting for. Then she turned and went back towards the house. At the point where the paths split, she paused. From here she could just make out the flash of grey light that was the lake beyond the trees. One path leads to Heaven, she thought, and one to Hell. But either way, her path did not include Will.

She came into the kitchen through the back door. Peggy was there, bustling about.

'Good morning, Anna, you're up early.' Her eyes went to Anna's bare feet. 'How's the ankle?'

'Fixed, I think.' She flexed her foot. It was a little stiff and sore, but nothing more.

'Don't you overdo it. Now, what can I get you on this lovely morning?'

'Just coffee, please.' Anna sat at the kitchen table. 'Thank you for preparing the food last night; it was delicious.'

Peggy looked across at her. 'I 'm glad you enjoyed it. Did Will manage okay?'

'Oh, yes.' Anna pretended to rummage in her bag to avoid meeting Peggy's eyes. 'It was beautiful.'

'I thought you'd slip and do yourself more damage on the way down with just those little lights, but Will was determined. Used all my jam jars, he did.' Peggy put a cup in front of Anna. 'And he got that old record player going?'

Anna nodded. 'That was lovely, hearing the music across the lake . . . It was magical, it really was. It couldn't have been better.' And it couldn't. She swallowed. What was she thinking, better than Oliver? I love Oliver, she thought.

'Ah, he's a good boy, that one. It's done the house good having him around, well, the two of you. It needs to have young people here again. Of course, it really should be lived in by a family. Perhaps young Oliver will bring his children up here.' Peggy sniffed. Anna hoped she had a noncommittal expression on her face. 'Not that he shows any signs of settling down, far too busy up in London.' Peggy's face broke into a wide smile as Will entered from outside. 'There you are, Will. What can I get you? Bacon and eggs?'

'That'd be great.' Will pulled out a chair and sat down opposite Anna as Peggy bustled to the kitchen range. He looked fresh and relaxed, his face glowing with health against his white shirt, his eyes warm as he looked across at Anna.

'I hear you gave Anna a good send-off last night,' Peggy said over her shoulder as she pushed bacon round a frying pan.

Anna's face felt as if it was burning up as she remembered. Clare would brave it out, she thought, or laugh it off. Hey, it was only a kiss, she'd say. Anna hunched into her chair. She wasn't like Clare.

Will raised his eyebrows. 'I hope that means you enjoyed it,' he said.

'Of course,' Anna said, trying to remain neutral despite her brain playing images of them together, locked in a starlight kiss. 'The garden's magical at night.' Their eyes met and she knew he was thinking what she was thinking.

'Now, Will, I want all those jars back, or there won't be any jam this year,' Peggy said, cracking eggs into the pan.

'Sure,' Will said, not taking his eyes from Anna. 'I'll round them up this morning.'

Anna didn't know what to say. She sat in silence, listening to Peggy gently humming as the bacon sizzled, and concentrated on the raised grain of the table as if it held the secrets of the universe. Anything not to make eye contact with Will.

'I love Bath for shopping, you've ever so lucky to live there,' Peggy said, putting a plate in front of Will. 'That's where I do my Christmas shopping. The WI take a coach down every year. Lovely, it is.'

'It gets crowded, though,' Anna said absent-mindedly. She was watching Will eating bacon and eggs. His shirtsleeves were rolled up and the skin on his arms was tanned and honey smooth, the hairs bleached white gold.

'Want some?' he said, holding up his fork.

'No thanks,' Anna said, embarrassed to have been caught watching. She drained her coffee.

'It's a shame you're going,' Peggy said. 'We've got quite used to having you around, haven't we, Will?'

'I expect Dr Carmichael has plenty to keep her busy.' Will gave her a questioning look which Anna didn't acknowledge. She wished she'd told them about Oliver before, then last night wouldn't have happened.

'Yes, I'm very behind with my work. I think this is the longest time off I've taken since I went freelance.' She gave a nervous laugh and stood up. 'I must go and pack my things.'

'Before you go, how did you get on with those recipe books? Find something nice for your sister?'

'I did take down a couple of recipes,' Anna said, desperate to escape from Will's presence, 'but I didn't quite manage to finish going through them.'

Peggy's face dropped. 'Oh dear, and I did say I'd find those bridal recipes for her. She'll be ever so disappointed.'

Anna didn't think it likely that Clare had remembered, but she could see it was important to Peggy. 'I'll finish them this morning.'

'That's all right then,' Peggy said, settling down at the head of the table like a comfortable tabby cat, and checking the clock. 'Fifteen minutes to go before I take madam's tray up. Oh, Will, before I forget, can you have a look at the washing machine? It seems to have gone on the blink and today's a perfect day for drying.'

'Sure,' Will said, rubbing the bridge of his nose.

'Lovely. I think there's time for just another cup.' Peggy reached for the teapot. 'More for you, Will?'

He shook his head, and Anna realised he was intending to follow her. The thought of having to face him, talk to him, galvanised her. 'Oh no, you stay here – there's no need to disturb yourself because of me.' Will looked puzzled now, and Anna's heart sank. Only cowards ran away.

'If you give me a shout, I'll bring your bag down when you're ready,' Will said.

Anna gave him a quick smile, not meeting his eyes, and escaped to her room. She slung all her possessions into the bag Clare had brought, socks, shirts, toothbrush, all higgledy-piggledy. Better a coward than face Will. She had to go. Checking the coast was clear, she crept down the stairs and tucked her bag into an inconspicuous place under the hall table, then gently pushed open the door to the dining room and closed it equally silently. Right. Only one box left.

She went through it quickly, not letting herself be distracted by stray thoughts of Will. Like the other boxes, most of the books were twentieth-century, and a few photographs, bookmarks and once a dried wild flower fluttered out, but nothing of any note. Quick. Finish before Will comes. She didn't want to talk about the kiss, the magical evening. She wanted to pretend it had never happened. Three-quarters of the way down the box she came across something more interesting, a brass-bound book of handwritten receipts. This was more like it. She sat, and turned the pages carefully as not all of them were bound into the cover. Yes, this was the book with the bridal recipes. She took out a pen and started to jot down those she thought might appeal to Clare – tinctures for shiny hair and bright eyes and a potion to keep a man faithful. Some were in the form of letters from a well-informed Aunt Tibbie, writing in the early 1820s, about various cures for childhood ailments, most of which featured goose fat and red flannel.

Will came in while she was working. He shut the door behind him and leaned against it. 'Are you avoiding me?'

There was no way out. Anna swallowed. Better get this over and done with. 'I'm really sorry about last night,' she said quickly. 'I shouldn't have kissed you.'

'Why not?' Will said.

'Because . . .' She couldn't tell him about Oliver. And besides, it wasn't all about Oliver. She sighed, and pretended to concentrate on the book. I don't know anything about you, she wanted to say. You won't tell me anything. But it was too hard to put it into words, especially when he was looking at her in that way. 'I just shouldn't have, that's all.' She looked up, head tilted. 'Hey, it was only a kiss,' she said in fair imitation of Clare. 'No big deal.'

'I see.' Will picked up one of the books and started to look through it, his expression hurt and upset.

Anna went back to her book, acutely aware of Will's presence. She wanted to hug him, say, sorry sorry sorry, I didn't mean it. But I did, she thought. I love Oliver. Will doesn't enter the equation. She willed herself not to look at him. Instead she turned the page, and found an envelope addressed in a slanting hand. Distracted, she took out the letter inside, scanned it, paused, then read it again. The writing was clear, though faded.

> *The Rectory, Templecombe*
> *15th May 1745*
>
> *Sir,*
>
>   *I must beg you not to address me further. My father has made his wishes clear to you.*
>
>   *Yr humble servant*
>   *Jessica Martin*

Anna looked at the envelope again. It was addressed to Arthur Farrell, Esquire, The Manor, Templecombe in thin copperplate writing, the black ink faded to sepia. At the fold red stains showed that it had once been sealed with wax, but this had long since crumbled away.

'What is it?' asked Will.

'I don't know,' Anna said, turning the pages of the book to see if there was another one. Six pages on there it was, sandwiched between a recipe for hair tonic and advice on insomnia. This one was simply addressed to A. Farrell. She opened it carefully, making sure not to tear the paper.

> *24th May 1745*
>
> *Sir,*
>
>   *You say you require but a simple 'no' and I will hear from you no more. Such a small word, but one I find it not in my power to utter, yet I know full well that my duty as a daughter demands such an answer from me. When you spoke of your garden, it set up such a desire in my heart to visit this place of beauty that I cannot bring myself to say the word I know should be spoken. But can I instead utter another little word and brave my father's wrath? I can. I do so and whisper 'yes'.*

Yr humble servant
Jessica Martin

'Anna?'

Her heart pounding, she searched through the pages. There had to be more. There were.

Sir

I obey an emotion of my heart, which made me think of wishing thee, my love, good night! So before I go to rest, with more tenderness than I can tomorrow, when writing a hasty line or two under Papa's eye, I wish thee a good night. O, I no sooner close my eyes than some invisible being bears me to you, my dearest friend. I long to be with you, and wish I could be with you in the Temple. O to be like the goddess Anahita and live there with you always. But I am but flesh and blood, not cold marble, and it tortures me to think of you and not be there.

If you please, you may write to Papa, but I fear it will do no good. Papa is averse to everything but I do assure you, your future shall be mine, and everything you shall do or say, I shall not question. I care not for Papa nor what they do say about you. I long for the day when I can explore your garden and visit the new house but for the present, goodbye, good night.

Yr humble servant
Jessica Martin

'Oh my God!' Anna pressed her hands to her face, feeling as if she was about to burst into tears.

'What is it?' Will said, sounding utterly bemused.

'This is it. This is what I've been looking for.' She handed him the letters.

'I can't make this out, it's impossible to read,' Will said, his forehead creased.

'Not impossible. You need to be used to it.' She picked the letters up and read them out to him, stumbling over the words in her haste. 'Do you see? That has to mean this house, it couldn't be anything else. The dates, the garden, the temple, everything. I can't tell you how this feels, it's just . . .' She wanted to sing and dance and skip about the room. 'Isn't it exciting?' She began searching for another letter.

'I thought last night was exciting . . .'

She came back to the present. 'Will. Don't.'

He slumped into one of the chairs. 'I'm sorry,' he said. 'I thought . . .'

Anna gripped the edge of the table. 'Please. It's not possible. I can't . . .' She couldn't look at him. The best moment of her life, and she felt like crying.

He took a deep breath. 'Tell me again about these letters.'

She read them out to him once more, feeling confused. She was grateful to him for letting her off the hook, so why did she want him to argue with her, to insist they talk about last night. She glanced up at him as he studied one of the letters. Last night . . .

'I don't think we should read them. They're private,' Will said, putting the letter down, his voice subdued.

'They're two hundred and fifty years old, it's in the past,' Anna said.

'They're still private,' Will said doggedly. 'We should respect that.'

Like she should respect his refusal to talk about his past? Anna pressed her lips together. 'I'm going to carry on,' she said, her chin in the air.

Sir,

Last night when we met, every nerve seemed to vibrate to the touch, and I began to think that there was something in the assertion of man and wife being one — for you seemed to pervade my whole frame, quickening the beat of my heart. And when I left this morning it was the separation of my humble frame, my heart being left behind with you, my love.

You asked me a question and I could not answer. But now that I sit down to answer you in the loveliness and depth of that love which unites us & which cannot be felt but by ourselves, I shall not fear, but shall come to the Temple as we arranged. I will be yours.

Yr devoted servant

Jess

Last night when we met . . . Anna glanced up at Will. Last night they too had been in the temple, had been . . . She could feel herself trembling, the letter gently fluttering in her hand. *For you seemed to pervade my whole frame, quickening the beat of my heart.* She could feel her own heart beating faster. Will was right; the letters were too personal, too close. She wondered what Jessica had looked like, how old she had been. She had obviously been young, perhaps too young for her parents to have considered her marrying. And yet she had been so sure of her love that she had been willing to go with Arthur to the temple. *And when I left this morning it was the separation of my humble frame, my heart being left behind with you, my love.* I'm leaving too. I'm going this morning, Anna thought. She stole a glance at Will. I don't know what I want any more. She slowly leafed through the pages of the old book looking for more letters, this time going right to the end. There was one more.

Sir,

I write in haste. Papa is adamant and I see that there is no choice but to take the course you proposed last night. But I tremble for what we are doing. Are you sure you will love me for ever? Shall we never repent? I fear, and I hope. This will be my last letter to you. What a thought! How terrible and yet full of bliss. You will love me for ever, will you not, my own husband, and I will always be your true and affectionate Jess. The week to come must be given to allaying suspicion and to preparation; and then Dearest, God willing I am your own for ever and ever.

Yr loving wife
Jess Farrell

'An elopement.' Will sighed. 'I suppose it was inevitable.'

'I so hope they married and lived happily ever after,' Anna said, with an intensity that startled her.

'They probably had umpteen children and became highly respectable.' Will's voice was quiet and reassuring.

'I hope you're right,' she said. 'There's a simple way to find out.'

Anna walked over the back lawn past the cedar tree towards the wrought-iron gate in the wall, as Will had instructed – Peggy had needed his help urgently as the washing machine was overflowing. The yew trees clustered together by the back wall, red bark peeling off in feathered strips, the dark shadows underneath the dense, low boughs cool and inviting. She turned at the gate to look back at the house and felt caught in time, as if once some other girl had hastened towards the village and then turned, hand still on the gate as if to establish she was going, but stealing one last, longing look at the house. A breeze rustled the leaves and they murmured above her head, soft whispers like gentle laughter. Anna held her breath, unwilling to break the spell, and then it was gone, as if that other girl had turned and slipped down the narrow path by the edge of the churchyard.

Anna undid the latch, thinking of the people who must have gone through the gate in the past, to and from the traditional triangle of big house, church and village. Not just the family in the house on their ceremonial Sunday visit, but the daily journeys of maids and stable boys, footmen and gardeners. Days off and outings and visits home. The path curved away from the house, towards the village, and opposite was a kissing gate to prevent sheep and other animals getting into the churchyard.

She crossed the path to the kissing gate and pushed through it with a squeak of rusting hinges. On this side the grass had been allowed to grow long, interlaced with sweet woodruff and white nettle. She dawdled, not wanting to go inside the church, yet certain that that was where she would find Jess. Gravestones leaned at drunken angles as if the occupants of the graves beneath had turned over and disrupted the earth. She knelt and tried to trace the name on one, fingers able to discern lines, a curve that might have been a D, but it was impossible to read, drowned in ochre, silver and green-grey lichen. She straightened and wandered on, reading names where she could: George, Alfred, Hepzibah. Beloved wife, cherished husband, gone but not forgotten. Tew, Pedway, Hughes. Perhaps Peggy's ancestors, though Hughes was a common enough name.

Nearer the church the stones were straighter, as if the dead lay more still there. Hard marble and granite overtook the soft native limestone. Lines remained sharp, names clear; modern graves, defined by granite chippings.

The church interior looked exactly as she'd expected. Dark oak pews ran like ribs off the central aisle. An elaborate flower arrange-ment stood by the pulpit on the left, and another next to the brass eagle with outstretched wings to the right. There was a table by the entrance with copies of the parish magazine, slim booklets on church and village history, an offertory box and visitors' book. Anna selected several of the booklets and dropped the appropriate coins into the box, hearing them rattle emptily around, then walked up the nave.

Near the altar were several large monuments. One was set into the wall, and resembled a four-poster bed with a woman lying on it. She was young, unless the sculptor had flattered her, and her head was turned slightly to one side as if she were sleeping and not cold marble. Her arms were folded to her chest, a posy of flowers clasped in her fingers. There appeared to be some sort of bundle tucked into the crook of her arm. Anna looked closer, then stepped back with a sigh.

The half-hidden bundle was a swaddled baby, very small, the face tiny and secret under the folds of material. Anna remembered what Bronwen had said about newborn babies, how they liked to be wrapped up tightly. It was commonplace for women to die in childbirth in those days, of course.

She bent towards the tomb, looking for the name. There it was. Jessica Farrell, beloved wife of Arthur Farrell, Esquire, of Templecombe Manor. Anna touched the effigy's cold fingers. Jessica had lived at Templecombe, had her baby there, and then died. Tragic, and yet an ordinary occurrence for a time when marriage meant childbirth within a year, and childbirth could easily be a death warrant. Poor Jess. Had she been pleased to be pregnant? Had she really been a beloved wife? Her husband had provided her with an impressive monument, but that might be simply an expression of his wealth. It didn't necessarily mean anything.

Don't be emotional about this, she thought as she walked back down the central aisle towards the entrance. It's work. At the table she paused and flicked through the visitors' book, looking at the comments and addresses. Most people had written anodyne remarks: lovely atmosphere, very nice. Anna turned to the last page, ready to add her own name and remark, then stopped. The last name to be entered sprawled across the page taking up three lines. Will Sutton. Just that, no address, no date, no comment.

Anna felt that summed up what she knew about him. No history, no location. Nothing. He's kind and funny and good company, but I know nothing else about him. She studied the signature. The firmness of the long stroke across the double t of Sutton told of someone who was very certain of himself; the heaviness of the ink showed decisiveness. She hesitated. There was a biro attached to the book with a piece of string, but Will obviously hadn't used it. Nor would she. She searched in her bag for her pen. Underneath Will's name she wrote her own in the allotted space. Anna Carmichael, Bath. She compared the two names, and was dissatisfied with her own: too thin and spiky in comparison, like architect's writing, a combination of using drawing pens to write with and the need for precision and legibility on plans. Now it seemed limited to have confined herself to within the printed lines. She wished her name had swaggered across several lines, as Will's had done. But there, she'd done it now, and at least it was legible.

'Any luck?' Will said, coming into the church.

'The monument by the altar.' She indicated it with a nod of her head, then sat in one of the pews. Will found the monument and knelt to read the inscription. Then he stood, and touched the cold marble statue. Anna watched him, and their eyes met. She knew what he was thinking: poor little Jess, so full of hope and expectation.

He walked slowly back to where she was sitting.

'Died in childbirth, poor thing, and the baby too. She was only nineteen.'

The girl of the letters had been so vital, so eager. Dust to dust, ashes to ashes. Anna looked up into the vaulted ceiling. The heavy roof beams were dark and oppressive. Of course Jess was dead. She could hardly be alive today, so what difference did it make if she died at nineteen rather than ninety?

Will sat next to her. 'Is your ankle hurting?'

'It's throbbing a bit. I wish she hadn't died so young.'

'Me too.' Will put his arm around her, and squeezed her shoulder. For a second she thought he was going to kiss her, but then why would he? She'd made it quite clear she wasn't interested.

Anna's head throbbed as much as her ankle. She'd so hoped Jess had lived happily ever after, but instead she'd died. Death for some, divorce for others; it all came to nothing in the end. She hadn't felt this bad since Richard had told her he was going. Will's arm was comforting and she wanted nothing more than to relax into it, make contact with another living human being. But Will was the one person in the world she couldn't relax with.

She stood up. 'The first letter was addressed from the rectory here, so we ought to look at the list of incumbents.'

The list was on the back wall, near the door and the visitors' book. In gold paint on a black background was written that R. Martin DD had been rector of the parish from 1744 to 1787.

'So Jessica was new to Templecombe,' Will said from behind her.

'Assuming she's his daughter.' Assumptions. Never make assumptions. She left the church and walked into the sunshine. She didn't want to go back to the house just yet, but nor did she want to stay in the graveyard. 'Let's look at the war memorial.'

There were more Hugheses on the war memorial just outside the wall of the churchyard, on a semicircle of green lawn surrounded by looped white chains. Anna walked round the monument, noting the names. Some she recognised from the churchyard. More Pedways, some Martins, five Tews. She hoped they hadn't been brothers.

'I expect many of these men worked at Templecombe,' she said, vividly aware of Will next to her. Her hand accidentally brushed against his.

Will looked up. 'How do you know?'

'The big house would have been the major employer in a rural area like this. Ducal houses could easily have over a hundred permanent staff.' She stared up at the cross on the top of the memorial. Facts were her salvation. 'When Capability Brown was redesigning the garden at Blenheim, they employed two hundred extra labourers, more than the largest contemporary factory, more than any other employer apart from the army.'

She put her hand on the memorial, thinking back to all those young men who had died in the trenches; undergardeners and stable boys who didn't return to the land. And the sons of the house, the future squires, they went too, leaving the estates to dwindle, allowing nature to reclaim the man-made landscape.

Her attention was caught by a butterfly fluttering over a buddleia growing in the drystone wall. She watched it meandering among the flower heads, moving from one raceme to another, apparently at random, coming closer and closer, and then it landed on her palm.

Anna kept still, hardly breathing, concentrating on the delicate beauty of the wings, the legs so light she could hardly feel them against her skin.

'Look,' she said, holding her hand out to Will.

'It's a Painted Lady.' He bent his head to examine the butterfly, touching her hand. 'They're surprisingly rare now. When I was a kid they were all over the place.'

The breeze dropped, and she could feel the sun on her face, Will's presence next to her, his hand lightly touching hers. 'Why won't you tell me anything about the past?' she whispered.

'Because I don't want to remember,' Will said, his eyes clouded. 'I – oh, there she goes.' The butterfly fluttered off, dancing to the next bush in the sunlight, the spell broken. He dropped her hand. 'Let's go back to the house.'

They walked across the churchyard, back to the kissing gate that led to the house. Will went through, then turned.

'I've always wondered why they're called kissing gates,' he said.

'I'm not sure what the origin is,' she started to say, but Will leaned forward over the gate, held her face in his hands and kissed her mouth. Before she could shut her eyes, he pulled away.

'And I'm not sorry at all,' he said, his eyes twinkling.

They walked towards the house, Will humming and Anna thinking about the etymology of kissing gates. Anything was preferable to thinking about the way he'd just kissed her, or the way she'd kissed him the night before. She touched her mouth, her emotions confused. I have to be rational, she told herself, trying to control the jumble of thoughts swirling round her brain. Rational. I am here to research the garden, not kiss the gardener. This is my fault. I shouldn't have stepped over the line last night. Will probably thinks . . . but she didn't know what Will thought. He never told her anything. Except about eels. *Anguilla anguilla.* She smiled to herself, remembering, as they went into the house through the back door. The kitchen was empty.

'Did you tell Peggy and Mrs Davenport about the letters?' Anna asked Will, pushing open the door into the hall. Then she stopped abruptly.

A man was standing in the hall, and as she came in, he turned and smiled.

Oliver.

Chapter 18

A nna felt the same lurch in her stomach as when the tunnel had collapsed under her feet, the same dreadful jolt. Oliver. All the cogs in her brain seemed to be rearranging themselves, while she struggled to keep up, make the right connections.

'What are you doing here?' she stammered.

'I came as soon as I heard,' he said, striding to meet her. 'Darling.' He held her face in his hands and kissed her. His mouth was on hers, where Will's had been just five minutes before, his fresh scent, cool and sharp as lemons, filling her senses.

'I expect they're in the drawing room,' Will was saying, coming into the hall behind her. 'Let's go and—'

The quality of his silence was louder than anything he could have said.

Oliver released her, and Anna slowly turned to look at Will.

'My grandmother tells me you're the hero of the hour,' Oliver said, his tone not entirely friendly. He pulled Anna to him with both arms around her and kissed the top of her head. 'Though what you thought you were doing, honey, beggars belief. Anyway, I've obviously got a lot to thank you for.'

What to say? How to explain? Will looked utterly shocked, his head thrown back and his jaw set tightly. Anna felt sick. She should have told him.

Will turned abruptly and disappeared back into the kitchen.

'God, that man's got all the charm of a cabbage. Poor you, stuck with him and the old biddies – for how long was it?' Oliver turned her around to face him. 'I tried to phone, text. Nothing. I finally got hold of Clare, who told me what had happened. What did you think you were doing? You're lucky it wasn't worse.'

'I know . . . Will saved me.' She felt numb.

'So he has some use.' Oliver hugged her. 'Mmm, I missed you. You'd love Prague, right up your street, lots of old buildings, although the food's not great.'

Anna put her hand to her head, trying to shift gear. Oliver was here. Oliver.

He held her chin and examined her face. 'You're not still grumpy about the weekend, are you?'

Anna tried to think. The weekend seemed years ago, so much had happened since then. Was it really just over a week? It seemed more like a million years, another lifetime. 'No,' she said, shaking her head, shaking Will away. This was Oliver. The man she loved.

Oliver stroked her hair back off her forehead. 'You'd be quite justified if you said you never wanted to see me again, my behaviour was unforgivable, but if I went on my knees and grovelled . . .' He knelt at her feet, looking wickedly mischievous rather than repentant. 'Lovely Anna, forgive me, forgive me.'

'Get up, you idiot,' Anna said, pulling him up, worried that Mrs Davenport or Peggy would come into the hall and see him.

He grabbed her legs, so she almost lost her balance. 'Say you'll forgive me.'

'Oliver! Get up.' She had to grab on to his shoulders to stop herself falling.

'Only if you say you forgive me.'

'Stop it! I'm going to fall! Oliver – I forgive you, okay?'

'It is so good to see you again,' he said, standing and folding her into his arms. 'I've missed you,' he whispered, his eyes dark. 'I really missed you.'

'I missed you,' she said, thinking about Will. But Will had been a mistake, an embarrassing error of judgement. Already the meal at the pavilion was fading, the garden by starlight dwindling in her memory. In Oliver's presence she was a different Anna, glamorous, confident. She had forgotten his energy, his drive, but now he was with her she felt the tempo of the house wake up, move from sleep to something alive. This was his home, this was where he belonged; his genes were woven into the fabric of the building. Will meant nothing in comparison. She didn't even know where he came from. She put her arms around Oliver's neck and kissed him. I love him, I love him, I love him, she told herself, thinking of the garden by starlight.

'But why didn't you say something, my dear?' Mrs Davenport asked, her expression bewildered. Anna shifted uncomfortably on the sofa next to Oliver, feeling extremely awkward. It wasn't exactly wrong to have a relationship with a client's grandson, but she felt it was unprofessional.

'I didn't want to presume . . .' she started before trailing off.

'My fault, Gran,' Oliver said. 'I should have said something. We were going to come down last weekend, but something came up and I couldn't make it. And then I've been off in Prague, and Anna's had her accident, so we haven't seen each other since.'

'I hope this means you'll come and see me more often,' Mrs Davenport said to him. 'You really ought to be getting more involved in the house. I won't live for ever, you know.'

He patted her hand. 'You can't die, Gran. You're all I've got.'

She laid her other hand on his. 'Sometimes you remind me very much of your grandfather,' she said. 'You behave yourself. Anna's far too good for you.'

'I know,' Oliver said, with a glance at Anna that made her squirm inside. What if he knew about her kissing Will? She hoped Will wouldn't say anything.

Mrs Davenport leant back in her chair. 'Has Anna told you about the discovery she made this morning? I was thrilled when Will told me.'

So Anna read the letters out to him, Mrs Davenport nodding and smiling. Oliver listened without comment, one leg crossed elegantly over the other, foot tapping like a cat twitching its tail. 'I've just come back from the church, and Jessica's buried there, so I've now got dates for the garden.' Anna paused for Oliver's reaction, but his face was expressionless. 'I wonder why Jessica's father was so against Arthur. I'd have thought he'd have been a good match for her.'

'Perhaps he thought she was too young,' Mrs Davenport said. 'She was little more than a child, after all.'

'Will these letters help with getting grants?' Oliver said, brushing invisible fluff off his trousers.

He'd asked the one question Anna hadn't wanted to answer. She glanced at Mrs Davenport before speaking. 'It will help,' she said, choosing her words carefully, 'because it's a romantic story, but I'm afraid the letters don't really tell us much more about the garden than I already knew, beyond a date. We need more evidence of structures, either in pictures or – even better – actually there.' She saw Mrs Davenport's face fall. 'I'll do the very best I can, I promise.'

'The trouble is,' Anna said later as she and Oliver walked around the garden, 'there simply isn't enough here that's visible. The pavilion and lake are lovely, but to be honest, they're commonplace; half the Georgian manor houses in the country have similar. The gateway's intriguing, because of the carvings and the possible link with John Wood and the building of Bath, and then there's my theory about Heaven and Hell, but I don't think it's going to be enough. I need something else.'

She saw a night light in a jam jar by the path that Will had missed and picked it up, turning it round in her hands. A magical evening, a moment of madness, a dream under the stars. She looked at Oliver. Here was reality. Not fantasy.

Oliver was staring out across the lake. He looked troubled, as if subconsciously he knew what had happened the night before. Not that anything had happened. A kiss was nothing, she thought, feeling waves of guilt. Please don't let him find out, she prayed inwardly. She tucked her hand into his arm. She would make it up to him. She loved him.

'I see someone's got a boat out,' Oliver said, still looking over the lake to where the dinghy was moored by the steps.

Anna didn't reply. She rubbed her cheek against his arm. She didn't want to think about Will rowing the boat across the lake, or anything to do with last night. The lake glinted below them, pavilion and clouds reflected in the surface. A duck landed, sending up a V-shaped wave of water. The clouds shattered, then, as the water subsided, gradually rippled back into the glassy mirror. Oliver's expression was strained.

'What are you thinking?' Anna said.

'I used to play here as a child. That might even have been my boat.'

'It must have been a wonderful place to explore.'

'It was . . .' He smiled at her. 'It would be a dream to restore the garden.'

'We could do it,' she said, smiling back at him. This was what she'd longed for him to say, to acknowledge that the gardens were worth restoring.

'Maybe,' he said, ruffling her hair. 'How's your ankle doing? I thought you were limping earlier.'

'It's a bit sore,' she said, touched that he'd noticed. 'I don't know how I'm going to manage if it carries on. I've got loads of garden tours coming up. In fact, the first one's the day after tomorrow. Hatfield House.'

'That's north of London, isn't it?' Anna nodded. 'And you've got other visits?' She nodded again. Oliver swept his hand through his hair, 'It must be easier to traipse around the country from London rather than Bath. Why don't you base yourself at my place?'

'I couldn't . . .' she said, completely taken aback by the suggestion.

'Why not?' He shifted his feet and looked embarrassed. 'I'm not saying move in with me for ever, but it seems to make sense, just for a couple of weeks, while you've got these visits to do, and your ankle's still weak.'

'That's so kind, but . . .'

'But what?' He screwed his face up. 'I know I was well out of order at your lunch, and I'm sorry. Really I am. So. Here's something I can do for you that maybe will make up a little for me being a prat.'

'That's so sweet of you.' She put her hand to her chest, feeling a rush of emotion. 'If you're sure . . .' Oliver nodded. 'Then I'd love to.'

He gave her a sideways look. 'I thought you were going to dump me after that lunch.'

'I thought about it,' Anna said.

He kissed her. 'Pleased you didn't?'

Anna smiled. 'Of course.'

They started walking back to the house. 'What's that in your hand?' Oliver said.

'Nothing,' she said, putting the night light in her pocket. 'Nothing important.'

They said goodbye to Mrs Davenport, who kissed Anna most affectionately. Oliver took Anna's bag and rucksack out to her car while she went to find Peggy. She went into the kitchen, but found it empty except for Will.

'I came to say goodbye to you and Peggy,' she said,

'Peggy's hanging out some laundry in the side garden,' he said tersely.

'Will . . .' This was worse than this morning. So hard to know what to say. 'I wanted to say thank you. And I'm sorry about…' She pressed her lips together. She wasn't sorry about Oliver; she was sorry Will had found out in the way he had.

'Are you really seeing him?' Will said, as if continuing a conversation they'd had before. 'Despite the fact he's a shit.'

Right. That was it. 'You know nothing about him,' she said in her coldest voice. 'Thank you for rescuing me from the tunnel. I'll go and find Peggy now.' She pushed past to go to the back door, but Will grabbed her arm.

'Okay, I shouldn't have said that.' Anna stared at the dresser, not wanting to speak to him. 'It's what I think, but I shouldn't have said it.'

'Let go of me, please.'

He let go of her arm immediately, but despite the opportunity she didn't leave.

'Why didn't you say anything?' he said.

Good question. Why hadn't she? Because, because . . . 'It's none of your business.' She shrugged, attempting nonchalance.

'True. But then I'm not seeing Oliver Davenport.'

'You don't own me. You saved my life, and I will never be able to thank you enough, but that's where it stops.' She couldn't meet his eyes. 'The garden yesterday was magical, but it was a fantasy, it's not real.'

Will examined his hands. 'What about Mrs D, and Peggy? Were you going to tell them?'

Anna began to feel angry at his accusations. 'I haven't kept it secret on purpose, it just never seemed the right time to say anything. And anyway, I don't have to justify myself to you. Oliver and I are both single, and what we do doesn't concern anyone else, certainly not you.'

'You're right. You're better off sticking with Oliver Davenport, who's going to inherit all this – and your precious garden – even though he doesn't value it.'

'You're wrong, you're so wrong. I'm with Oliver because – oh, I don't have to tell you . . .'

'You can't, can you?'

The derision in his voice stung and she whipped round to face him. 'He makes me feel great, okay? He makes me happy. He makes me feel like I can do anything, like I'm a different person.'

'You don't know what he's like,' Will said with contempt.

'And the sex is fantastic,' she flung at him.

Will flinched.

'It has nothing – nothing – to do with the garden.'

'That's good, because he's going to sell up to property developers the first chance he gets. He's had valuers down, and estate agents.'

She shook her head. 'That's a lie.'

Will's eyes were hard. 'Is it? Ask him. Ask him and see what he says.'

'Even if it was true, so what? This is his family's home, where he belongs. It's not yours, it's nothing to do with you.' She was suddenly consumed with anger. How dare he say these things to her? She wanted to hurt him, to hurt him so badly he'd never speak to her again. 'You come here from nowhere, you won't tell anyone anything about your background. It's really easy for you, isn't it, you can accuse people of things, and have people tell you stuff, but when it comes to sharing with others, oh no, that's too much for you, it's all got to be secret, nobody's allowed to know anything. So you can be as high and mighty as you like, and pass judgement, and all the time you could be hiding much worse things, you could have done anything. You could be a murderer!'

She stopped short, seeing the expression on Will's face. He sat down heavily on one of the kitchen chairs and put his face in his hands.

Anna knelt by the chair. 'Will, I'm sorry, I didn't mean to say you were a murderer . . .'

He looked up and gave a rueful smile. 'Why shouldn't you? After all, it's what I am.'

Chapter 19

Living with Oliver was a different world. He was right, it was much easier to get around the country from his flat, and oh, how blissful to come back, footsore and tired, to a temperature-controlled environment, limitless oceans of hot water, a fridge with an ice-maker. The best thing was the underfloor heating. Anna liked to walk across the antique limestone floors after a shower, leaving footprints that evaporated. The limestone, ripped up from some chateau no doubt, ran throughout, creating a seamless sense of space. It should have been hard and cold, but paradoxically was soft and warm. Skin temperature.

No cleaning or laundry worries either. The flat was serviced by a company which supplied a pair of women who efficiently dealt with all domestic issues. What food or household supplies they needed Oliver ordered over the Net and they were delivered by a cheerful lad who brought the bags right into the kitchen area. However, most of the time they ate out. Oliver never cooked. Anna discovered the instruction manual, still in its plastic bag, inside the oven. On the few occasions he didn't go out, he got a takeaway and watched television. He was riveted by Anna's confession that she hadn't got a television.

'What do you do in the evenings?' he said, flummoxed.

'Read, work, listen to Radio 4. Go out sometimes.'

He shook his head in amazement. 'You're a funny thing. Sometimes I feel like – well, you won't know who I mean because you haven't got a telly, but this man goes off and lives with primitive tribes in deepest darkest wherever. Sometimes I feel like that with you.'

'Thanks,' Anna said tartly, not entirely sure she was happy at being likened to a primitive tribe.

'I didn't mean it like that. Come here.' He gave his most charming smile and held out his arm, and she snuggled next to him. He flicked through the channels, image succeeding image in a colourful blur.

'Oliver . . .' She'd been wondering how to ask him, turning over different phrases in her mind. 'Have you had an estate agent round to Templecombe?'

'Mmm?' Oliver said, stroking her hair. Anna asked her question again, dreading his answer. 'Not recently,' he said. 'Why d'you ask?'

Anna felt faint. 'Someone said something, and I wondered, that's all.'

His encircling arm tensed. 'I bet it was that bloody gardener. The sooner he goes the better.'

'No, it wasn't him,' she said quickly. 'Just something I overheard and . . . well, I remembered the day we met, seeing you in the garden, when I was looking out of the attic window. It was you, wasn't it?'

Oliver kissed her hair. 'What a good memory you have.'

'Was it?'

He nodded. 'Yes. So?'

Her heart felt cold. 'You're not going to sell it, are you?'

'It isn't mine to sell.'

'Then why?'

He looked at her, as if gauging the situation. Anna waited. 'I wanted to know what the condition of the property was, what needs repairing, what's going to need serious work, how long it will remain habitable. My grandmother is old, as you know, and any moment things could change. She might have to leave Templecombe, in which case I need to be prepared. But I don't want her worried by any of this, which is why I lied about being in the garden that day.' There was a hard edge to his voice, neither indulgent nor playful. 'So whatever poison your little gardening friend has been telling you, I have only my family's interests at heart, and to be honest, it's none of your business. Okay?' He held her chin with his hand and searched her eyes. She nodded. 'Good. I'm going to have a bath.'

He snapped the television off and stalked to the bathroom, leaving Anna feeling guilty. Of course he was right. Why had she listened to Will? She should have known he'd say anything to disparage Oliver. She should have been loyal and stuck up for Oliver. She burst into the bathroom. Oliver straightened from where he'd been leaning over the taps.

'I'm sorry. I should have trusted you.'

'Yeah, you should have.' Oliver hugged her and Anna snuggled into his chest. 'Watch out for that guy. He's bad news.'

She wondered what he'd say if she told him Will was a murderer.

She hadn't known what to say herself. She'd stared at Will, and then Oliver had come in looking for her. She couldn't believe it, and wouldn't have if someone else had told her. But Will had said it himself. No wonder he didn't want to talk about the past, revive old memories. A murderer. She couldn't take it in. It buzzed in her brain, irritating, nagging. Gradually she began to invent scenarios – a wife with cancer, an aged parent, mercy killings and accidents. Will, the Will she knew, gentle, kind, caring Will, couldn't be a murderer. At night, when she couldn't sleep, she thought about him and what he might have done.

The sleepless nights surprised her, as she found Oliver's life

● ● ●   241   ● ● ●

exhausting. Most evenings he'd get back from work, quickly change, then they'd go out, perhaps to a corporate event or for dinner with friends, but always as part of a large crowd. Sometimes, if he'd been held up in the office, he'd call and get her to meet him. She'd take a taxi – impossible to go by tube in the high heels Oliver liked – and wait outside the venue for him to arrive.

'Funny thing,' he'd say, seeing her loitering on the pavement outside. 'Why didn't you go in? You know loads of people now.'

Anna would shrug. Knowing loads of faces was not the same as knowing people. The first weekend she stayed at Oliver's flat, they went to a white dinner party, where the sole sustenance on offer was a large bowl of coke in the centre of the table. Their host was a barrister, who must have sensed Anna's shock at his profession, as he launched into a lecture about middle-class drug use, finishing with: 'I'm not out on the streets mugging people for my supply, and it doesn't affect my work. It's no one's business but my own what I do at the weekends.' He waved an expansive arm. 'Rack 'em up and help yourself.'

Anna did.

The following Thursday evening, at the launch party for yet another new club, she was leaning against a wall, longing to go back to the flat. Her calves ached, her back ached and her brain ached with all the noise. Oliver was in full flow, talking, meeting people. Anna imagined his friends asking themselves what he saw in her, although they were all too polite to give any hint of such a thing around her. She wished she could be like them, confident and glamorous. Mind you, she'd bet none of them had been traipsing around gardens all day, answering questions. The noise had given her such a headache she could hardly think straight. And they still hadn't yet had any dinner. She drained her glass of champagne and headed for the loo, anything to get respite from the insistent noise.

A man was waiting in the corridor outside. He smiled when he saw her. 'Okay?'

Anna nodded. 'Tired. Busy day at work.'

'D'you need something?' He spoke pleasantly. Two months ago Anna would have shaken her head and gone into the loo, puzzled by what he meant. Now she paused.

'Here,' he said, his manner easy and relaxed. 'Free sample. My number's at the top.' She hesitated. Oliver would be furious if he knew. Anything went at weekends, but he was strict about keeping the week clean. But she was so tired. She took the packet from the man, her fingers trembling so much that she nearly dropped the little slip of paper with his number on it.

It was easy from then on. Just a little to get me over the beginning, she'd say to herself, as she did a line. Sometimes just knowing the support was there, that in her bag was the magic ingredient to transform her from a shy mouse into a sophisticated professional, was enough. Armed with chemical confidence, she got to know some of Oliver's friends better. Following Madeleine's recommendation, she had her hair transformed into a sleek, shining curtain, indulged in a visit to a nail bar, and invested in expensive make-up. There were a staggering number of body parts to worry about, from eyebrows to toenails, but gradually she started to look like the other women in Oliver's circles, polished and glossy.

She should have been happy – great boyfriend, lifestyle Clare would die for – but she felt edgy and restless, unable to concentrate. She raised the credit limit on her card again, and took out another one with a long interest-free period, hoping something would turn up. Perhaps there'd be more television work – they'd mentioned the possibility of another series, and even a tie-in book – and there was the Templecombe report. Anna felt a twinge of guilt. It was halfway through June and she still hadn't finished writing it up. She'd do it when she'd finished the last of the garden tours.

On the longest day of the year it rained, and the day following, drenching Anna as she trudged round Stourhead and Hestercombe. She sneezed all the way back in the coach, and when she got back to the flat the last thing she wanted to do was go out, but Oliver insisted. With really bad timing, he caught her just as she came out of the loo.

'Olly, darling,' she said, draping herself around him. He was lovely.

Oliver firmly took her wrists from round his neck. 'Keep it to the weekends like everyone else,' he said, a distinct frostiness in his voice.

'Sorry,' Anna said, pulling a contrite face she didn't mean. 'It's hardly my fault, I didn't want to go out in the first place.'

'Who supplied you?'

'No one,' Anna lied. 'Someone asked if I wanted a line in the loo, and I was tired so I said yes.'

Oliver narrowed his eyes, and for a second she thought he might insist on checking her bag, but he didn't challenge her. However, when they joined the others he kept his eyes on her. Like having a jailer, Anna thought resentfully, plotting escape. Of course she wasn't going to take any more, she didn't need to take any more, he was overreacting. As the evening wore on she started to feel cold and flat, sparkling Anna turning back into drab, dull Anna. All she needed was one teeny little line. But Oliver was watching. They went home early, Oliver still angry. Anna hardly slept that night, nose running, throat sore.

The next day they travelled in together, Oliver to his office in the City, Anna to meet the group she was taking to Stowe in the morning and Rousham in the afternoon. Her final garden tour until August. She thought they must look incongruous standing on the tube platform, him in a smart tailored suit, her in jeans and trainers, and a cagoule as the weather forecast was poor. She wondered if he was still angry with her, but he ruffled her hair on the escalator, and gave her a long, lingering kiss when their journeys parted.

The weather held for the trip to Stowe, and during the pub lunch, but the drizzle had set in by the time they got to Rousham.

Anna took them round, rain dripping off the end of her nose, thinking, this is where he kissed me first, that sunny spring day when everything was fresh and new. She wiped her nose with the back of her hand. Oliver had been furious with her the night before. If only she could relax more around his friends, if only she could be more like them. If only—

'Excuse me . . .'

Anna blinked. Blurred faces, many encased in pixie hoods, all under umbrellas, were staring at her, quite obviously waiting for her to say something. Her mind was blank. The last five, ten minutes – nothing. The faces waited.

'Could you repeat the question?' she said, feeling sick with the shock of not remembering. 'I didn't quite catch . . .'

There was a pause. 'You were talking about the terrace,' one of them said, pursing lips.

'Was I?' She gave a nervous laugh as she looked behind her. When had they got here? She couldn't remember. 'Well. This is the Praeneste terrace, named after the temple at Praeneste.'

'You've just said that.' Their faces were suspicious.

What else did she know? Nothing. The folder marked Rousham was empty. She could almost hear Oliver's voice: make something up, they won't know the difference. But I will. She stared at their faces through a haze of rain. I can't do it.

'Perhaps we should shelter for a little while,' Anna said, heading for the cloistered arcade, leaving them to follow. She was shivering under a layer of cold sweat and had to put her hands in her pockets to stop them shaking. Her memory had never failed her before. Never.

The coach driver managed to get lost on the way back, so by the time she got to the flat it was late. She stood in the hall, dripping. So much for glamour. But Oliver surprised her by looking after her, running a hot scented bath, wrapping her in warmed towels and making her a hot toddy – Peggy's recipe, he said.

'You look about six,' he said, sitting next to her on the sofa while she sipped the honey and lemon whisky. 'Like a poor little orphan.'

'I feel like an orphan,' Anna said, sniffing. Oliver handed her a tissue, and she blew her nose, beyond caring. 'Sorry about last night.'

'You've got to be careful or it gets out of control,' he said, pulling her towards him. 'Never mind. I've got a brilliant plan for the weekend. I've got Friday off, so I thought we could go down to Templecombe and you could hand your report in, and then go back to Bath and chill, maybe have a country pub lunch on Sunday, and then come back to London in the evening.'

'Sounds perfect.' Anna snuggled up to him. So lucky. Oliver started to massage her shoulders and neck, and she felt she could have purred with contentment. She dropped her head forwards, his strong fingers kneading the top of her spine. Massage. Shit. She sat up.

'Bugger. It's Clare's hen party on Saturday. We're going to a spa all day, and then to a club in Bristol in the evening. I'm sorry, Oliver, it would have been perfect.'

He stroked her cheek. 'Don't look so anxious, it's not the end of the world. I've got some friends who moved out to a cottage near Cirencester last year. I'll go and see them on Saturday while you're preening yourself, and then we'll meet up on Sunday.'

Anna worked flat out the next day, trying to pull together something approaching a professional report on Templecombe. The trouble was, there were too many gaps. She felt a pang of guilt. She really should have investigated the tunnel area more thoroughly, especially the chamber at the end. And the letters . . . The trouble with research was that it could go on for ever, one trail leading to another. You had to draw the line somewhere, and she had already spent enough time on the report. I am running a business, not a charity, she thought, as she wrote her description of the extant buildings. I can't make up what isn't there. I've done what I can. Her shoulders had seized up as she sat hunched over her laptop, and she rotated them, trying to release some of the tension. The bones clicked under her hand; she could feel them, hard knobbles on her shoulders. She'd lost weight over these last few weeks, despite all the eating out.

But no time to think about that. She had to finish the report. She worked on through lunch, trying to cobble something together by the time Oliver came back from the City. But the words wouldn't come. Her brain had seized up along with her shoulders. To try and get going, she checked her emails. Too many. She worked her way through them, replying only to those that needed attention.

From: *Gwyn Edwards*
To: *Anna Carmichael*
Subject: *Rock Stars and their Gardens*

What's up, Doc? No one's seen you for years.
   How do you fancy coming and being the cavalry for me next Tuesday 29th? Client swears it's Capability yeah yeah yeah. Should be good fee – client is Gene Machine.
   Gwyn

PS Full house for Monday. Let me know asap if you need any kit beyond the usual.

Anna stared at the screen. Monday. The conference. Her lecture was prepared, thank God, although she needed to do some work on it over the weekend, check the slides were in the right order, iron out a few sticky patches. And then Tuesday. She'd wanted to go back to London with Oliver, but a fee was a fee. She dreaded the arrival of her next credit card statement. She hit the reply button.

Been busy in London. Tuesday 29th sounds good. Expecting mega fee.
All set for Monday. See you there.
Anna

She noted the Tuesday in her diary, and started working again. She was still not finished when Oliver rang at half past five, wanting to meet her at a gallery off Piccadilly at seven. A quick scurry to get ready, her heels click-clacking on the stone floors, taxi, squeeze into overcrowded room, meet people, meet more people. Her head ached with the sound of chatter bouncing off cold white walls and reverberating in her brain. She needed help to get through, but Oliver would be furious if she . . . She clenched her fists. Of course she could get through without help. They were just people. Dinner, more talk about people and things she didn't know or care about, more noise, more people with shiny hair and perfect teeth. Then back home, and sex, and all the time the unfinished report weighed on her conscience.

She slid out from Oliver's embrace and wrapped herself in a dressing gown. The living room was cool and dark, so she put one of Oliver's sweaters on over the dressing gown. She booted up her laptop and waited, feeling she was going to collapse with tiredness. Oliver would go mad if he knew . . . but just one line would keep her going. He kept his supplies at the back of the bottom drawer. She hesitated, then pulled the drawer open.

She worked through until nearly five and then crept to bed, snuggling against a warm Oliver. But she couldn't stop shivering.

Chapter 20

Anna was watching Mrs Davenport's face as she read through the report when she heard the scrunch of gravel outside the house. She looked up as the Land Rover swung past the drawing-room window and out of sight beyond Oliver's car. Will. A door slammed. Then the front door, and footsteps. For a second she thought he was going to come into the drawing room. Her senses shot to red alert. Then the door under the stairs creaked. He'd gone through to the kitchen.

'Yes?'

Mrs Davenport was staring at her, and Anna realised she must have sighed rather loudly. 'Nothing,' she said with an apologetic smile. Mrs Davenport looked at her for a moment longer, a small smile creasing her face, then went back to the report. Anna could see she was nearly at the end. Just the summary and suggestions for future development left.

She wondered how her own future developments were going to go. Oliver had arranged to meet a surveyor to check over the stable area, which he thought might be dangerous after the heavy rain they'd had. 'Don't want something else collapsing,' he'd said. 'You got off lightly.' She shuddered. If Will hadn't come and rescued her, she might still be there, rotting away. An image flashed into her mind of Will, lit like a Rembrandt against the darkness of the pavilion. She smoothed her skirt over her knees, feeling it silky against her skin. That was all in the past. A mistake to be forgotten.

Mrs Davenport cleared her throat. 'I have finished reading the report.'

Anna's mind jerked back to the job. 'Is there anything you would like me to explain?'

Mrs Davenport paused, as if considering. 'No, it seems most comprehensive. Admirably so, in fact.'

'Good,' Anna said, relieved that she appeared satisfied, even if Anna herself felt it was clumsily written and lacked her usual thoroughness.

'There are a couple of things I would like to discuss with you, however.'

Anna's heart sank. 'Oh yes?'

'Yes, the future developments. Here,' and she pointed with a gnarled finger at the report, 'it gives a list of the areas to address should one should wish to proceed: grant applications, discussions with English Heritage and so on. Who does this?'

'It could be you . . .'

Mrs Davenport looked at her. 'I've never been good at filling in forms.'

'Or it could be your grandson.'

'Ah.' Mrs Davenport leant back in her chair. 'Oliver.'

'He could handle all that side of it easily, and you could bring in experts as you needed.'

'Such as yourself.'

Anna nodded. Mrs Davenport appeared to be thinking, her eyes focused on something far away. Anna let her own mind drift. It would be the ideal solution, Oliver running the project, Anna acting as adviser. She could imagine them working together to develop the garden, going to meetings, visiting other gardens for inspiration, standing side by side examining plans, hands touching . . .

Mrs Davenport stirred and Anna reluctantly left her imagination.

'The only building you've recommended for listing is the pavilion.'

'I'm really sorry. There just isn't enough extant to justify listing the other structures.' Anna clasped her hands, knowing Gwyn would have found a way, would have persisted. But she wasn't Gwyn.

'And your theory about Heaven and Hell?'

'There's no proof, it's pure speculation. When I first thought of it, I was in shock, I think, after the accident. I saw what I wanted to see . . .' Her voice trailed away and she looked down at her clasped hands. This had been the hardest part of all, but she'd talked it over with Oliver and he'd reassured her. She had to base her report on facts, not wild suppositions, however alluring they might be.

The skin on Mrs Davenport's knuckles was white. 'Is this enough to save the garden?'

Anna wanted to run away, anything not to have to deal with the disappointment she knew was coming. But she had to be honest. 'On its own, probably not.'

Mrs Davenport subsided into her chair. She looked old and shrunken inside her clothes. Anna knelt beside her and took her hands. 'Oliver will help, I know he wants to. And there's lots that can be done without the heritage organisations.' Mrs Davenport nodded, but didn't speak. 'Look at the amount Will's done, just on his own. We could enlist volunteers, and I'm sure Oliver could get sponsorship from someone in the City. We could—' She stopped as Mrs Davenport put a hand on her shoulder.

'You've been very kind,' she said, her voice quavering. Anna felt guiltier than ever that the report had been so rushed. 'And I know you mean well. But I know my grandson, and I don't think this is what he wants from his life.'

'No, he said he'd like to see it restored, he did.'

Mrs Davenport smiled and stroked Anna's hair. 'You're very young,' she said to Anna's surprise. 'Now, go and fetch me my bag, if you would.'

Anna got up and collected a large black crocodile handbag, much worn from use, from the top of the walnut bureau. She gave it to Mrs Davenport, who rummaged around inside and brought out a chequebook. She wrote out the cheque, payable to Dr A. Carmichael, in a shaking hand. 'For your work here.'

Anna took the cheque, knowing that it represented her mortgage repayments for the next six months. 'I'm sorry the report wasn't as you wanted it to be.'

Mrs Davenport shook her head. 'You warned me from the start that you had to be objective. And I appreciate your honesty.' Anna's conscience cringed. 'Now, I expect you want to find my grandson.'

Anna bent and kissed her cheek. 'I hope I'll be back soon,' she said softly.

'I always wanted a granddaughter.' Mrs Davenport smiled, but her eyes were sad. 'Now, run along, but before you go, would you be so kind as to ask Peggy to come through to me?'

She sat back in her chair, and closed her eyes, and Anna quietly left the room and went to the front door. No sign of Oliver outside. He must still be with the surveyor.

She found Peggy and Will in the kitchen, Will up a stepladder and handing platters and dishes down from the top of the dresser to Peggy, who was stacking them on the kitchen table. Will saw her and froze, a large willow-pattern dish in his hands.

'Hello,' Anna said, suddenly feeling very shy.

Peggy turned, her expression wary. 'Good afternoon, Dr Carmichael. Can I help you?'

Anna faltered for a second. She had obviously moved from being downstairs to upstairs since being with Oliver. 'Mrs Davenport asked if you would go to her.'

Peggy glanced up at Will, and Anna wondered how much she knew about his past. 'I'd better go.' She left the kitchen, wiping her hands on her apron.

Will's expression was guarded. He turned to put the dish back on the dresser.

'I'll take it,' Anna said, and lifted her hands up.

'You'll get dirty.'

Anna looked down at her flippy silk skirt and high heels, hardly how she'd dressed on her previous visits to Templecombe. 'I don't mind,' she said, and waited, her eyes fixed on him. With a sigh he bent down from the stepladder and held out the dish.

'Careful, it's heavy.'

She took it from him and placed it on the table.

'You've lost weight,' Will said abruptly. 'It doesn't suit you.'

'Thanks.' She shouldn't have been surprised by the anger in his voice. What had she expected, that he would give her his blessing to go off with Oliver? She looked up at him, wondering how he felt about her, but it was hard to tell with her eyes at about the same level as his knees. He handed her a dish in silence, then another. Anna looked at her wrists, thin and bony. All those dinners spent pushing expensive food around her plate, bored and wanting to go home, she supposed. Or the parties where food was forgotten. She felt tired and worn out, but she had to ask.

'Will, when I was last here you said . . .' She paused, not quite sure how to carry on.

Will steadied himself at the top of the stepladder, his hands gripped tight. 'I don't want to discuss it. Not with you.' His voice was controlled.

Stay calm. She put the dish on the table, playing for time. 'Why not?'

'Isn't it obvious?' He came down the steps and faced her. Her heart was pounding. 'All the time you were here, you were with him and you never said. That night in the pavilion, I thought . . .' He turned abruptly to the sink and began washing his hands in a torrent of water, scrubbing away the dust. 'You're not the person I thought you were, that's all.'

A stab of fury burned Anna's heart. She grabbed his arm and made him turn to face her. 'And what about you? What was I supposed to think? Did you expect me to fall in love with you when you won't tell me anything about yourself, where you come from, your past?'

'Who said anything about falling in love?' he spat back at her.

They stared at each other, shocked by how angry each was. What am I doing, she thought, talking about love with Will? Blood thumped in her ears, her hands were shaking. I love Oliver. She opened her mouth to speak, but the words wouldn't come. The silence grew between them.

'I'm sorry,' she managed, before stumbling towards the door, certain she'd never see him again. As she went through into the hall, she heard Peggy shouting from the drawing room.

'Will, Will, come quickly.'

Anna spun round. 'Will, Peggy's calling. I think it's urgent.'

He pushed past her, hands still wet, and crossed the hall into the drawing room. Anna followed.

Mrs Davenport was stretched out on the floor, her face white. Peggy knelt beside her, flapping with her hands.

Will felt her pulse. 'She's alive. Quick, call an ambulance.'

Anna ran back into the hall and grabbed the phone. When she came back, Mrs Davenport was covered in a blanket, her head on a cushion. Will looked up accusingly.

'What did you write in your report?'

'I . . .' Anna clutched at her chest as if she was having a heart attack.

'Did you say the garden couldn't be saved?'

'Not exactly . . .'

'But you knew how much it mattered to her.' His eyes were bright with tears. 'You've done Oliver Davenport's dirty work very well. I hope you think it's worth it.'

Chapter 21

'So how's the charming Oliver?' Bronwen asked, her voice dripping with irony.

'Charming, of course,' Anna said, turning her head so the masseur could get right into the knotty bit of muscle stretching across the base of her neck.

Bronwen, lying on the massage table next to her, grunted.

'I'm sorry he was rude to you and Nick. He'd stayed up all night and was really tired.' Anna prayed Bron would drop the topic. When the option to be done together had come up, she'd been relieved, as she'd never had a proper massage before and had been rather nervous about it. But now she wasn't sure: the masseur's hands on her shoulders skewered the pain points in her muscles with the same piercing directness as Bronwen's eyes.

'I hope he apologised.'

'Mmm,' Anna said, closing her eyes as if she was enjoying the sensation of the masseur pummelling up and down her spine. 'Of course.'

Bronwen shifted on the table. 'I hope that makes you feel better.'

'What do you mean?'

'Honestly! To turn up really late, and in that state.' Her voice became decidedly casual. 'Do you know what he was on?'

'Sorry? Didn't quite catch that . . .' Anna lied.

Bronwen sniffed. 'You want to watch out. I've met his sort before.'

Anna opened her eyes. 'You're talking in clichés,' she said. 'What's Oliver's sort supposed to be like? Sure, he's not like Richard, but that's a good thing, isn't it? I didn't realise it at the time, but I was stuck in a rut. We'd become more like brother and sister – no, like distant cousins, vaguely fond of each other, meeting with good will but forgetting the other's existence. I don't think about Richard any more.' As she said it, something struck her – I think about Will instead.

'I don't like to say this' – but you're going to, Anna thought – 'but I think you ought to be careful.'

'Is this the rebound speech? Listen, I love Oliver. He's funny, and attractive, and yes, he lives a different sort of life to me. So what? I'm fed up with always being the good girl.' She turned her head so she could see Bronwen's face. 'It's fun. I'm having a good time.'

'But *are* you having a good time? It's like he's taken you over. No one ever sees you any more. You seem really . . . edgy. I'm worried about you.'

'Don't be. I'm fine. Really.' She turned her head away from Bronwen.

They didn't talk any more, gave themselves up to the hands of the masseurs. When they'd gone, Anna and Bronwen sat up, towels wrapped around their chests.

'I feel all floppy,' Anna said. 'Like a rag doll.'

Bronwen touched her arm. 'Look, just tell me straight. Are you taking anything?'

'What are you talking about?' Although it was warm in the room, Anna felt cold.

Bronwen frowned. 'You know. Drugs.'

'Me?' Anna smiled, eyes on a spot just to the left of Bronwen's shoulder. 'Of course not.'

Bronwen bit her lip. 'I'm concerned, you're not like yourself.'

'Just because you don't like Oliver, there's no need to start accusing me.'

'I'm not accusing you.'

'Aren't you? You've just said I'm a liar, I'm on drugs—'

'Anna . . .' Bronwen put her hand on her arm.

Anna shook it off. 'Piss off. I'm fed up with everyone thinking they know me, telling me what I'm like. Just leave it.'

After lunch Anna avoided Bronwen. Instead she sat by the outdoor pool, chatting to Clare and her friends. They had a free run of the hotel's facilities, and although Anna didn't usually talk about things like pedicures and manicures, today they had a certain charm. It was Clare's day, and everything should be light and happy, not awkward and difficult.

'Is she okay?' Clare asked, gesturing with her head towards Bronwen, who lay stretched out on a sunlounger on the far side of the pool, sarong over her legs, book over her face.

'Sure,' Anna shrugged. 'I think she's tired.'

'God, it must be knackering, having a baby and all.' Helen, a friend of Clare's from work, stood up. 'I'm going to grab a sunbed. Anyone coming?' Her skin was already a honey brown, smooth and even, and she had a gold stud in her navel. Anna looked at her own arms. Despite spending a fair proportion of her working week outside, they never got a deep tan, perhaps managing a rich tea biscuit shade of beige. Perhaps if she tried a sunbed she'd go the same colour as Helen.

'Me,' Jackie said, also standing.

'And me,' Clare said. 'Coming?'

Anna looked across to Bronwen. There was something stiff about the way she was lying, but perhaps she was just sleeping. She shrugged. Why should she feel guilty? It was Bronwen who'd started it.

'I'll try it,' she said. Anything not to be left alone with Bronwen. She stood up and followed Helen.

The sunbed looked like a sandwich toaster. Perhaps I'll come out crisp, Anna thought, looking at it. Helen showed her how to operate the machine, then left Anna alone in the cubicle with the spray, the goggles and the token. It seemed quite a lot of paraphernalia.

Anna stripped and put the token in. The light flickered on, like a fly-killing lamp in a butcher's shop. She sat cautiously on the edge of the bed, expecting it to be hot, but it felt surprisingly cool. Carefully she lay down, trying to balance the goggles on the bridge of her nose, and pulled the lid down. She imagined she was an Egyptian princess lying in her sarcophagus. Queen Nerfertiti, floating on a bed made of light, but with the heavy stone lid pressing down on her. The machine ticked on. She wasn't sure where to put her hands. Anywhere near her body and she might give herself palm-shaped pale patches. She laid her hands flat, despite worrying about having tanned palms. Oliver, she felt, would be more forgiving of tanned palms than pale patches. Sweat trickled down her spine.

Imagine you're on a beach, cool breezes wafting the palm fronds, the sea lapping white sands. Imagine Oliver lying beside you, ordering the waiter to bring another fresh peach juice cocktail, complaining because the ice wasn't crushed . . . No. Go back to the beach, the swsh, swsh of the sea, the fronds wafting, a sea bird wheeling overhead . . . She relaxed a little, letting her legs flop apart. Oliver. She'd see him tomorrow. Mustn't drink too much tonight. Swsh, swsh, swsh. Oliver on the beach, lying on top of her, his hands touching her, the scent of jasmine and honeysuckle, palm fronds in the starlight, reflections on water, blond hair, dark eyes, the lean line from cheek to jaw, the hurt in his eyes when he realised she was with Oliver . . . What! She jerked her head upwards and banged her forehead on the lid. What was Will doing on her beach?

She settled back, feeling her skin prickle with the heat. She shouldn't have kissed Will. It had been magical, a magical end to a magical evening, but it had no place in reality. Strange to be thinking about reality while lying naked in a sandwich toaster. She scratched her hip. The reality was, she was with Oliver and Will wasn't important, however good he was at making feel guilty. She squirmed on the sunbed. Please let Mrs Davenport be okay. She'd looked so still and white, an oxygen mask over her face, when they'd taken her to hospital. She could see Will's brown eyes, hard and accusing.

Anna put her hand up to scratch her nose, and banged her knuckles on the lid. Who cared what Will thought? Will was a murderer and she was with Oliver. Oliver, Oliver, Oliver. Good-looking, charming Oliver. What did it matter if Bronwen didn't like him? Or Clare? They were so . . . so . . . provincial, that was the problem. Perhaps I ought to move to London. I wouldn't have to traipse up to the British Library for research, I could go to the theatre . . . art galleries . . . museums . . . She sighed. Unless she started earning vast amounts of money, London was impossible. She couldn't afford a broom cupboard in the same area as Oliver, and to get half the space she had in Bath, she'd have to go so far out into the suburbs she might as well still be in Bath.

She felt like a chicken fillet, poaching in its own juice. She flipped over on to her front with a squelch and draped the towel over her head. She should have stayed with Bronwen by the pool, made it up with her. Instead they'd all gone in and left her alone. Serve her right, Anna thought from inside her towelling tent. She shouldn't go around making comments about people, making judgements. She wriggled, her breasts squashed against the sunbed making a faint slurping sound. It wasn't any better face down. She flipped back over. Her face felt hot. Perhaps she should put the towel over her face. She decided against it. The machine carried on ticking.

Anyone would think I was mainlining heroin, she thought. A bit of coke every now and then didn't count. And it was only every now and then. Weekends, the occasional weekday. Okay, maybe it was a bit more than occasionally, maybe it was more like most days, but it wasn't as if she needed to take it, it just helped a little. An extra. People drank alcohol and no one thought anything of it. She wasn't addicted or anything like that. God, Bronwen was so provincial. Everybody took drugs in London. All Oliver's friends did and they held down serious jobs. Work hard and play hard.

Sweat trickled into her ears, and she dabbed at her hairline. I should have checked the tunnel area more thoroughly, she thought. But what difference would it have made? The chances of Templecombe getting any grants for restoration were remote. Oliver was quite right. It would have been just staving off the disappointment for later. She shifted around, slippery with sweat. It wasn't like Bronwen to be judgemental. Bronwen wasn't short of opinions and the force of personality to put them across, but it wasn't like her. In fact, she hadn't really been behaving like herself for ages, not since the baby had been born. Perhaps she was depressed, perhaps she was suffering from post-natal depression.

Anna pushed the lid up and slithered off the sunbed. She quickly put on her robe, then bundled her clothes under her arm and went out to the pool.

Bronwen was still lying on the sunlounger, but had shifted round so her back was towards Anna. She could have been asleep. Or dead.

'Bron?' Anna said softly, not wanting to disturb her. 'Are you awake?'

Bronwen turned her head slightly. 'I am now.'

'Oh. Sorry.' She waited, but Bronwen didn't say anything more. 'I wanted to check you were okay.'

'I'm okay.'

'Oh.' Anna felt stupid standing there, wearing nothing but a thin cotton robe with her belongings in a bundle in front of her like a refugee. 'Well, if you're sure . . .'

Bronwen turned a little further, then did a double-take. 'What have you been doing?'

'I went on a sunbed.'

Bronwen gave a bark of laughter. 'You look dreadful.'

Anna sat on a lounger, her hands to her cheeks. 'They do feel hot,' she said.

'Hot? Lobster! Have you looked at yourself?' Anna shook her head. 'How long did you do it for, anyway?'

'I don't know, Helen set the machine up. It seemed for ever.' She scooped a handful of water and splashed it over her face and neck. Eau de Chlorine.

Bronwen shrieked. 'You twit, you're supposed to build up the amount of time you spend on it, not go the whole hog straight away.'

'I came to see if you were okay,' Anna said, standing up. 'Obviously you are.'

'Hey, Anna,' Bronwen called after her. 'I'm sorry.'

But Anna pretended to ignore her.

Anna woke on Sunday morning with bells ringing in her head. She gulped down the glass of water by her bed and staggered to the front door, a film of cold sweat covering her skin.

Oliver removed his finger from the door bell. 'You took your time. Christ, what happened to your face?'

'Can't remember. A sunbed, I think. How's your grandmother?'

'She's okay. Comfortable, I think, was the word.'

'Thank God.' The guilt eased but her whole body still felt as if she were St Lawrence being martyred on his gridiron.

'You're better sticking to pale and interesting,' Oliver said, dropping the Sunday papers on to the side with a thump. 'I thought you said you weren't going to drink last night.'

'I wasn't . . .' That had lasted about five minutes. 'Jeez, I've got such a hangover.'

'No, really?'

Anna groaned. 'I can't take irony this early in the morning.'

Oliver grunted. 'I hope it was worth it.'

Flashes of the night rushed past like a photomontage sequence in a film: swaying girls, arms draped around each other's necks, legs skittering down the pavement. She put her hand to her head. Had she really told that bouncer she couldn't fall in love with him because she loved Another? Probably a good thing her memories were hazy. She could just remember Clare demanding they drink the entire cocktail menu, but after Capirinha things had gone a little hazy. Clare.

'Must check Clare's okay,' she mumbled. She trudged up the stairs to the top of the house using the banister rail to heave herself up. Clare was lying fully dressed across her bed and snoring for England. Yes, she could vaguely remember pushing her up the stairs, the pair of them giggling like maniacs because Clare's legs and arms had suddenly become wayward like rubber bands. On the landing Anna paused. Back to bed, or see Oliver?

Bed won. She crawled in and pulled the duvet over her head. Lovely bed.

Oliver tugged at the duvet. 'Wake up.'

She snuggled further down. 'Go 'way.'

'I have gone away. I've been sitting downstairs for the past two hours reading the papers while you've been snoring like a pig.'

'I don't snore,' she said, peering out at him through crusty eyes. 'Have I really been asleep?'

'Yup. Come on, wake up. I'm hungry.'

She levered herself upright. 'What's the time?'

'Half twelve.'

'No. Really?'

'Do wake up, I want lunch.'

Anna put her hands on her stomach and shut her eyes. 'I couldn't eat a thing.'

'I'm starving.' She could hear the irritation in his voice and kept her eyes shut. 'I could have been having roast beef with my friends, but I came back specially because you insisted, and now you smell like a brewery and have all the animation of a basin of tripe. God knows what you've been up to.'

Anna wished she knew too. No she didn't. Best not to know. 'How's your grandmother?'

'You've already asked me that.' Anna nodded. So she had. Oliver looked as irritated as her stomach felt. 'She's a tough old bird, she'll live. Now do get up, I've booked a table at the Richmond Arms, and at this rate we'll miss last orders.'

She didn't have the strength to protest. She pottered to the bathroom and washed as quickly as her poor coordination allowed. The skin on her face felt heavy and seemed to have dropped two inches. It was a curious mix of red overlying grey. She bunged some foundation on top. Dracula's bride stared back at her. She looked down and saw *I survived Clare's hen party!* emblazoned across her chest. She wasn't convinced.

Oliver drove fast to the pub in order to catch last orders. Anna thought he would drive more slowly if he realised how close she was to being sick down the sleek black side of his car, but decided, in the circumstances, that keeping her mouth shut was a better idea. He ordered for both of them, and the food came quickly.

I wish I hadn't drunk so much, she thought. I wish I felt more together now. She tried to concentrate on what Oliver was talking about. Some friends getting married, second time for her, third time for him. She sipped mineral water and tried to eat. The meat swam in bloody gravy, the fat starting to congeal in grains on top.

'Do you know,' she said, giving up on the food, 'the average duration of a marriage today is about the same as in Shakespeare's time.'

'Is that so?'

'Mmm. Then it was death that finished marriages. Now it's divorce.'

'Really.'

'Marriage was a death sentence for women. Get married, get pregnant, and die. That's what happened to Jess at Templecombe. She fell in love and then she died.' She hugged herself, feeling as if her bones were brittle. 'Happily ever after probably did mean just that; the chances were they'd be dead within the year, no time for the romantic fantasies to be shattered.'

Oliver stared at her. 'What are you going on about?'

'Death and marriage.'

He blinked. 'That's a bit morbid.'

'Is it? Sorry, I'm not good company at the moment.' She rubbed her aching forehead. She felt grey, grey and cold and clammy. 'Can we go now?'

'We've only just got here.' He sighed, fished around in his inside pocket then reached under the table and tapped her knee. Her hand went under the table, met his. Her fingers felt the hard, sharp edges of a neatly folded packet. 'Emergency rations.'

Anna gripped the packet in the palm of her hand so the corners dug into the soft flesh. He raised his eyebrows and smiled, and she smiled back.

Anna came back from the Ladies feeling perkier. She didn't want to eat, but watched Oliver. God, he was good-looking. She ran her hand up his leg under the table and leaned forward.

'Let's go back and fuck each other's brains out.'

Oliver choked on his roast beef. 'Keep your voice down,' he said, half laughing but looking round. 'Stay cool.'

'I don't want to be cool. I'm hot. Hot hot hot.' She inhaled deeply, then stretched her arms up. Her fingers tingled, the blood rushed around her veins, she could feel it, whoosh, round the blood went, round and round. 'Harvey discovered the circulation of blood in seventeen . . . seventeen . . . seventeen something. Why don't I remember? I should know that. Why don't I remember? Do you remember?'

'I don't think I ever knew, sweetheart.' He grabbed her hand. 'Anna? Anna, listen . . .'

'You're shaking my hand.'

'I know, listen . . .' He lowered his voice so she could only just hear. 'How many lines have you done?'

'Umm . . .'

'Don't say.' He held up one finger. She thought, then shook her head. Two. Another shake. Three. Four. She nodded.

'Okay.' He pushed his plate away. 'Let's go.'

He went to the bar, Anna clinging to his hand. 'I felt so dreadful, really, Olly, I did, I felt awful . . .'

'Sure. Do you want to wait outside while I pay up, bit of fresh air?'

'Oh nooooo, I want to stay with youuuuu.' She ran her hand down his back. Such a nice back. Nice and strong. He was lovely. Lovely.

He grabbed her hand. 'Stop it,' he said, quite sharply.

Anna frowned. Poor Olly, he looked all worried. She stroked his forehead. 'Don't worry, Olly. It's going to be brilliant.'

Chapter 22

'Wake up!'

Someone was shaking her shoulder.

'Anna? Can you hear me? Wake up!'

Anna managed to persuade one eyelid to peel up. She squinted at the fuzzy figure standing before her. Fuzzy, and female. Clare.

'Where's . . . ?'

'He's buggered off. Said he had to be back in London for a meeting.'

Anna subsided back into the bed. 'You saw him then.'

'And how.' Clare plonked a cup of tea beside her bed. 'Apparently you have a fucking crap shower and a fucking lousy heating system.'

The irritation in her voice penetrated the regurgitated porridge that Anna's brain had become. 'Sorry,' she mumbled. Her tongue had somehow got stuck at the bottom of her mouth. It was all too much. She closed the eye that was open.

'C'mon, Anna, wake up.' Clare shook her shoulder again. 'What's the matter with you?'

'Don't feel well. Got a cold.' She sniffed. 'Not getting up.'

'I thought you were doing that conference thingy up at the uni.'

Shit.

'What day is it?'

'Monday.'

Oh, shit.

'What's the time?' She couldn't see the alarm clock through her bleary eyes.

'Eight twenty. Look, I've got to get going or I'll be late for work, but are you okay?'

'Mmm. No. Yes. Oh, shit.' She closed her eyes as tightly as possible to stop herself being sick.

Clare put her hand on her forehead. 'You're freezing. Do you want me to phone Gwyn?'

'No, he'd never forgive me.' Anna struggled to sit up, the room swimming around her. Clare came into focus. Her face was creased with concern.

'Yesterday, when you came back . . . I don't want to pry, but are you taking something?'

Anna swung her legs round so she was sitting on the edge of the bed. Clare passed her the tea and Anna took a sip. A wave of nausea shuddered through her. She closed her eyes.

'Anna? I know you don't want to talk, but we're all worried about you.'

'No need to be.' Anna forced her legs to push her upright. 'It's just a cold.'

'Some cold. Look, I'm not going to have a row with you like you did with Bron, but you need help, not some guy supplying you with—'

'It's a cold, okay?' Anna groped her way to the door, pushing past Clare. 'Everyone knows summer colds are always the worst.'

'You sounded okay last night.' Clare's tone was dry.

Last night. Last night. What had happened last night? She'd think about that later. 'Just going to have a shower . . .'

'Your boyfriend's nicked all the hot water.'

On the way up to the university she remembered. She'd felt invincible, astride Oliver, surging ahead as if cresting the waves; she could do anything, she ruled the world. Oh no. She hadn't. Not 'Rule, Britannia'. Oh no. Oh God.

'You're late.' Gwyn, his expression as black as his hair.

'Sorry, sorry, sorry.'

'You're in the main lecture theatre.' He was rushing her down the corridor. 'Have you got your slides?'

'In my case.' Her hands trembled as she opened it and hauled out the carousel. She felt hot, cold, waves of nausea. Waves. Oh shit.

'Gwyn, I've got to go to the loo.'

'You haven't time.'

'I've got to.'

'Jeez. Okay, I'll set up your slides.' She thrust the carousel at him. 'Two minutes, that's all.'

She turned and rushed back to the Ladies and dry-retched into the pan. Oh God. Hot tears filled her eyes. Giving talks was bad enough, but she couldn't, couldn't. Not like this. Her hands were shaking, she felt sick, she could hardly stand.

'Anna!' Gwyn's voice. A thump at the door. 'Come on. They're waiting.'

'Just a minute.'

Her fingers frantically searched the bottom of her bag. There had to be some left, she hadn't used it all, she was sure, there must be some. There it was. Thank you, God.

'Anna!'

'Coming.' She unfolded the stiff paper, her hands shaking so she spilled a little. No time to worry about that. Quick, quick, chop it, line it. She bent her head.

'Sorry about that,' she said to Gwyn two minutes later. 'I've got some sort of bug.'

'Are you okay?' Gwyn was frowning at her, silly man.

'Fine.' She grinned at him. Talking in public was a doddle. 'Absolutely brilliant.'

*

'What's going on?' Gwyn tossed a pebble off the edge of the bridge and watched it fall into the water below with a plop. They had come to a stop at a Palladian bridge, the furthest point of the landscape garden. For seven hundred years the house had been the seat of the Turberville family, but was now owned by an ageing rocker.

'What do you mean?' The ripples spread outwards in widening circles, making the lone duck on the water bob up and down.

'You know.'

'No.' Anna flipped a pebble over the edge. Plop. 'Shall we carry on?'

'We need to talk . . .'

Anna stooped for another pebble. 'You sound as if you're about to tell me off. Good thing you're not my big brother.' She gave a little laugh. 'You'd have been awful as a big brother, no wonder Bronwen's always trying to boss me around. Oops. Sorry, duck.' The duck, disturbed by the velocity of Anna's last pebble, took off, the splashing of webbed feet on the water disturbing the stillness of the sweeping landscape ahead of them.

'Anna . . .' Gwyn touched her arm.

Anna stared up towards the great house, golden grey in the afternoon light, the two colonnaded wings on either side stretching out from the central block like arms reaching across the top of the valley.

'They had such confidence in the future,' she said. 'We're only seeing these gardens at their best now, two, three hundred years on from when they were designed.'

Gwyn leant on the balustrade. 'What gets me is the way they shifted the earth around. A hill there, a river there. Let's put a wood up on the crest of that hill, and there it is. Done.'

'Like the Pyramids, lots of people working for pennies.' She pointed across the valley to a group of trees at the crest of a gentle slope. 'That's a nice clump of trees. It makes a good frame for the view back towards the house.'

'Yes, there's a watercolour back at the house of this view.' Gwyn stared at his hands clasped in front of him. 'This guy you're seeing . . .'

A breeze started, making Anna wrap her jacket around herself. Her cold hadn't gone and the miserable chill went straight to her bones. The trees swayed, branches fluttered, ripples scudded across the lake. The house was reflected in the water, honey stone floating on the surface.

'Oliver.'

'It's going well?'

'Yup.' She blew her nose noisily. 'It's great.'

'Bron thought you didn't have much in common.'

'Bronwen should mind her own business.' Anna almost said that Gwyn should mind his own business too, but she stopped herself. She leant back against the balustrade, feeling cornered. 'You're all ganging up against Oliver and me, and I don't know why. You should be pleased for me, he's the complete opposite of Richard.'

'Does he take drugs?'

'None of your business.' She picked some lichen off one of the columns.

'It is if he's giving them to you.'

'He isn't,' she said shortly. Gwyn scratched his head but said nothing. Anna rummaged in her pockets for a clean tissue, then turned back to look at the mansion, framed but isolated within the landscape. 'At least Gene Machine won't have the neighbours complaining about the noise levels. What do you think he's going to do with it all?'

Gwyn shrugged. 'He'd hardly got his key in the door when English Heritage were round asking the same question. You know they'd tried to save it for the nation? Couldn't raise the funds.'

Anna nodded, wiping her nose, happier now they were on safer ground. 'But they must be pleased it's gone to a single owner rather than being carved up into flats.'

'Apparently he came round when he was a kid, and promised himself that one day he'd own it.'

'Really? That's a good story.' Anna said. Drat, her nose was streaming.

Gwyn outlined the contours of the slope with his hand. 'I think there must have been a carriage drive across to that bridge, and then up to that building on the other side,' he said.

'Maybe.' Anna looked, weighing up the options. 'Yes, it'd make sense. What's the documentation like?'

'Pretty good. Of course, he's got a receipt from Mr Brown.'

'Oh dear. How much for?'

'Eighty-four pounds exactly.'

'Oh dear,' Anna said, this time with real feeling. 'Something tells me he's not going to want to hear about Mr Brown's fees.'

'That's why you're here.'

'And there I was thinking it was my charming personality.'

''Fraid not.' Gwyn put his arm around Anna's shoulders and squeezed. 'I'm worried about you,' he said. 'We all are.'

'Don't be.' She turned so his arm slipped off her shoulders. 'It's a nice bridge. It looks like a copy of the one at Wilton.'

'Near enough.'

She put her hand on one of the columns that supported the roof. Someone had carved a heart, the initials OT and LJ, and a date: 1854. She traced the heart shape with her finger, then the O. O for Oliver. 'I know he's different from us, but that's part of it. I've been good for so long, it's fun being bad,' she said, her voice soft.

'So long as you're in control.'

'But I am.'

'You weren't yesterday.'

She leant forward on the parapet, picking moss off the edge.

'Sorry about that. I think I was still hungover from Clare's hen party.'

'It must have been some party.'

'It was.'

He cleared his throat. 'Is it coke?'

'No.' She dropped another pebble off the edge of the bridge, her shoulders hunched. She hoped Gwyn would drop the subject as easily as she had the pebble.

There was a pause, then Gwyn said, 'Let's head back to the house.'

Anna shivered and dug her hands deep into her pockets as they walked round the lake, grass swishing under their feet. 'He'll need to get his grazing sorted out soon,' Gwyn said. 'The place should be covered with sheep.'

Anna looked sideways at him. Had Bron called him and told him to say something, or was it . . . 'Yesterday,' Anna said, choosing her words carefully, 'it did go all right, didn't it?'

Gwyn stopped and stared at her. 'No. It didn't.'

'Oh.' She laughed nervously. 'I always find public speaking difficult.'

'I know.' Gwyn looked up at the scudding clouds. 'I put a lot of work your way. But I can't if you're not . . . reliable.'

'I see.' She licked her lips, feeling the corners crack like paper cuts. 'Monday was a one-off. Clare won't have a hen party again – at least, I hope not.'

'I can't make allowances just because—'

'I don't want anyone to make allowances for me. If my work's not good enough...' She shook her hair out, pretending not to care.

'People notice, Anna. Not everyone's as naïve as you are.'

'Is that what you think? I'm being naïve?'

'Jeez, Anna, you might as well have a fucking sign on your head.' His voice rose. 'You may think you're being discreet, but you're not.'

'I don't know what you're talking about.'

'I can't put any more work your way.'

Anna gasped. For a second she thought the world had stopped. Then the blood surged back into her brain and beat against her ear-drums with a sickening thud thud. She turned to him, eyes wide, not believing what he'd just said.

Gwyn shrugged. 'I'm sorry.'

She pushed her fists deep into the pockets of her coat. 'You have to do what you think is best.' She held her head up, biting her lower lip to stop it trembling. What was happening to her? Everything seemed to be going wrong. Life was supposed to be fun and exciting, not bleak. She felt small and insignificant against the sweep of the landscape, the lowering sky. But she would manage. She had to manage. Oh god, why was everything going wrong?

'Hey, hey.' Gwyn hugged her, and she let him. He was comfortingly large, his arms secure, his hands on her hair gentle. He reminded her of Will, the way he'd looked after her, being happy at Templecombe. It seemed a long time since she could remember being happy.

She waited until her breathing was under control, then pulled away. 'Sorry.' She'd run out of tissues, and had to re-use one to wipe her eyes.

He looked down at the ground as if deciding something, then back up at her. 'All I want to say is, does he make you happy? Because it doesn't seem to me that you're happy. And haven't been since you met him. That's all.'

'It's got nothing to do with Oliver . . .' Anna stopped, and stared at her hands, knowing she was close to breaking down completely. Her skin was paper dry, stretched taut across her knuckles, red-lined and sore. She couldn't read Gwyn's expression. Not disapproval, but something else. Embarrassment?

He patted her shoulder. 'Come on, let's get back to the house.'

They walked across the landscape, discussing the positioning of viewpoints and vistas and whether a heap of rubble could be the remains of a temple or was just a field shelter. Gwyn helped Anna climb up the ha-ha, heaving her up the walled bank and on to the formal lawn in front of the house.

They looked back down the valley, at the lake and the bridge where they'd been standing. Clouds sped across the sky, throwing fast-moving shadows over the landscape, the grass billowing on the hillsides catching the light then turning dark, like shoals of fish escaping a predator. Anna took in a deep breath of the clean, fresh air.

'I'm sorry if I've let you down,' she said. 'I didn't mean to, it's just . . .'

'We're worried about you. Me, Bron. Clare and Steve. You disappear for weeks on end, you're sharp with everyone, having rows – Bron's really upset, you know. Clare says when you are around you're wrecked, and your work . . . I can't cover for you again. I was in two minds about cancelling this.' He waved his arm, indicating the garden.

Anna rubbed her forehead. 'I won't let you down.'

Gwyn looked at her. 'No more shoddy work?'

Anna shook her head.

'Okay.' He nodded at her as if gauging her response. Then his manner changed. 'So. Are you going to tell the wild man of British rock that Capability Brown charged eighty-four pounds for an initial consultation only and all the receipts in the world can't alter that fact, and that therefore this is not a Capability landscape, or am I?'

Anna's car wouldn't start and was towed off to a local garage, leaving her bereft. Gwyn gave her a lift home.

'Will you be okay?'

She nodded, although she felt as if she was made of brittle glass. 'Of course.'

He hesitated as if he was going to say something, but changed his mind. He kissed her cheek. 'Take care, Anna.'

She let herself into her house, ready to shatter into a million little pieces. The post lay scattered on the mat and she collected it. Lots for Clare, acceptances to the wedding she guessed. Not much for her except bills, and one envelope addressed in scrawling, bold writing she recognised. Will. She picked it up, not sure if she could face whatever Will had to say to her. No, she'd do the bills first. She couldn't feel much worse.

She discovered she could.

How had she managed to spend all that money? She went through the list. Shoes. Clothes. Restaurants. Hundred-pound withdrawals from the cash machine – and she never seemed to have any cash. She knew where it had gone – up her nose, at £50 a wrap. Even if she used Mrs Davenport's cheque, she'd not clear the debt. She slumped against the wall, sliding down until she crumpled on to her knees, her face in her hands, and howled.

She had ruined everything. She had neglected her friends, damaged her health, wrecked her professional reputation, and for what? An attempt to compete with people she didn't even know, and a bill she couldn't pay. When Clare had gone, how would she pay the mortgage? Perhaps she'd lose the house. She'd been professionally negligent, and an old lady was dying, and Will despised her, and she'd never work again, and her friends hated her and there was no point to living. So much for being Cinderella; the ball was well and truly over. She cried even harder.

When she'd got to the hiccupping stage, she picked up Will's letter. At least it wasn't a bill. Her heart suddenly leapt. Perhaps he wasn't writing to accuse her; perhaps he was writing to say . . . What nonsense, she thought. Will despises you. Her hand was shaking as she opened the letter. Inside was a photocopy of one of Jessica's letters, with the words 'the goddess Anahita' highlighted in Day-Glo yellow, and a print-out from the Internet. Scrawled across it were the words: *Shouldn't you look into this? Will.*

Not an accusation. Not a declaration either. She started to read the print-out.

Anahita, the Immaculate One, was one of the ruling deities of the Persian Empire. She embodied the physical and metaphorical qualities of water, especially the fertilising flow of water from the fountain in the stars. The Greeks associated Anahita with Aphrodite, the Goddess of Love. Zoroaster was specifically commanded by his male god to honour her.

She looked at Jessica's letter again. What was a Persian goddess doing in an eighteenth-century landscape garden?

Chapter 23

Oliver rang that evening. 'How was your day?'

'Mixed,' she said, thinking of Gwyn, of Anahita. She wondered what Oliver would say if she told him that one of her best friends had said he couldn't recommend her for work any more. She had a horrible feeling that he wouldn't be interested at all, would pass it off with platitudes. Everything was happy and shiny in Oliver's world. 'I'm a woman on the edge of a nervous breakdown.'

'You should have stayed in London with me.' He laughed. 'Come up tomorrow, I'll soon sort you out.'

Did she need sorting out? You've not been happy since you met him, Gwyn had said. But she hadn't been happy before, she'd been sore and bruised over Richard. Oliver had made her forget Richard. She was having a good time. She stretched her right hand in front of her. It shook. She couldn't stop it shaking.

'I can't come up tomorrow.' Her voice sounded robotic. She tried to pull herself together. 'How's your grandmother?'

'Much better, apparently, but they're keeping her in for a few more days.'

Anna felt her shoulders relax with relief. 'When are you coming down to see her?'

'I can't get away right now, too much work. And I hate hospitals. Be an angel and go and visit for me.'

'Surely . . .' She was startled that he wasn't coming down, but stopped herself from saying it. It wouldn't make any difference, after all. Oliver did exactly what Oliver wanted. 'I was thinking of going to visit her anyway. I've made some new discoveries I wanted to tell her about.'

'Oh yes?' Oliver's voice sounded distant.

'About the garden.' She snuggled into the phone, longing to share the news with someone. 'Listen, you know in one of the letters Jess mentions the goddess Anahita. Well, I've been doing some research, and Anahita was the central goddess in Persian mythology, and the partner of Mithras, the bringer of light.'

'You've finished the research.' His voice was heavy.

'I should have looked into this before.' Anna remembered how he'd reassured her that she'd done quite enough, there was no need to go further. 'I'm looking into it now.'

'No.'

Anna thought she must have misheard. 'Sorry?'

'Stop it. You've written the report, and that's the end of it. You have nothing to feel guilty about, you know. You're not to blame for my grandmother's heart attack.'

Will thinks I am, Anna thought, but didn't say. 'It would make all the difference if it was true,' she said slowly. 'Imagine a garden based around a Persian goddess. She was adopted by the Zoroastrians too, as the female part of the spirit, so perhaps Arthur was a Zoroastrian. It would be unique – Grade I listed, no problem.' Silence from the other end. 'Oliver?'

'This is complete crap,' Oliver said, words enunciated clearly down the telephone line. 'You said yourself it was nothing but speculation, and without any proof all it was was theories. There isn't any proof, so stop it. Now.'

'But—'

'Anna. No.' There was a pause.

She tried again. 'But—'

'No.' He took a deep breath. 'I appreciate you're trying to make things better by going back on your report, but honestly, all you'll do is confuse and upset a very sick old lady. Do you want to cause my grandmother any more distress? Do you want that? Because that's what will happen.'

Anna thought of Mrs Davenport's white face. She bit her lip and said nothing.

'So. You'll visit my grandmother for me?'

'Yes, of course, I've said I will.' She twisted the phone cord around her finger.

'And you promise you won't upset her by talking about this.' He paused. 'Anna?'

She sighed, and untangled the cord. 'No, I won't say anything.'

'Good girl.'

Mrs Davenport was in a side ward. She looked so still, Anna went back and checked with the nurse on duty that it was all right for her to visit. Mrs Davenport opened her eyes as Anna peered round the door.

'Come in, my dear,' she said, her voice thin but steady.

'I brought you these, but they look a bit redundant,' Anna said, holding out a mixed bunch of summer flowers. There were already four vases of flowers, three modest like Anna's bunch but one an extravagant riot of colour. Anna recognised the style.

'Oliver.' Mrs Davenport nodded. 'Always the big gesture.'

Anna felt she needed to make excuses for him. 'He wanted to come but he's busy at work, so he asked me to visit instead.'

Mrs Davenport smiled. 'And you're not busy?'

Anna shrugged. 'Yes, but – I wanted to come.'

Mrs Davenport nodded, and indicated the chair by her bed. 'I'm pleased. Do sit down.'

Anna sat. 'I feel guilty about you being here. If I hadn't written the report . . . Will says it's my fault.'

'My dear . . .' She held her hand out to Anna, who took it. 'You mustn't feel like that. The house is old, and I am old, and we are crumbling away together. It was not your job to invent what you couldn't find. William is a dear, good boy, but he is quite wrong. If anyone is at fault it is I, for I let the garden disintegrate and become overgrown when I could quite easily have maintained it.'

Anna frowned. 'I assumed it had become overgrown during the Second World War, because all the men were away fighting.'

'The garden died then, but not because of that. No, it was after the war that I gave up . . . You're sure you want to hear this?'

Anna settled in her chair. 'Please.'

Mrs Davenport paused as if collecting her thoughts, eyes fixed on some point on the opposite wall. Then she gave a big sigh, and began.

'I was born just before 1914, so in a way wars have defined my life. My father survived the war, but he and my mother had no further children. I had a blissful though rather lonely childhood. But then, when I was sixteen, a new gardener joined the staff.' She smiled, as if remembering, before continuing. 'His name was Tom, and I fell in love. Before long I was expecting a child. In those days being an unmarried mother was a dreadful thing. Tom was dismissed immediately, and my parents sent me off to relatives in Northumbria, where I had the baby. They took her away immediately, I never even held her.' She stopped and closed her eyes, her skin paper white. Anna didn't know what to say. She held Mrs Davenport's frail hand in both of hers. The old lady sighed, and continued.

'I was sent away to finishing school in Switzerland, and when I returned, everyone pretended nothing had happened. It was easier to fall in with my parents' plans and be a debutante than try to find Tom. I threw myself into having fun, parties and lunches and balls and dinners, all the time feeling I'd died inside. You've seen the photographs from that time. Several young men proposed, but I turned them all down. And then there was Quentin Davenport. He was charming, and sociable – Oliver is very like him. He made me feel that perhaps I could have a life, so I married him.' Her hands twisted the blanket.

'Things went wrong from the start. My father died shortly after the wedding, and I inherited Templecombe. I assumed we'd settle there, especially as I was expecting Oliver's father at that point, but Quentin hated the country. He wanted to let out the estate and live in London. We argued constantly about Templecombe, and about money. Then the Second World War came and he went off to fight. I returned to Templecombe with my son, Oliver's father, knowing that my marriage was over.

'Then one day I was in the garden when I saw a strange man walking by the pavilion. I went to challenge him, to find out what he was doing, and it was Tom. He'd come back to visit his family in the village. We began to meet again when he was home on leave, using the pavilion. He was on leave for Midsummer's Eve in 1944, and I put lanterns and candles out in the garden for him. That evening we decided I'd ask Quentin for a divorce.'

She stopped, and to Anna's horror one tear slid out from her eye. 'Tom was part of the British 1st Airborne Division sent to take the bridge at Arnhem. He died on the twenty-second of September 1944. They called it Black Friday, and there didn't seem any point in living.'

'I'm so sorry,' Anna whispered, feeling useless, inadequate. The room was quiet, the curtains wafting gently in the breeze from the open window. A bee buzzed in, attracted by the flowers. Mrs Davenport gave a sad smile, continued.

'Quentin lived. I didn't ask for a divorce in the end. There didn't seem any point, and in those days there was still a stigma attached to divorcees. We lived separate lives, Quentin in London and me here. I tried to trace my baby, but it was too late. So I let the garden die. My son was never interested in it – maybe he associated it with unhappiness. He went to London as much as possible during the holidays and moved there once he'd left school. He died a year ago, and I realised that there was no one left who remembered the garden. And suddenly it all seemed a waste, a waste of love, and that's when I decided to try and reclaim something of what had been there. I hoped Oliver would be interested, but I think not. He is his father's son.'

'But Oliver *is* interested in the garden,' Anna said, leaning forward.

'Oliver is interested in you, my dear,' she said, patting Anna's hand. 'It is not the same thing. No, when I am gone, Oliver will sell up. And perhaps that's as it should be. Someone else can restore the garden, or make a new one. We sometimes have to let go . . .'

'I'm sorry I couldn't write the report you wanted,' Anna whispered.

'But you did. I am delighted you discovered the letters. I always knew it was a garden meant for lovers. I suppose I hoped it would work its magic on your last night at Templecombe. I could see William was falling in love with you, and I thought you were . . .'

Anna dropped her head. Will. Falling in love.

'Never mind. I should be pleased for my grandson.' Mrs Davenport stared into the distance, her eyes cloudy, and Anna sensed she wasn't thinking of Oliver. 'William reminds me of Tom, you know. Something about the way he stands. But I know it's just an old woman's fantasy. William is not Tom's grandchild. My baby – my daughter – is lost, and the garden will follow.'

'Don't say that.'

'But it's the truth. When you get to my age, the truth matters.'

Anna longed to tell her about Anahita and what she'd discovered. Oliver had said it would only confuse and upset the old lady, but she wondered if that was true. Mrs Davenport was tired and physically frail, but there was nothing wrong with her mind. She wavered, then decided. Find out first, and then tell her. She'd have to explore the tunnel again.

There was a sound at the door. She turned and saw Will and felt her spirits rise at the sight of him, then drop as he shied away from meeting her eyes. Of course. What else did she expect?

'I'll come back later,' he said quickly.

'No, Will, stay,' Anna said, getting up. 'I'll go. Thank you for telling me your story,' she said to Mrs Davenport. She kissed her soft creased cheek. 'I will save the garden for you.'

Anna left, registering Will standing well back to avoid any physical contact with her. She went downstairs and loitered in the foyer. She almost missed him as he strode through after twenty minutes, having to run to catch up with him.

'Will, please, I need your help,' Anna said.

'Not interested,' Will said, going through the automatic doors.

'To find Anahita,' she called after him just before the doors shut.

He stopped on the pavement outside. Turned. The doors swooshed open. 'What do you want?'

'A lift to Templecombe.'

'You're kidding,' Will said. He looked at the canoe, looked at the lake, then back at the canoe. 'It'll never take our weight.'

'It doesn't have to take our weight, just our things,' Anna said. She bent down and gave the canoe a tug. The bottom scraped over the pavilion floor. 'Come on, give me a hand.'

Will didn't move. 'What about us?'

'We're going to swim.'

'Now you *are* kidding.'

Anna straightened up. 'You've swum in the lake before.'

Will dug his hands in his pockets. 'Yeah, I've swum it. Once, when it was an emergency. I don't intend to do it again.' He'd been silent on the journey to Templecombe and she knew he hadn't forgiven her. But she needed his help.

'At least give me a hand with this.' She tugged at the canoe.

Will bent and picked up the other end. 'You're mad.'

'Maybe.' Oliver would kill me if he knew what I was doing, she thought, and immediately remembered Will admitting he was a murderer. She looked at his tanned face, the blond hair tousled as usual. Whatever Will was, she knew he was trustworthy.

They eased the canoe out through the French windows and down the bank to the edge of the lake, where Anna had left the notebook, ruler and pens she'd bought from the hospital shop, along with towels and a torch. She looked at the water. Although it was a sunny day, it looked cold as glass. Eels and mud. She shivered.

'Second thoughts?'

Anna shook her head. 'Nope. I should have done this ages ago.' She bundled her equipment into an old picnic rug she'd borrowed from Peggy. It wasn't ideal, being thick and heavy, but the reverse side was made of a sturdy waterproof material. She thought she remembered the chamber floor being dry brick, not earthy at all, but although she wasn't going to say anything to Will, she wasn't convinced that the canoe wouldn't leak.

Will watched her. 'What if the roof collapses again?'

'Then you'll have to come and rescue me,' she said. 'Right. Let's get her in the water.'

They pushed the canoe into the sludgy water, Anna keeping hold of the rope. It floated. Anna looked across to the mouth of the tunnel. She bit her lip. What had seemed a brilliant idea at the hospital now seemed distinctly stupid. But then, this was all about being stupid. She hesitated for a moment. Ah well, Will had seen her in bra and pants before, and it claimed on the Agent Provocateur care label that they were washable in cool water. If anything was certain, it was that the water was definitely going to be cool. She pulled her T-shirt over her head and undid her jeans, then stuffed them into the bundle along with her gym shoes, tied the rug loosely at the top like a gigantic plum pudding, and dumped it in the canoe.

Will look dumbfounded. 'You're not going in like that.'

'Yup.' Anna tied her hair in a high ponytail, looping the ends round so it made a bun, all the while thinking, I must be mad. One toe went into the water, and involuntarily she snatched it back.

'Cold, isn't it?' he said pleasantly.

'Refreshing,' she said. She took a breath, then stepped into the water. Mud oozed up between her toes. Don't think about eels. The cold made her skin goosebump all over, but she took another step in.

'I can't believe you're doing this,' she heard Will mutter behind her, but she didn't turn round. Holding the rope firmly, she launched herself into the water.

Shhhiiiittt. Instant numbness. Desperate to get the blood circulating again, she doggy-paddled for five, six strokes before catching hold of the side of the canoe to get her breath back, not wanting to put her feet down even though she thought she could still stand. Her skin tingled all over. A splash made her head turn.

'It's even colder than before,' Will panted beside her. He slung his bundled clothes into the canoe.

'I thought you weren't coming,' she said through chattering teeth.

'Got to save you from yourself.' He grinned at her, and it was as if they had gone back to the past, to her accident, to the night at the pavilion, all the arguments forgotten in the excitement of the adventure.

'Come on then.' She launched off from the side of the canoe.

It wasn't far across the lake, although holding the canoe rope in her fist made swimming awkward. The tunnel entrance appeared to be a heap of rocks jutting into the lake. Hart's-tongue ferns grew out of the rock, the strap-like fronds obscuring the shape so it looked like a natural rocky outcrop from the valley side. But there it was, the arch that led to the tunnel.

Anna stopped and trod water. 'I'm amazed you found the entrance the night I fell,' she said over her shoulder to Will.

'It's amazing I heard you,' he said, treading water beside her. Anna didn't want to think about her lucky escape. Instead she took one last look at the bright sunlight, then swam under the arch. Four, five, six strokes, and she was against the edge of the pool. Looking back, she saw the arch as a crescent of light, emphasising the darkness within. Then she swung herself up and out of the water and on to the brick floor of the chamber. She could hear Will doing the same.

The air was cold and dank, pitch-black except for that single crescent of light. She pulled the bundle from the bottom of the canoe, shivering like a greyhound, and spread the blanket out on the floor, searching for a towel. Teeth chattering, she towelled herself half dry then handed Will the towel. It was surprisingly hard to pull on her jeans and T-shirt in the dark but she managed, ignoring the sludge that clung to her skin and the horrible clamminess of her bra and pants. Dressed and feeling exhilarated from the bracing swim, she knelt and searched the blanket again, fingers feeling for the torch. There. 'That's better.'

Before the light beam, the chamber had seemed merely dark. Now it loomed blackly around her, as if all colour had been sucked out of it. She swung the beam round and caught Will getting dressed, the light sparking his hair.

'You know the roof's likely to collapse on us,' he said.

'Go back if you want to,' Anna replied, grinning at him. She lifted the torch and moved the beam round.

A white face leered out of the darkness, ghastly in the gloom, the bright light highlighting green streaks. The shock made her almost drop the torch.

'What the—' Will behind her, sounding as shaken as she felt.

She ran the torch across the statue, noting the wings, the fluted dress tight around the waist and over one shoulder, leaving one breast exposed, the long hair flowing abundantly, and above the smiling face a crown.

Anahita.

'What's she doing here?' whispered Will. Of course, he'd also seen the Internet photographs.

'Who knows? Maybe Arthur had trading connections in the Middle East or India.'

'I thought she was Persian, not Indian.'

'She was, originally, but Zoroastrianism is a major religion in India, so perhaps . . .' She shrugged, although Will couldn't see her. 'Who knows what went on in Arthur's mind? Maybe he was a devout Zoroastrian, or maybe he acquired the statue because he liked the look of it.'

'Do you think this was the temple that Jess referred to in her letter?'

'Yes. I'm sure it is.' Anna hesitated. 'Did you read about the temple practices on the Net?'

'Ritual intercourse.' Will paused. 'Sounds interesting.'

'Oh, it'll be some fertility ritual,' she said, deliberately offhand, as she touched the statue's feet. Anahita the goddess of water, and Mithras the bringer of light. Fire and water. She felt very conscious of Will standing next to her in the darkness. Once she had thought of him like a Rembrandt, haloed with light and warmth. They were standing in darkness, but she could still sense his warmth. Mrs Davenport had said he was falling in love with her. But that was before he had known about Oliver. Now he despised her. Didn't he? But he's here – helping me . . .

She swung the torch round, wondering if there would be a statue of Mithras, but the rest of the chamber was empty. It was oval, about twenty feet at its longest point, with the statue of Anahita at one end and the pool at the other. At the pool end, opposite the statue, a spring gushed from the wall, trickling over the mossy rock wall, the water glistening. Quartz pieces had been set in the rock, glittering white in the torchlight like thousands of tiny stars.

'The fountain in the stars . . .' Next to the spring she could see the opening that led to the tunnel, the neat small bricks that made the arch over it, the blackness that absorbed the torchlight. She shivered. This would have been her tomb but for Will.

'If she's the water, then where's the fire?' Will's voice was hushed.

Anna moved the torch round at waist height. 'Look.' There were three oval basins on the wall, similar to the ones on the gateway.

Will moved forward into the light and felt the basin. 'There's some oil still in it, and the remnants of a wick. I wonder . . .' He came back towards her, then stumbled slightly. Anna instinctively put out her hands, and the torch fell to the ground with a clatter and went out.

'Drat.' She crouched down and patted the ground, searching for the torch.

'Hang on,' Will said. She heard something rattling, then a small match flame blazed.

'Oh,' she breathed. Thousands of crystals set in the arched roof caught the tiny flame, magnifying it, reflecting it back and forth, fire lights sparkling and dancing like a million diamonds. Whorls of shell cupped the flame reflections as if they were tiny spirits contained within miniature worlds.

'Damn,' Will said, and the match went out and they were in darkness again, an unbearable darkness after the light. She waited. Then he lit another match, held it up and the crystals shimmered with light again. Between them she could make out the flat pans of abalone shells, the light on the mother-of-pearl making iridescent flickers until the match went out and all was darkness once more.

And then the intimacy of the light again between Will's cupped hands as he lit another match, then another, the ceiling springing into life as he held the flame up, the flickering light making the reflections dance. The flame started to gutter, smoky shadows swallowing up the light as it flickered to faintness. One final flare and then it was gone.

'Mithras was born in a cave with a ceiling like the starry sky,'

Anna whispered, remembering her research. 'See if you can light the basins.'

The light from the matches illuminated Will's face as he bent over the basins, trying to persuade the wicks to light. There was smoke and a faint, heady scent like incense, and a leaping flame that dwindled as sharply as it had flared up. 'They catch but don't want stay lit,' he said eventually. 'And that was the last match.'

'We should have used them to find the torch,' Anna said.

'We'll find it.' Will made his way back to her. 'I didn't hear it go in the water. Besides, wouldn't you rather have seen the ceiling? It's incredible, and just think, it's been here all this time.'

Anna felt overwhelmed with guilt. She should have been here before, should have explored. Her instincts had told her the chamber was worth investigating and she had ignored them, submitting a sub-standard report instead. Mrs Davenport had nearly died from the disappointment. She looked up to the roof. This alone warranted conservation; it should have been included in her report. Her work had been shoddy. No wonder Gwyn didn't want to use her again.

What had happened to her that she hadn't checked this out before making her report? She knew the answer, a dark worm of shame inside her. She had been seduced by a lifestyle, an image of herself that wasn't true. It was fake, unreal. She wasn't that person, that Anna. Only the boring old Anna was true. Hot tears trickled down her face.

'Hey, are you all right?'

Anna gulped. 'Fine,' she said, pressing her hand to her mouth so he wouldn't know she was crying. She heard him shuffling back.

'Anna?'

'I'm fine,' she said, but her voice was a squeak in the chamber.

He touched her, his fingers gentle on her wet face. 'Don't cry.' He hugged her in the darkness. 'It'll be okay.'

'I've been so stupid,' she sobbed into his chest.

He patted her shoulder awkwardly. 'You weren't to know.'

'I did know,' she said. 'All along I've known this was important, that I had to explore, and I put it off. You were right, I have been negligent. It's all my fault.'

He hugged her close. 'No, no, I shouldn't have said that.'

'But it's true. I've always been proud of my work, of being professional . . .' Anna couldn't finish. She realised Will was still holding her, and pulled away. 'Sorry. I shouldn't have done that.'

'You're always saying that to me.' She could hear the smile in his voice.

Anna looked up in the darkness, remembering the magical interplay of light. Will the bringer of light. Will who had saved her. Will the murderer.

'Will,' she whispered into the darkness. 'Are you really a murderer?'

A long silence while she waited, nerves strung out. Then he spoke, his voice heavy with pain. 'Yes. I killed my father.'

Anna gasped, she couldn't help it. The cave seemed very dark and for a second she felt disorientated, as if she was going to lose her balance. Not Will. She wouldn't, couldn't believe it. She steadied herself. 'Can you tell me?'

He was silent and she'd almost given up when he finally spoke. 'I'm a vet. Or used to be one.'

She was so taken aback she almost fell into the pool. 'A what?'

'Is it that surprising?'

Anna rearranged Will in her mind. A vet. Yes, she could see it, his confident and assured manner. And that explained his professional air when he'd examined her ankle after the accident, and why Mrs Davenport and Peggy had deferred to him. They must have known. 'What happened?'

At first she thought he wasn't going to answer. When he did his voice was husky. 'I can't remember when I didn't want to be a vet. Dad's family had been farmers for ever, so I grew up around animals. I should have taken over the family farm, but instead I went to veterinary college, went into practice near where I grew up, got married. Everything was going to plan, and then, boom. Foot and mouth.'

Will was married? He couldn't be. She was bewildered by how shocked she felt, one surprise after another. She wrenched her mind back to what he was saying.

'I think it's impossible to understand unless you were there. We were slaughtering whole herds of healthy animals, and then seeing the bodies piled up, stinking, waiting to be burnt.' His voice dropped. 'For a lot of small-scale farmers, their livestock is like family, their lives are intertwined. Some couldn't take it and killed themselves. My father . . .'

'Oh Will,' Anna whispered.

'Our farm was next to a farm suspected of the disease. That meant our animals had to be slaughtered in case the infection spread. He begged me . . .' Will cleared his throat. 'He begged me, but I insisted it had to be done according to the rule book. There were so many farms, so many animals, it was so frantic that it would have been easy to be sloppy. The rules were being broken all the time. But because it was my family farm it had to be done correctly so no one could say I was favouring one farm above another. My professional duty.' He gave a short laugh. 'My father blew his brains out the day after we slaughtered the animals. I killed him.'

'Of course you didn't, it wasn't your fault . . .'

'I know, I was only obeying orders.' He spoke with a bitterness she couldn't begin to comprehend. All she could do was reach out in the darkness and hug him, feeling small and ashamed that she'd wept earlier when her problems were all self-inflicted and trivial. Will's grief was on a much larger scale and beyond his control. She could feel him trembling and hugged him tighter, reassuring him again and again that it wasn't his fault, wanting desperately to take some of his pain and anguish.

After a while he pulled away and took a deep breath. 'The tests showed that none of our livestock were infected after all, but it was too late for them – and for my father. Things went back to normal, or as much as they can when the heart of a community has been ripped out. I couldn't work, couldn't do anything. All I could think of was my father. My wife said she couldn't live with me like that, and left, and my practice told me to take a sabbatical year. I travelled around for a bit, and ended up here.'

'Are you going to go back?'

'I don't know. Being here has helped, being with . . . I was in a bad way when I first turned up. Mrs D. and Peggy have been wonderful.' She heard him sigh. 'So now you know. Pretty pathetic really.'

'Don't be stupid,' Anna said, hugging him again. Professional duty. He had done his professional duty, and his father had died. Spoilt and self-indulgent, she had paid lip-service to professional duty and Mrs Davenport had nearly died. She could feel his heartbeat against her cheek as they clung to each other, Will's arms around her. I have to save Templecombe, she thought. I have to. I have to make amends. His hands were touching her hair. She nuzzled his neck, inhaling his warmth, couldn't help brushing her lips against his skin, feeling the pulse on his neck.

She felt him press his head to her hair, felt his gentle kiss as he murmured her name. She closed her eyes, rubbing her cheek against his shoulder like a cat, her hands splayed on his back, lost in being with him, being here, being now. His fingers felt her face like a blind man's, searching, and she caught his hand to her mouth, kissing his palm, roughened with work, dragging his finger along the inside of her lower lip. Hands together, palm to palm, stroking, touching. He bent his head and kissed the inside of her wrist, tongue running a line of electric heat against the veins. Her body felt heavy, lulled into stillness, thinking of nothing except the softness as skin explored skin, his touch tender and loving.

She realised she could make out his face, tawny like a lion's. She turned, puzzled, then realised that one of the basins had caught fire, sending flickers of light dancing over the rough walls. Gradually the flame burnt more strongly so the chamber filled with a rosy glow, bouncing off the crystal ceiling, and a strange, exotic scent, both sweet and heavy, perfumed the damp air. They stood, eyes drinking each other in, equally caught in the moment. There was no hurry; time no longer danced in circles, but stood still for them.

Dreamlike, Will pulled her T-shirt over her head, and she slipped his shirt from his shoulders, the sheen on his skin gleaming like satin in the firelight. The noise from the spring sounded like thousands of tiny bells. Her skin was silvery white and she trembled as he reached for her, not from fear or worry, but feeling held in the goddess's hand, on the edge of something powerful.

Will's head bowed over her breasts and she arched her back as his mouth teased the still heaviness away, replacing it with something sharp and intense, electric. Her body rippled with the light reflected from the sparkling water. She pulled him down on to the blanket, not questioning what they were doing, only knowing it was right. It was as if they were following a pattern laid down long ago, their bodies entwining in the dance, the oldest dance, her hands on Will's back, taking him to her, feeling him, two halves of a whole becoming one.

She cried out, and he paused, suspended in the dream, then began moving slowly, plunging deep into her soul, her being, and she was water, water against him, snow melting in the fire, the crystal stars making rainbows of the light and dazzling her eyes, and everything flowing to her centre, making her whole, making her one with Will. She dug her fingers into his back, with the watching goddess smiling faintly, blessing them. Her mouth found Will's, no longer gentle but hungry, devouring, burning; she was kissing his mouth, his hair, his neck, and the lights shone gold and red and rainbows poured into her body as she arched and Will cried out and she was falling, falling, falling . . .

Will's eyes were honey-flecked like tiger's-eye stones, but warm and soft. His face, washed golden with the light, was relaxed, younger than she'd seen before, the sadness gone. He was smiling slightly, and as they stared at each other the smile grew, and Anna could feel her own face lift with the enchantment of being with Will. He was beautiful, more beautiful than anything she'd seen before.

He had wrapped the blanket round them so they were safely cocooned, arms about each other, legs still entwined, cuddling close against the chill air, lost in time. He kissed her eyes, her nose, her mouth, loving kisses gentle and soft. She felt awash with emotion. Nothing would ever, could ever be that perfect again. All there was was Will and his arms about her. She kissed him, his mouth soft and sweet. She felt as if everything had been washed away, the scars healed, and once again she was reborn, but this time she was back to herself, another restoration.

'Anna,' Will breathed, his hand tracing the line of her cheek. 'Anna, Anna, Anna.' He caught his lower lip in his teeth and shook his head as if amazed. His eyes were wide, pupils dark in the firelight. Anna smiled at him, feeling her own eyes shining.

'Will,' she whispered. Everything jumbled around her head, warm, fuzzy feelings glowing in her heart. Oh, Will. Everything she was, or could be, or ever had been was summed up in that single word. She felt overflowing with emotion, soft and tender. Nothing could touch them in their world. Up above the crystals shimmered in the firelight, and she was perfectly happy.

Will was smiling at her, and she reached out and touched his glowing face. He sighed, as if about to speak, when suddenly his expression changed, hardened, fixed on something beyond her shoulder. He pulled back, away from her, and Anna felt cold.

'What is it?' She touched his arm but he sat up, looking infinitely tired and sad. 'Will?' She could hear the bewilderment in her own voice, the edge of panic, and she sat up too, clutching the blanket to her. She felt bereft, the change in his mood was so abrupt, so sudden. What had happened? What had he seen? She looked around wildly, searching the chamber. The statue, the stars, the spring, all was as before. The flames flickering on the walls, darkening tongues of red and gold. Her eyes frantically scanned the walls. Then—

A name, carved into the brickwork near one of the basins. A name, the lettering rough and sketchy, perhaps etched with a penknife, but still distinct.

O Davenport. 1981.

Chapter 24

'You knew.' She spoke the second he came out of the lift.

'Anna! What are you doing here? I thought you were in Bath.' Oliver bent to kiss her, but she shied away, emotions churning. 'Hey, what's up?'

'You knew it was there, and you said nothing.' She felt sick at how Oliver had betrayed her. He'd known all the time that the temple was there but had said nothing. Nothing.

'I don't know what you're talking about, darling.' He looked her up and down, then glanced along the hall. 'Let's get inside. You look as if you could do with a shower.'

She'd been so angry, she'd got Will to drive her straight to the station and taken the first train to London, then a taxi to Oliver's flat. There she'd waited for him, pacing up and down the hall, ignoring the glances of his neighbours. Everything was confused: Oliver, Will, the temple. She looked down at her arms, seeing the streaks and smears of lake mud. No wonder the neighbours had looked horrified. She followed Oliver into his flat and waited while he slung his suit jacket over a chair, pulled off his tie and dumped his briefcase.

'Drink?'

She shook her head. 'You knew it was there.' In her emotional confusion it was the one clear thing she could hang on to. Oliver had known all along about the temple.

'As I don't know what "it" is, I can't say.' He got a bottle of lager from the fridge and flipped the metal lid off, his cool elegance a complete contrast to Will's scruffiness.

'The temple.' Will had been silent as he'd driven her to the station, but she had been quiet too, overwhelmed by what had happened. Suddenly she felt a squeeze of anxiety. Perhaps it had been a mistake to leave him. They needed to talk about what had happened. But she had to confront Oliver.

'You mean the pavilion? Of course that's there, where else would it be?' The beer was so cold it frosted the glass with condensation. 'Sure I can't get you something?'

'The temple to Anahita by the lake.' That afternoon she had . . . She closed her eyes for one ecstatic second, remembering, then snapped them open. This had to be done before she could think about Will. She had to settle things with Oliver.

'You've lost me.' Oliver took a sip, then put the bottle carefully down on the granite surface. 'Shall I run you a bath? You look as if you've been swimming in the lake,' he said, and laughed.

'I have been.'

'Be serious.' He was indulgent, humouring her as he strolled to the bedroom door.

'I am. I swam out to the temple and explored.' Already the afternoon seemed a long ago, a time of magic and mystery. Anna clenched her fists, trying to keep control of her emotions. 'As you did, all those years ago.'

Oliver paused. When he turned his expression was neutral, his voice even. 'Why do you say that?'

'I saw your name. You'd scratched it into the wall.'

'Ah.' He stared at the ceiling, then at her. Anna scanned his face for some reaction to being caught out, but there was nothing. 'If you don't want a shower, I'll have one.'

'Oliver . . .' She grabbed his arm to stop him leaving the room. 'We need to talk, I need—'

'What? Look, I've just come back from work, I want to shower, change and then I'm going out. Do come if you want, but I think you ought to change first.'

'You can't just walk away from this.'

He gave her a hard stare. 'Watch me.' He stalked through the bedroom into the bathroom and flipped the shower on at full power.

Anna followed him, determined not to be deflected. 'Why didn't you tell me?'

'Tell you what?' He paused while taking his shirt off – a new one, Anna noticed with a corner of her mind. 'Okay, yes, I can vaguely remember exploring the garden as a kid. And if my name's there, I suppose I put it there. I can't remember.'

'You expect me to believe that?'

Oliver shrugged, and let the shirt drop to the floor in a crumpled heap ready for someone else to pick up. 'I don't care whether you believe me or not. It doesn't make any difference.'

Anna wheeled round. 'It makes all the difference. If I'd known I would have investigated further, I would have—'

'But you didn't. You've done your report, and that's the end of it.' He undid his trousers. 'Strictly speaking, you were trespassing in going back.'

'Oliver!' She couldn't believe what he was saying. It was outrageous, it was impossible, it was horrific. How could he?

'Let's not quarrel.' He carried on undressing, unselfconscious as a cat. Anna stared out of the window.

'Quarrel? You've just told me I was trespassing. I suppose you think I'm trespassing now.' She pressed her fists to her mouth, unable to believe what he was saying.

'Don't be silly, of course I don't. This is such a stupid thing to argue about.' His voice was as smooth as milk of magnesia, designed to mollify upsets, smothering them with creamy richness.

Anna slapped the wall with frustration. 'It isn't stupid to me.'

'It's only a garden, and an overgrown one at that,' Oliver said. She could hear him washing himself.

'Your grandmother wanted it restored.'

'There are lots of things that people want. They don't all happen.'

'But this *could* happen.' She paced the bathroom. 'We could apply for grants, we could get funding for conservation, maybe even restoration . . .'

'We?'

'You.'

'Not interested. The house and garden are an anachronism. No one lives like that any more. I can't wave a magic wand and make the world as I'd like it to be – and to be honest, I don't want to live the life of an eighteenth-century squire. That was then and this is now. You can't live your life in the past, things have to move on.'

Anna tried to take in what he was saying. To her the garden and the people were inextricably linked, the past weaving in with the present. She'd thought he shared that view. He'd said something about how it would be a dream to restore the garden, something about a private kingdom. Realisation hit her like a sledgehammer to the guts. 'You remembered, didn't you, that day we stood by the lake and you talked about having a boat when you were a child. You remembered then, and you didn't tell me.'

Oliver turned the shower off, and the sudden lack of noise was startling. 'Your memory's too good,' he said, grinning at her as he came out. She didn't smile back, just stared at him. His grin snapped off. 'Pass me that towel.'

He wrapped it round his waist then went through to the bedroom. His back was tanned against the white of the towel, his hair sleek and dark like an otter's, but compared to Will he was as cold and smooth as the polished granite surfaces in the kitchen. Anna's insides contracted thinking of Will. Poor Will, carrying all that guilt and pain about his father. She couldn't begin to imagine how he must be feeling. And now . . . I shouldn't have come here, she thought. I should have stayed with Will, made sure he was all right. But she'd had to come.

She followed Oliver back to the living room, rubbing her arms to try and warm up. Concentrate. Don't think of Will now. Oliver had collected his drink and was sitting on the sofa. His gaze was direct. 'I did think about telling you what I could remember. And maybe I should have said something.' He acknowledged that with a nod to her, and she felt slightly mollified. 'But the idea of restoring the garden was a fantasy, an unrealistic dream. It seemed better not to encourage it.' He shrugged.

Anna wanted to understand. She wanted to understand this man she'd slept with, lived with, thought she was in love with. She perched on the arm of the sofa. 'Why?'

He leant forward, his hands clasped around the bottle, and looked up at her. 'I've always known that wasn't for me. Living in a house like Templecombe, playing lord of the manor. That's not what I want.'

'It's your heritage.' Oliver snorted at that, but it was true. Surely he valued what he was privileged to have. He had to. 'Your ancestors built the place, built the house, built the garden. It's as much part of you as of anyone else.'

'No, it's not. I wasn't brought up with it. My grandmother looks at the house and sees herself. I look at it and think of the running costs, and how much it'd cost to repair the roof and fix the guttering.'

'It can be restored, we could bring it back to life.' Yes, it was difficult, it was impossible, but people did the impossible every day. It could be done.

He shook his head, his demeanour that of a Fra Angelico saint, patience mixed with suffering at man's stupidity. 'Where's the money to come from?'

'There are grants – you could get sponsorship, you know enough people.'

'Sponsorship? Why would anyone want to give a privately owned garden that sort of money? Join the real world, Anna. There isn't some cosy, publicly funded quango waving a chequebook; everything has to be paid for with hard cash. My cash.' He stopped, and rubbed the back of his neck. 'The reality is, I can't afford to restore the house and garden. It's too far gone.' She started to butt in, to say that Heligan and Hestercombe had been restored simply because of one person's vision of what could be, but he stopped her. 'Even if by some miracle you managed to wangle grants to cover the costs of restoration, it would still have to be maintained. Worse, you have to let Joe Public traipse around. I've no interest in struggling just to keep the slates on the roof.'

'Will says—' As soon as the words came out of her mouth, she knew it was a mistake.

'And he's an expert?'

'No, but—'

'As soon as I can I'm chucking him out.'

Anna was stabbed with panic. 'You can't.'

'I can.' He gave her a hard sideways look. 'Why? What do you care what happens to him?'

Because he is everything, she wanted to say, but that was impossible. She looked at Oliver and realised he was a stranger. 'I never knew you could be like this.'

'Oh, grow up. What have you been doing, living some fantasy where I pay for everything and you waft around playing Marie Antoinette in the garden? No one has a God-given right to live in a place like Templecombe; families come and go. That's life. It's not static, it moves on. There's no reason why Templecombe should stay preserved like a museum.' She flinched, recognising the truth of what he said but not wanting to hear it. Oliver took her hand. 'Darling Anna, you are beautiful and sexy and terribly clever, but you live on a different planet to everyone else. It's part of your charm, but you need to realise that other people have to live in the real world. I was never going to chuck in everything and go and live at Templecombe.'

'I thought . . .' Had she really been living on a different planet? She looked at him, unwilling to give up the vision of restoring the garden. How could she have been so wrong about him? 'You kept saying how bored you were with your job, how you wanted to do something different.'

'Yeah, but I meant something different in the City, perhaps move into consultancy. Gardening's not an alternative. Never has been.'

'I've been so stupid,' Anna said slowly.

'A little unworldly, perhaps,' Oliver said, kissing the palm of her hand. 'But it suits you.' He reached over to the desk and pulled out the bottom drawer where he kept his supplies. 'You look tired.'

Anna jumped up and backed away. 'No,' she said, shaking her head. 'No.'

'It's up to you.' Oliver shrugged, and closed the drawer. 'Now. Quickly go and have a shower, and we'll go out.'

Just like that. As if everything was back to normal. Anna looked at him, really looked at him, and there he was, charming, handsome, superficial, shallow. She'd always known that, right from the beginning, and he'd always been quick to admit he had no hidden depths. She just hadn't wanted to believe it. The garden didn't matter to him at all; it had been her, projecting what she wanted to see. He hadn't taken her seriously; she'd been his funny little thing, a doll to dress, a novelty toy to play with. But she wasn't. She would be the person with the vision, who would make the impossible happen. Maybe Templecombe couldn't be saved, but if it was worth saving then it was worth trying to save, even if it all ended in failure.

'I can't do this any more,' Anna said. 'You see, I may be from a different planet, I may well be naïve and unworldly – in fact, I know I am – but that's who I am. And maybe my dreams and hopes are unrealistic, but I believe in them. This is the real Anna, mud and all.

I can't pretend to be someone else.' She picked up her bag, knowing that whatever happened, what she had thought she'd felt for Oliver had been burned out of her, leaving her clean and whole. 'It's been fun, but I don't fit in with your world. And to be honest, I don't want to.'

Oliver stood too. 'Are you saying goodbye?'

'Yes.' Strange how it didn't matter at all. Even if she and Will hadn't found the temple, even if she hadn't found Will, this would still be happening. Perhaps it showed how little their lives coincided, how the threads that had brought them together had proved to be as insubstantial as candyfloss. Anna took one last look around the flat, her final glimpse of a different world, then stood on tiptoe and kissed Oliver's cheek. The scent of cool lemon lingered in the air as she went to the front door and opened it.

'Anna. Stay the night, and we'll talk about it,' he said.

She shook her head, swung her bag up on to her shoulder and walked to the lift.

'I don't want you to go.' He leaned against the door jamb. There was no doubt, white towels did suit him.

'But I have to.' Anna pressed the lift button, and the doors opened. 'I have a report to write. A garden that needs restoration.' She stepped into the lift.

His expression changed. 'Anna, you're not to bother my grandmother. I forbid you—'

''Bye, Oliver.'

The doors closed.

Chapter 25

The village church was small, the nave Norman. The oldest arch, by the chancel, had a strange serpent twisted around one of the capitals. Anna traced it with her eyes. Christian man triumphs over the pagan gods and goddesses, the worship of dragons and earth mothers. The Minoan earth goddess held snakes in both fists. Idly she wondered if the Reverend Martin's opposition to Arthur Farrell as a suitor was based on his religious principles. It would fit. And perhaps in some dusty corner of the attic, or some scholarly archive, she'd find the answer.

After seeing Oliver she'd rushed home to write her new, revised report and sent it off to Mrs Davenport. She should have received it several days ago. Anna nibbled her thumbnail. Would the old lady tell Will about the new report? Perhaps she wasn't back from the hospital. Perhaps Oliver had somehow intercepted it. No, now she was being paranoid – although she wished she'd sent a copy to Will. She'd thought about it, just to let him know that she'd rewritten the report, but that would have breached client confidentiality. She'd tried calling the house to speak to him a couple of times, but only Peggy had answered, the warm burr of her accent edged with frost. Yes, Dr Carmichael, of course she'd pass a message on to Will. Yes, Dr Carmichael, she'd passed the previous messages on. Anna checked her mobile for missed calls, but it was blank.

She replayed their last meeting in her mind. Will had been virtually silent on the drive to the station, but he must surely have understood why she'd got to confront Oliver about the temple. He couldn't not want to speak to her, not after what had happened in the temple. Perhaps Peggy hadn't passed the messages on. Will must have been in emotional turmoil when I insisted he drive me to the station, Anna thought. He'd just told me about his father's death and then we . . . She closed her eyes. From despair to ecstasy. And then I left him alone to go to Oliver. But he knew I had to sort the garden out. He knew that. He was the one who made me go back to the temple after all. He knew I wasn't leaving him to go to Oliver – well, I was, but not in that way. He knew that.

Anna realised she'd bitten her thumbnail down to the quick, and clasped it tightly in her fist to stop it aching. She looked around, wondering how long the wedding rehearsal was going to go on for. Clare and her mother were still having a heated discussion about something, while the vicar stood between them, head bobbing like an umpire at a tennis match. She wondered when exactly her mother had started planning this wedding – at Anna's birth probably. She'd missed out there, and unfortunately Clare had unshakeable ideas of her own. Anna checked her watch. The rehearsal was supposed to be over in half an hour, and they'd hardly started.

She swivelled back in her seat, and watched her father sitting in one of the front pews chatting to his niece, whose children were acting as bridesmaids and pageboy. Three children under seven, and a whole year younger than Anna, Julie had done the right thing, the Carmichael thing, by marrying early. It had seemed to Anna so romantic when she and Richard had rushed off and got married, so spontaneous, so much part of their being in love, but instead she had been conforming to her family's values. No, she thought, shaking her head. That's not what marrying Richard was about. I needed the affirmation that someone valued me for what I am.

Her father laughed at something Julie said, his face creasing in wrinkles, enjoying talking to a pretty young woman. The reception was being held at his golf clubhouse and he was going to make a speech. She wondered what he'd have said if Clare was marrying a worshipper of Anahita instead of a property developer.

Steve slid in next to her. 'I was just thinking about you,' Anna said, smiling.

'Good things, I hope.'

'I was thinking how well you fit into our family. Oh, looks like there's some action.' Anna stood as Clare walked up the aisle towards her father. Steve rubbed his hands together. 'Nervous?'

'A bit.' Steve stood too. 'About this, though, not the future.'

No, she could see their future clearly. They'd settle down and Clare would fuss over him, just like their mother, but bossier. It must be what he wanted. Anna linked her arm in his. 'I always wanted a brother,' she said, remembering how envious she'd been of Bronwen having Gwyn.

He smiled. 'You're bringing Oliver to the wedding, Clare said.'

'Mmm.' Anna hadn't told Clare she'd split up with Oliver. She hesitated, wondering if she should say something to Steve, but before she could, Clare clapped her hands together. 'Okay, everyone, can we get started, please?' The children were ushered in from outside where they'd been playing; the adults took their places, Steve and his best man at the front, Clare, Anna and their father waiting in the lobby with the children, waiting for the signal.

Just as the organ started to play, Anna's mobile rang.

'Anna . . .' Clare rolled her eyes.

She didn't recognise the number – was it Will? 'Sorry, sorry – carry on, I'll be back in a sec.' She raced outside the church. 'Hello?'

'Dr Carmichael?'

Not Will. 'Speaking.'

'I'm from Braithwaite, Keaton and Braithwaite, solicitors of Milbridge. I'm sorry it's such short notice, but our client has requested your presence at a meeting next Tuesday, the twelfth, at nine a.m.'

'And your client is?'

'Mrs Veronica Davenport. The meeting will be at Templecombe Manor.'

Anna paused. 'I'll be there,' she said.

Anna borrowed Clare's car for the drive to Templecombe. She went down the familiar long drive and turned the corner, her heart lifting with pleasure at the sight of the house, and the balustrade, and the clear blue sky beyond that once she'd thought had been the world's end. And Will. She'd see Will. Then her heart sank. Oliver's black BMW was outside the front door.

She hadn't seen or heard from him since leaving his flat. Awkward. She'd assumed that the meeting was something to do with her report, but now it crossed her mind that perhaps Mrs Davenport had asked her to be there for some attempt at reconciliation, assuming she knew they'd split up. No, that couldn't be right, or why the solicitor? It didn't make sense. She got out, and rang the doorbell.

Peggy answered the door, her expression less than welcoming. Anna could have been a stranger. 'Good morning, Dr Carmichael. If you'd like to follow me.'

Anna trailed behind Peggy's forbidding back to the dining room. Oliver's dark head turned quickly. She gave him a brief smile, which he didn't return. Presumably he was angry about the new report; she didn't flatter herself it was because she had left him. No sign of Will. But it was hardly likely, with Oliver there.

'Dr Carmichael, I'm so pleased you could attend.' Mrs Davenport, seated at the head of the table, smiled at her. Her skin was pale, almost translucent, like a pressed wild flower, but her voice was firm. 'This is my solicitor, Mr Braithwaite . . .' She indicated the burly young man with sandy red hair next to her, who stood and held out his hand. 'And of course you know my grandson Oliver.'

Anna shook the solicitor's hand but Oliver didn't offer his. 'You're looking well,' he said from the other side of the table. 'Cleaner than when I last saw you.' Anna smiled, determined to be pleasant, but didn't answer.

'Oh, Peggy, before you go,' Mrs Davenport said, 'could you please ask William to join us?' Anna's heart did an involuntary back-flip.

Oliver swung round to his grandmother as Peggy left the room. 'What's he got to do with this?' he said. Mrs Davenport raised her eyebrows and Oliver sat back in his seat.

The solicitor shuffled his papers. No one spoke. Anna looked at Oliver, drumming his fingers on the table. He wasn't a bad man, just not the one she'd thought he was. Once they'd said they loved each other, but that was like children playing with words, with no deep significance. She doubted if Oliver had any deep significance. He was charming, glamorous, exciting, but remote to her, like being behind glass.

The door opened and Will entered. 'You wanted me?' His eyes flickered as he registered Anna. He looked wary and closed, the vulnerability she'd once seen hidden. She tucked her hair behind her ears. Oh yes, she wanted him. But did he want her?

'If you wouldn't mind,' Mrs Davenport said, smiling at him. 'Please, do sit.'

The choice was next to Anna or Oliver. Will pulled out the chair at the foot of the table instead, away from both. A sign of his feelings?

Mrs Davenport turned to the solicitor. 'Mr Braithwaite . . .'

The young man cleared his throat. 'I have been asked here today to represent my client, Mrs Veronica Davenport, in matters concerning the house and garden at Templecombe Manor, in particular concerning the future. My client is aware that the house and garden are in a considerable state of dilapidation and will require a serious degree of investment to restore them to a habitable condition. To this end, she has decided to dispose of various items, viz. the Dutch flower painting in the hall, the Baccarat paperweights, the snuffboxes . . .'

The list continued. Anna recognised many of the items. She glanced at Oliver. His eyes were fixed on his grandmother's face and a muscle twitched in his jaw. But he said nothing. She couldn't look at Will, but she sensed his presence as if he was sitting next to her. Oh, to know what he was thinking, how he felt. If only they could have spoken beforehand. Had Peggy really passed on her messages? She clenched her fists and tried to concentrate on what the solicitor was saying about the garden.

'The sum of monies raised by the sale of these items, estimated at around two hundred thousand pounds, should be enough to secure the short-term future of Templecombe. However, my client is also concerned with the long-term future of the house and garden. According to the conservation report recently delivered by Dr Anna Carmichael, there is a possibility of receiving grants from various UK and EU heritage funds. My client hopes that Dr Carmichael will be available and willing to take charge of the grant applications, and the initial stages of restoration, as director of the project.'

Oliver looked at Anna and she held his gaze for a second, then turned to Mrs Davenport and nodded her agreement. Inside she felt as if she might blossom into a thousand flowers. The garden would be saved. She turned to Will, a grin starting to spread over her face, then deflated. He wasn't looking at her; his eyes were riveted to the polished tabletop.

Mr Braithwaite continued. 'The report makes it clear that the probability of obtaining grants is severely diminished while Templecombe is in private hands. Therefore my client is gifting the house and garden to a charitable trust.'

'What!' Oliver was on his feet.

'Sit down,' Mrs Davenport said sharply.

'I can't believe you're going to do this to me – this is my house, my inheritance.'

'You don't want it,' Mrs Davenport said. 'You'll have it sold before I'm cold in my grave.'

'This is what you've wanted all along,' Oliver spat, pointing his finger at Anna. The anger in his voice made her head reel. 'All you've been after is the garden. You won't get away with it, I'll get an injunction, I'll get power of attorney, I'll stop you—'

Will sprang to his feet, fists clenched. 'It's nothing to do with her, it's about what your grandmother wants. You're angry because we've done what you should have, look after your grandmother and not yourself.'

'How dare you—'

'Oliver!' Mrs Davenport's voice sliced across the tension. 'Sit down or I'll cut you out of my will completely.'

Oliver took a sharp intake of breath. Anna thought he might storm from the room. She'd never seen him so angry, his handsome face distorted with the effort of controlling his temper. She glanced at Will, who was still standing, his jaw set, his eyes fixed on Oliver. *We*, he'd said, and despite the tension Anna felt a momentary glow. We.

Oliver gave a snort of disgust, then slumped down on to his chair. His shoulders relaxed slightly, and he gave a little nod to his grandmother, as if acknowledging her control. Anna felt a twinge of guilt. If she hadn't rewritten the report . . . but Oliver had never valued the house and garden. Mrs Davenport looked at Will, who also sat. The storm had passed. Then the old lady turned to the solicitor, who continued.

'It is proposed that the charitable trust will have six trustees. Veronica Davenport. Oliver Davenport. Kevin Braithwaite, of BKB solicitors. George Sampson, of the accountancy firm Davies, Sampson. Dr Anna Carmichael.' The solicitor cleared his throat. 'And William Sutton.'

'What? This is—' Oliver shook his head as if in disbelief.

Anna looked at Will, who was also shaking his head. 'I can't . . .' he said, looking towards Mrs Davenport. 'You need someone who knows what they're doing.'

'I need someone who is loyal,' Mrs Davenport said. 'Someone I can trust.'

Will clasped his hands in front of him. 'I can't accept,' he said softly. 'There are . . . personal reasons.'

'But what about the temple?' exclaimed Anna. 'You know what it means. We discovered it together, both of us. Will?' He turned his head away from her, leaving her confused. 'I don't understand.'

'I know you don't.' Will closed his eyes for a second, then turned to Mrs Davenport. 'You do, though.'

Mrs Davenport nodded, her face soft, and Anna wondered if she was seeing the lover Will reminded her of. 'You don't have to decide now,' Mrs Davenport said. 'Think about it.'

Will hesitated, then nodded. 'I'll think about it,' he said, but he didn't sound as if he intended to change his mind.

'Thank you.' Mrs Davenport closed her eyes for a second. 'And now I'm feeling a little tired. I wonder if I could ask you to leave for a short while.'

They stood. Anna glanced at Oliver, wondering what he was thinking. He'd lost Templecombe. Surely that mattered to him. But his face was blank, controlled. Then she turned, sensing Will's eyes on her. His gaze dropped as soon as he realised she'd caught him watching her looking at Oliver. What is it you're thinking? she wanted to say, but Will had turned away.

Mr Braithwaite was holding the door open for them to leave when Mrs Davenport spoke again.

'Oliver – stay with me . . .' She held out her hand to him, and Anna saw it was trembling. Oliver hesitated, then took it, and dropped a kiss into her palm.

Mr Braithwaite closed the dining-room door behind Will and

Anna and let out a sigh. 'Good thing that's over. I'm afraid the grandson was none too happy about the situation,' he said cheerfully. 'Well, it can't be helped.'

'There's coffee and tea in here,' Peggy said, holding the drawing-room door open. Will shook his head and went out of the front door, not looking at Anna.

'Some coffee would be good,' Mr Braithwaite said, rubbing his hands and going through to the drawing room.

'Dr Carmichael? Coffee?'

'Thank you, Peggy, I'll come through in a minute,' Anna said.

Peggy looked as if she might say something, then stopped herself with a shrug and followed Mr Braithwaite into the drawing room. Anna was about to follow Will when the door behind her opened and Oliver emerged. She paused. More unfinished business that needed resolving.

'Is ... is your grandmother okay?' Anna said, stumbling slightly.

Oliver considered her and for a second she thought he was still angry. But instead he turned to the Dutch painting. 'I've never liked this picture,' he said. 'Always made me think about death.'

'It *is* about death,' Anna said standing next to him. 'It's a memento mori. The caterpillars and bugs are eating the flowers, the apple is rotten with maggots. Even when life is perfect, it's dying.'

'That sounds cheerful,' Oliver said. 'Good thing it's going then.'

Anna hesitated. 'Do you mind?'

'Shit, don't be stupid. Of course I mind,' he said, and spun away from her to the stairs. He stopped abruptly, his hand on the newel post. Anna waited, Oliver turned and managed a wry smile. 'But she's right. I would have sold up.' He slapped the newel post. 'It's never been part of me, and it's very much part of her. So . . . so, it's hers to do what she wants with.' He looked around the hall, and his ancestors stared back at him. 'By the way, I didn't sleep with you just to influence your report.'

Anna gasped. 'It never occurred to me . . .' she said, horrified. He couldn't have. No. To go through all that, and for him to . . . No, he couldn't.

'Well. I didn't.' Oliver looked shamefaced for the first time since she'd met him. 'Okay, maybe a bit.'

'Oliver!'

'Ironic, isn't it? You ending up with the garden and me out in the cold, despite . . .' He looked at the flagstones, then up at her, hair flopping over his forehead, the most charming expression on his face. 'I did like being with you. It was fun, wasn't it?'

Anna resisted being charmed. 'You're a shit, Davenport. Did you know that?'

'So they tell me.' He winked at her, the easy charm leaving her cold. 'But a lovable one.'

'You don't know what love is,' Anna said, and walked out of the house.

Will was standing by the balustrade, staring out into the valley beyond, his hair ruffled by the breeze. When they'd first met Anna had been the one standing there, thinking about her future, about Richard and the past, about moving on. And then Will had appeared.

'Don't jump,' Anna said, and she could hear the smile in her voice.

Will raised his head, but made no comment.

'I rang. Did . . .' Anna swallowed, feeling suddenly dizzy, unsure of the ground beneath her feet. 'Did Peggy pass the message on?'

'Yes.'

Oh. So he simply hadn't called back. Anna stood beside him, wanting to ask him how he was, how he was feeling. What she meant to him. The sky ahead was blue, deep blue, a perfect summer's day, and she couldn't think where to begin. Stick to safer ground. 'Why won't you become a trustee? Mrs Davenport needs someone like you on board, someone she can trust.'

He glanced at her. 'Can't she trust you?'

'Of course she can, but when she's gone the solicitor and accountant might well be neutral and then it'll be Oliver against me.' There. She'd said Oliver's name.

'So I'm to be the buffer between you and Oliver. Mmm, that does sound attractive.' A muscle flickered in his jaw.

'Will . . .'

'You and your boyfriend will have to sort out your differences yourselves. You can't ask me to be involved.' His tone was harsh.

'He's not my boyfriend.' She felt suddenly close to crying. 'How could you think that, after what happened between us? Is that why you didn't call me back?' She pressed her lips together and tried to regain control. 'I went to London to see him, to confront him about the temple, about him knowing. No other reason.' Will shoved his hands into his jeans pockets. Anna picked a bit of crumbling stone off the balustrade. 'Oliver and me – we're from different worlds, and I don't belong in his. I never belonged.' But she'd dived headlong into his lifestyle, his values. It had all been her choice, all those parties, and socialising, and throwing money around. Inhaling it.

'He's always here, though, isn't he? Even in the temple . . .' Will gazed into the blue, blue sky as if the answers were to be discovered on the faint wisps of clouds.

'Please be a trustee,' Anna said. She couldn't stop herself from touching his arm, and having touched him she couldn't let go. 'Please stay.'

'Anna . . .' Will's eyes were screwed up.

'There won't be much work involved, you just have to approve applications and sign a few forms every now and then. You wouldn't have to go to the meetings if you didn't want to, you could assign a proxy vote and . . .' She swallowed, knowing it was all irrelevant to what she wanted to say. 'Stay with me,' she whispered.

He held her shoulders, examined her face. Her eyes searched his in return, desperately seeking some sign of his feelings. But they were opaque, and she couldn't read what was in them. Will let his hands fall.

'What happened . . . in the temple. It wasn't real.'

'It was,' Anna said.

'Not like my father's death,' he said sharply. Anna flinched. 'That's real. Do you know what it looks like, a man's brains spattered across a barn floor? That's reality. It's not pretty gardens and starlight.'

'But it happened,' Anna said. 'It was real.'

Will shook his head. 'You know better than anyone that these gardens are designed to manipulate your emotions. It succeeded.'

Anna's heart gave a leap. Did that mean he loved her? 'I'm sorry I left you that day, but all I could think about was confronting Oliver, finding out what he knew about the garden. Were you . . . okay?'

Will shrugged. 'Sure. I mean, I'd just had my insides taken out, mangled up and then dumped by the roadside, but no problem.'

'I had to find out . . .' Anna hung her head.

'Look, really, it's not a problem. You're dedicated to what you do, to the garden, and that's great.' Will watched a bird fly past and settle in the bushes by the path to the garden. 'It was better that you weren't around. I did a lot of thinking and talking to Peggy. And then some more thinking. I thought about you swimming across that bloody lake, and how determined you were. How you didn't run away, but came back to confront the situation, to make amends . . . and how I've been running away.'

His tone was final. Anna's emotions were all confused, building up inside. 'I think I love you,' she blurted out, not sure where it had come from.

'Oh, Anna . . .' Will touched her cheek, stroked a wisp of hair off her forehead, and she waited, hardly breathing, hardly tilting her head against his fingers. 'You don't love me, you love the garden.'

She shook her head, but he put his finger to her mouth. 'The garden is magical, but it's not real life.'

'It was real. It happened. It was the best thing that's ever happened to me,' Anna cried. 'I love you.'

'But you put the garden first.' Will ran his hands through his hair, his face grim, and her heart plummeted into cold depths.

'I'm leaving,' he said into the vast emptiness in front of them. 'I'm going back.' And Anna realised it really was the end of the world.

Chapter 26

Anna and Clare drove down to their parents' house the day before the wedding, Clare talking non-stop, already in a state of high excitement.

'Now, do you want me to drop you at your hotel?'

Anna shook her head, not caring any more whether Clare knew. 'No, I'm staying at home.'

'What about Oliver?'

She shrugged. 'I expect he's in London.'

Clare frowned. 'But he's coming down for the wedding . . .'

Anna shook her head. 'No.'

Clare yelped. 'What about my seating plan?'

'Sorry, but it wasn't a major consideration when we split up.'

'Split up?' The car swerved erratically, narrowly avoiding an overladen Lada. 'You never told me!'

Anna felt incredibly tired. 'It didn't seem important.'

'Oh.' Anna sensed Clare going over various possibilities – poor you, why didn't you say, lucky escape. In the end she said, 'You could have brought someone else.'

'Like who?'

'Like . . . the gardener bloke at that house. He was all right.'

'You mean, I should just have said, "Will, I haven't got an escort to go to my younger sister's wedding and I have to go with someone.

Please, please, be my man"?' She remembered Will standing at the balustrade, looking out into the void, and her heart contracted. 'I don't think so.'

'It would have been a good excuse, you could have got to know him better.' Clare sighed heavily, obviously torn between her seating plan and being sympathetic.

I do know him better, Anna wanted to cry out. I do know him better, but I've been stupid and not seen it until it's too late and he's leaving.

'It's a bit of a pain, I'll have to rearrange the tables. Couldn't you have hung on to Oliver until after the wedding?'

'Clare!'

Clare was silent for a few seconds, then launched into the saga of the wedding flowers. Anna let the information about freesias and lilies wash over her. She wanted Will so badly, her whole body felt in pain. Heartsick. She hadn't known what that word meant before.

When they arrived at Sundowners, Clare bounced into the house, Anna trailing behind. Their mother came into the hall, arms outstretched.

Valerie hugged Clare. 'I can't believe it's here already. My little girl . . .'

'Mu-um,' Clare said, wriggling out of her mother's embrace, so reminiscent of the teenager she'd once been that Anna laughed despite her depression.

'Anna, darling, lovely to see you. And have you brought . . . ?'

Anna kissed her mother, feeling the soft powdery skin against her cheek. 'No, I'm on my own.' Alone, except for the thoughts of Will that stayed with her constantly.

'They've split up,' Clare said, picking up a parcel from the hall table and tearing at the tape.

'Oh dear.' Valerie's face creased. 'What about the seating plan?'

Anna gritted her teeth as the familiar waves of teenage angst swept through her. She wanted to stamp her feet and shout, what

• • •   318   • • •

about me? Perhaps she only had value when she had a man in tow.

'We'll just have to rearrange it, Mum,' Clare said, holding up a glass bowl. 'Look what the Swinglers have sent. Isn't it gorgeous?'

Anna left them to it and went upstairs to her old bedroom. It was still recognisably hers, with the walls the pale cream colour, delicate as bone, she'd chosen to go with the curtains with the geometric pattern that reminded her of the ladder back of a Charles Rennie Mackintosh chair. Woefully inappropriate for a cottage, her mother had said, trying to push Anna towards cabbage roses – so pretty! In Anna's absence her mother had diluted the austerity of the room with a lacy pink bedspread and plump, frilled cushions nestled in an overstuffed, armchair, the velvet upholstery faded to a colour that reminded Anna of uncooked sausage bulging through its casing. Her books, her pictures, her clothes – all gone.

Downstairs she could hear noises, and her mother calling up to her. The relatives must have arrived. Her bedroom was going to be taken over by Auntie Pat and Uncle Frank. Once, at a family party, she'd overheard Auntie Pat say 'Of course, she's terribly clever' as if it were a disability. Anna looked around the room as she left. It wasn't hers any more.

The noise levels in the house rose as the day wore on. Julie and the children arrived, Auntie Pat asked Anna's advice about building a water feature in her garden, Uncle Frank rumbled on about blackfly in his greenhouse. Anna did her best; she'd given up trying to explain she wasn't a gardener. Tea and fruit cake gave way to supper, everyone crammed round the dining room table, the children at a separate picnic table squeezed into the corner. Valerie fussed about making sure everybody had enough to eat and insisting that they start immediately, which meant that the first people to be served had nearly finished by the time she finally sat down to eat her own meal, only to leap up immediately to offer them seconds.

'Sit down, Mum,' Clare said, flicking her hair back. 'You'll give yourself indigestion. And I want to run through the arrangements for tomorrow.' She pulled out a large file with colour-coordinated tabs.

Anna looked up and caught her father's eye. A nearly imperceptible tilt of the head at Clare and Valerie, the flicker of an eyelid. 'I've taken to calling your sister Wellington,' he whispered. 'This wedding's going to be run on military lines.' He pushed back his chair. 'Shall we have coffee in the sitting room?'

Valerie shot up. 'Coffee! Gordon, I'm so sorry, I'd quite forgotten. And we've still got our pudding bowls.'

'Sit down, Mum, I'll do it,' Anna said, getting up. She stacked the bowls and took them through to the kitchen, leaving Clare and Valerie deep in discussion over what to do if the cars didn't arrive on time. She filled the kettle, and started on the washing-up, feeling like Cinderella consigned to the kitchen. And where's my handsome prince, she thought, come to whisk me away? She couldn't even muster a pumpkin. Will's not going to happen, she told herself. It wasn't real, just a fantasy. He's off somewhere sorting out his life. She rubbed her eyes with the back of one soapy hand. I hope he's okay. Even if I never see him again, I hope he's going to be okay.

No one seemed to notice she'd taken a long time making the coffee. Anna distributed cups to Auntie Pat and Uncle Frank, settling down in the sitting room, Julie having taken the children upstairs to bed in the spare room, then took a tray through to Clare and Valerie, still talking in the dining room.

'We'll be there in a minute,' Valerie said, looking like a flustered chicken at the receiving end of Clare's foxy determination. '*Gardeners' World* will be on shortly.'

Anna went back into the sitting room. She placed a coffee beside her father's armchair. 'There you are.'

He smiled up at her. 'I hear you've caused havoc with the seating plan.'

'I know. It'll be written on my gravestone.'

He squeezed her hand. 'Sorry things didn't work out for you.'

Anna shrugged. 'Yeah, well, you've got to kiss a few frogs, I suppose.' Oh, Will.

'Never mind. Don't want both my girls going away.' He patted her hand. 'Leave the best till last, eh?'

Anna smiled weakly. 'I don't know about that.'

'Put the telly on, will you?'

'It'll never fit,' Anna said automatically, remembering the old family joke. She turned on the television.

'Call your mother, *Gardeners' World* will be on any second.'

'Here I am,' Valerie said, coming in, puffing slightly. 'Has it started?'

They all settled themselves down to watch. Anna could hear Clare talking on the phone in the hall, she guessed to Steve. So this is how I'm spending the night before my younger sister gets married, she thought. Sitting on the sofa, squished between my mum and Auntie Pat, watching *Gardeners' World*. Would it have been any better being with Oliver, if she hadn't found the temple, hadn't discovered Will? Eating expensive food, drinking expensive wine, wearing expensive clothes. Pretending to be someone else.

Clare's voice rose and fell, the television droned on, her father started to snore. Uncle Frank looked as though it would take a crane to shift him from his armchair. Anna couldn't imagine Oliver in such a setting; he didn't belong. But do I? And if not here, then where? The garden at Templecombe? With Will? She wondered if he was right, if it was just the garden casting its spell. She'd fallen for Oliver at Rousham. Perhaps I should turn to urban planning, she thought. It'd save a lot of heartache.

Valerie gave a squeak. Anna looked up to see her pointing at the screen. 'It's you! Gordon, wake up, Anna's on the telly. Clare, Clare . . .'

Anna stared at herself on the television, unable to hear over the noise of her father harrumphing awake, and Clare rushing in wanting to know what the fuss was about. Her mother shushed like a steam kettle, making more noise than anyone. There was Anna, talking about Capability Brown. And then she was gone. The opening credits of a comedy programme started.

'It must have been a trailer,' Anna said, bewildered. 'I didn't think the programme was being aired for ages.'

'Oh, Anna,' Valerie said, hand to chest and eyes shining. 'You never said.'

'It's nothing important,' Anna said. 'I'm only the consultant on it, not the presenter.'

'You looked lovely. Darling, I'm so proud.' Valerie was as pink as the peonies on the curtains.

'I think I looked awful,' Anna said, scarlet with embarrassment.

'It'll be in the *Radio Times*. I'll have to order lots of copies.' Valerie's eyes were dreamy, as if she was seeing a vision of herself distributing thousands of copies to the WI.

'Mum, no,' Anna said. 'I'm only on for two seconds.'

'I'd like a copy, Valerie,' Auntie Pat said. 'Make that two, I expect Julie'll want one too.'

'Signed, of course,' Uncle Frank chipped in.

Auntie Pat gave Anna a dig in the ribs. 'Aren't you funny, sitting there like a little mouse, not saying anything.'

'I didn't know it was going to be on—'

'I'd have told everyone I was going to be on telly.'

'I didn't know—'

'What's the noise about?' Her cousin Julie, back from settling the children to sleep. A chorus of voices explained. 'Anna, on the telly! Did you get Hamish McCarthy's autograph? He seems ever so nice on the box, I bet he's a really nice person.'

'He is—'

'You are a dark horse,' Auntie Pat said. 'Fancy not saying anything. I'd tell everybody. You always were an odd little thing, ever so quiet.'

Uncle Frank leaned over. 'It's always the quiet ones you've got to watch. Still waters, you know. Still waters.'

*

Anna lay on top of an inflatable mattress that was slowly deflating on Clare's bedroom floor, listening to Clare's regular breathing, and staring at Clare's ceiling. It had been months since she'd last slept through the night, the combination of coke and anxiety not being a soporific one. She'd thought she'd return to her usual sleep pattern once she'd stopped taking coke, but it hadn't happened yet. Instead she spent the quiet hours planning strategies for the garden restoration, and trying not to let her mind wander towards Will. Perhaps Mrs Davenport would eventually persuade him to become a trustee . . . No, she mustn't think about Will. He had gone. Count sheep instead, fluffy white sheep jumping fences, tripping and needing the vet . . . She sighed. Not thinking about Will took so much effort.

'Anna? Are you awake?'

'Yes,' she whispered back. 'Can't you sleep?'

'Too excited.'

Anna wriggled round to look at Clare, aware of the minute hiss as air escaped from some unknown puncture. 'You ought to get some sleep or you'll look dreadful in the photos.'

'They'll just have to touch them up. Digital cameras, you know.' She sounded just like the naughty little sister Anna remembered. Anna reached out and squeezed her hand. 'What's that for?' Clare said, squeezing back.

'For being my sister, and for being happy.' She tried to make out Clare's expression in the soft darkness of the room. 'You are, aren't you?'

'Utterly.' Clare stretched her arms out like a sensuous kitten. 'It's utterly blissful getting married. I do recommend it.'

Yes, Anna could remember getting married, full of hope, full of expectation, no idea of what was to come. 'I really, really hope it works out for you,' she said quietly. 'Just because it didn't for me doesn't mean it won't for you.'

SARAH DUNCAN

Clare was quiet for a while. Then, 'Bron said she thought all that stuff with Oliver was sort of rebound.'

'I don't know.' She didn't think it was rebound, more learning about other lives she might have lived if she hadn't met Richard. 'I wanted to be someone different.'

'Glad you're back to normal.'

Anna didn't say anything. She didn't feel normal, whatever that might be. An image of Will floated into her mind, Will bending over to look at the butterfly in her hand.

'I was sort of a bit pleased you went off the rails. You've always been so bloody perfect,' Clare said in a small voice. 'It's been hard knowing you were Mum and Dad's favourite.'

Anna came back to the present. 'What? But you're their favourite, by a mile . . .'

Clare snorted. 'I'm not – they're always going on about you, what you've done, how clever you are . . .'

'They don't.'

'They do. God, there have been times I've hated you, all that "why can't you be more like Anna" stuff. And at school – turning up to parents' evenings and everyone agreeing it was a shame I couldn't be more like you . . .'

'I'd no idea,' Anna said into the darkness. 'I wanted to be like you. You were pretty, and popular, and . . . I thought you fitted in more. I've always felt outside the family, not really part of it. Not belonging.'

'You're mad,' Clare said. 'Mum and Dad are just bursting with pride about you. And now you've even been on telly.'

'S'funny,' Anna said. 'I've worked and worked, but all anyone cares about is a few seconds on the box.'

'You've certainly upstaged me,' Clare said. 'No one's going to be looking at me tomorrow, they'll all be clamouring for your autograph.'

'Don't be silly,' Anna said. 'No one will have taken any notice.

And if they have, what does it matter? All that matters is you and Steve, being together, and being happy. That's all that matters, in the end. Loving someone and being loved.' Anna opened her eyes wide to stop the tears from coming. 'I'm so happy for you,' she said to Clare, meaning every word, while inside her heart broke into little pieces.

Valerie cried from the beginning, but Anna sat dry-eyed. No tears left, she supposed. The vicar talked about relationships, and her thoughts turned to Richard. The registry office had done its best, but it couldn't compare to High Church Anglicanism, the beauty of the marriage service. Richard. She felt nothing. No pain, no guilt. Perhaps a faint twinge of regret. Whatever there had been had gone, burnt out in the relationship with Oliver. She thought of the Breughel painting of Icarus falling into the sea while everyday life carried on around, the farmer ploughing with his oxen, uncaring of the drama unfolding in the ocean. Icarus flew too close to the sun, and died, his wings falling apart as the soft wax melted in the heat. He wanted more, wasn't content with what he had. But unless some of us had aspired to more, thought Anna, we would never have progressed from the plough and the oxen, would never have got this far. Perhaps the price was that some crashed and burned.

And then there was Will. Lovely Will, with his burden of pain and guilt. She hoped the garden had helped to heal him. Anna stared fixedly at Clare's bouquet, given to her to hold for the duration of the ceremony. The tumbling flowers were scented, lilies and tuberose, sweet and heady like incense. Perhaps Will had gone back to his wife. Perhaps his wife would finish the healing process. I want him to be happy, Anna thought. Even if . . . She bit her lip. She couldn't let the words form in her head.

Valerie gave her a prod. It was time for Anna's reading. She stood up and made her way to the lectern. She looked at the congregation: her parents, Bronwen and Nick, Gwyn, aunts, uncles, family, friends. Then at Steve and Clare. Her little sister's eyes were shining. Anna cleared her throat, and started reading the Shakespeare sonnet Clare had requested.

> Let me not to the marriage of true minds
> Admit impediments. Love is not love
> Which alters when it alteration finds,
> Or bends with the remover to remove . . .

When she sat down again, her mother squeezed her hand. 'You read that beautifully,' Valerie whispered.

Anna nodded, lips pressed together. Will had gone back to his family, his life. His wife. He had gone and she had to accept it, however she might feel. He wasn't coming back.

Clare spoke her vows in a clear voice, Steve's deep and firm. With my body I thee worship . . . Ancient words, spoken with sincerity.

'I now pronounce you man and wife.'

There. It was done.

People might not have noticed Anna's appearance on television the previous night, but Valerie kept them informed, so it seemed to Anna that everyone at the wedding had at least heard of her 'performance'. She kept saying that it had been only a few seconds on a trailer for an obscure programme for BBC4 that no one was ever going to watch, aware that the more she protested, the more modest people assumed she was.

'I'm not being modest, honestly,' she kept saying. 'Yes, he's very nice. No, I'm not doing any more. Yes, you do hang around a lot. No, I didn't get his autograph.' She escaped to where Bronwen was sitting. Bronwen squeezed her hand.

'How you doing?' Her warm eyes meant Richard, memories and regrets. 'Okay?'

'The past is the past. Yes, I'm okay.' Anna nodded, picking at a thread of fabric coming off the edge of the tablecloth, not wanting to tell Bron about Will. Perhaps she never would. 'I'm really sorry about the way I behaved at Clare's hen party,' she started to say, but Bron stopped her with a hug.

'Think nothing of it.'

'Oliver and I . . . we've split up.' It seemed a lifetime ago.

'Wow.' Anna could see the conflict as Bronwen tried to overlay a sad and sympathetic expression on top of one of pure delight. 'What brought that on?'

'Where to start? We're very different people, I suppose.'

'He wasn't the man for you,' Bronwen said confidently. 'Now, the sort of man you need is . . .'

As she talked, Anna listened with half an ear. When Bronwen paused for breath, she butted in. 'But do I need any man? I've got my job, my own house, friends for company.'

Bronwen hesitated. 'Love?'

Anna shook her head. 'I don't think it's for me.'

'Oh lovey, you just need to find the right man.'

'You could be right.' She scanned the marquee, not seeing, her mind full of Will.

'Perhaps you ought to look a little closer to home.' Bronwen raised her eyebrows in a meaningful way.

For one glorious second she thought Will was there. 'What do you mean?' She looked again, clocking uncles and cousins, friends of Clare's, friends of Steve's, Gwyn and Nick putting the world to rights. No Will. Stupid of her to have thought even for a second that he might have been there. Bronwen didn't even know about him. It was better that way. It would be easier to forget him.

'Isn't there a film where one of the characters says that bridesmaids always get laid?' Anna said, unclipping the wreath of pink and white artificial flowers Clare had insisted on, and shaking her hair out. It was the tail end of the evening and the older guests had gone home, although the dance floor was still full of couples slow-dancing to 'Lady in Red'. She hummed along a little. 'Amazing how this track always gets people dancing.'

'Except us.' Gwyn picked the wreath up from the table. 'You should always wear one of these.'

'Huh. I think it was part of a fiendish sisterly plot to make me look daft.'

'It suited you.'

Anna squinted across at him. 'You must have drunk one hell of a lot if you think that.'

Gwyn smiled, turning the wreath round in his hands. 'You looked cute.'

'Cute!' Anna mimed being sick. 'No, I'm not into girlie pink.'

Gwyn looked around him. 'Not like Clare, then.'

It was like being inside a gigantic marshmallow. The marquee was lined with ruched pink and white silk. The table decorations were pink carnations with sprays of gypsophila; pink and white balloons hovered like cherubim in the tented ceiling; the cake had been adorned with scrolls of pink icing and pink sugar roses. Everything was pink, including Anna's dress. It hadn't been designed for sitting down. She tugged at the satin bodice, trying to make it comfortable round her waist.

'It's in *Four Weddings and a Funeral*, that line, isn't it? One of the characters says to a male friend that she was promised that bridesmaids always get laid, but that she hasn't been, and her friend offers and she says she's not that desperate. And then, later that night, they do get together and theirs is the next wedding.'

'So she does get laid.'

'Yup.' Anna yawned. 'Clare kept threatening to pair me off with various guys, but I guess they were put off by the dress and the wreath. She even chucked me her bouquet.'

Gwyn undid his bow tie. 'So you'll be next.'

Anna shook her head. 'I ducked. Jackie caught it.'

The couples on the dance floor were shuffling like zombies to 'Je t'aime', as if they could devour each other through full body contact. She wanted to be one of them, eyes shut, mind floating, absorbing the warmth of another person. She sighed.

'Today's been really strange. I think people expected me to be . . . I don't know.' She shrugged, searching for the right words. 'I suppose people expect me to be jealous or upset or something, because I'm divorced and Clare's my younger sister.'

'And are you?'

'No, of course not.' And she wasn't. She didn't think she'd feel any emotion again, ever. 'But everyone seems to expect it, so I sort of feel I ought to be upset. And that is upsetting.' She sat up straight. 'D'you know, at least three people have patted me on the back and said, never mind, dear, it'll be you next time.'

Gwyn laughed. 'Perhaps it will,' he said lightly.

Anna shook her head. 'I think I've missed my chance.'

'Hey, Oliver wasn't the guy for you.'

'Oliver?' She focused on Gwyn, her mind rearranging itself. 'Oh yes, Oliver. No, he wasn't, was he?' She rubbed her face with her hands. Of course, they all thought she was getting over breaking up with Oliver, only leaving Oliver hadn't made a single dent on her heart. And I thought I was in love. But it was nothing compared to . . . No. She had to stop thinking of Will. He was over, gone, to be forgotten.

'I'm giving up falling in love, I only get it wrong,' she said. 'From now on I'm going to concentrate on being sensible. I'm going to find someone I like, someone I can respect, who's a friend. We'll like the same things, of course, and he'd have to be a bit attractive, but we wouldn't be in love. Like an arranged marriage.'

'Doesn't sound very romantic.'

'That's the point, it wouldn't be.' Anna realised she had shredded a carnation, pink scraps on the white cloth. 'I don't want romance any more. I've been really stupid these last months, thinking I knew better than everyone, not seeing what was right under my nose.'

'Or up it,' Gwyn said drily. Anna felt herself go scarlet. He put an arm round her shoulder. 'Don't be so hard on yourself. The way I see it, you forgot to have your mad experimental stage when you were a student. You're just catching up with the rest of us.'

'I shouldn't have done it.' Oh, there was so much she shouldn't have done. She touched Gwyn's hand. 'I'm so sorry for how I was. I know it must have put you in a difficult position. But I'm okay now.'

'No matter,' Gwyn said, giving her shoulder a squeeze.

But it did matter. Just thinking about it made her lungs ache. She turned her back on Gwyn. 'You couldn't loosen the lacing on this wretched dress, could you? I can't breathe.'

He edged his chair closer. 'Um . . .' His voice sounded uncertain.

'Undo the bow at the bottom, and then pull the strings. Like rugby boots,' she added, thinking that Gwyn was probably a dab hand at those, if not quasi-Tudor outfits. She could feel his fingers tugging at the loops, and the dress ease from round her ribcage. She pulled her hair to one side so he could easily reach the top. His fingers were touching the nape of her neck, the very top of the dress. And then, so lightly she thought she might have been mistaken, his lips kissed her neck. She turned. 'Gwyn?'

And he kissed her properly.

Extraordinary to be kissed by someone she knew well, someone who was familiar. Extraordinary, and not unpleasant. Quite nice, in fact. And darling Gwyn was everything she wanted in a man, a good friend who shared her interests, whose sister was her best friend, who knew and liked her own family. Yes, this was the moment when she was going to discover that her long-time good friend was the man of her dreams, just like in the film. She kissed him back, willing the kiss to become more than quite nice.

But it didn't.

And she realised yet again that she had been talking nonsense, that all the friendship and niceness in the world would not compensate for the lack of charge between them, that she would swap all the time in the world with Gwyn for one kiss with Will, however painful and hopeless it might be. And it *was* hopeless, because Will didn't care for her. But he had done, once. *I could see he was falling in love with you,* Mrs Davenport had said. What did it matter, he had gone, and he wasn't coming back. She'd blown it and she knew it. But knowing with her head was quite different from knowing with her heart. She pulled away from Gwyn.

Their eyes met, hers trying to make him understand what she didn't understand herself. And his expression changed as he realised that this wasn't the start of something new. She shook her head. 'I'm sorry. I can't . . .'

He dropped his head into his hands. She touched his shoulder, but he shrugged it off and her hand fell limply to her side. They sat in miserable silence, while the music played love songs and those who'd got lucky danced on.

Chapter 27

Summer, the following year. The volunteers had cleared the vegetation by the pond, exposing the stone rim. There was no possibility of diggers getting down the path, so the pond had to be dredged by hand, bucket after bucket of thick black sludge being pulled out and passed along a line. It was always a surprise to Anna that there were people who willingly spent a week's precious holiday on manual labour of the most unpleasant kind, in exchange for board and lodging. And this work *was* unpleasant. The rotting humus stank as it dried on the slopes, and everyone was soon smeared with black, even Anna, who was directing operations and not up to her waist in murky water.

The foundations of the bridge were visible now, just nudging the surface. Anna knelt by the edge and felt the pond wall with her hands to see if the pool was natural or clay-lined, but there was still too much mud to tell. She pushed her hair back off her forehead, leaving another black smear, trying to gauge the work rate. She hoped that by the end of the week the foundations would be entirely exposed, but at this rate it could be touch and go. She'd only got these volunteers for a week, so she needed to push on before work stopped. And there was a meeting of trustees that afternoon, so they'd have to manage without her for an few hours. At least the volunteers seemed to have understood what they were supposed to be doing. She poked the mud with her forefinger. Bad timing, but it couldn't be helped; it was the only time Oliver could squeeze them in on his way to some more glamorous destination.

Mrs Davenport had succeeded in persuading Will to become a trustee, but he'd never come to a meeting. He'd gone back to his veterinary practice, according to Mrs Davenport, so perhaps he was too busy. Anna had given up hoping. Of course he wouldn't come. He'd accused her of putting the garden before him, so he'd hardly be in a rush to save it. She winced, remembering Will's expression, infinitely sad, as he told her she'd fallen in love with the garden, not him. Echoes of Oliver and Richard, both accusing her of being more interested in gardens than in them. Ah well. At least a garden didn't leave.

She wiped her muddy hands on her trousers. No. Better not to be involved. You didn't get hurt that way. It had taken her long enough to get over Will, but she'd managed it. She was back to her usual self, the quiet academic, in love with her work. It was better like that. Will, Oliver, Richard – they didn't matter. Restoring the garden was what mattered.

'Anna . . .' She looked up. All the mud was being sieved in case of finds, water swooshing through, and one of the volunteers on sieving duty, an elderly man with a mud-spattered face, was waving something at her.

'What have you got?' she said, clambering up the slope towards the path.

He held out his hand. It appeared to be a coin, heavily corroded. Not gold then. Anna weighed it in her hand, trying to guess if it was a lead penny. 'Well spotted. Bag it up and we'll send it to the expert – we could do with a few more to send him.' Coins meant dating evidence, along with pottery, and who knew what Arthur Farrell might have dropped or placed in the water. The more she learnt about him, the stranger his beliefs seemed, a mishmash of fact, fantasy and wishful thinking. But no weirder than John Wood's beliefs of the same time.

She checked her watch. Peggy would be bashing the gong for lunch in a few minutes, and then it would be time for the volunteers to down tools and head back to the house for a simple but plentiful meal eaten outdoors off trestle tables. She crossed her fingers. They'd been lucky with the weather so far, although judging by the glowering clouds she didn't think the luck would hold.

Anna looked up towards the house, and for a moment she didn't recognise the man coming down the path. He was wearing a suit, and his blond hair was neatly cut. Then her brain surged with energy, the synapses snapping. Everything else went hazy, her focus concentrated on the man walking down the path, and as if she'd shouted out loud, Will stopped and their eyes met.

He was here. Easy to pretend he didn't mean anything, easy to tell herself she was over him, easy – until he was here. And in that second she knew that nothing had changed for her. Love is not love that alters when it alteration finds, or bends with the remover to remove . . .

Anna felt breathless as Will broke eye contact and walked down towards her. She'd spent enough time thinking about him, and now he was here she didn't know what to do. Shake hands, kiss him, what? Shriek 'Take me, take me'? How stupid of her to think she could get over him. She stood still, hands by her side, and waited, feeling poised on the edge of a precipice. He hesitated about three feet from her. He didn't seem sure of what to do either.

'You look smart,' Anna said, breaking the silence. She'd forgotten how dark his eyes were, like best-quality chocolate, bitter and sweet at the same time.

'You look . . . muddy.' He smiled, but Anna felt too nervous to smile back.

She wiped her hands on her jeans, suddenly conscious that she must look like the Creature from the Black Lagoon. 'I was going to change during lunchtime.'

'I didn't think you'd attend the meeting like that.'

Oh! 'You've come for the trustees' meeting.' That explained his suit.

He nodded. 'I thought it was about time I pitched up. It's been a long time.'

'A year.' A lot could happen in a year. People changed. He had changed, no longer the tousled Will she remembered. It wasn't just the suit; he appeared reserved. Distant.

'Would you . . .' She paused, feeling self-conscious in a way she had never been with him before. 'Shall I show you round, or would you prefer to go by yourself?'

Before he could answer, a loud clanging noise came down the valley. 'Lunch,' she explained. The volunteers stopped work, stretching and easing tired backs. They walked up the path between Anna and Will, chatting, laughing, all mud-smeared, good-humoured as they headed for the house.

Anna and Will were left alone.

'Show me what's been happening,' Will said.

She took him down to the pond, explaining how they had to proceed in manageable stages, each stage being a complete project in itself. 'Of course, I'd like to go straight in and work on the temple, but these things take time – and money. But I hope we'll be able to start work on it as part of the next phase. Some students from the archaeology department came and helped, so I've managed to record it properly at least.' She could hardly breathe. 'It doesn't seem much, I know . . .'

'You've done a lot. Will you clear this end of the tunnel?'

'If there's time. I'm hoping I can get a date for when it was blocked. My guess is that someone barricaded the chamber off for being blasphemous.'

He looked around at the pond. 'Is this still Hell?'

'I think so. It looks like this area was created after the temple, so maybe he added Hell after Jessica's death.' She looked down into the murky water, as unclear as Will's thought processes, and her own. Over the past year she'd made an image of him, and now he was here and he wasn't the same. The Will of her memories was a transient gardener; and this man was a confident professional. Will had moved on. 'Let me take you round the rest of the garden.'

They walked up the path to the gateway, which was covered by scaffolding. Anna explained that she'd enlisted an MA student from Bristol University to research the symbols as part of her dissertation, and was waiting to hear the results. 'A friend of mine who works for one of the major landscaping companies is currently preparing a report on the landscaping work.' At least her relationship with Gwyn was back on its old footing after a sticky patch. It had been helped by Gwyn's new girlfriend, whom everyone liked, a cheerful physiotherapist who drank pints like a man. 'And towards the end of the summer holidays I've got more archaeology students doing a dig to see if there ever was a landing stage by the lake. Oliver managed to get sponsorship from a sweet manufacturer, so they'll be fuelled by E numbers and sugar.'

Oliver's name hung in the air between them. Will cleared his throat. 'How are you finding the other trustees?'

Was he asking about Oliver, or was it a straightforward question? She glanced up at him, but his face gave nothing away. 'Mrs Davenport's very much in charge – have you seen her yet?'

'She doesn't seem to have changed at all.' Will hesitated. 'She told me where to find you.'

Had he asked? No, more likely he wanted to see the garden. After all, he was a trustee. The pavilion on the other side was perfectly reflected in the lake like a floating castle. Heaven, shimmering across the lake in unattainable perfection. She wondered if Arthur had looked across and remembered Jess, like some knight of old keeping vigil for his loved one, lighting the candles and making the walls flame while he waited in the cold, yearning for her, condemned to loneliness. Waiting, waiting.

She shivered. 'Let's walk on.'

They walked in silence round the path towards the pavilion. There were so many things she wanted to ask him, about his life and whether he'd managed to accept what had happened. But it was hard to articulate, So, Will, do you still feel like a murderer? She concentrated on her role as director of the restoration. 'It seems to be going pretty smoothly so far. The Dutch flower painting made loads at auction, over double the estimate. Did you know?'

Will nodded. 'The house seems empty without it.'

The house seems empty without you, Anna wanted to say. 'It's sad, but the sale has meant we can get started on restoring the garden, without waiting for grants.' They were at the pavilion steps. Will walked up and peered in. Once they had kissed there. Was he remembering that? That magical evening, when time had seemed to stop . . .

'You've not moved everything back to the house, I see,' Will said, interrupting her thoughts.

'I sometimes sleep here.'

'Not at the house?'

'If I can't sleep, I come here . . .' Her fractured sleep patterns had never recovered, but it was easiest in the pavilion, surrounded by the garden. Her heart was thumping, the memories of that evening very close.

Will sat on the top step and looked out across the lake. 'It's beautiful. I'd forgotten . . .'

Anna sat too, two steps down from Will, the dull ache she'd felt since he'd left intensified in his presence. 'How are things going? With your practice, I mean.' If she leant back her head would touch his knees. She sat upright. A fat drop of rain landed on her head, then another on her hand.

'It's been hard, but I suppose I'm back to normal.'

Normal. What did normal mean? Anna couldn't help but glance at his hands. No wedding ring, but that didn't mean anything. She felt sick, but had to ask. 'Your wife?'

'Wife? Oh, you mean my ex. She's remarried – a GP from Manchester.' He gave her a sideways look. 'I wouldn't have gone back to her, even if she'd been interested. Not after the way she behaved.' Anna was surprised by the harshness of his voice. Not that she knew anything about his wife's behaviour, but she hadn't expected him to sound so unforgiving after what must have been some years. She wondered if he harboured grudges. I hardly know him, she thought. Only what took place here in the garden, and we've agreed that that was far removed from any sort of reality. The surface of the lake shimmered with tiny ripples as scattered raindrops fell.

'I think we ought to go inside,' Anna said, standing and walking up the steps past Will. She pushed the pavilion door open. 'It's a shame it should rain when you visit; you won't see the garden at its best.'

'I can remember,' Will said, following her inside the pavilion and looking around. The light was cool grey, reflected off the stone floor and walls, nothing like the glowing russets and golds when he'd slept there. The night he rescued her she'd thought he should have been painted by Rembrandt, but now in the clear light he more resembled a Dürer etching as he stared out of the French doors to the lake beyond.

'It's been interesting, going back to being a vet instead of being a gardener. Made me look at what I wanted from life, what mattered,' he said, not looking at her. 'I was thinking about moving south. There are too many memories at home. Nothing's the same any more.'

'Everything changes,' Anna said, frantically trying to work out what he meant by moving south. Did that mean Surrey, or Birmingham? Or Templecombe? The thought made her heart quicken as the rain started to fall heavily, disrupting the surface of the lake so the reflected images were lost.

Will turned to her. 'Hey, you've been doing well, you're always on the telly.'

Anna grimaced. 'Hardly. I think they've run out of ideas for gardening programmes and have decided to have a go at garden history.'

'I saw your book.'

'The TV tie-in? Or the one on Repton?'

'Two books? Very grand. The television one.'

'It did surprisingly well.' Perhaps garden history was the new sex after all. 'I'm negotiating a deal at the moment to film the restoration here at Templecombe.'

Will's eyes met hers, and he gave his head a slight shake as if in amazement. 'You've changed – television, deals, negotiations.' His tone was regretful. 'It sounds very high-powered and glamorous.'

'I haven't changed,' Anna said quickly. 'I haven't changed at all.' They stared at each other and she longed to know what he was thinking.

Will moved, breaking eye contact. 'How's your sister?'

'She got married just after I saw you last.' That last meeting when he said she'd fallen in love with the garden and not him. She'd spent enough time since then wondering if he was right, but standing here with him she knew he was wrong, quite wrong. 'She's expecting her first baby at Christmas.'

'And Oliver?' he said very casually.

'Oliver's going out with a six-foot model from Estonia,' Anna said, equally casually. 'He's never here.'

'Is the temple accessible now?' Will said after the tiniest of pauses. 'I'd like to see it again.'

'You'll have to swim,' Anna said, gazing out to the lake. It looked freezing cold, slate blue, with the wind rippling the surface so the reflections became blurs of light and colour. Her heart ached with wanting him, knowing it was impossible.

'Perhaps not. I've already done it twice.'

'Third time lucky?' Anna spoke lightly. She'd thought seeing Will again would dispel the memories. No one could live up to what she remembered. But here he was, and she felt just the same. She glanced up at him. He may have felt something for her once, maybe that midsummer evening with the fairy lights glowing in the dusk, but it would be too late now. He had moved on, adjusted, adapted, while she was stuck in the past again.

She traced a raindrop down the window with her finger. 'Do you remember that evening in the pavilion, when you brought all the little lights down and we rowed across the lake? You told me about eels, and the full moon, and Aristotle. I've always wanted to know if that was true.'

'Would I tell you a lie?' Will said. Anna shook her head. 'Well, then.'

The only sound between them was the rain lashing at the glass.

Will cleared his throat. 'That was a beautiful evening.'

'Not like now.'

'No.' Will hesitated, as if choosing his words carefully. 'Do you remember when we last saw each other?' That last time, when she'd blurted out that she loved him, and he'd turned her away. 'You said something then . . . I've not been able to forget. I wanted to know if it was true, what you said.'

'Oh yes.' Anna said sadly. 'And you said—'

'I know what I said.' Will cleared his throat again. 'The thing is . . . what I wanted . . . what I wanted to know was, well . . . Oh, never mind.' He rubbed the back of his neck in a familiar gesture.

'Was your question, do I still feel the same way?' Will nodded, not looking at her. Anna thought about lying, about hiding the hurt behind a flip response. No. Better to be honest. 'Oh yes. I still love you.' She shrugged, making a joke of it. 'Well, that's life. Can't be helped.'

He made no response, carried on staring out at the rain.

Anna died inwardly. Too painful. Move on. Everyone else managed to. She put her hand on the door handle. 'Let's go back. This rain doesn't look like it's going to let up, and I must change before the meeting.'

'Anna . . .' He caught her hand as it turned the door handle. 'Are you running away?'

She shrugged, unable to speak, his hand on hers.

'What are you frightened of?' Will said gently.

'Being stupid,' she whispered, unable to look at him. 'I've been stupid so often . . .'

'You're not stupid,' he said. 'Anything but.'

Anna moved her hand from Will's to the glass, feeling it cold against her palm, hardly daring to hope. 'What are *you* frightened of?' she said.

'Hamsters.'

'What?' The answer caught her by surprise and she laughed.

'All vets are,' Will said with an apologetic shrug, but the twinkle in his eyes was just as she remembered. 'They've got a really vicious bite, and the more scared they are, the harder they bite, and worse, you've got some kid watching you with enormous eyes as you're yelling blue murder and trying to flick little Hammy off your hand.'

His voice trailed away. The raindrops pelted the windows, blurring the view of the garden into impressionistic sweeps of green and grey. Will looked out at the rain, his face serious. 'When I came to Templecombe I thought I'd never feel anything again. Then you arrived, and . . . That day, when I saw you with Oliver . . . it hurt. The woman I thought you were no longer existed, she was someone I had imagined. Then in the temple – I didn't trust what had happened. I couldn't. It was too perfect, too incredible. I didn't deserve it.' He sighed. 'When I left I didn't intend to come back. I had to sort my life out, and you weren't part of it. Or so I thought.' He stopped and turned to her. 'I know I've got no right to come back here and expect . . . hope . . .' His voice was very soft and gentle, so quiet she could hardly hear him. 'I miss you.'

He misses me. He misses me. Anna stared at the grey rain, but inside she felt as if a million fireworks were exploding, filling her soul with flashes of light and energy and joy. He misses me.

'I miss you too . . .' They were standing very close to each other. She'd only have to move her other hand a little to touch his chest. Like this. She looked into his warm eyes, hardly able to believe he was with her. He'd come back.

'Will . . . am I being stupid if I do this?' Anna slid her hand to his shoulder.

He smiled, and her heart lifted. 'No.'

She swallowed. 'Or this?' She touched the back of his neck and tilted her face towards him.

'No,' he said, his mouth inches from hers.

'Or this . . .'

'Stop talking and get on with it.'

Anna sighed happily. 'Okay.'

Author's Note

The house and garden at Templecombe are entirely fictional, but the other gardens mentioned in the text exist as described and are all open to the public, unless otherwise stated. My favourite is Rousham in Oxfordshire, which has to be one of the most romantic gardens ever. Next would probably be Hestercombe (Somerset), which as well as the landscape garden also has stunning Victorian and Edwardian formal gardens. Stowe (Bucks) and Chiswick House (London) are politically themed gardens so you'll need a guidebook to get the most from them. Heligan (Cornwall) is probably the best-known restored garden although it's later than the others and is a garden of secret valleys and lush foliage rather than sweeping romantic landscapes. Go out of season to avoid the queues. I've only been to Stourhead (Wiltshire) in pouring winter rain so it shouldn't have been romantic, but luckily I had the right companion. The grotto at Templecombe was inspired by a mixture of the grottoes at Stourhead, Heligan and Goldney Hall (Avon). Goldney Hall is part of the University of Bristol and only open to the public on a few days in the summer. A good book on grottoes is *Shell Houses and Grottoes* by Hazelle Jackson (Shire Books). The last garden I drew on was Stancombe in Gloucestershire which is privately owned and usually only accessible on garden tours. The Temple overlooking the lake inspired the pavilion at Templecombe, although the pavilion in my imagination was rundown, and in reality the Temple is a super-luxurious retreat that can be rented for short breaks and holidays. Go to *www.thetemple.info* for pictures and information. Finally, I recommend Tim Mowl's book *Gentlemen and Players: Gardeners of the English Landscape* (Sutton Publishing) to anyone who wants to find out more about these wonderful gardens.